STRANGE BUILDINGS

STRANGE BUILDINGS

UKETSU

TRANSLATED FROM THE JAPANESE
BY JIM RION

PUSHKIN VERTIGO

Pushkin Press
Somerset House, Strand
London WC2R 1LA

HENNA IE 2 -11 NO MADORIZU-
© UKETSU 2023

English translation rights arranged with
ASUKA SHINSHA, INC. through Japan UNI Agency, Inc., Tokyo

English translation © JIM RION 2026

First published by Pushkin Press in 2026

1 3 5 7 9 8 6 4 2

ISBN 13: 978-1-80533-629-7

All rights reserved. No part of this publication may be reproduced,
stored in a retrieval system or transmitted in any form or by any
means, electronic, mechanical, photocopying, recording or otherwise,
without prior permission in writing from Pushkin Press

A CIP catalogue record for this title is available from the British Library

The authorised representative in the EEA is
eucomply OÜ, Pärnu mnt. 139b-14, 11317, Tallinn, Estonia,
hello@eucompliancepartner.com, +33757690241

Designed and typeset by Tetragon, London
Printed and bound in the United Kingdom by Clays Ltd, Elcograf S.p.A.

Pushkin Press is committed to a sustainable future for our
business, our readers and our planet. This book is made from
paper from forests that support responsible forestry.

www.pushkinpress.com

1 3 5 7 9 8 6 4 2

STRANGE BUILDINGS

On a cold, windy day, I walked through the streets of Umegaoka towards my friend the draughtsman's flat. I was carrying eleven files.

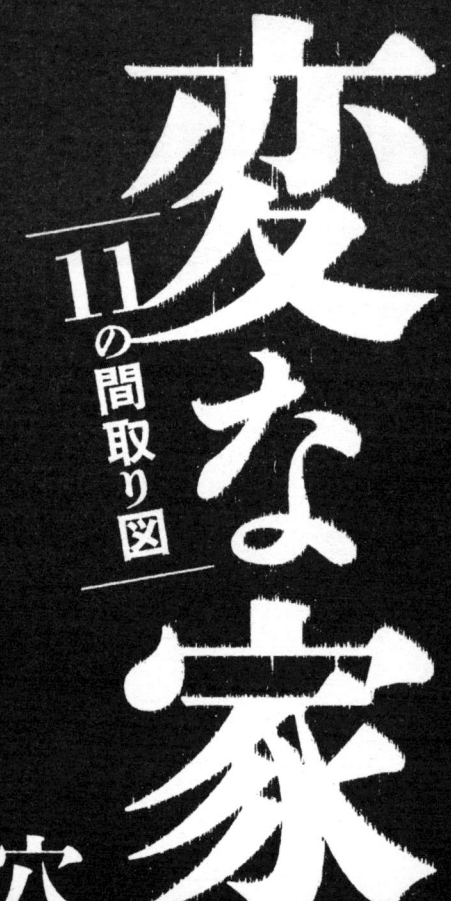

変な家
11の間取り図
Uketsu
雨穴

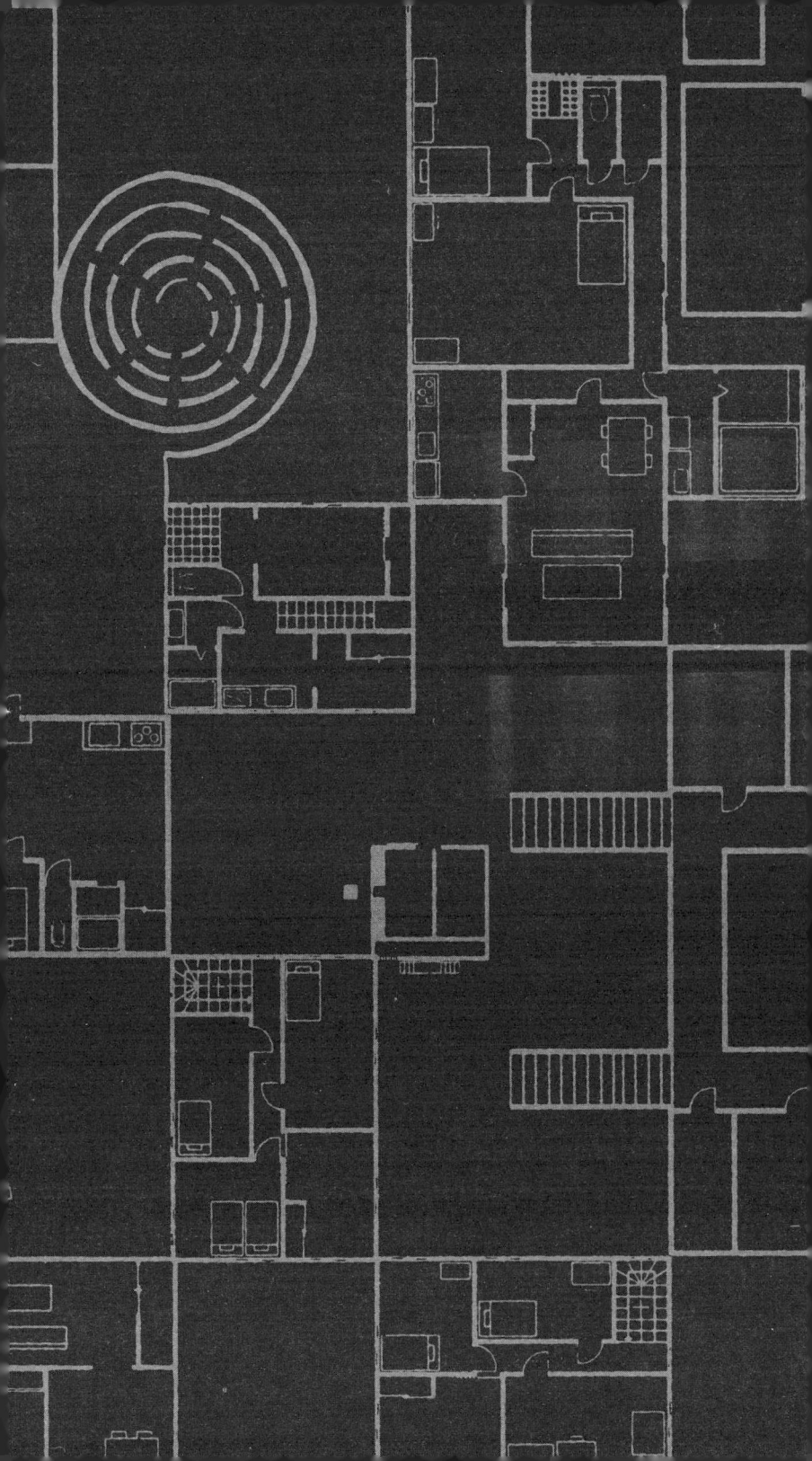

My book *Strange Houses* came out a while back.

It exposed the stories behind some strange floor plans that my friend, an architectural draughtsman, and I investigated. Together, we uncovered the chilling reason that the houses had been built and the terrifying things that happened there.

I am happy to say that *Strange Houses* was well received and read by a great number of people, with the result that many of those same readers began sending me their own 'house' stories:

'I read your book. The fact is, my house has a strange floor plan, too…'

'Once, when I went to play at my grandmother's house, I heard odd noises coming from an empty room…'

'There was this weird pillar at a bed and breakfast I once stayed at…'

It turns out there are far more 'strange houses' around Japan than I could have ever imagined.

This second book consists of my research into eleven of those many, many strange buildings.

At first glance, their stories seem totally unrelated. But on careful reading, they begin to intertwine, telling one incredible tale.

I encourage you try to spot the connections yourself as you read.

CONTENTS

FILE 1:	The Hallway to Nowhere	13
FILE 2:	Nurturing Darkness	43
FILE 3:	The Watermill in the Woods	69
FILE 4:	The Mousetrap House	83
FILE 5:	The House Where It Happened	105
FILE 6:	The Hall of Rebirth	135
FILE 7:	Uncle's House	157
FILE 8:	The String Phone	167
FILE 9:	Footsteps to Murder	189
FILE 10:	No Escape	209
FILE 11:	The Vanishing Room	227

Kurihara's Deductions — 255

FILE 1

The Hallway to Nowhere

17TH OCTOBER 2022

Record of research and interview with Yayoi Negishi

I was sitting in a café in Toyama Prefecture, with a woman across the table from me.

Her name was Yayoi Negishi. She was a part-time worker in her thirties, living in Toyama City. She and I were meeting because she said she had some long-standing worries about her childhood home.

Her son, Kazuki, would soon be turning seven. She told me that one day, he had brought home a copy of *Strange Houses* from his elementary school library. Apparently, the floor-plan on the cover had caught his eye.

However, he'd struggled with the decidedly adult book and couldn't read many of the words, so he asked his mum to read it to him. Negishi promised to do just that, but for only ten minutes a day, just before bed.

She told me that as they progressed through the book, though, it started to stir up old memories. Slightly unsettling memories that had been buried deep in her subconscious.

NEGISHI: There was something odd about the house I grew up in. But the place was torn down ages ago, and things are so busy now that I just stopped thinking about it. I suppose I had actually buried those memories. But as I read that book, little by little, they came back to me. Memories of that house and my mum.

Negishi's expression darkened at the mention of her mother.

NEGISHI: Ever since, it's all I can think about. While I'm doing the washing up, while I'm at work, all the time. I thought talking to whoever wrote that book might help me feel better, so I contacted your publisher.

It's not like I'm expecting you to uncover some hidden truth. I think I'm just hoping that telling someone will help free me from the burden of my own past. But really, I'm just putting you out. I'm sorry.

AUTHOR: No, not at all. I've been talking to lots of people about all kinds of houses and floor plans ever since my book came out. It seems that collecting stories about strange floor plans is becoming my life's work.

And it sounds like your story certainly falls within that field, so it's no trouble at all. In fact, I like the idea that your taking part in my little hobby like this might also help bring you some peace. Two birds with one stone, and all that.

NEGISHI: I'm glad to hear you say so.

Negishi took out a notebook and opened it on the table between us, revealing a house floor plan drawn in pencil. There were obvious traces of lines rubbed out and sections scribbled over. It seemed clear that she had been slowly dredging up faint memories as she drew, rubbing out and redrawing over and over as she recalled details.

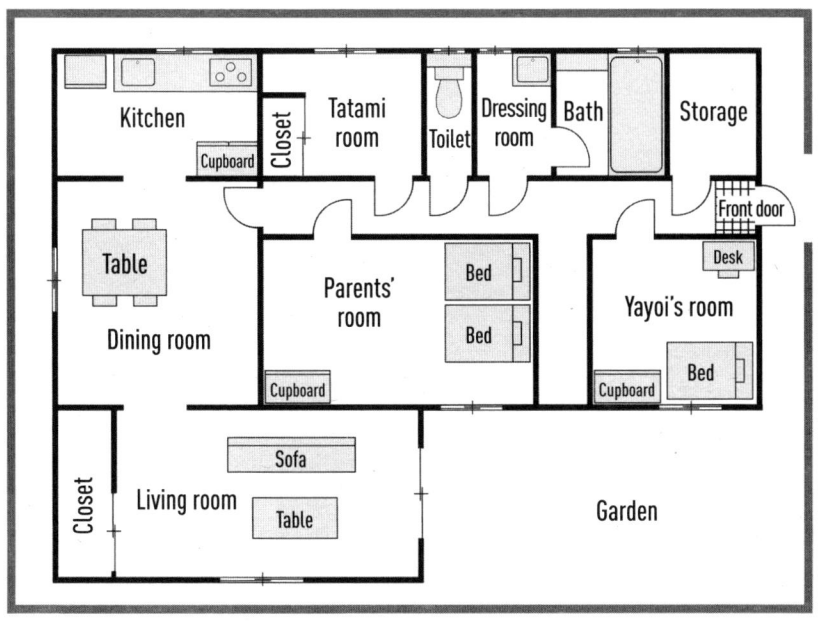

Note: Recreated by the author from Yayoi Negishi's drawing

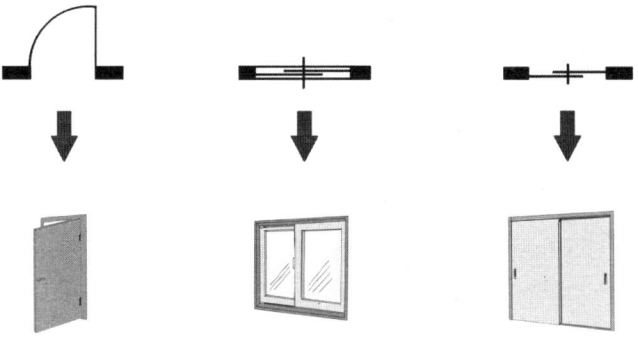

NEGISHI: My childhood home was in a residential neighbourhood in Takaoka, Toyama Prefecture. It was a single-storey house. It never felt uncomfortable or poorly laid out, but this section right here always struck me as odd. Even as a child, I wondered about it.

She pointed at one part of the drawing.

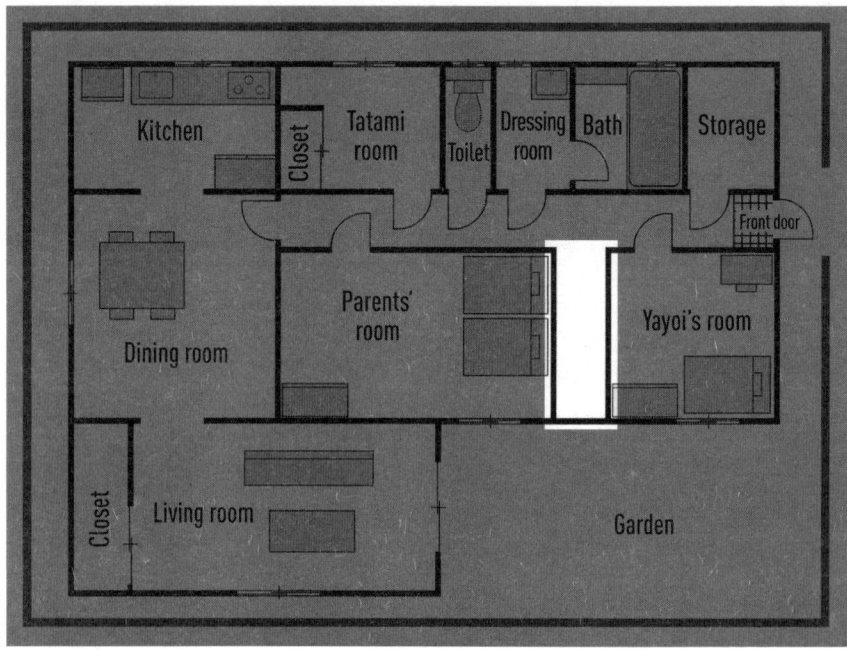

NEGISHI: What is this hallway for?

AUTHOR: How exactly do you mean?

NEGISHI: It doesn't lead anywhere. It's a dead end. And if it weren't there, my parents' room could have been that much larger. It always bothered me. Why on earth did they waste that space when they built the house?

When she put it that way, it did seem odd. The spot was too narrow to serve as storage, and there were no doors or windows there. You could only call it a 'hallway to nowhere'.

NEGISHI: I did ask my dad about it when I was a child. Just once. I asked what it was there for.

For some reason, he changed the subject. It was like he didn't even hear me. Him ignoring my question irritated me, and I threw a bit of a tantrum. I kept at him, whining and asking over and over, 'What is it there for?'

Dad doted on me, and normally he'd have given in immediately, but that time he simply refused. He wouldn't say a word about it.

AUTHOR: It sounds like he must have had a very strong reason to avoid speaking about it.

NEGISHI: I can only assume so. My parents both helped the construction company to set out the floor plan, so he must have known why they included that hallway. So, when he was so reluctant to tell me… I started to feel like he was hiding something.

AUTHOR: And what about your mother?

Negishi's expression darkened again.

NEGISHI: I never asked her. Or, rather, I suppose I couldn't. We didn't have that kind of relationship.

In my experience, you couldn't truly understand the secrets of a house without understanding the people living there first. I had a feeling that Negishi's problem with her mother would be key to unlocking the mystery in this case.

AUTHOR: Would you be willing to tell me about your mother? Only as much as you're comfortable with, of course.

NEGISHI: All right. When she was speaking with the neighbours or my dad, Mum was a normal, cheerful person. But with me—and only me—she was always terribly strict. I can barely remember her offering a word of praise, and she would blow up at me over the smallest thing. I suppose that probably sounds like your usual strict mother, but there were times when I caught her looking at me with something like fear in her eyes…

I came to wonder if she was actually afraid of me… Or maybe she just didn't like being around me. All I know was that her attitude towards me wasn't normal.

AUTHOR: Do you have any idea why?

NEGISHI: No. I honestly don't. It was always like that. As far back as I can remember, I simply felt that my mum didn't like me. It was just the way it was.

Now, though, I don't think it was that simple. Mum had a harsh side, but she could also be overprotective.

I was born prematurely. I was small and frail, apparently, and I think that's why she was always asking me if I was all right, or if I was hurt or something. Oh, and she was forever asking, 'You didn't go near the big road, did you?'

AUTHOR: The big road?

NEGISHI: Right. I should probably explain that, too. Our house faced a main street to the south. There were other houses to the north, east and west, with narrow lanes between us.

Mum always said, 'No matter what, you're never to go on the big road. If you have to go anywhere in the neighbourhood, use the lanes.' The pavement along that main street was really narrow. I could see the danger, of course, but we didn't live in a big city or anything, so the traffic wasn't very heavy. I always thought she worried too much. Anyway. If I didn't do as she said, she'd scream at me, so I listened.

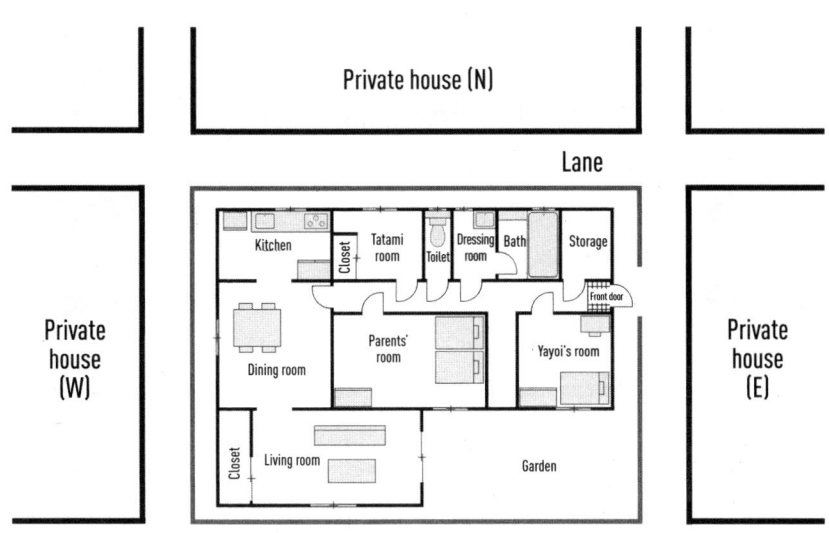

So, on the one hand, her mother smothered her with criticism, and on the other with overprotective rules. I suddenly had a thought. Could it be that Yayoi's mother simply didn't understand how to show love?

I know that there are parents who struggle to find ways to appropriately express love for their children, even though they want to. Instead, they are so fixated on being 'responsible parents' that they become overprotective.

But children can often sense the tension of that struggle, which can cause communication to break down. Which then leads to impatience, irritation and distance on both sides. Some parents respond to this with overprotectiveness as well, which only adds to the child's stress. And, if that was the case here, I had another thought.

AUTHOR: Ms Negishi, what you said has given me an idea. Could it have been your mother who proposed this hallway?

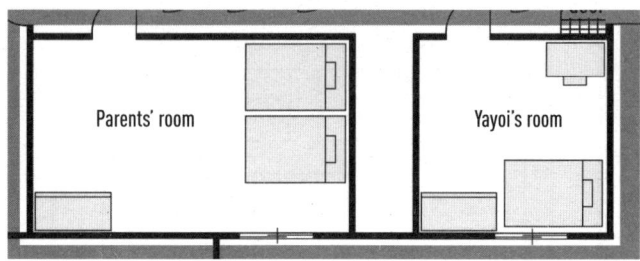

The hallway in question was between the parents' bedroom and hers. Maybe its true purpose was to create some distance between the two rooms?

While overprotective parents seem to want to keep their children close, they may secretly want the opposite. This hallway might have been a kind of barrier born of that unconscious emotional contradiction.

I tried to explain, as gently as I could, so as not to hurt her feelings. But when I finished, she slowly shook her head.

NEGISHI: No, I don't think so. Honestly, the same idea occurred to me. That maybe Mum wanted to get away from me. But it doesn't fit. This house was finished in September 1990. That's only six months after I was born.

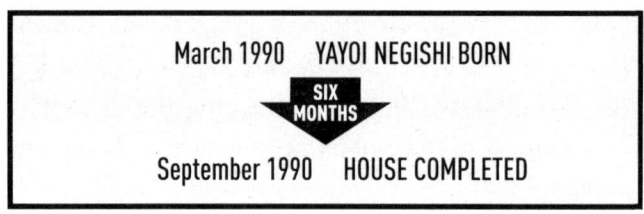

NEGISHI: I don't care how much they rushed it, there's no way they could have gone from house planning to completion in six months. So, this layout had to have been decided well before I was born. I just can't believe she wanted to put space between us that early.

I had to agree. It was hard to imagine a parent craving distance from their child before they were even born.

NEGISHI: I'm sorry, I should have told you that earlier.
AUTHOR: Not at all. But that fact does offer an important clue.
NEGISHI: It does?
AUTHOR: From the timing, I'd say that your parents decided to have this house built when they found out they were having a baby.
    So, in a sense you could almost say this house was built for you. In which case, this hallway may very well have been there because of you, specifically. I can't say for sure, though.
NEGISHI: If that's true, I really should have got my parents to tell me.
AUTHOR: Forgive me, but… About your parents. Are they…?
NEGISHI: They both passed away years ago.

She went on to describe their final days.

NEGISHI: It was in the winter of my third year at elementary school. The three of us went out to dinner. My mum suddenly said she had a headache, then she collapsed on the spot. We called the emergency services, but it was during the big year's-end holiday, so all the ambulances were already on dispatch. It took for ever for one to arrive.

When Yayoi's mother got to hospital, the tests revealed she'd had a stroke.

The delay in response meant she was bedridden from that day on. Yayoi's father quit his job to care for her, working part time and piecemeal when he could, barely sleeping. Yayoi herself had to help with housework while keeping up with school.

Things went on like that for two years. When Yayoi was eleven, her mother contracted pneumonia and died. Her father also fell ill and died soon after, as if he simply couldn't bear losing his wife after those two painful years of caregiving.

NEGISHI: After that, I went to live with some distant relatives. Our house went up for sale, but there were no buyers. I heard that it was torn down to make way for a block of flats.

She took a sip of coffee, then put her cup down with a loud clink.

NEGISHI: After they died, I found a couple of odd things while going through their belongings. First there was the money—an envelope in my mother's drawer stuffed with 10,000-yen bills. Sixty-eight of them. I guess it was her secret stash or something.
AUTHOR: 680,000 yen. That's quite a stash.
NEGISHI: When Mum was still healthy, she worked part time at a bento shop. It wasn't an impossible amount for her to have saved up, but I was surprised, because she never struck me as that fixated on money. Still, if that had been all, I wouldn't have thought much of it, but…
AUTHOR: What else did you find?

NEGISHI: A doll. A wooden doll all wrapped up in newspaper and hidden in the closet in the tatami room. I don't know who it belonged to—Mum or Dad.

    The odd thing is, the doll… It was missing one leg and one arm. Like it was made that way, not broken.

AUTHOR: Really?

NEGISHI: I thought it was creepy, so I threw it out. But to this day, I don't know what it was for, or why it was missing those limbs.

The mysterious hallway, the mother's behaviour, the hidden money, the misshapen doll. This seemingly unrelated, fragmentary information spun around in my mind.

A sudden clattering sound brought me out of my reverie. I looked down and saw that Negishi's hands were shaking, making her cup rattle against its saucer.

AUTHOR: Are you all right?

NEGISHI: Yes, sorry. I just feel so anxious all of a sudden.

AUTHOR: You do? Why now?

NEGISHI: The truth is… We still haven't got to the real reason I wanted to talk to you today.

· · ·

Negishi stared down at her still-trembling fingers and went on, her voice nearly a whisper.

NEGISHI: I couldn't stop thinking about the secret of that house, even after my parents died. It stayed with me, on and on. I started reading books on architecture, taking notes of everything that seemed important. For years. Then, I finally found what I think is the answer.

AUTHOR: You're saying you already solved the mystery?

NEGISHI: Yes, maybe. But there's no proof. And more than that… If my answer is right, then the whole thing was so dark, so miserable, I just… I've tried to put it out of my mind. To forget it.

But I couldn't. All through the years, even after I'd grown up, got married and had my own children. Whenever something happened that reminded me of it, I would find myself afraid. Like right now. Just trying to talk about it, I get… Like this. So nervous. I just want to run away from it all.

At the very start of our interview, she'd expressed the hope that telling me her story might free her of the burden of her past. This answer she was tiptoeing around must have been the 'burden' she meant.

And she was hoping that telling me about it would ease her anxiety.

AUTHOR: This must have been hard for you. To be honest, I'm not sure if I can judge whether the answer you've found is correct or not.

Still, talking about it might help you feel better. So, please, let me hear your story. At your own pace.

NEGISHI: Thank you.

She gently cleared her throat and began.

NEGISHI: So, why did they build this 'hallway to nowhere'? At first, that was all I kept asking myself. But then, one day, I realized that I might have been looking at it all wrong.

Maybe it wasn't a 'hallway to nowhere'. Maybe it was a 'hallway to somewhere that had disappeared'.

Negishi took a biro from her bag and drew something on the layout.

AUTHOR: A door to the garden?

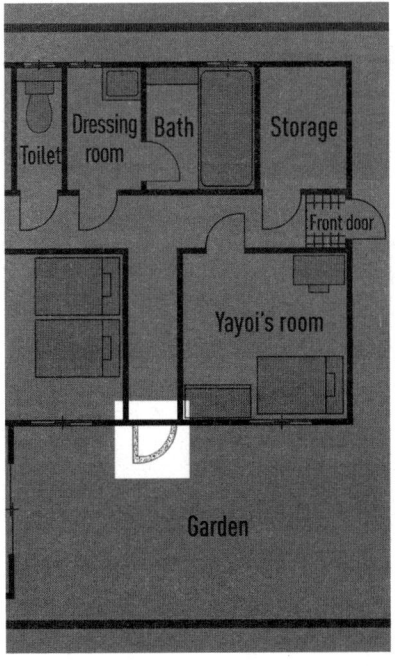

NEGISHI: That's what I thought at first. That they'd originally planned to put a doorway at the end of the hallway. But there's already a door to the garden from the living room. Why would they need another?

Also, if they eventually decided against the door to the garden, why keep the hallway? Then, I thought of another possibility.

She picked up the biro again.

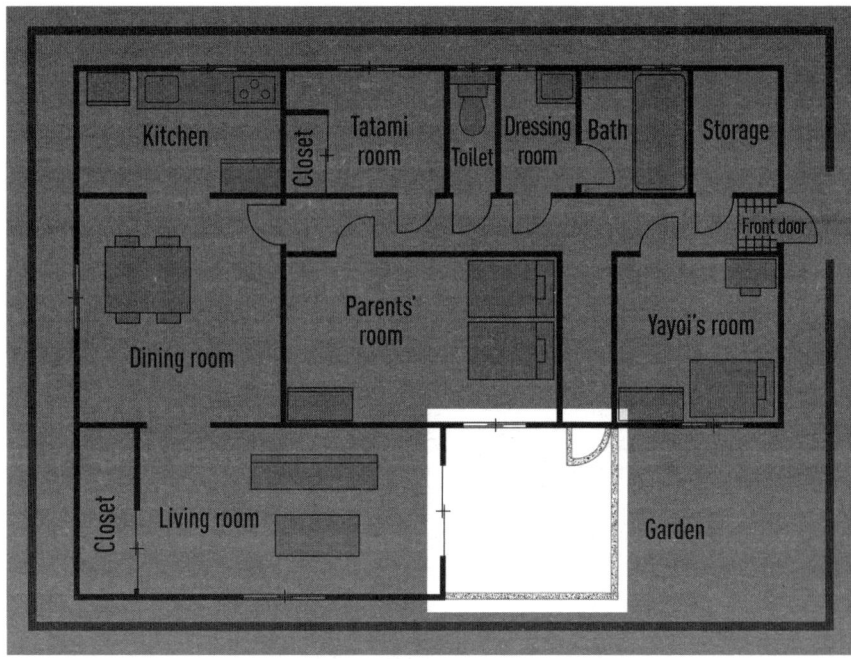

AUTHOR: Ah, a room...

NEGISHI: The original plans for the house included another room, which this hallway led to. But just before construction started, they made a last-minute change and removed the room, leaving just the hallway behind.

AUTHOR: But suddenly removing a whole room is a huge change.
NEGISHI: Right. Which means there must have been an important reason, something that made it necessary. For example… the loss of a family member.
AUTHOR: What?!

Negishi explained that this room must have been intended for a relative: a grandfather, a grandmother, an uncle, an aunt, a cousin… Whoever it was, just before construction started, that person must have died.

AUTHOR: But even then, why remove the whole room?
NEGISHI: Normally, you probably wouldn't. So, whoever it was wasn't a 'normal' person to my parents. They must have been special.
   While I sat pondering who it could possibly have been, I noticed something else.

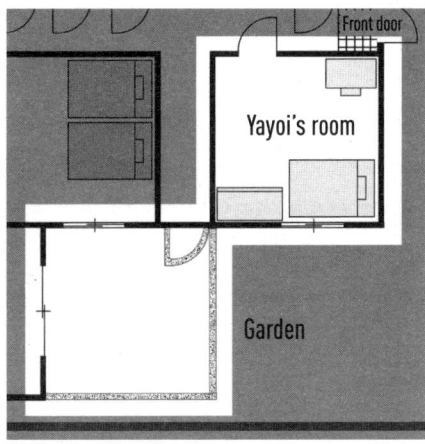

NEGISHI: This room kind of looks like mine. It's about the same size, and it faces the garden, the same as mine. Like… a twin.

My heart skipped a beat.

NEGISHI: Like I said before, I was born prematurely. Two months before the due date, and by caesarean. From what they told me, it was a risky birth for both mother and child.

My parents never liked to talk much about my birth, but I started to think that maybe I'd had a sibling. A twin. But something happened while my mum was pregnant, and she had to have emergency surgery. And one of us… I mean, I was born safely, but my twin couldn't be saved.

AUTHOR: So, you think this room was supposed to be for another child, one who died…

NEGISHI: That's what I'm convinced happened. And my parents decided to hide the fact that I'd ever had a brother or sister from me. Now that I'm a parent, I think I can understand that. It could be traumatic for a child to learn they'd had a sibling who died before they were even born.

AUTHOR: And your parents decided to remove the room to prevent you from noticing and starting to suspect something.

NEGISHI: Right, in part. But I imagine the main reason was that they wanted to forget it themselves. Every time they saw that room, they would have been reminded of their devastating loss.

I could certainly see how that would justify removing that room at such a late stage.

NEGISHI: And if this is all true, I also think it explains my mum's treatment of me. She was overprotective because she didn't want to risk losing another child.

But at the same time, she might have been afraid of me. I was like a living fragment of that other child, after all. My simply being there must have reminded her of what she'd lost. Thinking of it that way also helps me understand the doll. The missing arm and leg are like a metaphor for the pain of losing one half of the twins she was expecting.

Negishi reached into her handbag and took out a picture.

NEGISHI: I found a bundle of old photographs in my dad's drawer when I was putting their house in order after they passed away.

They all showed the house under construction. I guess he wanted to keep a record of the progress. Here's one of them.

The photograph showed the frame of an unfinished house. There was a sign out front reading: 'Under Construction: Housemaker Misaki'. That must have been the company handling the project.

But what truly drew the eye was a small red object in the foreground.

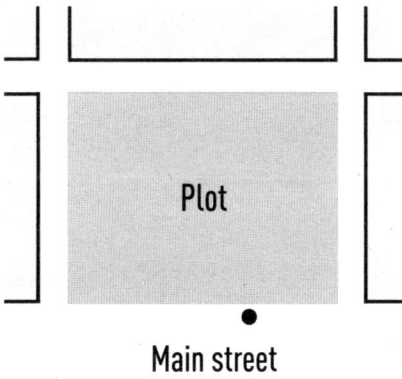

It was placed on the kerb at the edge of the main street, which would put it at the bottom of Negishi's drawing.

By squinting, I could just make out that it was a glass cup with a single flower sticking up out of it.

NEGISHI: I think my parents must have put it there in memory of that other child.

But something about that felt off.

Of course, I could understand parents putting out flowers in memory of a deceased child, but would they do it there, in front of a construction zone? No matter how you looked at it, the placement was odd. It felt less like a memorial to their own lost child, and more like…

. . .

NEGISHI: Well, what do you think? From your objective perspective, am I onto something?
AUTHOR: Well… Your deductions are logical and persuasive. But there are a few points that bother me.

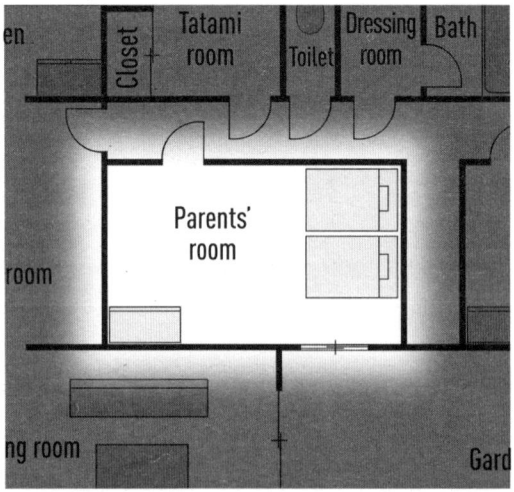

AUTHOR: For example, if there were a room here, your parents' room couldn't have a window in that spot. This wall wouldn't have been an outside wall then.

Your parents worked with a construction company to plan the house, right? With professionals involved, I can't see them planning a room without an external wall and window to let in light.

NEGISHI: Hmm. I see what you mean...

AUTHOR: And another thing. I have my doubts about the possibility of making such a major change just before construction. It would have meant redesigning the roof, for example, and they'd have already ordered all the materials. It would have taken a lot of time and money. I'm not at all sure the construction company would have agreed to it.

NEGISHI: That... That's a good point.

AUTHOR: All in all, then, I don't think your answer is the right one.

I was not as sure of my reasoning as I sounded. But if I left any room for doubt, I knew Negishi would only continue struggling with the anxiety of it all, haunted by the ghost of a departed sibling who might never have even existed.

And in that case, it would be kinder to quash her theory here and now and free her from the curse. It was what she wanted... Or so I thought.

No sooner had I spoken, though, than I was surprised to see her face fall.

NEGISHI: Thank you. I suppose I'm relieved to know my theory is wrong, but at the same time, it's kind of sad. Disappointing, even. I think I've just realized that this theory of mine was born out of hope.

AUTHOR: What do you mean?

NEGISHI: I still don't like my mum. Even after all these years since she passed, I still haven't changed my mind. I don't think she was a good mother. And I hate that.

I just want to be able to tell myself that the way she treated me wasn't her fault. That there was a good reason for how harsh she was with me.

. . .

We stepped out of the café into the bright light of the setting sun. We parted, and I walked towards the station.

So, Yayoi Negishi's search for answers was motivated by a desire to let go of her resentment of her mother. That made sense.

In which case, I thought it would be best for her just to try to forget. There was no reason to go on suffering for the sake of a mother who had long since passed away. I grew ever more certain that I had been right to refute the explanation she had come up with.

But there was still one thing that I couldn't stop thinking about.

That red flower in the picture. What was that? Who had put it there, and why?

Negishi thought her parents had left it for their lost child. But that surely wasn't true. The placement was all wrong. It was on the street.

Memorial flowers left on the street… That usually meant…

Fireworks went off in my brain. An explanation seemed to just appear out of nowhere.

Could it be? If I was right, it would also explain the hallway to nowhere.

I opened a map app on my phone and looked up the nearest library.

It was a thirty-minute walk from the café. They had an archive of the local newspaper there. I started searching the papers from 1990, the year the Negishi house had been completed.

I soon found the article I was looking for.

30TH JANUARY 1990 | MORNING EDITION

A fatal accident occurred yesterday, 29th January, around 4 p.m. in Takaoka, Toyama Prefecture. The victim was local elementary-school student Yunosuke Kasuga (8). The boy was walking along the main street when he was hit by a truck backing out of a work site. The truck was loaded with construction materials. The driver reportedly said, 'It was hard to see, and I just didn't notice the boy.' The man is an employee of Housemaker Misaki and...

The article included a picture of the street where the accident happened. I recognized it from the photo Negishi had shown me earlier.

It was just as I thought. That hallway to nowhere had appeared because of this accident. I left the library and immediately rang Negishi.

NEGISHI: Yes, hello?

AUTHOR: Ms Negishi, I have a favour to ask you. Could you please contact Housemaker Misaki? It's the company that built your house. I think we should go and talk to them in person.

NEGISHI: In person? But my parents had that house built over thirty years ago, and we've not contacted them once since then. I doubt they'd be willing to meet with me after so long, and there probably isn't anyone left at the company who would remember a job from so long ago anyway.

AUTHOR: I wondered about that too, but I've just looked through some old newspapers and made a huge discovery. I'm sure they won't have forgotten your family. You're a very important person to that company.

NEGISHI: What on earth do you mean?

AUTHOR: The truth is…

I explained what I'd found, and she agreed to contact the company. Just as I'd expected, they recognized her name. When she'd said she wanted to talk to someone who remembered those days, they put her in touch with a Mr Ikeda, the head of human resources.

We made plans to meet him at the company's headquarters on Friday of the following week.

· · ·

And so, that Friday afternoon Negishi and I found ourselves in the visitors' room at the head offices of Housemaker Misaki.

Mr Ikeda sat across a small table from us. He was a short man in late middle age and had a friendly face. He stared at Negishi for a while before speaking.

IKEDA: Well, now… You're the little miss all grown up, are you?

AUTHOR: Are you saying you know who this is?

IKEDA: Sure. I've known her since she was still in her mother's belly.

Back then, I worked the shopfront, handling customers directly. I was the one who handled your parents' enquiry when they came in hoping to have a house built. We talked quite a bit, and your father used to rub your mother's belly and beam. 'We're having a girl!' he'd say, just as happy as can be. I remember it so well.

But… Then came the accident. As a company, that's a shame we'll never forget.

AUTHOR: That's actually what we came to talk to you about. Can you tell us about the accident?

IKEDA: Of course. Let's see, it was after the ground survey and just around when we were putting up the frame.

One of our employees ran over a boy walking on the street in front of the property.

AUTHOR: Did the boy die on the spot?

IKEDA: Yes. It just never should have happened.

Negishi produced the picture she'd shown me.

NEGISHI: Were you the one who set out this flower?

IKEDA: Not just me. We put out fresh flowers and offered a prayer every day all through construction. We knew, of course, that wouldn't absolve us of anything. We were, and still are, ready to do whatever we can to support and compensate the boy's family. But at the same time, we felt guilty for your family's suffering, as well.

There was a fatal accident right in front of their new house, and it was our fault.

AUTHOR: That's why you changed the plans and moved the location of the front door, isn't it?

IKEDA: You know about that?

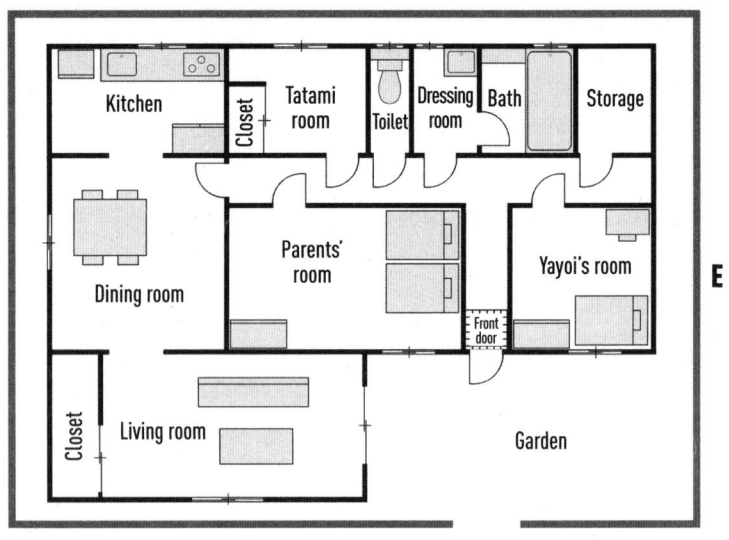

● **Accident**

Ikeda went on to explain that the front door was originally intended to be on the south side.

The accident had happened right in front of where that door would have been. Even people who don't believe in ghosts would be troubled by the idea that their front door opened onto the site of a fatal accident. Ikeda said that Mr Negishi was in a rage over it.

But it was Mrs Negishi who seemed to take it the worst. Then, she proposed an alternative plan.

She suggested that construction of the house could continue only if the location of the front door was changed.

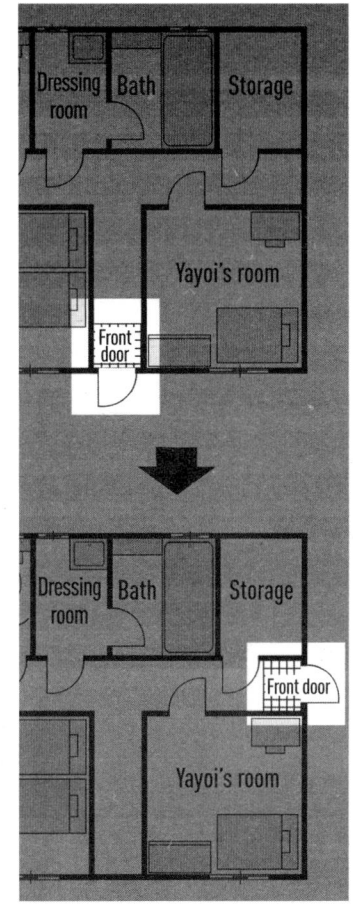

The proposed new location was at the end of an existing hallway, so it would be easy to add the door. The company assumed all the costs for it.

And so, what was originally the entrance hallway lost its role and became a hallway to nowhere.

They had discussed expanding one of the

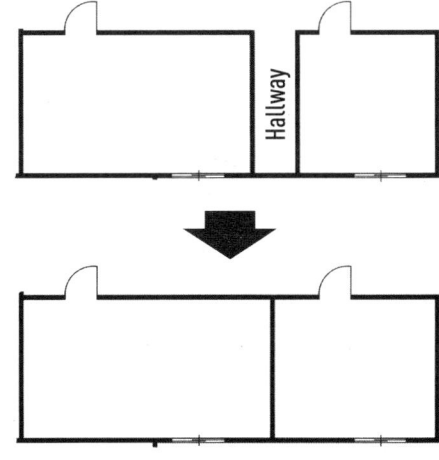

rooms to use that space, but earthquake-resistance requirements made it difficult to reduce the number of load-bearing internal walls.

Ikeda kept saying how impressed he had been by Mrs Negishi's 'wonderful proposal'. I could see what he meant. The simple change meant that the family wouldn't have a view of the accident site from inside the house. I had a feeling, though, that Mrs Negishi might also have had another motive.

Perhaps by moving the front door so it didn't open onto the main street, she was hoping to keep her own child from bolting out of the door and into traffic when she was older. She wanted to avoid the risk of another accident.

> Mum always said, 'No matter what, you're never to go on the big road. If you have to go anywhere in the neighbourhood, use the lanes.'

That insistence was based on the stark knowledge that this street was dangerous. It had already been the site of one death.

The fact of the accident itself was sad enough. But with this new information, I hoped that that Yayoi Negishi could take some comfort in knowing that her mother had truly been worried about her.

She hadn't known how to show her love. She had shouted, she had kept her daughter at arm's length. But in her heart of hearts, she had cared for her child. Or so I thought at first. Soon, though, another puzzling fact came to light.

· · ·

After going over the incident in detail, Ikeda seemed to remember something all of a sudden.

IKEDA: Ah, yes, there was something I wanted to ask you, Ms Negishi.
NEGISHI: Me? What is it?
IKEDA: Do you know why your mother wanted that odd renovation?
NEGISHI: What renovation?
IKEDA: Ah, so, you weren't aware… The fact is, about five years after the house was built, your mother came to us one day, without your father. She had the strangest question. 'Can you tear out the room at the south-east corner?'
NEGISHI: Tear it out?
IKEDA: We do sometimes remove parts of houses. We call it 'floor-space reduction', but taking a whole room off a building is quite rare. I asked why she wanted it done, but she wouldn't tell me.

From her manner, I got the impression that she wanted the job done quite urgently, so I drafted an estimate for the work. It was expensive, though, and I think that convinced her to give it up. Still, I wonder what it was all about…

I couldn't help thinking about the 680,000 yen she'd had in cash in her drawer.

That might well have been money she'd been stashing away to cover the construction costs.

AUTHOR: The south-east corner is… Which room was that?
IKEDA: It was right next to the front door…

NEGISHI: It was my room.
AUTHOR: What?!

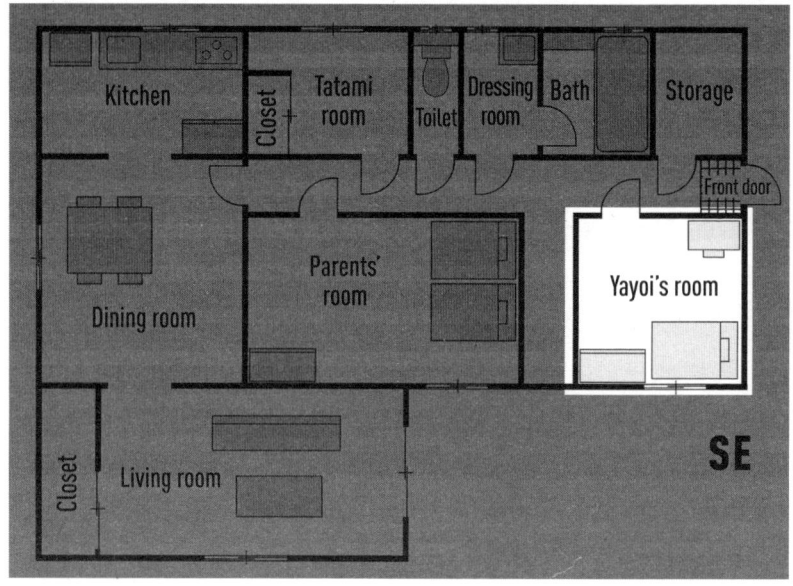

The room at the south-east corner was indeed her bedroom. But then…

NEGISHI: I knew it. Mum hated me.
AUTHOR: No, wait, that can't be right! After all, she was so worried about you getting hurt on the street like that.
NEGISHI: Then, why?

Why did she want to remove her daughter's bedroom?
Try as I might, I could not come up with a satisfactory answer.

END OF FILE 1: THE HALLWAY TO NOWHERE

FILE 2

Nurturing Darkness

6TH NOVEMBER 2020

Interview with Tatsuyuki Iimura

You may have heard of the term 'forensic clean-up'.

It refers to the cleaning and disinfecting of rooms that have been scenes of crimes or accidents, or where somebody has died alone and their body has lain undiscovered for a long time.

Normally, when someone dies, their families or friends arrange a funeral and have the body cremated within a few days. However, in the case of somebody who lives on their own and has no relatives or close friends, it can be weeks or months before somebody finds their body. In the meantime, it begins to decompose and leaves behind stains.

It is the job of 'forensic cleaners' to erase those final traces of lives that once were.

My interview subject for this file is Tatsuyuki Iimura, a man who has worked as such a cleaner for nearly ten years.

He originally worked in construction before switching jobs in his mid-forties.

IIMURA: Fact is, I just got too old for it. In my thirties, didn't matter how hard the day was, I'd get home and have a few drinks, get a good night's sleep and wake up good as new. But past forty, it sticks with you, the exhaustion does.

It built up, little by little, and I guess one day, it just got too much. I woke up in the morning and just couldn't move. I was admitted to hospital, but that was it for me. My body got weak, and I just couldn't handle the labour anymore.

But I'm not cut out for desk work, either. So, an older co-worker pulled some strings and got me this forensic clean-up gig.

Iimura popped some edamame into his mouth and took a swig of beer.

IIMURA: So, forensic clean-up. Basically, it's setting people free from a house. Most folks think it's the opposite. 'A person leaves the house dirty, and you have to clean the house up.'

That's like saying houses come before people, which is bollocks. Houses are there for people, not the other way around. People always come first. That's something I learnt as a builder, and I keep it in mind in this work, too.

When it's time for the departed to move on, whether it's to heaven or hell, if any bit of them is left in the house, it'll hold them back, see? So, we go in and scrub it all from the house, so they're free. That's the job, as I see it. Interesting, right?

Sorry, mind if I order another beer?

I had been put in touch with Iimura through a friend, who thought he might be able to provide me with some information I was looking for. And so, here I was in this bar in Shizuoka Prefecture to interview him.

I found these details of his job as a cleaner fascinating, but I could sense the conversation drifting away from what I had come to discuss. So, after he'd ordered his second beer, I steered Iimura back towards the topic at hand.

AUTHOR: So, Mr Iimura, I understand that you helped with the clean-up at the Tsuhara house. I was hoping to talk to you about that.
IIMURA: Oh, that's right. Sorry for rambling on like that.

．　．　．

In 2020, a boy of sixteen allegedly killed three members of his family at their home in northern Shizuoka City.

The victims were the boy's mother, grandmother and younger brother. His father was out at work at the time. A neighbour heard the mother's screams and called the police, but the three were already dead by the time officers arrived on the scene. The boy did not resist when the police took him away.

The murders had been committed using a single kitchen knife. There was a half-chopped pile of vegetables in the kitchen, so police believe the boy must have taken the knife from his mother while she was cooking and used it to attack his family.

The three bodies were found as follows:

MOTHER: Discovered in the kitchen with a single stab wound to the chest. Clothing showed signs of a struggle.
GRANDMOTHER: Discovered lying in her own bed with eyes closed. Stabbed multiple times through the blanket covering her. She was generally confined to bed because of difficulty walking, and it is believed that she died without a struggle.

YOUNGER BROTHER: Found in the doorway between the kitchen and the hallway. The knife was still in his abdomen.

The alleged perpetrator suffered multiple cuts to his upper body. He was arrested after receiving treatment at the hospital.

He made several statements to the police, with explanations including, 'I was feeling irritated,' 'I had no hope for the future' and 'Mother and grandmother never got along. It was hard to be in the house.'

Alongside the usual opinion pieces in the media about 'The epidemic of hopelessness afflicting Gen Z' and 'A breakdown of communication in the family home', there was some speculation that there might have been something wrong with the layout of the Tsuhara house.

This speculation never got much traction and soon faded from public discourse, but it caught my attention. I was in the middle of writing *Strange Houses*, and of course I had floor plans on my mind.

I did a bit of research of my own, but, try as I might, I didn't manage to turn anything up. In fact, I never even found a copy of the Tsuhara house floor plan.

When I was about ready to give up, I had a thought.

When police investigations finish, houses that were murder scenes are subject to forensic clean-up. So, maybe people involved in that clean-up would know how the house was laid out.

And that is why I had come to interview Iimura.

IIMURA: There were ten of us on that job. Usually, forensic clean-up teams have eight members at most, but that one was different. Things being as they were and all.

AUTHOR: Was it a difficult job?

IIMURA: It was. The stretch from the kitchen to the old woman's room especially. It was just a lake of blood. We had to replace the floorboards there. That was rough. Course, it's always rough physically, but that one… It was hard on the heart. You know one of the victims was a kid?

AUTHOR: Yes. The killer's younger brother, right?

IIMURA: There was this small puddle of blood at the entrance to the kitchen. Kid-sized. It was hard even to look at it. I've got a boy of my own, with the ex.

AUTHOR: How terrible…

IIMURA: Sorry, didn't mean to put a damper on things. Oh, right, you said you wanted a floor plan for the Tsuhara house, didn't you? I brought a copy. I suppose that's worth the price of some edamame.

Iimura pulled a folded-up piece of paper from his pocket. He spread it out to reveal a floor plan.

IIMURA: This is the Tsuhara house.

AUTHOR: Really? How did you get this?

IIMURA: There are copies all over the web. I just picked one and printed it out.

That was odd.

I'd searched all over the internet and never found a copy of the Tsuhara house floor plan. But if Iimura was so sure, after having actually been inside that house, I didn't doubt it. I must have just been looking in the wrong places.

GROUND FLOOR

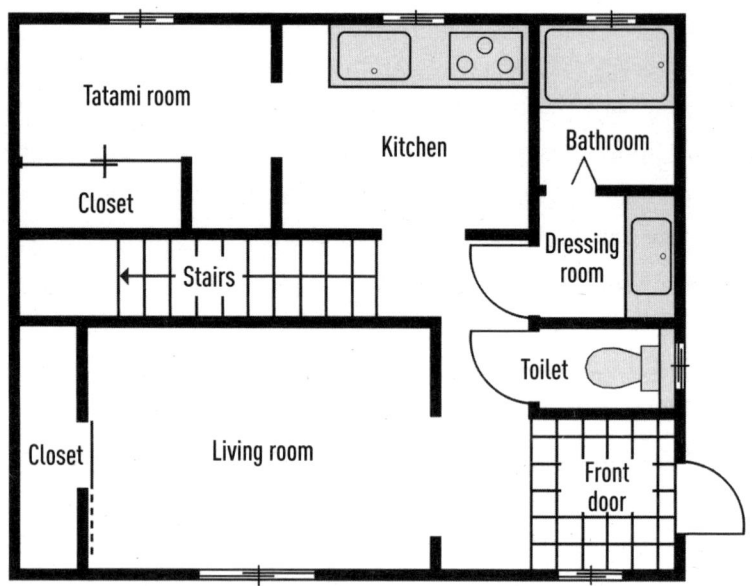

FIRST FLOOR

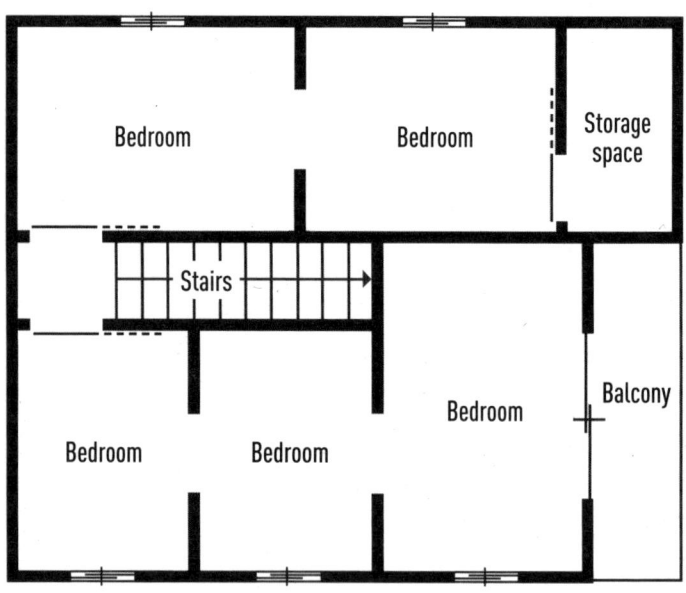

IIMURA: It really is a terrible house. You live in a house like that too long, it'll drive you nuts. It was unfit to live in, that place.

AUTHOR: Unfit to live in? What do you mean?

IIMURA: Just look at this layout. Isn't it obvious?

AUTHOR: I'm sorry, it just looks like any other house to me.

IIMURA: Well, just you try imagining living here. Take the ground floor. You're having your dinner in the living and dining room. But there's always this foul stink in your nose, killing your appetite. You know why?

The kitchen, bath, and all the other stuff we call 'wet areas' are concentrated on the north. The north side never gets enough sunlight, so it never really dries out even in the dry season, and in summer it gets stuffy and mouldy.

On top of that you got your usual toilet smells mixing in and wafting down the hallway to the living room. And there's no door there, so no way to keep the smell out.

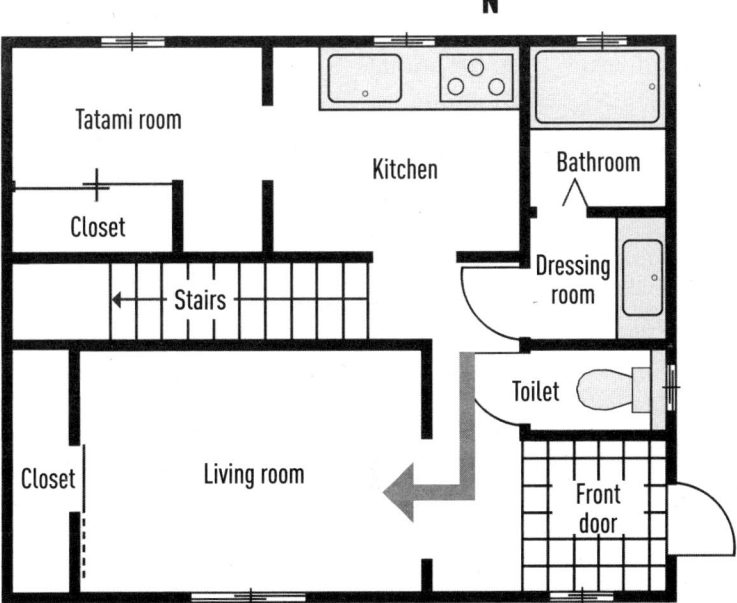

AUTHOR: Why do you think there's no door to the living room?

IIMURA: I imagine the builders were cutting corners. There are all kinds of nasty little tricks to keep construction costs down.

AUTHOR: I see.

IIMURA: And there are other problems with not having a door to the living room.

You know how some folks come and ring the bell around dinner time, collecting money for the newspaper or trying to spread the good word or what have you. Imagine it here. You open the front door, and your dinner and your family are all right there for the world to see. Not a hint of privacy.

At the very least they should have put the entrance to the living room on the kitchen side, but the stairs take up all that space, so they couldn't, I suppose.

You get poor layouts like this when you try to build a house on too small a plot. Which just means it's easy to end up with a bad design like this here in Japan. Lots of small plots.

Of course, you get some really good architects who do it right, but whoever drew up these plans is a joke.

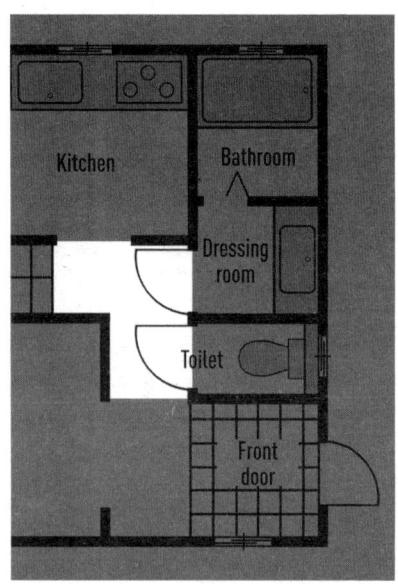

Look here how the entrances to the kitchen, dressing room, and toilet, are all clustered together.

I bet that caused a lot of trouble, a lot of fights. People always bumping into each other.

AUTHOR: Now you point it out, it does look like an unpleasant place to live.

IIMURA: Right? And the first floor is even worse.

This floor space is good for three, maybe four rooms. But they crammed five in there. Which means they didn't have space for a hallway.

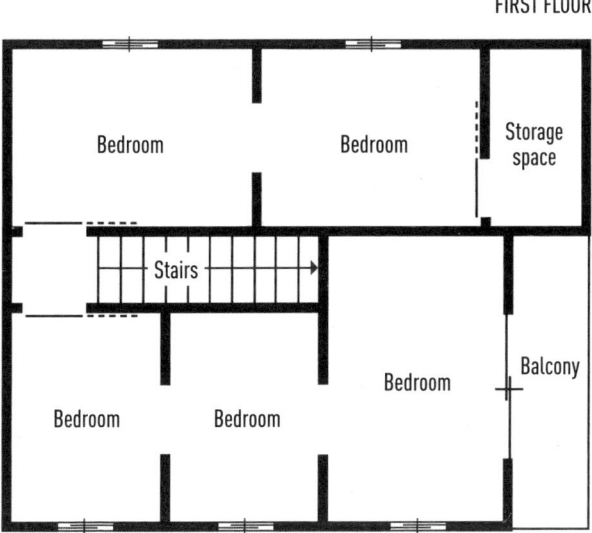

FIRST FLOOR

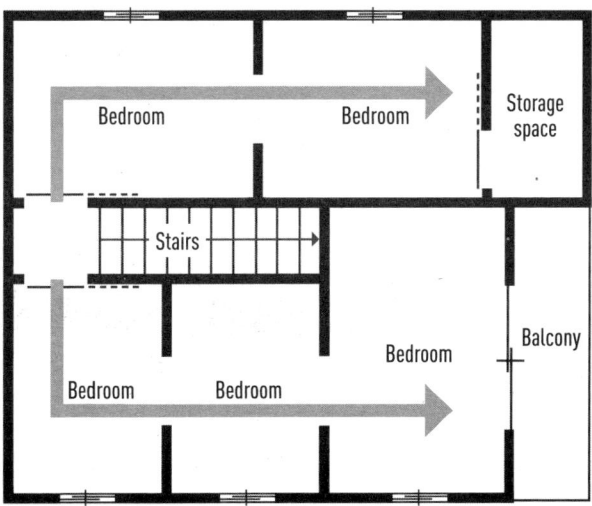

Without a hallway, if you want to get to the room at the back of the house, you have to pass through the rooms at the front. So, those bedrooms also served as a corridor. And look, no doors here, either. Not a hint of privacy.

AUTHOR: That would be really uncomfortable.

IIMURA: It also bothers me that the balcony doesn't face south. You want to hang your laundry out to dry on the balcony, you need it to face south. Nothing dries laundry like decent southern exposure.

I could feel my own interest in the house fading bit by bit. Iimura's explanation was certainly convincing. He had been a housebuilder himself, so I trusted his ability to judge the design of a house from just looking at the plans. And perhaps he was right—maybe this had been a bad house to live in.

Still, it felt like a stretch to go from 'a bad house to live in' to 'a house that would drive someone to murder'. Perhaps sensing my scepticism, Iimura cleared his throat and went on, his tone slightly muted.

IIMURA: Of course, spending a day or two in this house wouldn't cause any problems, I reckon. But you live here for five or ten years, and those little stresses pile up day after day. Eventually it drives you crazy. It might sound like I'm making it up, but that's the kind of power houses have.

AUTHOR: You think so?

IIMURA: I do. But still…

His voice dropped to a near whisper.

IIMURA: All that just now, that was just me guessing. The real issue is what actually happened after the Tsuhara family started living here. You got kids, by the way?

AUTHOR: No, I don't.

IIMURA: Well, try to imagine. So, when you've got a kid of two or three playing at home, what do you think is the most important thing to do as a parent?

AUTHOR: Hmm… I suppose making sure there's nothing dangerous around?

IIMURA: Well, that too, but there's something else that's just as important. Maybe even more so. The answer I'm thinking of is 'keeping them in sight'.

When kids reach a certain age, around two or three, they start to want some independence, to play on their own. But at that age, you can't leave them completely on their own. So, they usually play in the living room.

The kitchen and living room in most houses in Japan are connected. Parents can keep an eye on their kid, and the kid has the feeling of playing alone, along with the reassurance that Mum and Dad are still close by.

But in this house, you can't see into the living room from the kitchen. In fact, there's no good play space you can keep an eye on from the kitchen.

That Tsuhara boy must have grown up feeling anxious all the time, don't you think?

AUTHOR: Hold on… There's this tatami room next to the kitchen. Isn't that perfect for a playroom?

IIMURA: It would be, maybe, but that was the grandmother's room.

Granny's room… Something about that flicked a switch in my brain.

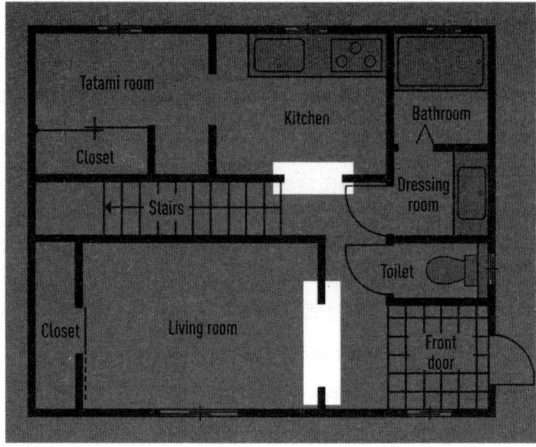

MOTHER: Discovered in the kitchen with a single stab wound to the chest. Clothing showed signs of a struggle.

GRANDMOTHER: Discovered lying in her own bed with eyes closed. Stabbed multiple times through the blanket covering her.

YOUNGER BROTHER: Found in the doorway between the kitchen and the hallway. The knife was still in his abdomen.

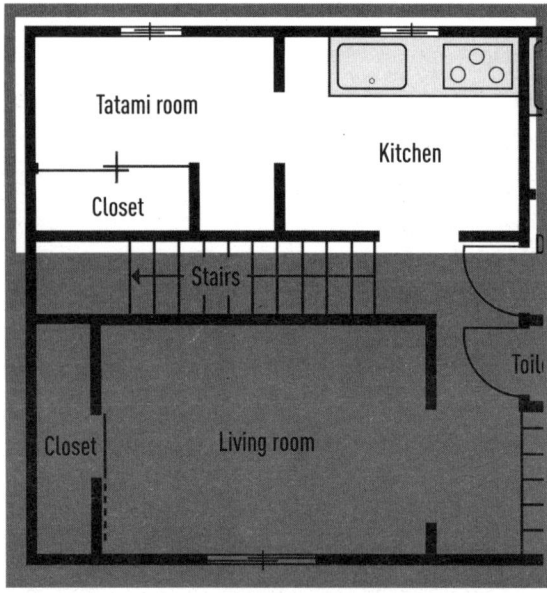

The grandmother was killed in her room. The mother and younger brother were killed in the kitchen.

The murders happened in two adjoining rooms. I couldn't help imagining the scene.

IIMURA: The old woman was Mr Tsuhara's mother, I understand.

From his wife's perspective, every time she stepped into the kitchen, the old woman would be right there. That would be grating even with a blood relative, but with her mother-in-law it must have been absolute misery.

And the old woman's legs were bad, so she was practically bedridden. Mrs Tsuhara would have been forever breaking off from her own work to help her mother-in-law to the toilet. She must have felt plenty stressed and irritated with it all.

Children pick up on things, especially their parents' moods. I just can't imagine those kids playing happily while their parents were always on edge. They wouldn't have felt relaxed around their mum while she was so wound up, but if they played in the living room, then they would have felt alone and anxious…

I doubt there was anywhere in this house where the Tsuhara boy could feel at ease when he was a child.

The boy had even told the police that his mother and grandmother didn't get along.

IIMURA: Then, when kids get older, they want their own rooms. And that was another problem. The Tsuhara boy's room was right here.

Iimura pointed to the storage space on the first floor.

IIMURA: I got a look inside when we were cleaning. There was a desk and a lamp, with a futon on the floor. The boy must have liked football, because he had J League posters on the wall.

AUTHOR: But why was he staying in the storage space?

IIMURA: Process of elimination, I expect. Like I said, none of the rooms on the first floor offered any privacy. Which would have been just about hell for a boy in his teens.

The only 'room' with a door was this storage space. I doubt the boy liked it in there. A cramped, dark room with no windows like that. It'd be enough to depress anyone. But where else could he go?

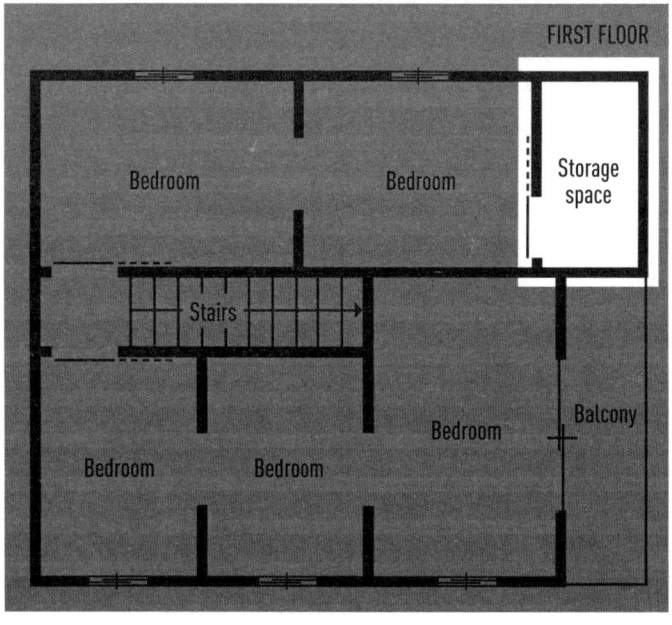

A childhood full of anxiety and loneliness. An adolescence spent in cramped darkness. And a house entirely lacking in comfort.

Could all these have combined to slowly warp the young Tsuhara into a murderer?

IIMURA: Of course, I wouldn't go so far as to say that anyone who lived in this house would end up a murderer. I suspect the boy had something in him from the start. The house just brought it out. Nurtured the darkness in his heart, I guess you could say.

AUTHOR: I wonder if this tragedy would have happened if he'd lived somewhere else.

IIMURA: I wonder… Anyway, the Tsuhara boy isn't the only one in the world with darkness in his heart, and this house isn't the only one of its kind.

AUTHOR: What do you mean by that?

IIMURA: Exactly what I said. There are over a hundred houses like this across Japan.

AUTHOR: Really?

IIMURA: Yes. You've never heard of Hikura Homes? It's a construction company running out of central Japan, the Chubu region. All of us in the business know it's crooked as a dog's hind leg. This is what they do.

First, they draw up a floor plan. They design it for, say, a hundred-square-metre plot. Then, they go all over the area, buying up as many hundred-square-metre plots as they can, then build the same house on each one, like stamping them out of a machine.

Using the same design for hundreds of houses means they can cut costs by ordering materials in bulk, and they can sell these mass-produced houses at low prices. They're commodities, in other words.

Which in itself isn't an issue. Other companies build to set plans, sure. The problem is, Hikura's basic design is bad. So, they're mass-producing bad houses just like this one.

AUTHOR: So, the Tsuhara house is just one of these mass-produced Hikura Homes properties?

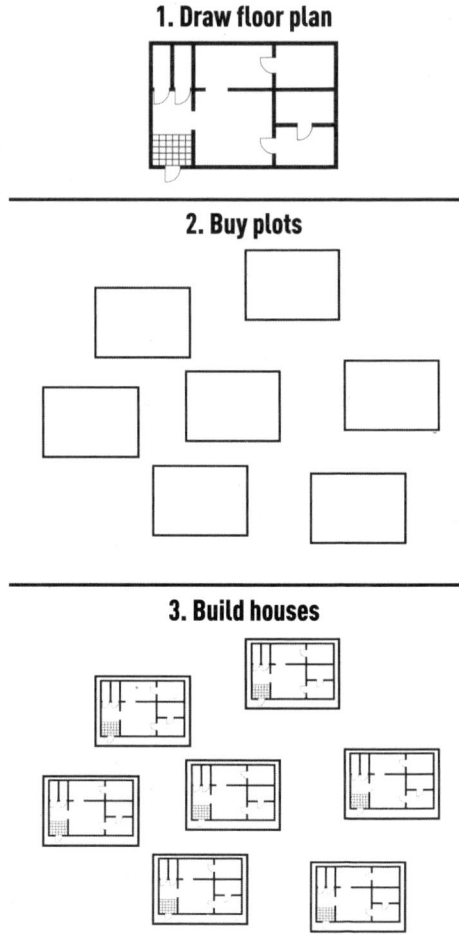

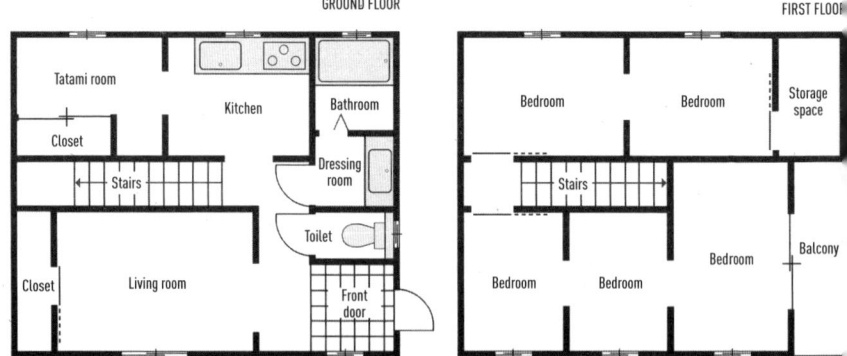

IIMURA: It is. I've lived in the Chubu region for years now. I can't tell you how many of their flyers I've seen. They all have the floor plan and some lines like:

'New-Build Detached Houses—Two Storeys, Six Bedrooms with Living/Dining and Kitchen—15 Million Yen'. That's enough to get your attention.

Your typical single-family home starts around thirty million yen. That means they're selling at around half the market price. And with six bedrooms? Most folks would call it a real bargain. But this is what they get.

Tiny rooms, crammed into the plan just so the numbers in the ad look impressive. Doors sacrificed to cut costs. Not a thought given to comfortable living.

Flashy ads, high pressure sales, no hint of service or care after the sale's done. That's the kind of company they are. I can just picture the Tsuharas, with two young kids, their heads full of dreams, falling for the story the salespeople spun.

I finally understood what Iimura had meant by 'There are copies all over the web' when he gave me the floor plan.

He must have just downloaded it from a property website. There were probably houses like this up for sale all over the country.

And some day, another person like the Tsuhara boy might end up living in one. The thought gave me a chill.

· · ·

After Iimura finished his second beer, he ordered a vanilla ice cream for dessert.

IIMURA: Sorry, I seem to have talked up an appetite.
AUTHOR: Not at all. You've given me some really valuable information.

I have to say, though, I'm surprised that Hikura Homes has stayed in business, what with that reputation for poor quality you mentioned.
IIMURA: They're good at playing the media game. And their PR budget is huge. So long as they keep up a good image in the media, customers will keep taking the bait—hook, line and sinker.
AUTHOR: I see...
IIMURA: It wasn't always like that, though. Hikura only started focusing on the media after a big scandal.
AUTHOR: What scandal was that?
IIMURA: Let's see... I think it was when I was still an apprentice... So, maybe the late 1980s?

There were some dark rumours going around about the Hikura president. That he'd abused some little girl when he was young. They turned out to be unfounded, in the end, but the TV and tabloids were all over it for a while, so everybody heard about it. These days I guess you'd say it 'went viral' or whatnot.

And rumour being so powerful, it even hit Hikura's market share. There, I have to admit, I feel a little bad for them.

Then along came Housemaker Misaki, their biggest local rival, to take advantage of it all and expand their share of the market. It took Hikura over ten years to regain all that lost ground.

And I guess the lesson they took from that was, the truth is powerless against the media.

. . .

When I got home, I looked up Hikura Homes on the internet.

The search bar suggestions included phrases like 'Hikura Homes terrible', 'Hikura Homes scam' and 'Hikura Homes religious'. I followed a few of those and a quick read confirmed Iimura's claims. Hikura really did seem to have a reputation for selling low-quality homes, and their customer ratings were terrible.

Then I checked the company's own website.

Under the header 'Great homes, better prices' were pictures of famous influencers throwing parties in elegant living rooms.

There was a video lower down on the page. I hit play and was greeted by a well-known movie actor murmuring, 'Hikura Homes can make your dreams come true,' in her most seductive voice, with a chart-topping pop song playing in the background.

I could only think of Iimura's comment—'the truth is powerless against the media'.

Having suffered at the hands of the media, Hikura Homes decided to use those same media to paper over its own poor reputation.

At the edge of the site, I spotted a link that read 'A Message from Our Leadership'. I clicked through, and the new page had two photos at the top. One was of the company chairman. He was an older man with an aquiline nose and glasses. A caption gave his name as Masahiko Hikura. The other picture showed a middle-aged man with short, cropped hair. This was the president, Akinaga Hikura.

I didn't need the names to see they were father and son. Akinaga had his father's face, especially the nose.

I shut down my computer, then once more took out the floor plan that Iimura had given me.

In 2020, this house—or one just like it—had been the scene of a tragedy. The victims were the mother, grandmother and younger brother of the alleged perpetrator, a boy of sixteen.

A neighbour heard the mother's screams and contacted the police, but the three were already dead before the officers arrived on the scene. The murder weapon was a kitchen knife. The boy presumably took it from his mother while she was cooking and used it to attack her and the other two victims.

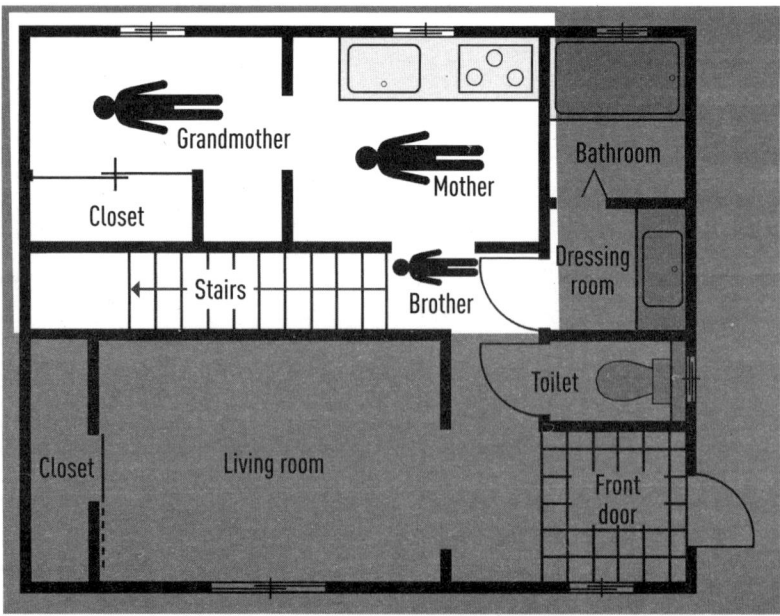

MOTHER: Discovered in the kitchen with a single stab wound to the chest. Clothing showed signs of a struggle.

GRANDMOTHER: Discovered lying in her own bed with eyes closed. Stabbed multiple times through the blanket covering her.

YOUNGER BROTHER: Found in the doorway between the kitchen and the hallway. The knife was still in his abdomen.

The accused suffered multiple cuts to his upper body. He was arrested after treatment at hospital.

Something started to bother me then. What order were these people killed in?

The fact that the knife was still in the brother's abdomen meant he had to have been killed last. So, what about the other two? I stared at the floor plan as I ran through the crime in my mind.

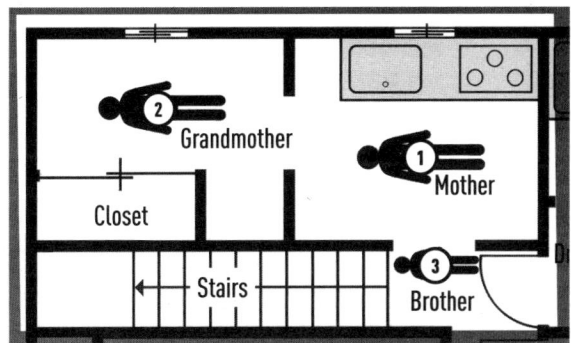

The Tsuhara boy takes the knife from his mother as she is cooking and, after a struggle, stabs her.

He goes to the tatami room and stabs his sleeping grandmother.

He stabs his brother when the boy comes running to see what has happened.

That order seemed to make the most sense. But then something else started to bother me. Why didn't the grandmother wake up? The boy's mother had screamed so loud that the neighbours heard. There's no way the grandmother would have slept through that. In which case...

'Grandmother: Discovered lying in her own bed with eyes closed.'

It didn't fit. Well, then, was the grandmother killed first?

> The Tsuhara boy took the knife from his mother while she was cooking, went into his grandmother's room and stabbed her to death.
>
> ⬇
>
> His mother ran to stop him. She pulled him away from the old woman and dragged him back to the kitchen as they struggled, before he stabbed her in the chest and killed her.
>
> ⬇
>
> Then, he stabbed his younger brother to death when he rushed in to see what was going on.

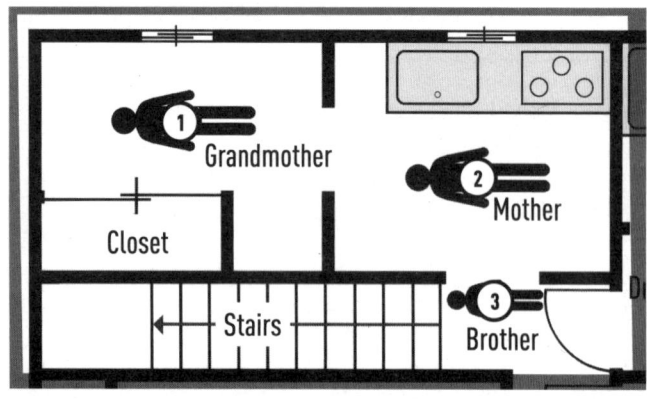

That would help explain why the grandmother's eyes were still closed when she was found. But it also raised another question.

How did the boy receive his injuries?

If the fight with his mother started after he killed his grandmother, then he would still have been holding the knife. And as a sporty boy of sixteen, he would be strong, probably just as strong as his mother, if not stronger.

And yet, the mother had no injuries apart from the single stab wound to her chest, while the boy had cuts all over his upper body, which would imply that it had been his mother who was holding the knife when they were fighting.

That led to a chilling thought. The story we had been telling ourselves fell apart.

It wasn't the boy who'd killed his grandmother: it was his mother.

The poor relationship with her mother-in-law. The exhaustion of caring for her. A house not fit to live in.

All those stresses just built up, and finally, she'd had too much. She walked into the next room, kitchen knife in hand, and thrust it into the old woman as she lay in bed.

The boy happened to see it. He ran in to stop his mother.

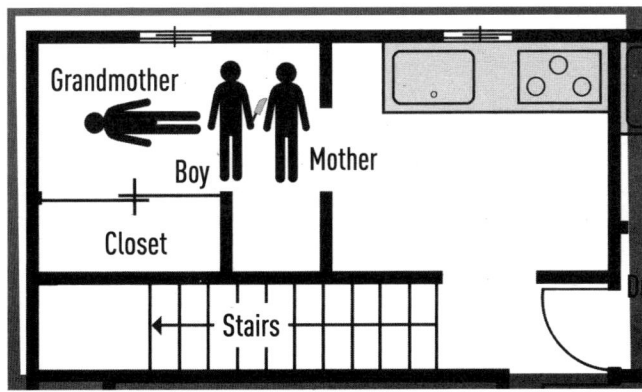

He struggled to pull his mother away and dragged her back into the kitchen.

The knife in his mother's hands struck him again and again, wounding him all over his upper body.

The stretch from the kitchen to the old woman's room especially. It was just a lake of blood.

Could the boy's blood have been in that lake, too?

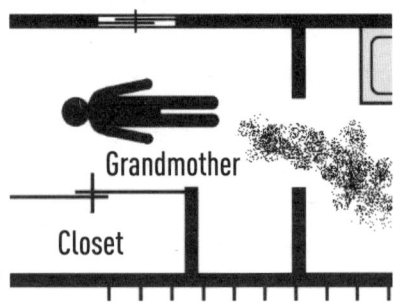

Then, in the fierce struggle, the knife ended up in his mother's chest. A mistake? A pure accident?

The younger brother came running when he heard the screams.

The older boy may have panicked at the thought that his brother had seen what happened to their mother and struck out blindly with the knife...

It was all just speculation. But, still... Maybe this house had nurtured more darkness than just the boy's...

END OF FILE 2: NURTURING DARKNESS

FILE 3

The Watermill in the Woods

Excerpt from an old book

There is an old book called *Records of Beautiful Sojourns*.

It is a collection of accounts by various people of their travels in Japan in the early twentieth century. It was published in 1940 but went out of print almost immediately. I was lucky to find a copy myself.

The excerpts I include here come from a chapter called 'Memories of the Hani Region'. It was written by a woman named Uki Mizunashi, who was just twenty-one years old at the time. The Mizunashi name may be familiar to some because of the pre-war steel-industry giant Mizunashi Zaibatsu. Uki was the sole daughter of the Mizunashi family.

'Memories of the Hani Region' recalls a summer she spent escaping the heat of the city at her uncle's home in the mountain cool of rural Nagano. There is one section that is particularly unsettling.

It describes how she came across a strange watermill on a walk in the woods near her house. The following excerpt is taken from that section.

However, please note that I have updated some of the more outdated or obscure wording used in the original, and the illustrations are my own, based on the descriptions Uki Mizunashi included.

EXTRACT FROM *RECORDS OF BEAUTIFUL SOJOURNS*,
CHAPTER 14: MEMORIES OF THE HANI REGION
(BY UKI MIZUNASHI)

23rd August 1938

After three days of rain, the weather had finally cleared, so I informed my aunt that I would go out for a walk and went into the woods. The ground was quite wet, so I went slowly, watching my feet lest I slip and fall. Soon, I found a small wooden hut before me.

The building had a large wheel affixed to the outside. When I was young, I had visited a relation's house in the far northeast of Japan and seen something similar there. So, I knew at once that it was a watermill.*

The sight aroused pleasant memories, so I stood and stared for a good long while before I noticed something odd. There was no water anywhere near the waterwheel. As the name implies, a waterwheel requires running water for power, from a river or a sluice gate.

But look as I might, there was no source of water to be seen. I soon began to doubt that the hut was, in fact, what I'd

* **What is a Watermill?**

Illustration based on common designs.

A building with a waterwheel attached to the outside.

The flow of water in the adjacent stream turns the waterwheel. A system of gears then transforms the wheel's rotation into power for grinding grain or weaving cloth.

Japan still used waterwheels widely until the 1960s.

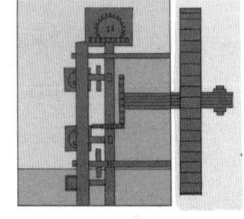

The internal structure of a watermill.

taken it for. Perhaps the large wheel was simply there for ornamentation. As I pondered this oddity, I walked around the hut, until I found a small, barred window to the left of the waterwheel.

I looked through and saw a room. It was wider than it was deep, and inside it was a dizzying variety of gears in a complex arrangement that looked almost like a work of art.

I had seen a similar room at the other watermill, though it hadn't been quite so densely packed, so I concluded that the waterwheel was not, in fact, simply ornamental.

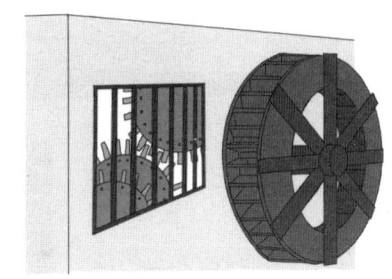

Note: Image created from description in excerpt.

I examined the surroundings once more, and noticed that there was a small, shrine-like structure to the left of the building, so I walked over to it.

It had a lovely peaked and gabled roof and was still relatively new. The wood was clean and pale. Inside was a stone statue. It was a woman, or goddess, holding a round fruit in one hand.

The goddess stood facing the hut. I folded my hands and paid my respects, then went round to the other side of the building, where I found a door.

It was a simple sliding door of wooden planks. Despite knowing that I shouldn't, I gave in to curiosity and slid it open to look inside. There I saw a small room, about three tatami mats in size, of bare wood.

There was no sign of the complex gears and axles glimpsed through the barred window, so I assumed that area must have been walled off from this one.

There was no furniture inside the room, no decorations or windows on the walls. It was like a rectangular wooden box, entirely featureless apart from the door and a large hole in the wall to my right.

I call it a hole, but it did not go all the way through the wall. Indeed, it was more of an alcove—a perfectly square depression in the centre of the wall, large enough that I felt if I curled up, I could fit my whole body inside. I tried to imagine what possible purpose it could have served. It might have been suitable for a flower vase, but who would decorate this bare, isolated room with flowers? It seemed wholly inappropriate.

As I stared into the little room, I began to have the most peculiar feeling. It felt as if what I'd seen outside and what I was seeing inside did not fit together. Then I understood. The room was much smaller than it should have been.

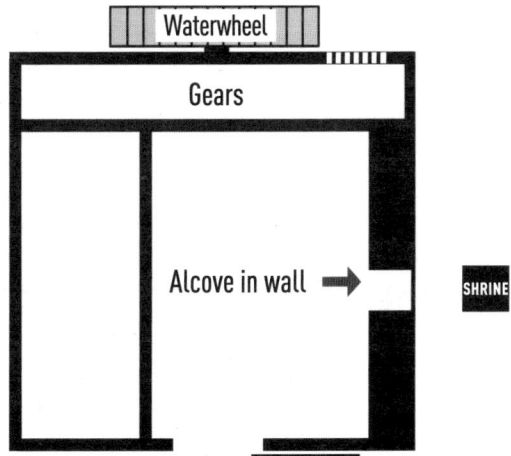

There must have been another room to the left of the one I was facing. However, I could find no door in that wall. I imagined there must be a way in from the outside, so I undertook to check all the outside walls.

Yet when I walked all the way around the opposite side of the building from the shrine, I found no door before I came once more to the waterwheel. I had made a full circle of the hut, and all I had learnt was that it was truly a strange little building.

A waterwheel with no water. A senseless alcove in the wall. A room with no door. It was like something from a dream.

I feared that if I stayed any longer in that place, it could well unsettle my mind. I resolved to quash my curiosity and return to my uncle's house.

But when I tried to move, I found I could not. I looked down and realized that as I stood and pondered, I had sunk into the mud left by the night's rain and was stuck fast.

I braced with my right leg as I pulled to remove my left foot from the mud, and with a squelching sound it finally came free of the sodden earth. But it did so with such vigour that I lost my balance and nearly fell.

I put out my hands to steady myself and they came to rest on the waterwheel, so I managed to avoid soiling my kimono.

However, my relief was short-lived. A great squealing sound suddenly filled my ears, and I found myself falling forward. My weight was causing the waterwheel to turn!

The gears showing through the window began to spin and whirr like massive insects. In a panic I jerked back from the wheel and leant against the wall.

My heart was pounding in my throat. I took a few deep breaths and stood there, trying to regain my calm. I do not know for how long I was there, but as my pulse slowed, I found myself wondering something.

The wheel had turned, and with it the gears had spun. Was it not possible, then, that they had moved something else in turn?

In the watermill I'd seen at my relatives' house in the north-east, the turning of the waterwheel had powered a grain thresher. I'd also heard about looms powered by waterwheels.

But I had seen nothing inside that looked like it would move when the gears turned. It was a watermill with no function. What could it possibly mean?

I recalled that terrible squealing sound that had accompanied the wheel's motion. It had not come from the wheel itself, nor the gears. It seemed to have come from deeper in the building. And at that thought, an image formed in my mind as if by itself. Could it be?

I walked slowly along the wall, taking care not to slip or get stuck. I went past the little shrine and once more approached the opposite side of the shed.

And when I approached the door, I found I had been right.

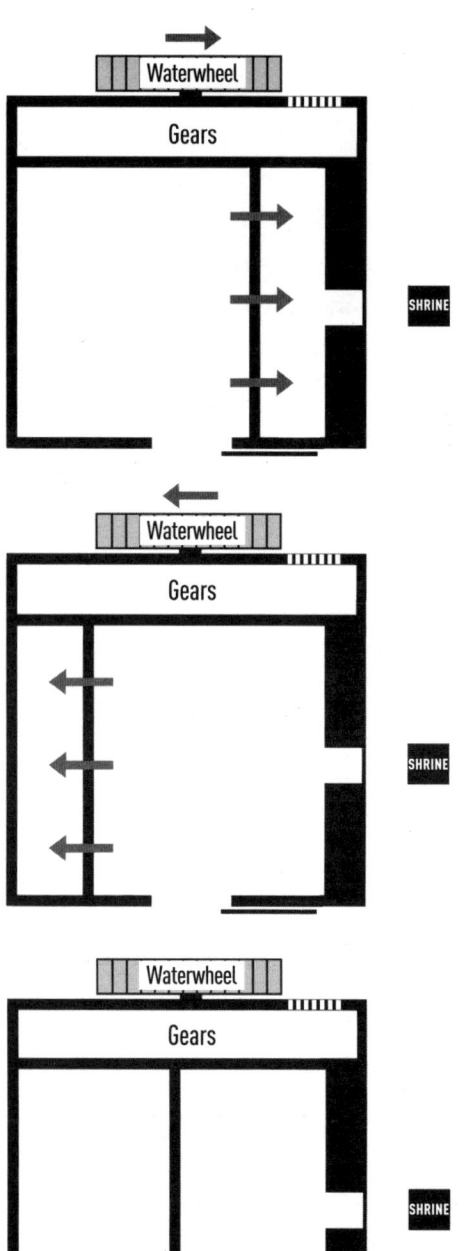

To the left of the doorway was now a small gap that had not been there before. The doorway had not grown wider. The left wall of the room inside had moved forward.

Clearly, turning the waterwheel moved the wall inside the room in the direction of the wheel.

When I had unintentionally turned the wheel just now, it had caused the hidden left-hand room to expand and so revealed the entrance.

A moving wall... The idea called to mind something I had once read in a book. Edogawa Ranpo's *The White-Haired Demon*—a story about a man obsessed with vengeance after his friend steals his wife. To take his revenge on the friend, he prepares a special room, quite small, with a ceiling that can be raised and lowered.

From outside the room, the killer slowly lowers the ceiling on his victim, who is sealed inside with no escape. The trapped man can only shriek in terror as the ceiling slowly descends, until his body... Oh, what a terrible story! Simply thinking of it gives me a chill.

So, did that mean this little watermill was built as an execution chamber, like that in *The White-Haired Demon*?

If you trapped a person in either of the rooms inside, then turned the wheel... But no, no one would ever build such a terrible thing in truth. It must have some other purpose.

I banished my horrific thoughts and stepped closer to the door. Wanting to see what kind of room that hidden left space might be, I peeked through the narrow gap. When I got close, a terrible stench filled my nose.

It was like rotten food mixed with the smell of iron. A sickening smell. As my eyes grew accustomed to the dark, I made out something lying on the floor inside.

It was a snow-white bird.

A female egret lay dead on the floor. Some terrible person must have trapped it in there as a cruel prank. Unable to get out, it had starved to death. Judging by its condition, it must have been in that room for some time. Its feathers were falling out, the tip of one of its wings was missing, its flesh was rotting, and a pool of scarlet and black fluid spread out around it.

Terror filled me, and I fled that place.

That evening, after dining with Uncle and Auntie, I meant to ask them about the watermill. It was not their property, of course, but, as it was so close to their home, I thought they might know something about it.

However, the moment I began to speak, the baby began to cry in the back room and Auntie rushed to check. It had been struggling from the operation, and the stump of its left arm was festering.

Over the next few days, their time was taken up at the hospital, so in the end I was unable to ask about the watermill before I returned home.

[*Section omitted*]

The next year, I married and had my own daughter. My life became so hectic that memories of my time in the countryside faded. However, that walk after the rain remains fresh and clear in my mind to this day.

And sometimes I wonder.

Who trapped that poor egret?

Why would anyone do such a terrible thing?

And what was the true purpose of that watermill?

The first two questions remain a mystery, but I do have a theory about the third question, the watermill's true purpose.

That day, the sight of the moving wall had prompted some gruesome thoughts about *The White-Haired Demon*. I brushed them off as preposterous speculation, but later I began to suspect that perhaps I was not so wide of the mark.

Which is not to say I believed that mill was used for executions. But perhaps something similar? That is what I began to consider.

What I wondered about in particular was that square alcove in the wall of the right-hand room. What was it there for?

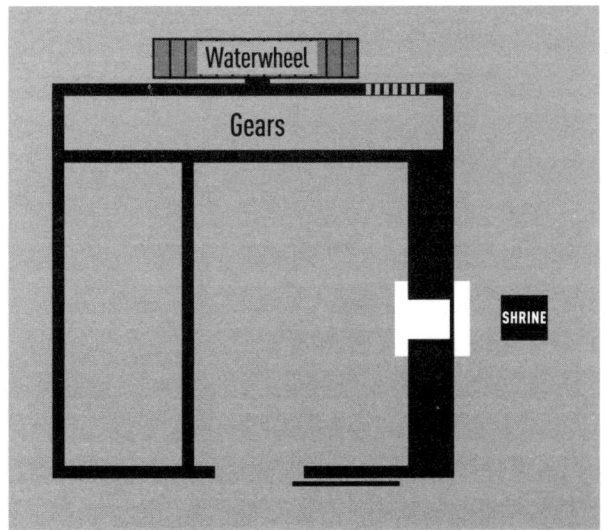

Let us imagine someone was imprisoned in that right-hand room, and then the waterwheel turned. As the wall closed in, whoever was trapped inside would grow terrified of being crushed. What would he or she do, then?

Might they not escape into that alcove, curling into a ball?

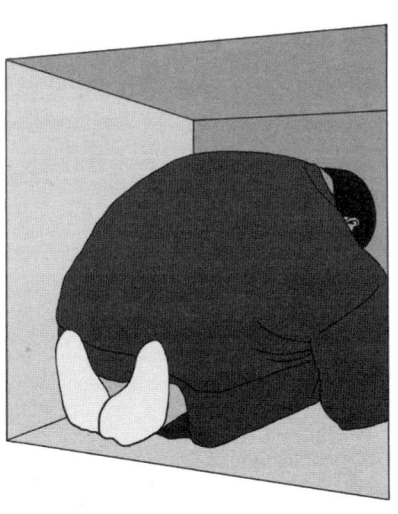

They would kneel, their head bowed down between their knees. The position of someone begging forgiveness for some transgression.

And in the direction of their prostration was the shrine. The stone statue of the goddess. Why put such a thing there? I believe its position was very deliberately chosen.

That watermill was built to force wrongdoers into paying penance. Some transgressor who refused to repent would be forced to kneel and bow to the goddess there. That was the purpose of the room.

No doubt some deeply religious community had built it in secret, out there in the woods. That is what I came to believe.

This all happened long ago, of course, and it most certainly was nothing more than a fantasy of mine.

END OF FILE 3: THE WATERMILL IN THE WOODS

FILE 4
The Mousetrap House

13TH MARCH 2022

Interview with Shiori Hayasaka

'I always knew, deep inside, that one day the time to tell this story would come.'

Shiori Hayasaka looks down over the city from the broad expanse of glass nearly filling her office wall.

At thirty-three years old, Hayasaka runs her own company from this Roppongi high-rise office. Here, she and ten employees create web apps that earn the company several hundred million yen a year. With her long light-brown hair, her precise make-up and perfectly fitted brand suit, she is the very image of the modern female CEO.

It is a Sunday, so Hayasaka and I are alone in her office. I am here to interview her because of a certain house and the fatal accident that occurred there.

HAYASAKA: I went to a private middle school for girls in northern Gunma Prefecture. You know the type, a school for 'little princesses' from well-to-do, important families.

    The other students were all daughters of local company owners or government officials or landowners. In other words, all quite wealthy. And I always felt embarrassed around them.

At the time, her father was a division manager at an automotive manufacturer. It was a perfectly respectable position, but Hayasaka says that her 'family standing' resulted in subtle discrimination at school.

HAYASAKA: No one ever said it out loud, but it was obvious to them. There are different ranks even among the wealthy, and classmates form little cliques along those lines. School castes, I think they call them

I was right at the bottom. They looked down on me as a 'company man's daughter'. They mocked me for all sorts of things, like how my shoes weren't the right brand, and when we made groups for school outings, the other girls would shut me out. They'd say, 'If we go around with you, we won't be able to go to the good shops.'

AUTHOR: They sound rather merciless.

HAYASAKA: That's the exact word for it. My parents worked incredibly hard to make sure I went to a good school, but in all honesty, it was a mixed blessing.

Actually fitting in and making the most of your time at a school for the wealthy requires far more money than just the cost of tuition. Students need to be decked out in designer goods to prove their status. If they aren't, the others will make their life miserable.

Hayasaka takes a pack of cigarettes out of the designer bag at her side.

'Do you mind?' she asks me before putting her lighter to one. The lighter looks to me like solid gold.

HAYASAKA: But even so, there was one girl who was nice to me. Just the one. Her name was Mitsuko. We ended up in the same class in our first year. Mitsuko was in the highest caste, too. Her father was the president of Hikura Homes, one of the largest construction companies in the region.

She was the most darling child. Long black hair in pigtails, delicate pale skin and big bright eyes.

One day, during a free period, she just came up and talked to me. I forget what we talked about, but I do recall we had a lot of fun doing it. After that, we got closer and closer. We talked and even kept a joint 'exchange diary' together, where we'd take it in turns to write down our thoughts.

One day, I happened to mention how much I loved the manga *Clever Pepper Girl* and it turned out she did, too.

I was so happy to find someone to share it with, and from then on manga was all we talked about. But if I'm honest, thinking back, I was the one doing all the talking. Mitsuko would just listen and smile.

Things went on like that every day for two months or so. Then, just before the summer holidays, Mitsuko made me an offer.

She told me, 'During the holidays, why don't we take turns having sleepovers at each other's houses?' I was happy, but also a bit worried. We lived in a small house. My own room was only six tatami mats. Thinking back now, I'm sure it wasn't that big a deal, but back then I just didn't feel comfortable inviting round someone as wealthy as Mitsuko.

I wrestled with the decision, but in the end I agreed. It was *Clever Pepper Girl* that decided me. I had the full collection of paperback editions and most of the merchandise.

Even if my room wasn't luxurious, I thought that would be enough to make Mitsuko happy. We could stay up late talking about it. I had this idea that our shared interests could overcome any social divide between us. I was... naive, I suppose.

Hayasaka exhales a cloud of smoke and sits staring out the window for a moment before speaking again.

HAYASAKA: We decided whose house we'd stay at first with a game of rock, paper, scissors. Mitsuko won, so I would be staying over at her place. I still remember how I felt that day, the first Saturday of the summer holidays, when I took my bag and left the house. It was my first ever sleepover at a friend's house. I was so excited.

But when we arrived at the gate in front of her house, all the excitement just vanished. I had been expecting a big house, but what I saw was just... It was beyond anything I could have imagined. It looked large enough for a hundred people to live in, and the garden was like the English parks you see in movies. The only word for it was palatial. It showed me just how desperately wide the divide between us truly was.

When I rang the bell, an elegant man in dress shirt and tie came to the door. I was full of nerves when I told him why I'd come, but he was perfectly kind. He said, 'We've been expecting you. The young mistress is in her room upstairs. I'll show you the way.' He escorted me into the house.

I remember thinking he must be some kind of servant. Normally that would have come as a shock, but I remember accepting it pretty readily. It would have been more odd for that house not to have had servants. That's just how extravagant it was.

Hayasaka drew a rough floor plan on her note pad.

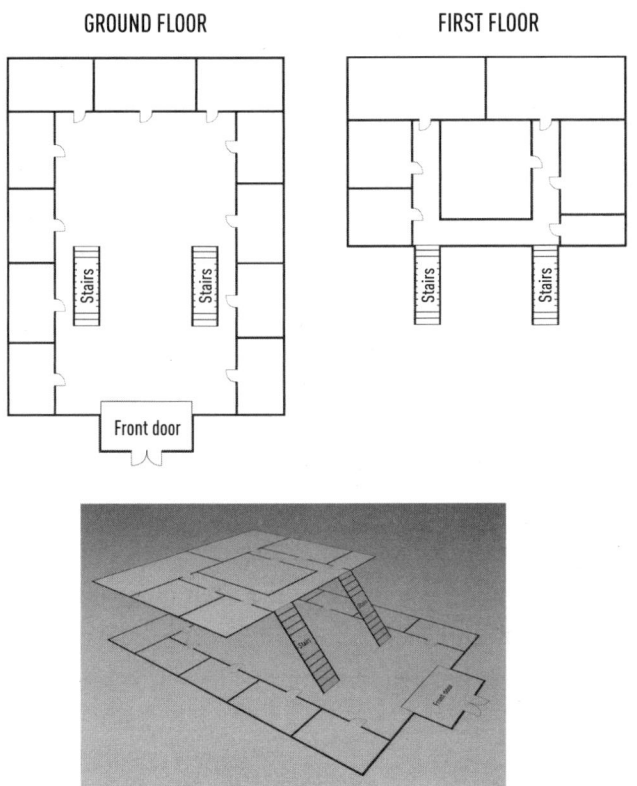

HAYASAKA: Going in the front door, you were faced with two staircases, one each to the left and right. The servant told me that the ground floor had guest rooms, servants' quarters, the kitchen and so on, while the family mostly stayed on the first floor.

AUTHOR: Speaking of family, was it just Mitsuko and her parents?

HAYASAKA: No, actually. Her parents lived in a second home quite far away due to her father's work. At that time, the only ones living in this house were Mitsuko and her grandmother. They told me, in fact, that the house was built especially for those two.

AUTHOR: An estate like that, for just two people. That's something else...

HAYASAKA: I understand that Mitsuko's father designed it himself. Like I said, he ran a housing company. As a child, I just assumed it was normal to build houses for your own family when that was your business... I remember feeling quite impressed at the thought.

Looking back on it now, though, he was probably only able to use Hikura Homes for his own needs because it was a family-owned company based in the countryside. There was no one to pay attention or point out that company assets aren't personal property.

When we went up the stairs, Mitsuko was waiting outside her room for me. My mother had been quite insistent that I make sure to greet Mitsuko's family properly, so I asked her to show me to her grandmother's room. It was in the centre of the first floor.

When Mitsuko opened the door, a lovely, sweet fragrance came wafting out. I think Grandmother Hikura must have been burning incense. Inside, the room was decorated with beautiful furniture and paintings,

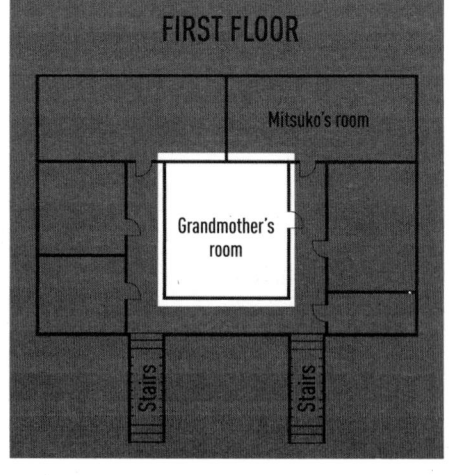

and her grandmother sat in a chair reading. She seemed far too young and beautiful to be called 'Grandmother', though.

She was wearing a long skirt that hung to the floor, hiding her legs completely, and was wrapped in a flower-patterned cardigan. She had long white gloves on her hands. It felt like I was looking into the world of a painting. She looked up from her book and smiled at me, saying, 'Welcome to our home!'

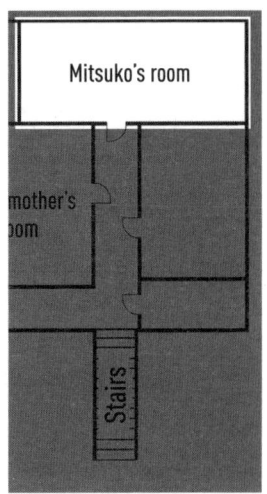

After that, we went to Mitsuko's room. It wasn't decorated as luxuriously as her grandmother's, but it was all still much more than what any normal family could afford. The first thing that caught my attention was an enormous wardrobe standing at the back of the room. We had wardrobes at home, of course, but trying to compare them seems almost insulting. It was so elegant. After that, the two of us sat in her room snacking and talking for a couple of hours.

Mitsuko said she was going to the toilet and left the room. Sitting there alone, I couldn't help staring around the room in curiosity. Everything was so fascinating. It was full of rare toys, imported cosmetics, and all kinds of wonderful things, but I could not get over that wardrobe.

I went over to it and could see in every detail just how different it was to mine at home. The patterns carved into the doors, the lustre of the finish… It was just so wonderful. I had to sigh. I remember being so impressed that even the most common parts surprised me. Like, when I saw the keyhole, I thought, 'Oh! You can lock it! How wonderful!' but of course that's nothing unusual at all.

I stood there, looking at it for a while. I started wondering what could be inside. I knew I shouldn't, but I tried the door. It was ill mannered of me, of course. I could have just waited and asked her to show me.

I pulled the handle, and the door opened silently. It was packed with books. It wasn't a wardrobe at all. It was a bookcase.

There were literary works, reference books and foreign-language dictionaries. Once more, I was impressed. I remember thinking, 'Rich kids certainly do read difficult books.'

But as I looked at the books lined up there, I noticed something odd. There weren't any copies of *Clever Pepper Girl*, the manga we had bonded over. There weren't any manga books at all. I just stood there in confusion until I heard footsteps in the hall.

I didn't want Mitsuko to catch me prying, so I hurriedly closed the door and went back to where I'd been sitting.

After that, we had dinner in the dining hall. I was worried when her grandmother didn't appear, but Mitsuko said that she always ate alone in her room.

Then we spent an hour or so watching a film in the home cinema until bath time. After that, we changed into our pyjamas and went to bed. I remember feeling sad, thinking about how our fun day was coming to an end. I wanted to stay up, talking all night, but when we turned off the lights, my eyelids grew heavy, and I drifted off.

I don't know how long I slept. When my eyes opened, the room was pitch dark. I could hear Mitsuko's slow, deep breathing beside me. I thought back on everything that had happened that day and it was like going through a box of treasures. It was all like some kind of dream.

But... There was one thing that I couldn't ignore, like a little bone stuck in my throat. The bookcase.

It just seemed so strange to me that there wasn't a single volume of *Clever Pepper Girl*, even though she'd told me she how much she loved it. Or maybe there had been, and I'd just missed them. And at that, I thought I should take another look.

I'd packed a little torch in my bag, so I took it out and used it to light my way to the bookcase. I reached out and pulled the handle.

But it wouldn't open.

I pulled again, harder, but it didn't budge. Then, my eye came to rest on the keyhole. I felt a chill run down my spine.

Had Mitsuko somehow noticed that I'd opened the door and then locked it to keep me from looking again? I suddenly had the feeling that someone was watching me from behind. I spun to look at the bed.

Mitsuko was still lying there, breathing deep and slow, asleep.

I suddenly felt like the most wretched sort of person. So what if there weren't any *Clever Pepper Girl* books in the bookcase? She could be storing her manga in some other place entirely. They might have an entire library somewhere in the house.

And still, I had got out of bed in the middle of the night and gone poking around like a sneak-thief. I felt so guilty.

HAYASAKA: Then, the next thing I remember is Mitsuko waking me up.

It was just past five in the morning, but she told me, 'Let's play some more, since we're almost out of time.' She had already set up a card game, so I rubbed my eyes and got out of bed.

We played cards for a while, then I had to go to the toilet. I stepped out of the room and saw her grandmother in the hallway.

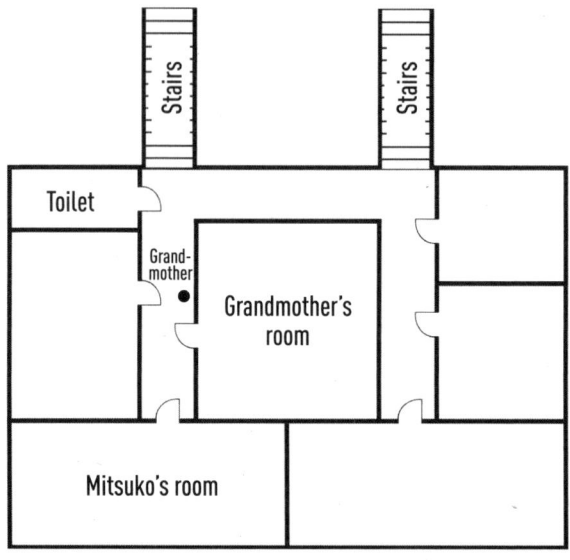

She had her back to me, facing the stairs, her right hand resting on the wall. She was trying to walk, but looked as if she might fall over at any moment. I think she must have had a problem with her legs.

She was still wearing that skirt, so long it dragged on the floor. I was worried that it might trip her up, so I rushed over to help.

She tried to wave me off and said, 'I'm fine. The toilet is just there.' But I couldn't just leave her like that, so I told her that's where I was going as well, so we should go together. I tried to lend her my shoulder to lean on, but she insisted. 'Never you mind me. Go on ahead. Wouldn't want you to wet your pants!'

To be honest, I really was about ready to burst, so I did what she said and went on ahead. Oh, how I regret that.

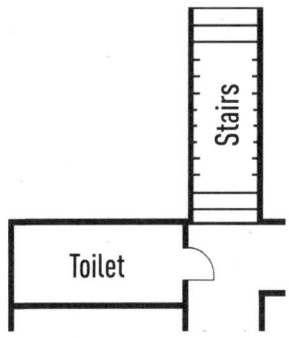

HAYASAKA: I used the toilet and washed my hands, but just as I was about to step out into the hall, I heard a loud 'thud' just outside the door, then the sound of something heavy rolling down the stairs, growing fainter as it got further away. I threw the door open. Mitsuko's grandmother should have been standing there, but she was nowhere to be seen.

I knew I should search for her. So, I went back to her room. To this day, I wonder why I did that. Maybe I was trying to avoid facing what I knew must have happened.

Of course, she wasn't in her room. I stood there for a moment, unsure what to do, then I heard a commotion from the ground floor. The servants were shouting and rushing around. I could hear someone talking on the telephone.

An ambulance came right away and rushed Mitsuko's grandmother to the hospital.

I didn't see her get taken away. I was afraid to look. Afraid to see what had happened to her. So, I kept my distance, hanging my head and averting my eyes. How selfish and mean of me, closing my eyes to what was happening when my friend could not…

And even so, when Mitsuko and I parted that day, she was the one to apologize to me. 'I'm sorry something like this had to happen.'

I could only think what a kind, gentle girl she was, worrying about me, when surely she was the one suffering. And how miserable and pathetic I was.

All I could think of was myself while Mitsuko was in such pain. And the whole time, I just kept repeating to myself the same thing. 'It's not my fault.'

. . .

HAYASAKA: I learnt two days later that Mitsuko's grandmother had passed away in hospital. She'd struck her head in the fall, and the injury was just too severe.

The day after that, the police came to speak to me. It wasn't that they were suspicious or anything like that. They just wanted to know how it had happened.

I told them everything I'd seen. The police didn't blame me for not helping Mitsuko's grandmother that morning. But... neither did they say what I most wanted to hear, that it wasn't my fault.

Hayasaka stops to stub out her cigarette in an ashtray.

HAYASAKA: After that, Mitsuko and I drifted apart. I mean, of course we did. It didn't matter what we talked about, we couldn't forget what happened that morning. She never did come to sleep over at my house in the end. So, that is what happened to me.

She stops talking, and her eyes seem to bore into mine.

HAYASAKA: So, what do you think? About the old woman's death?
AUTHOR: From what you just told me it sounds like a simple accidental death. She fell down the stairs.
HAYASAKA: Was it really an accident, though?
AUTHOR: ...

I have no response to the sudden question, and the silence drags on. She is the one to break it.

HAYASAKA: I'm not saying anyone actually pushed her down the stairs. Nothing like that. I came out of the toilet immediately after the sound of her fall, and no one was there.
    Mitsuko's grandmother fell on her own. That's a fact. But still...

Hayasaka points to the floor plan.

HAYASAKA: Don't you think this spot here is terribly dangerous?

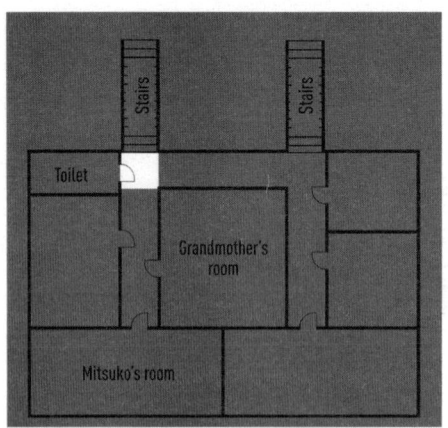 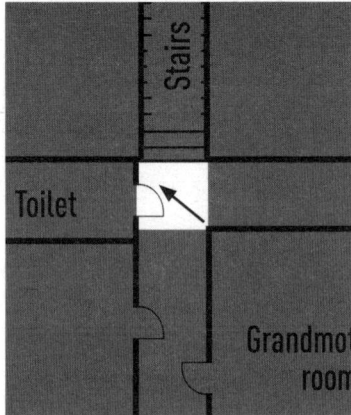

HAYASAKA: When I saw her that morning, she was making her way to the toilet, supporting herself with one hand on the wall to her right. If you follow that path forward, then it leads to a space without any wall to support herself on.

AUTHOR: I see. Here, between the end of the wall and the toilet door.

HAYASAKA: So, she would have to take her hand off the wall and walk unsupported until she could grab the toilet door handle. That hallway is a good two metres wide. That's a long way for someone in her condition.

I think she must have lost her balance and fallen in that space.

AUTHOR: That seems a reasonable conclusion. But isn't that exactly what makes it an 'accident'?

HAYASAKA: Is it? This house was built specifically for Mitsuko and her grandmother. In which case, you'd expect it to be designed with their needs in mind.

I can't imagine designing a house for an older person with this kind of dangerous space. I mean, she had difficulty walking, so shouldn't they have had some handrails in the hallways or perhaps an en-suite toilet in her room?

There was nothing like that in this house. No sign that any thought had been given to her well-being.

AUTHOR: Well, when you put it that way…

HAYASAKA: Mitsuko's father built this house. The president of Hikura Homes, a housebuilder. I simply can't believe that the president of a company whose main business is building houses would make mistakes like that.

So… I don't think they were mistakes.

AUTHOR: Which would mean…

HAYASAKA: Wouldn't you say this house was built specifically to cause Mitsuko's grandmother to have an accident?

AUTHOR: Um…

Once, I might have said such a thing was impossible, that she was overthinking it. But I know better now. Three years ago, when researching for *Strange Houses*, I had seen a house built specifically for murder.

HAYASAKA: Hikura Homes is a typical family-run business. As an older member of the family, the grandmother must have had a lot of influence in the company. She was probably a thorn in the president's side.

AUTHOR: So, you think that he wanted to kill her to get her out of the way?

A tightly sealed company structure where family members held all the rights. It is easy to see how this might lead to resentment between relatives.

And, in that case, it certainly seems plausible that someone might resort to this sort of 'ill-treatment', which crossed all kinds of lines but stopped short of outright murder…

HAYASAKA: You know those old-fashioned mousetraps? You know, where you put some food in the middle, and, when the mouse or whatever steps on the trigger, it snaps shut and kills it?
AUTHOR: Sure I do.
HAYASAKA: It's the same idea. You set the trap and just wait for your target to set it off. You're not killing them directly, so you keep your hands clean.
AUTHOR: Murder without the risk…
HAYASAKA: And then, just by coincidence, the trap was sprung when I came to stay over.
AUTHOR: I see.
HAYASAKA: Well, anyway, that's what I used to think.
AUTHOR: What?

Hayasaka takes her lighter from the table, then stands and looks out over the city from the window again.

HAYASAKA: Lately I've been wondering if that's really how it was. Isn't it all just a bit too much? The day I just happened to be staying there I just happened to meet her grandmother in the hallway just before she happened to fall down the stairs and die? There are far too many coincidences.
AUTHOR: But if those weren't just coincidences?

HAYASAKA: Then someone must have triggered the trap intentionally.
AUTHOR: And... Who...?
HAYASAKA: There's only one person it could have been. Mitsuko.

Her face is dead, devoid of expression when she says this.
For some reason, it sends a chill down my spine.

HAYASAKA: So, do you think any of it was true?
AUTHOR: Any of what?
HAYASAKA: Do you think Mitsuko was really a fan of *Clever Pepper Girl*?

Whenever we talked about manga, it was always just me talking. Mitsuko only listened. I thought she was just being kind and letting me talk my heart out, but... Maybe she'd never even read it.

So, a few months later after all that, I just happened to overhear something. Mitsuko was talking to another girl in class, and she said, 'As if I would ever read manga! That's for poor people, isn't it?'

Something clatters as it falls to the floor. The gold lighter.

HAYASAKA: I... I think I was being used for something. It's all just so odd. Mitsuko invited me to come and stay. That's like a princess inviting a beggar to her palace. No matter how many times I might invite her to my house, it would never balance out. She must have had some ulterior motive.

That day, the bookcase was unlocked. But, at night, it was locked. When did she lock it? We were together all that evening and into the night. I remember we even went to the toilet together. So, the only time she could have locked it was later, between when I fell asleep and when I woke up.

So, after she was sure I was asleep, she got out of bed and locked the bookcase.

AUTHOR: Why would she do that?

HAYASAKA: Maybe she hid something in there. Like, say, a walking stick.

AUTHOR: Oh!

A walking stick! Why didn't I think of it myself? If Mitsuko's grandmother did have problems walking, then you would expect her to use a stick, wouldn't you?

Mitsuko sneaked into her grandmother's room in the middle of the night, took the old lady's walking stick and hid it in the bookcase. The next morning, when her grandmother woke up to go to the toilet, she looked for her stick but couldn't find it.

So, what did she do? The toilet was close, so perhaps she thought she could make it.

Maybe she wasn't aware of how dangerous that space was, since she normally walked it with a stick. So, thinking that the distance was nothing to worry about, she tried and...

AUTHOR: Mitsuko removed the bar holding back the mousetrap spring...

HAYASAKA: That's what I think happened.

AUTHOR: But she was just a middle school girl. Twelve or thirteen years old. She was too young to be involved in company business, surely?

HAYASAKA: I'm just speculating, but surely her father put her up to it.

Maybe he told her that if she hid the stick, he'd buy her whatever she wanted or something.

Since she was so young, she might have given in to temptation and just done what she was told without much thought about it at all.

HAYASAKA: And if that's the case, then I think I know why I was invited. To serve as her alibi. I think maybe the plan was for me to be able to say, 'Mitsuko and I were playing cards in her room when the accident happened.' That's why she woke me up so early.

When I went out into the hallway and saw her grandmother, it ended up being a happy accident. Me actually being a witness would make for an even better alibi.

And why me? It must have been because I was poor. She probably considered me disposable because I was in the bottom caste. It's pathetic. Truly.

Hayasaka starts pushing the fallen lighter around with the tip of one high-heeled shoe.

The pure gold glitters.

HAYASAKA: This lighter's pretty flashy, right? Like I'm carrying a sign saying, 'new money'.

I got tired of the view from this window in three days. The expensive clothes, the imported perfume, the brand bag, it's all ridiculous. Why is everything money buys you so ridiculous? But I have to have it all. I have to wear the symbols.

Because I want to show Mitsuko and everyone like her. I want her to know. I want to tell her, 'I don't live like a princess on my parents' money. I did this all myself.'

> **END OF FILE 4: THE MOUSETRAP HOUSE**

FILE 5
The House Where It Happened

AUGUST 2022

Record of research and interview with Kenji Hirauchi

The summer of the year after I first published *Strange Houses*, a man came to consult me about his new house.

Kenji Hirauchi, an office worker in his mid-thirties, had just moved to Shimojo in Nagano Prefecture. He told me he'd bought a somewhat old house in the mountain village a few months ago.

The house was on the outskirts, about an hour by bus from his office in the centre.

His commute was long, but there were supermarkets and other shops within a short walk of the house, so all in all the location was not too inconvenient. The house was near some woods, which were criss-crossed by hiking trails with beautiful views of the surrounding countryside, which fitted well with his interests in walking and photography. But he was most attracted by the relatively low property prices compared to the city.

When the estate agent had told him that the house was twenty-six years old, he had imagined something quite run down, given that most houses in Japan don't make it past thirty years, but when he went to see the property, it seemed barely lived in. He decided to buy it on the spot.

But not long after he moved in, Hirauchi discovered something strange.

One evening, lazing around in bed, he started looking up maps of 'Incident Properties' on his phone. These maps show places where bad things have happened: murders, fatal accidents and the like. They're usually on unofficial sites maintained by users. The most famous in Japan is called Oshimaland, but there are several others with a similar setup.

He was using a special app called Dark Spots Japan. He'd just learnt about it that day when chatting with a co-worker at lunch, so he installed it after work just to have something to talk to his colleague about.

When he opened it up, he was presented with a map of Japan. Locations with 'dark histories' were marked with stars. Tapping them would open up a window with details.

The first thing he looked up was the student flat where he'd lived in Tokyo. He zoomed in on Tokyo, then the Kinshi district and found his old flat on the north side of Kinshicho Station. Three houses down from his flat, there was a star.

He tapped it.

LOCATION:	Kinshicho, Sumida-ku, Tokyo
DATE:	26th May 2009
PROPERTY:	Two-storey detached home
DETAILS:	This house was the site of a family murder-suicide. There are rumours that shadowy figures can be seen through the windows at night.

Hirauchi was impressed by the accuracy.

He had known about the murder-suicide in that house and remembered all the commotion in the neighbourhood at the time, with police, media and gawkers filling the streets. He'd even heard the rumours—true or not—that neighbours were spreading about shadows moving in the windows of the empty house after that.

Clearly, someone who had lived, or was still living, nearby had posted the information.

After that, he searched out a few more dark spots that he already knew.

The old, abandoned hospital he and his friends would dare each other to venture into during the summer holidays.

The suicide spot on the island of Shikoku that one of his favourite streamers had talked about.

The highway tunnel near his house where five people had died in a car crash.

They all had stars. His curiosity even drove him to check Honno-ji temple in Kyoto, and, sure enough, there it was: '21st June 1582. Oda Nobunaga was killed in a plot to overthrow his rule.'

He was totally convinced of the app's accuracy.

He played around with the map for a while until he noticed that it was already past midnight. He had to work the next morning, so he knew he should go to sleep, but, before he did, there was one more spot he wanted to check.

He scrolled to Nagano Prefecture.

He wanted to see if there was a star somewhere near his own house. He wasn't so much curious to find out as anxious to set his mind at ease.

As he zoomed in on the area around his new house, he spotted a single star.

He zoomed in further to see exactly where the star was. As he did, the map became clearer, until he was able to make out individual houses. He was overtaken by a peculiar feeling. He knew this road. He knew those houses.

He gasped. The star was over his own house.

· · ·

'Here, let me show you,' Hirauchi said and tapped at his phone.

When I first read his email, I had fully intended to make the trip to Shimojo.

But he told me he had a sudden work trip to Tokyo coming up, so I asked him to drop by my Japanese publisher's offices to discuss his situation.

I sat across the table from Hirauchi in the visitor's conference room, with my editor Sugiyama beside me. He held up his phone, and we examined the screen.

From the map, the area looked like a lonely one. It was more than seventy per cent forest, with just a handful of houses dotting the green. And among them was a single bright-yellow star. It seemed oddly out of place.

Hirauchi touched the star, and a detail window popped up.

LOCATION:	Oaza, Shimojo, Nagano Prefecture
DATE:	23rd August 1938
PROPERTY:	Privately owned house
DETAILS:	Woman's corpse found

1938. Almost ninety years ago.

Hirauchi's house was only twenty-six years old, so the incident happened long before it was built. So, did that mean the woman's body was discovered in a house that had previously stood on the same spot?

HIRAUCHI: I know it might be faked. Anyone can post anything on these kinds of apps, so someone could have made it up as a joke or something. But, I don't know, it feels too realistic, somehow. I just don't think it's a prank.

AUTHOR: I agree. I think if someone were going to make up something as a prank, they'd go further than that. It'd say, 'This house was the site of a mass murder' or 'A headless ghost has been seen here at night.'

HIRAUCHI: Exactly. It doesn't seem like they were trying to make it scary. It's just a simple statement of fact. That's what makes it feel real.

AUTHOR: So, has anything strange happened in the house since you moved in?

HIRAUCHI: No, not at all. I'm not one to 'sense the spirits' or see ghosts or anything, to be honest. But still, I must say it feels creepy now. Just the thought that someone died there, even so long ago, you know, I can't help imagining things at night after I turn off the lights.

AUTHOR: Hmm…

Sugiyama had been sitting there, listening silently, but chose that moment to speak.

SUGIYAMA: If you just want to know if something actually happened there, we should be able to confirm the facts, at least.

He pointed at the detail window still visible on Hirauchi's phone.

LOCATION:	Oaza, Shimojo, Nagano Prefecture
DATE:	23rd August 1938
PROPERTY:	Private house
DETAILS:	Woman's corpse found

SUGIYAMA: The first questions that come to mind are: who posted this and how did they know about it? Generally, you get two groups of people posting on these kinds of apps.

The first are people who live nearby and have first-hand knowledge of whatever happened. I imagine whoever posted about the murder-suicide in Kinshicho was in that category.

The second group are those who learn about the incident from books or the internet. Obviously, that's the case with the person who posted about the Nobunaga incident at Honno-ji.

We can assume that whoever posted this incident is in the latter group too. If it were someone who had first-hand knowledge of the incident, they'd have to be nearly a hundred years old. It's certainly not impossible for someone that old to have gone to all the trouble of installing the app and posting the information, but I find it highly unlikely.

AUTHOR: That means that there must be information about it out there somewhere.

I tried searching for 'Shimojo Nagano Prefecture woman's corpse 23rd August 1938' on my own phone.

I got no hits.

AUTHOR: There's nothing online, at least.

SUGIYAMA: Well, even the net has its limits.

AUTHOR: Meaning?

SUGIYAMA: At the last publisher I worked for, I was assigned to a rural history magazine. An older worker told me, 'If you really want to learn about the countryside, forget the internet.'

   He insisted that all the rural organizations holding the historical information we were interested in are made up of older people, and they just don't put their information online. They aren't interested in digitalization or any of that stuff. So it's no use looking on the net to find out about something that happened out in the countryside.

   Honestly, my experience totally confirmed what he said. There were things that I spent hours searching for online to no avail, but when I went on-site I was shocked how much I learnt with barely any effort. It happened all the time.

AUTHOR: So, what you're saying is, it's time for some foot-slogging.

· · ·

The next day, I went with Hirauchi to Nagano.

It was a four-hour trip by Shinkansen and then a local line to the station nearest Shimojo. After we arrived, our first stop was the library, a twenty-minute walk from the station.

The information signs said they had a newspaper archive on the first floor.

AUTHOR: I think newspapers are the best place to start. They would surely have carried some mention of a body discovered in the local area.

HIRAUCHI: Do you think they'll still have papers from that long ago?

AUTHOR: Certainly not the original papers themselves, but there's a chance they have some kind of copies.

We were in luck. The library had reproductions of local newspapers going back one hundred years. We started our search from the August 1938 editions, sharing the work as we went through different papers.

After about two hours of searching, we still hadn't come across any mention of a woman's body being discovered. However, Hirauchi did find something interesting.

18TH OCTOBER 1938

HEAD OF AZUMA FAMILY, KIYOCHIKA AZUMA, DIES

Kiyochika Azuma, head of the influential local family, passed away in his room at the Azuma manor. The cause of death was reportedly hanging. Kiyochika has no direct heirs, so authorities are still unsure who will inherit the Azuma family estate.

AUTHOR: The 18th of October 1938. That's about two months after the woman's body was supposedly found. But who was this Kiyochika Azuma, anyway?

HIRAUCHI: Actually, just the other day I went out on a walk taking photographs, and I found a stone marker reading 'Site of the former Azuma Estate'.

AUTHOR: So, the manor house was nearby... I don't know if it's connected, but it might not hurt to look into the Azuma family. What do you say?

We started to search the library for any books that might contain information about the family.

Before long, Hirauchi found a section of the library dedicated to local history. There were dozens of books there, all on one shelf. We browsed through and found one titled *History of the Great Houses of Nanshin*.

AUTHOR: Nanshin?
HIRAUCHI: It must mean southern Shin Province. It's the old name for Nagano Prefecture.
AUTHOR: Then it will cover Shimojo, too. From that article's mention of an 'estate', it certainly seems possible that the Azuma family could have been a 'great house' of the area. Let's take a look.

There were only a few pages with any mention of the Azumas, but we learnt the following:

The area where Hirauchi lived was once completely covered in forest. There was a small village at the eastern edge of the forest, while the Azuma manor stood on the western edge.

The Azuma family had been the rulers of the area in feudal times. After the feudal system was abolished, they remained a powerful local family, as one of the 'great houses'.

However, in 1938, the head of the family, Kiyochika, committed suicide and plunged the family into disorder. It never recovered, and, in the chaos of the Second World War and the post-war period, it lost all its money and influence completely. Finally, the manor itself was torn down in the early 1980s, the woods it had controlled began to be cleared, and private homes appeared on the family's former holdings. One of those houses was Hirauchi's.

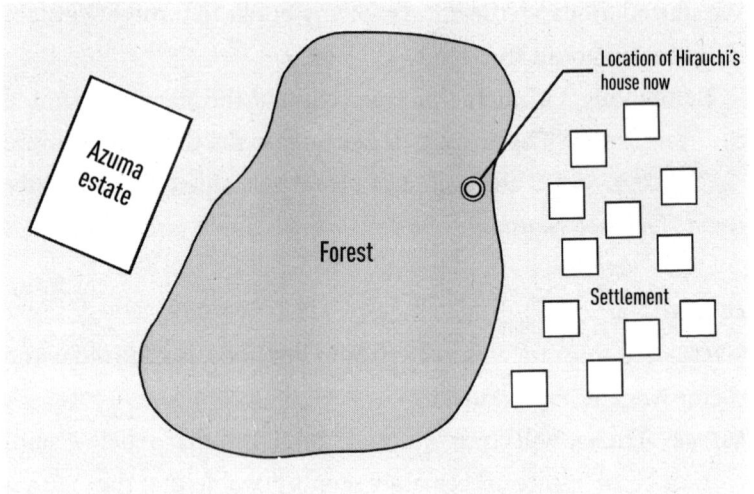

HIRAUCHI: So, when the woman's body was discovered in 1938, the place where my house stands was still unsettled forest.

AUTHOR: So it would seem. I doubt there were any houses in the woods at that point. So the entry must be at least partly wrong.

LOCATION:	Oaza, Shimojo, Nagano Prefecture
DATE:	23rd August 1938
PROPERTY:	Private house
DETAILS:	Woman's corpse found

AUTHOR: The woman's body couldn't have been discovered in a house, but perhaps it was found in the forest. Maybe it was buried there.

HIRAUCHI: So, someone dug her up?

AUTHOR: Which definitely suggests she was murdered. And if that was the case, we could perhaps link it to Kiyochika Azuma's suicide like this.

- Kiyochika Azuma kills a woman → buries her in the woods near his manor
- The corpse is found
- An investigation begins
- Kiyochika feels the law closing in, kills himself

AUTHOR: So, Kiyochika Azuma killed a woman and buried her in the woods near his manor. The body was found by someone on 23rd August 1938, and the police began to investigate. As the investigation went on, Kiyochika was afraid of being caught, so he killed himself.

HIRAUCHI: It's a neat picture.

AUTHOR: But, if that's the case, there's something else I wonder about.

HIRAUCHI: What's that?

AUTHOR: How exactly did the person who posted that information on Dark Spots Japan find out about it? If even local newspapers didn't mention it, I can't imagine it being reported anywhere else.

Which I think indicates the case simply wasn't made public. And so, how did the poster find out about it?

HIRAUCHI: I see.

While we talked over all these problems, the library's closing time approached. We chose five books that looked to have potential, including *History of the Great Houses of Nanshin*, and Hirauchi checked them out.

The librarian seemed a bit surprised by someone checking out five books on local history at once. She said that if we were researching local history, we should visit the town's historical archive and museum. It was another twenty-minute walk, but she assured us it stayed open until evening, so we decided to head that way.

It was housed in an old private home that had been renovated into an exhibition and archive space. It had very few written records. Most of its collection consisted of photographs, some of local scenery, others documenting everyday life in the town in the past.

We didn't get the sense that there would be much to learn there, so we were about to leave, when an elderly man came out of the back. He was wearing a badge that read: CURATOR.

CURATOR: Oh, I hope you'll forgive me for not coming out sooner. We don't get many guests, and you took me by surprise. I was trying to whip up some tea for you.

He held out a tray bearing some cups of tea and a small cake cut in half.

It seemed we would be staying a while.

CURATOR: Whereabouts are you visiting from?
HIRAUCHI: I've lived in Nagano for the past ten years.
AUTHOR: I'm here from Tokyo.
CURATOR: Is that right! You know, young people just don't have much interest in local history these days. It makes me happy

that you came all the way out here. Is there anything I can help you find, or anything in particular you want to know about?

HIRAUCHI: Well, actually, we're researching a man named Kiyochika Azuma. Do you know anything about him?

CURATOR: Let's see, Kiyochika would be the old lord of the Azuma manor. I'm not really all that familiar, but there's a man in the neighbourhood named Kyuzo, a friend of mine, who might be. His grandmother used to be a maid up at the Azuma place, and she did like to tell tales.

AUTHOR: Really? And he lives near here?

CURATOR: He does, and he's not at all a busy man. I'm sure he'd come by if I asked.

He immediately picked up the phone. After a surprisingly brief exchange, Kyuzo agreed to come over. Hirauchi and I were astounded by this tight-knit rural information network.

'If you really want to learn about the countryside, forget the internet.' We were seeing just how true those words were.

Kyuzo arrived about ten minutes later. He was a white-haired man about the same age as the curator.

AUTHOR: Sorry for asking you out here just to talk to us…

KYUZO: Not at all, it's fine! I'm retired, so it's not like I have anything else to do. So, what was it again? You're wondering about the old Azuma family?

AUTHOR: That's right. We're looking into Kiyochika, from the Azuma manor. We learnt over at the library that he killed himself in 1938. We were hoping to find out why he did it.

KYUZO: Oh, that. It was woman trouble. An affair, you know.

AUTHOR: An affair?!

KYUZO: My old granny, rest her soul, used to talk about it all the time.

Kiyochika's wife was a greedy one, the way I heard it. The only reason she married Kiyochika in the first place was to get at the Azuma family's money and power. She set about spending all the money right away, and she took hold over the manor and servants like they were hers alone. And it was like Kiyochika wasn't even there. He ended up with that monster of a wife on one side, and his folks on the other, saying, 'You good for nothing fool, how could you bring her into the family?' Granny said it wore on him something terrible.

The only one around who gave him any comfort was a maid, name of Okinu. Granny said she was a pretty young thing, and, well, nature took its course, I suppose. Kiyochika fell for the girl. And it seems she was happy enough, too, being loved.

But then the wife found out. She got worried Okinu would take her place, so she used her influence and ordered the staff to kill her. Okinu managed to get away in the nick of time, though, leaving Kiyochika all alone. He hanged himself on account of the loneliness… Or that's what I was told, at least. Granny always called him 'Poor old thing'. Okinu, too.

AUTHOR: Where did Okinu go after she escaped?

KYUZO: That I don't know. Might have returned to her family or ended up dead in the wild.

HIRAUCHI: I've heard that a woman's body was found in the woods near the manor or thereabouts. Have you ever heard of such a thing?

KYUZO: Hmm. Not that I recall. But if it's true, then maybe Okinu never got away after all.

- Kiyochika Azuma has affair with Okinu.
- Kiyochika's wife discovers infidelity, in a rage orders Okinu's murder.
- Okinu escapes the manor.

We thanked the two men and left the museum.

It had got quite late, so Hirauchi invited me to stay at his house. We bought a simple dinner at the supermarket by the station and took the six o'clock bus towards his neighbourhood.

As the bus drove on, the buildings outside the window thinned out and were replaced by thickets of bushes and trees. After about an hour, we reached the stop nearest his house. The sky was darkening, and the calls of night insects filled the air.

The road we followed towards his house was unpaved. We passed a house only every few minutes, and none of them seemed lived in. They were probably holiday homes.

Finally, his house came into view. It had a very 'lonely house in the woods' vibe. At twenty-six years old, it showed some age, but the previous owners must have taken good care of it, because it was not at all run-down. Overall, it struck me as a lovely home.

But when we stepped inside, it immediately felt strange.

GROUND FLOOR   FIRST FLOOR

There wasn't a single window on the ground floor. So, even with the lights on, it had a dim, gloomy atmosphere.

HIRAUCHI: When I came to view it, the estate agent told me the ground floor used to be a storehouse. That's why there are no windows.
AUTHOR: That's an unusual construction choice.
HIRAUCHI: Well, there are lots of farmers out here, so I guess they need storage space for their tools and such. I don't, of course, so I have my bedroom down here.

He then gave me a tour of the house. As he did, one room gave me a very odd feeling. It was a square room in the north-east corner of the ground floor. When I stepped inside, it felt almost overwhelmingly… off.

AUTHOR: Mr Hirauchi… Doesn't this room seem odd to you? It's so small…
HIRAUCHI: Oh, you noticed? The first time I came in, I noticed it felt quite cramped. A while after I moved in, I actually took a tape and measured it. Just like I felt, it was a bit narrower than the next room. The difference is about eighty centimetres. The exterior wall is that much thicker here than elsewhere in the house, it seems.

Using his measurements as reference, I redrew the floor plan. Hirauchi said that he assumed the thick wall was needed to make space for piping or the like, but I couldn't see why any piping would have been necessary there.

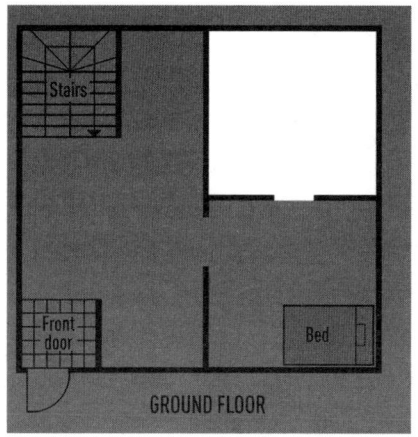
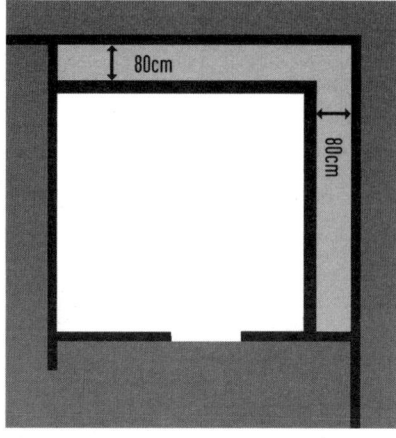

Later, we had dinner upstairs. Hirauchi cooked up some Nagano-style soba, which we ate with tempura of some local vegetables we'd bought at the supermarket. It was all so delicious, it could have been from a gourmet restaurant.

As we were enjoying some after-dinner tea, my phone suddenly rang. It was my editor, Sugiyama.

AUTHOR: Hello?
SUGIYAMA: Sorry for calling so late. Can you talk?
AUTHOR: Yes, of course. What's the matter?
SUGIYAMA: It's about Hirauchi's house. I got in touch with an author I know who researches Nagano history to ask if she knew anything. She told me about an old book that I think could have something to do with that map entry.
AUTHOR: What book is that?
SUGIYAMA: It's called *Records of Beautiful Sojourns*, a collection of travel journals from the 1920s and 30s. It has one chapter, 'Memories of the Hani Region', which describes a strange experience on 23rd August 1938.

I'll send you some photos of the pages from that chapter. I think you should read it.

The pictures he sent were of a yellowed old book. The chapter heading read: *Records of Beautiful Sojourns*, Chapter 14: Memories of the Hani Region (by Uki Mizunashi).

It told how the author went for a walk in the woods and came across a strange watermill.

SUGIYAMA: The Hani region is where you are, right, in southern Nagano? Which would mean it includes Shimojo village. But you know what really got me curious is the part where the author talks about finding the corpse of a bird inside the mill.

> A female egret lay dead on the floor. Some terrible person must have trapped it in there as a cruel prank. Unable to get out, it had starved to death. Judging by its condition, it must have been in that room for some time. Its feathers were falling out, the tip of one of its wings was missing, its flesh was rotting, and a pool of scarlet and black fluid spread out around it.

SUGIYAMA: That raised some red flags the moment I read it. Because, how on earth did this Uki know that the egret was female? The body was rotting and the feathers falling out. It was in terrible shape, in other words. And staring at it in some dim little room, I think she'd be lucky to figure out what type of bird it was, much less its sex.

But she definitively calls it female. Just for the sake of argument, let's say that she's right about it being an egret. Knowing the sex, though?

Personally, I think this is some kind of metaphor. She actually saw something else when she looked into that mill, but she didn't want to put it into writing. So, she used the bird as a stand-in.

I've got no proof, of course, but I think what Uki actually saw that day was a woman's body.

AUTHOR: Ohh...

SUGIYAMA: And if that is true, then it matches up to that post on the map.

LOCATION: Oaza, Shimojo, Nagano Prefecture
DATE: 23rd August 1938
PROPERTY: Private house
DETAILS: Woman's corpse found

In 1938, the whole area was still undeveloped forest, so we'd assumed that the post was mistaken about the body being found in a house because there couldn't have been any houses there. But Uki Mizunashi had come across a watermill in the woods at that time. If we changed the word from 'house' to 'watermill', then everything matched.

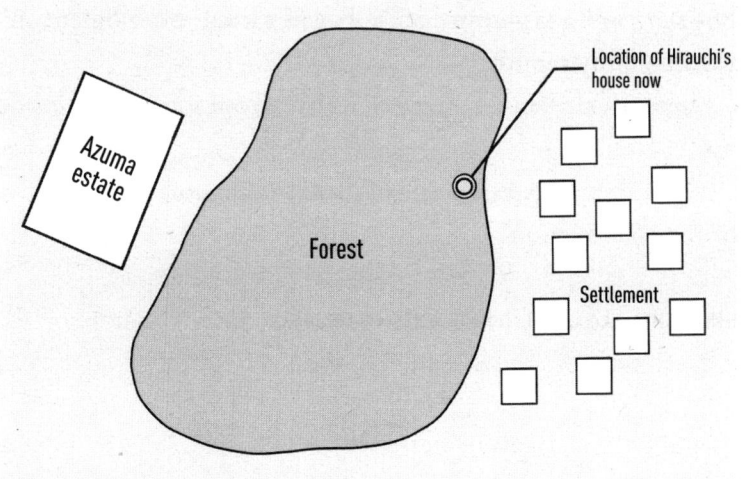

SUGIYAMA: The only problem I see is, Uki didn't mention the precise location of the house where she was staying, so we can't know if it was near where Mr Hirauchi's house is now.

AUTHOR: No, I think you must be right. We did some research at the library today and learnt this whole area used to be covered by forest. The trails through what remains of that forest run right past Hirauchi's house. It also seems there used to be a little settlement nearby, so if Uki walked from there into the woods, she would have passed by the spot where his house stands now. It all fits.

SUGIYAMA: I see. Then, I guess that settles it. We've found the case referenced on that website. So, are you still in Shimojo?

AUTHOR: I am. The time got away from us, so Mr Hirauchi is letting me stay with him.

SUGIYAMA: I hope you don't think I'm overreacting, but... be careful, all right?

AUTHOR: Oh, don't worry, I'm fine. It's not like the place is haunted. And the body wasn't actually found in this house anyway.

But for some reason, my pulse began racing the moment the words left my mouth.

A nameless unease seemed to well up from somewhere inside me.

After I hung up, I showed Hirauchi the pictures of 'Memories of the Hani Region'.

HIRAUCHI: So, this is what happened, then.

Okinu left the Azuma house and escaped into the woods.
↓
She found the watermill while she was wandering in the woods.
↓
She hid there to shelter from the elements, but with nothing to eat or drink, she starved to death in the hut.
↓
Uki found her and wrote about it in this book.
↓
Someone read the book, figured out what Uki had really seen and posted it on the Japan Dark Spots map.

AUTHOR: The story all seems to fit together.
HIRAUCHI: But then, who sealed Okinu in that room?
AUTHOR: What do you mean, sealed her?
HIRAUCHI: That's what must have happened, right?

Hirauchi picked up a piece of junk mail and sketched a diagram of the mill.

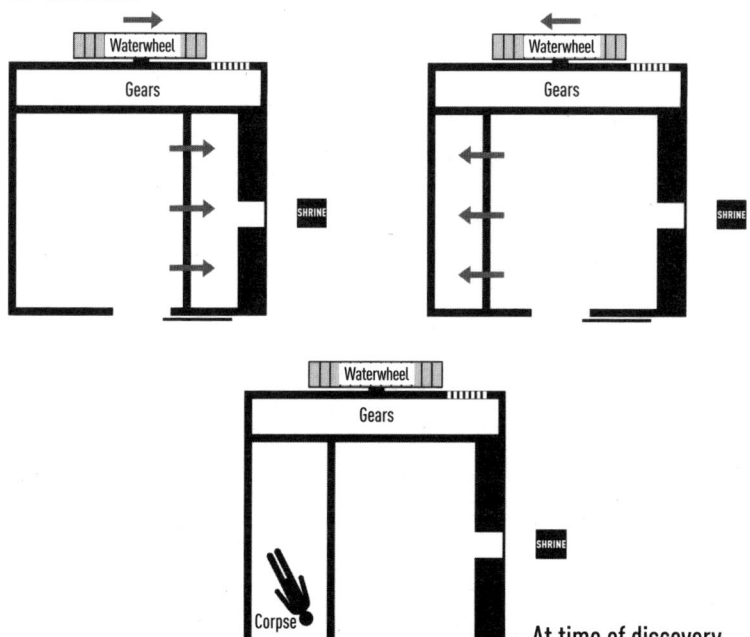

HIRAUCHI: The internal wall moves when you turn the waterwheel, right?

So, there's no way to move it from the inside. When Uki found the watermill, Okinu's body was sealed inside the left-hand room.

Which means that someone must have turned the waterwheel to close it up after Okinu was dead.

AUTHOR: You're right. But who would do such a thing? And was it really after she was dead?

HIRAUCHI: Maybe not. I wonder what on earth that watermill was really built for.

AUTHOR: Surely it was built by people from the village nearby. I don't know what to make of Uki's idea about it being a place to force people into repentance, though.

The two of us sat there, staring silently at the diagram for a time. As we did, I began to feel something niggling at me. A sense of déjà vu, almost.

AUTHOR: Mr Hirauchi... Is it just me, or does this watermill remind you of that room downstairs?

HIRAUCHI: Honestly, I was just thinking the same thing.

We both rushed downstairs.

That cramped room on the north-east corner. The one that was eighty centimetres narrower in two directions than the room next to it.

HIRAUCHI: You don't think...?
AUTHOR: Let's check and see.

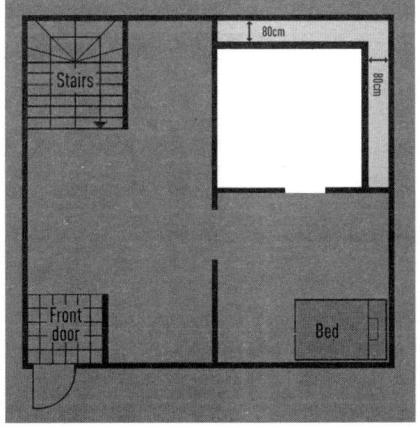 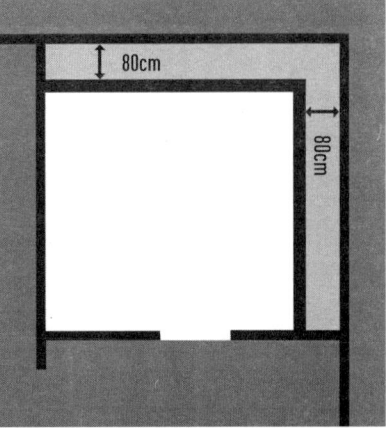

I started tapping on the eastern wall, one of the 'thick' ones. It made a solid, thudding sound. I slowly tapped across the wall, moving towards the centre. When I hit a certain point, the sound clearly changed.

It became a light, echoing *tonk-tonk*. Which meant that the spot in the middle was hollow.

> There was no furniture inside the room, no decorations or windows on the walls. It was like a rectangular wooden box, entirely featureless apart from the door and a large hole in the wall to my right. I call it a hole, but it did not go all the way through the wall. Indeed, it was more of an alcove—a perfectly square depression in the centre of the wall, large enough that I felt if I curled up, I could fit my whole body inside.

The idea seemed so outrageous as to be impossible, but every clue we found appeared to point the same way.

This house had been built around that watermill.

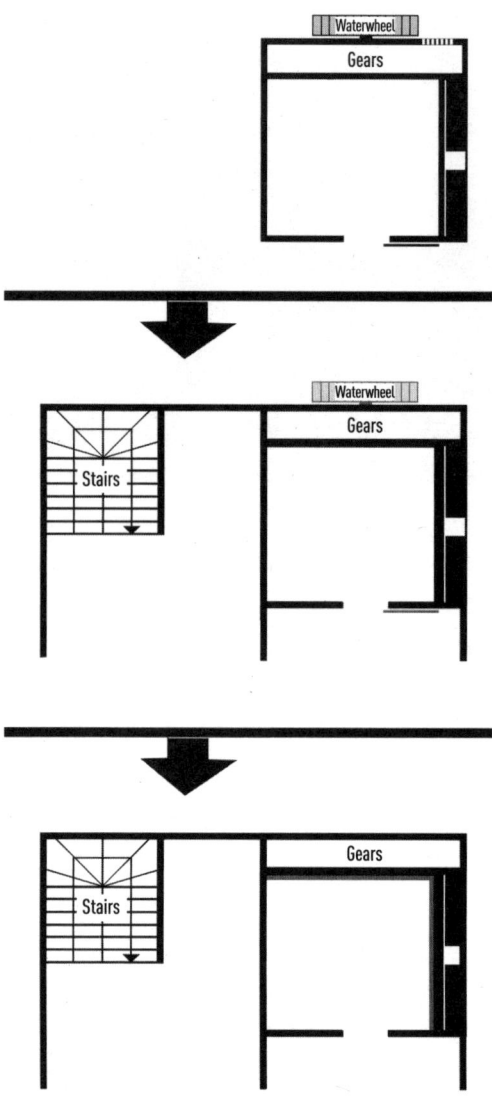

HIRAUCHI: Who on earth would do such a thing? And why?

But, wait, it can't be true. The estate agent told me this house was built twenty-six years ago. Uki found the watermill over eighty years ago. Surely, they can't just lie about things like that, can they?

AUTHOR: Did the estate agent say anything else? Offer any elaboration?

HIRAUCHI: How do you mean?

AUTHOR: I have a friend who's an architecture draughtsman. He once told me that estate agents do have a legal obligation to disclose the age of a building. However, there are actually different ways to calculate that age.

For example, if they have a building that was originally built ten years ago with an extension made five years ago, they are required to state the age as ten years.

But if the extension also involves major reinforcement of the original structure, then they can count the building's age from the date of the extension.

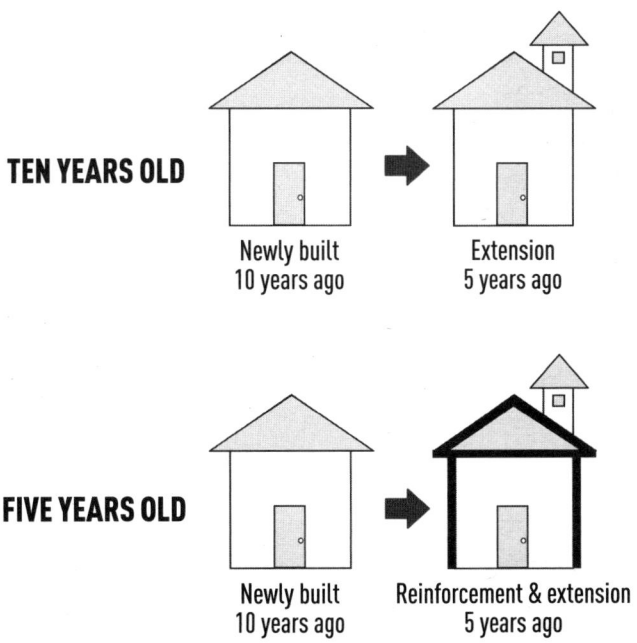

HIRAUCHI: What?

AUTHOR: In other words, if you have a building that was originally built ten years ago, but had extension work that included major reinforcement five years ago, then the estate agents can say the building is only five years old.

HIRAUCHI: That's ridiculous!

AUTHOR: Of course, the agents are supposed to explain that parts of the building are older than that, but the law isn't clear about how they should do so, meaning some less ethical agents might try to hide that info in a load of technical jargon to keep their customers from catching on.

HIRAUCHI: Now that you mention it, if I'm honest… There was some really complicated stuff that I didn't pay much attention to. But seriously… Are you saying this room…?

So far, I had felt a certain distance from the grisly discovery mentioned on that map.

For me, it had all been something in the distant past. Even if it had happened on this plot of land, there was nothing connecting it to us… That is what I had thought. I was wrong.

The building was right there all along.

. . .

Honestly, I didn't want to stay in that house a moment longer.

I felt like running away. But the last bus had already gone, and there weren't any hotels or anything nearby. So, Hirauchi and I spent the night upstairs, talking. Neither of us slept a wink.

The next morning, we set out for the bus stop together. As we were passing one of the houses I had taken for an empty holiday home, an old woman came out and wished us a good morning. We stopped to talk.

As it turned out, she had lived in the area for many years. She was an early riser and early sleeper, so the lights in her house were out by seven in the evening most days. That's why it always looked dark and empty when Hirauchi came home from work.

Given that she had been living here for years, I thought she might know something about the house, so I asked.

WOMAN: That house, is it? It was already there when we moved in, so I can't say when it was built, but I do know that no one lived there until Mr Hirauchi came.
AUTHOR: It was empty that whole time?
WOMAN: I believe so. If anyone was living there, surely I'd have run into them once or twice on the road, don't you think? But I never saw a soul.

But… I did see some building work they did over there, so maybe someone was living there and I just never noticed.
HIRAUCHI: What kind of building work?
WOMAN: Oh, it must have been twenty years ago or so. They did a lot of work. The house has two floors, right? When we moved in, it only had one. I remember thinking when they were all finished, 'Oh, they doubled it!'

If that was the case, the building wouldn't have had any amenities like a kitchen, a toilet or a bath before then. It wouldn't have been fit to live in.

> When I came to view it, the estate agent told me the ground floor used to be a storehouse.

So, the 'storehouse' the agent mentioned was all there had been.

Twenty-six years ago, someone had extended the watermill into a 'storehouse'. Then, a few years later, someone had added a second floor and turned it into a home.

Why do such a thing? The more I thought about it, the more confusing it became.

END OF FILE 5: THE HOUSE WHERE IT HAPPENED

FILE 6

The Hall of Rebirth

AUGUST 1994

Article from a monthly tabloid magazine

Once, there was a large religious hall standing at the foot of Mt Yake in western Nagano Prefecture. Known as the Hall of Rebirth, it was the spiritual base of a cult known as the Rebirth Congregation.

The cult broke up years ago, and the building has been torn down, so the only way to learn anything about it is through archival records. When I was searching for just such records, I found an article from the August 1994 issue of a defunct tabloid magazine, which is perhaps the only existing undercover report from inside the Hall of Rebirth.

It appears that the article had originally been planned as a two-part series, but after the first part was published, some business entity complained to the magazine publishers. The publishers pulled the second part, and it never saw the light of day.

And so, the only thing I have to show you now is Part One.

Please note that I am quoting the text exactly as it appeared in that magazine.

REVEALING THE SECRETS OF A MYSTERIOUS CULT
UNDERCOVER IN THE REBIRTH CONGREGATION HOME BASE! PART ONE

WHAT ARE THEY *REALLY* AFTER?

The Rebirth Congregation, a cult based in Nagano Prefecture, claims to follow the teaching of a leader known as Midori Hikari, the Living Goddess, whom they call the Holy Mother. 'Living gods' are common enough in cults, whose leaders often hope to inspire devotion by claiming to be flesh-and-blood deities. In other words, they say, 'I am your god! Bow to me!' and the worshippers fall at their feet to do just that.

In that sense, the Rebirth Congregation is no different from most other cults, but it does seem to have some unique features.

TARGETING PEOPLE WITH 'SPECIAL CIRCUMSTANCES'

In my career, I've gone undercover in all kinds of cults, and each time I've met different kinds of believers. There are wealthy family men and broke singletons. Graduates from elite universities and high-school dropouts. Their backgrounds, ages, genders, careers, interests—they're all different, and I have learnt that you simply cannot point to any one group and say, 'These people are vulnerable to cults.'

But I have heard that members of the Rebirth Congregation do have some very particular 'special circumstances' in common. But what could that mean?

A CULT WITH NO BRAINWASHING

Cults often brainwash believers using 'mystical powers' (i.e. simple trickery) and sometimes even violence or illegal drugs.

But reports of the Rebirth Congregation suggest that the cult gets a grip on its followers and even convinces them to part with wads of cash for some mystery product, without resorting to any such tricks.

Now, these mystery products aren't just the usual dodgy magical vases or mystical crystals that other cults flog. The Rebirth Congregation seems to be selling something that costs in the range of millions—even tens of millions—of yen.

This cult has used telephone cold calls and word of mouth to amass hundreds of followers. If you imagine that they're all parting with sums of the size mentioned above, that gives you a rough idea of the piles of dough they must be raking in. The numbers are astounding and inspire not a little envy in the author's heart.

UNIQUE DISCIPLINE

The Rebirth Congregation has a special facility in western Nagano that they call the Hall of Rebirth.

There, they hold four sessions a month where the faithful gather overnight for some kind of special training or spiritual practice. What that actually consists of, though, is still a mystery.

A 'special practice' only carried out a few times a month... This is almost certainly the secret to how the cult deceives members into spending fortunes on its products. To uncover this truth, I—your intrepid undercover cult reporter—infiltrated the Hall of Rebirth for this report.

Of course, infiltrating the facility required me to join the cult, or at least to appear to. That is always the hardest part. Most cults are very keen to keep their practices secret, so they tend to investigate potential members thoroughly, trying to catch any potential spies. Even a veteran cult-investigator like me often gets sniffed out and turned away at the door.

The Rebirth Congregation, though, seemed relatively lax on that front. I called them on the phone, told them my name, age and the answer to a certain question—a question directly related to the true nature of the cult, so I'll be holding on to that for Part Two, planned for our next issue—and swore my obedience to the leader. Just like that, I was a member.

And that wasn't all. I was able to reserve a spot at the next session at the Hall of Rebirth right then. It went so smoothly that it almost made me nervous.

The day of the gathering, I took the train to Nagano.

The estate owned by the cult sits on a wide plain surrounded by breathtaking mountains. At the very centre of the grounds stands an imposing white building. This is the rumoured Hall of Rebirth—which I'll just call the Hall for brevity's sake. It has a strangely misshapen look, more apt for a work of contemporary art than a religious facility.

A few dozen believers had arrived on the grounds ahead of me and were making their way towards the Hall, so I followed them. We entered a long, narrow, tunnel-like structure emerging from the building, which led to an assembly hall.

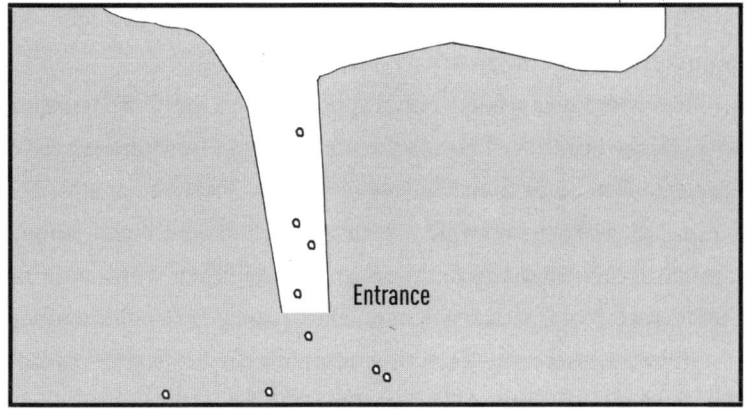

As I emerged from the tunnel I saw a semicircular stage to my left, with rows of folding chairs set up facing towards it in the middle of the hall in front of me. To my right was a crimson-coloured structure that looked like some kind of sculpture or art installation. The believers all bowed deeply to it before sitting down in one of the chairs. It was clearly an important religious symbol for the cult.

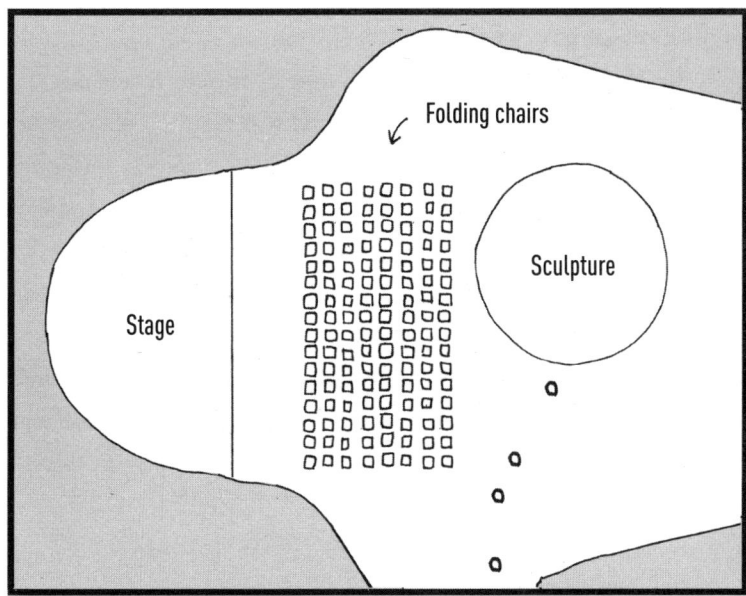

The chairs filled up in about thirty minutes, but the believers kept coming, forcing many to stand in the back.

The crowd was a fairly equal split between men and women, with a large number of couples among them. Many of the believers looked to be in their thirties or forties. They sat or stood in silence, their backs straight, staring at the stage. It was a sight familiar from my many undercover reports. They were awaiting their leader. It was, in a sense, the default mode for a cult member.

However, there was one way in which they differed from all the members of other cults I had seen so far. Most cults require their members to wear some kind of uniform, what they usually call 'vestments' or some other religious-sounding word, for their rituals or practices. These people, though, were all dressed in their own clothes. In fact, they all seemed to be sporting pricey designer outfits—in wildly varied levels of taste. As I looked more closely, I saw that their watches, necklaces and other accessories were just as flashy and expensive.

That made sense to me. The Rebirth Congregation extracts millions of yen from its members, which of course requires that they be reasonably wealthy.

Before long, someone took the stage. However, it was not the leader of the cult, the Holy Mother. It was a suited man in his mid-forties.

Deep frown lines in his brow, sunken eyes and a prominent aquiline nose. I had seen that face before. It was Masahiko Hikura, the president of one of the region's largest construction companies, Hikura Homes.

I had heard rumours that the Hikura Homes president had some important role in the Rebirth Congregation cult and was supporting it financially. And here was the proof.

Hikura stood in the centre of the stage and began speaking, his voice almost menacing in its slow, measured pace.

Below is a transcript of his speech taken from a secret recording I made.

'By your presence here, I know you are well aware. Aware of your sin, and of how your poor children have inherited that sin. Children born out of their parents' sin. Children of sin. That stain will bring profound suffering and surely drag you to hell itself.

'Sadly, your defilement can never be erased. However, it can be lightened. Reduced. Through faith and the sacrament, you can ease your burden. Dilute your impurity here, in this hall. And, tomorrow, you can go home, your stain faded, and introduce your children to the sacrament.'

He was a skilled speaker, like you'd expect of someone in charge of a major company. The message itself, though, was orthodox in the extreme. You could almost call it commonplace.

First, you use scary words like 'sin', 'defilement' and 'suffering' to create fear in your audience, then offer them a way out. That was what he meant by 'Through faith and the sacrament, you can ease your burden'. In other words: 'Our cult will save you.'

As cult-leader sermons go, it was standard stuff, but the believers listened raptly to Hikura. They nodded along, as if each word was meant for them alone, and I saw some eyes welling with tears.

I had heard that the Rebirth Congregation didn't brainwash its members, but I was beginning to doubt that. These people were clearly under some kind of powerful influence.

When Hikura finished speaking, a few acolytes—members who ranked higher than those in the crowd—emerged from the darkness and herded us to stand in a long queue.

It seemed we were being led to worship, to stand in the presence of Midori Hikari. The living goddess, the Holy Mother herself! What kind of person was she?

The queue of the faithful in front of me led into the crimson cylinder. Presumably the Holy Mother was inside. So it was a shrine, rather than just some huge art installation.

The acolytes opened a door into the shrine and allowed the members to enter in groups of five. Each group spent about ten minutes inside, so progress was slow.

Everyone that came out of the shrine wore an expression of deep fulfilment.

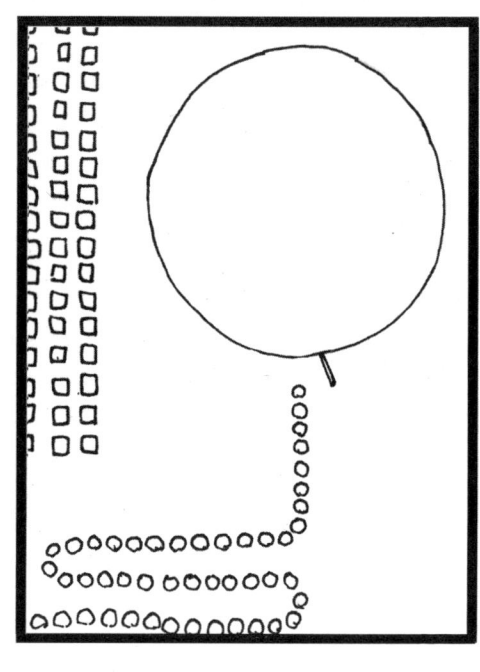

I began to suspect that the cult's style of brainwashing, whatever it consisted of, happened inside there. After about an hour, my turn came, and it was time to find out.

Let me first describe the shrine's structure. The interior consists of a narrow spiral path leading to the centre, where the Holy Mother sits. There are windows in the walls which allowed the five of us to glimpse her as we made our way around the spiral.

The path was unlit, but a small spot of light spilt over the Holy Mother, so we could just make her out in the gloom. When I got my first glimpse, I must admit I doubted my own eyes.

But as we approached the centre and I could see her better, I knew I had not been mistaken.

The Holy Mother was missing her left arm and right leg.

THE HOLY MOTHER

I had heard that the Holy Mother was in her fifties, but she looked to be no older than in her early forties. Her features were finely sculpted, her long hair was black and lustrous, and her skin was smooth and clear.

Her right leg was missing below the hip, while the left leg she used to balance herself on her simple stool was long and slim. She was utterly motionless. She wore only a simple white cloth wrap, leaving her barely covered. I don't know if I would call the vision she presented 'sacred', but she had an unusual beauty that drew the eye like a magnet.

When we arrived in the centre, the other four people present knelt before the Holy Mother, and I copied them. The Holy Mother looked my way and said, her voice quiet and gentle, 'I see this is your first time. Practise the sacrament with care.'

She went on, speaking to all present.

'You, and you, and you, and you, and you, newcomer. You all suffer under the weight of your sin. But be at ease. All will soon be well. You know my story. I was born a child of sin. I lost my left arm to my mother's sin. I lost my right leg to save a child of sin. With what is left of this body, I wish only to save you and your own children. Now, it is time for rebirth. Over and over again.'

The believers all gazed on the Holy Mother with rapture.

When she finished speaking, we returned the way we came and left the shrine. The next group of five took our place. The man standing at the rear of that group caught my eye. He had an odd, intense expression that was unlike the other believers.

Now, let me give my honest opinion of what happened inside that shrine. To my experienced eye, it was all just a clichéd stage play.

The windows along the path offering glimpses of what lay ahead were obviously calculated to give us the sense that we were proceeding towards a hidden goal of great value. Walking along that darkened spiral pathway past those lighted windows was also slightly disorientating. The penitents, slightly dizzy and lost in the dark, catch glimpses of their heart's desire in the gloom as they draw nearer to the light. When they reach the middle, there she sits: a woman wrapped in beauty and solemnity, her body, so unlike theirs, displayed for all. Every element is carefully arranged for maximum mesmerizing effect.

This is classic stagecraft, using techniques common in all kinds of entertainment, not just religious organizations.

And then there's the Holy Mother herself. My guess is that she's just a figurehead. I didn't sense from her any of the powerful charisma needed to lead a cult. She is probably paid by the real leaders to be their public symbol.

Some ancient cultures considered people with physical defects divine incarnations, objects of worship, and the Rebirth Congregation is just following that example. This woman is not the mortal incarnation of a goddess with one leg and one arm; she is being presented as a goddess because she is missing a leg and an arm. She is, of course, just a woman.

That shrine is a tool to transform this mere woman into a goddess, but cheap tricks like that aren't enough to brainwash people.

At the most, it might bolster the faith of believers who've already been brainwashed. But the shrine was not the secret I was looking for.

THE CULT'S SHOCKING RITE UNVEILED!

Soon after my own experience in the shrine, a voice suddenly came ringing out from its depths. It sounded like a man shouting in anger. I listened intently and was able to make out what he was saying.

'You lied to me, Holy Mother! You promised my son would be saved!'

A few acolytes immediately rushed into the shrine, and a minute or so later they dragged a struggling man from the door. It was the man who had been standing at the rear of the group after mine, whose odd expression I'd noticed. He had a striking face that would probably have been handsome were it not twisted in rage.

The handsome man was still shouting. 'You fraud! If you're truly a goddess, tell me why? Why did my boy, my Naruki, have to die? I'll kill you! I'll seal your heart for ever!' The screams went on even as they dragged him outside.

None of the other members seemed particularly bothered. They merely stared on with a look of mild distaste.

The hall fell quiet after the heretic was removed. An acolyte asked my group of five to follow him to the room where the ritual would be held. The ritual room was in the centre of the building, but to get there we had to go back outside and re-enter the building through a different door. It struck me as an oddly inconvenient design.

We took the long, narrow tunnel outside then walked along the wall for about five minutes to the next entrance.

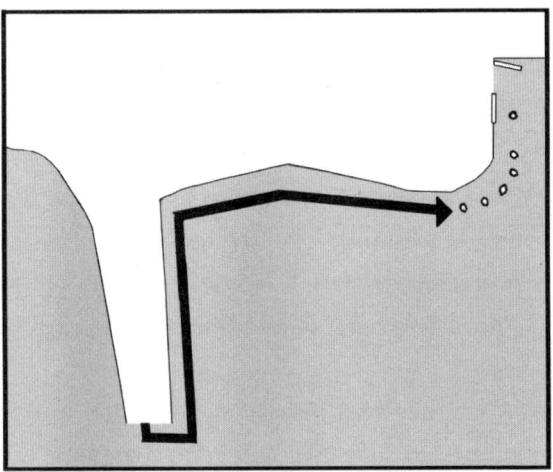

We stepped into a wide lobby area with a single door, presumably leading to the ritual room, on the far side. We walked in single file through the lobby.

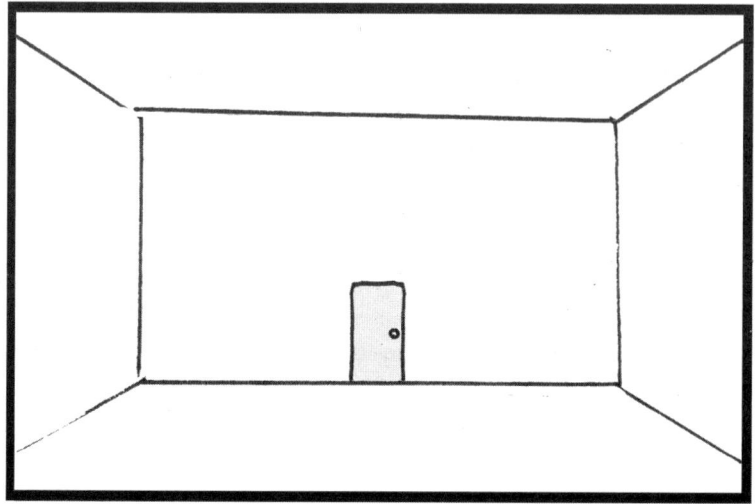

This ritual or practice or whatever it was, held just a few times a month, had to be what was brainwashing the members, and I was sure it had to be something pretty extreme. Something I'd never seen before. My pulse sped up. Finally, an acolyte opened the door.

The scene before me was not at all what I had imagined.

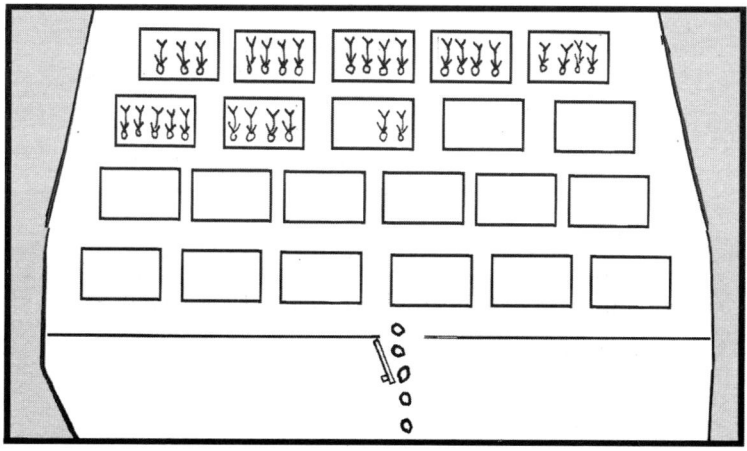

It was a huge room filled with what looked like large beds. The groups that had arrived before us were already lying down, four or five to a bed, and seemingly sleeping peacefully. The other members of my group quickly went to the next open beds and lay down themselves. I had no choice but to follow suit, so I joined them. The others closed their eyes and appeared to drift off. I thought to myself that this must just be preparation for the true ritual.

After a while, the door opened again, and the next group came in. They did as we had done. Time passed, and the beds slowly filled. When there was no more space on the beds, the believers began to lie on the floor. Large as the room was, it still began to feel claustrophobic and crowded.

While this was happening, I lay there, feigning sleep, wondering the whole time when the real ritual would begin, but, wait as I might, nothing happened. Eventually, night came, and everyone stayed as they were. Around the time my watch read four in the morning, I began to get an odd idea.

Could sleeping itself be the sacrament they had spoken of?

It was the only thing that made sense. If this act had no deeper significance, then the members were all making the trip out here just for a nap. But what an odd practice.

Sleeping as a sacred rite… I'd never heard of a religious cult like that. What could it mean? Even as I pondered it, I found myself falling asleep.

WHAT AWAITED ME OUTSIDE

I woke up just after ten the next morning. When I looked around, I saw that many of the faithful were still asleep. Apparently, you could lie in as long as you wanted! The place was beginning to seem more like a hotel than a cult hall.

I got out of bed and opened the door. Acolytes were stationed outside, passing out tea and sweet buns. Those were welcome, since I hadn't had a bite to eat since the morning of the day before. I stood in a corner of the lobby and tucked in. That's when I noticed a long hallway to the left side of the entrance.

I call it a hallway, but on inspection I saw it was a dead end, with no doors on any side. It was simply a cul-de-sac that stretched about a dozen metres.

As I looked at the hallway, an idea occurred to me. I began to suspect something about this cult and its Hall of Rebirth.

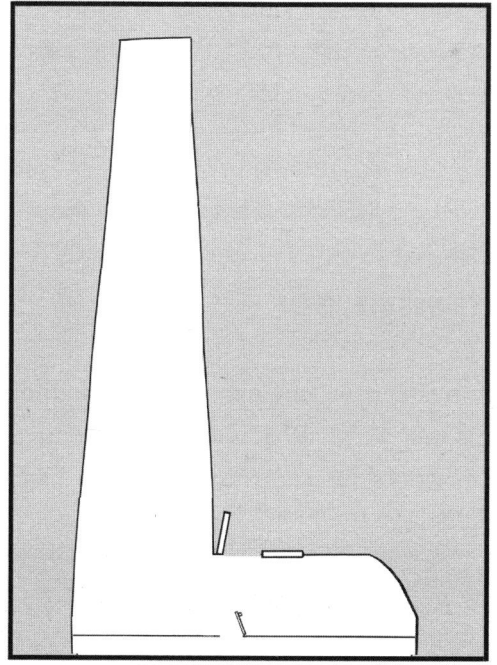

Some of my cleverer readers might be able to figure out what I'd spotted after examining my clumsy sketches scattered throughout this article.

After I finished my bun, I left the hall and witnessed something truly unexpected.

The broad lawn outside was now lined with long

tables. Cult members, the people I had just spent the night with, lined one side of each, with acolytes in white vestments sitting across from them. The acolytes were speaking intently to the members across from them.

When I got closer, I could see the tables between them were covered with floor plans. And that is when it all fell into place.

My suspicion in the lobby had been correct. This was all about...

Well, it appears I've run out of space. You shall just have to wait for Part Two to learn the rest!

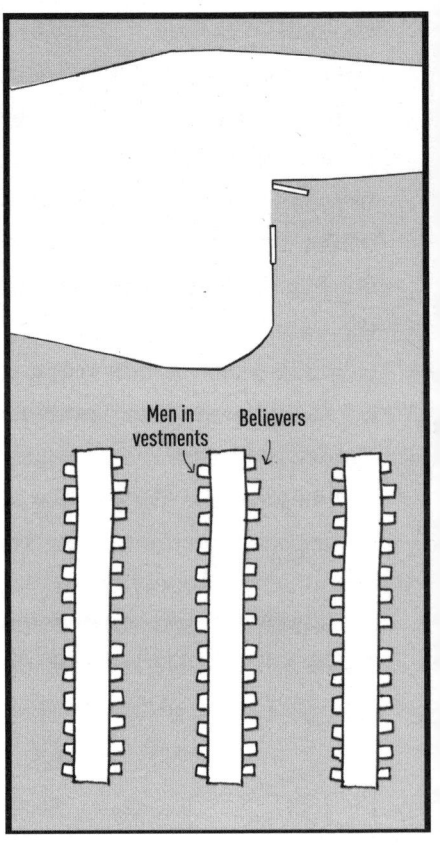

COMING NEXT ISSUE

What is the true goal of the Rebirth Congregation? How do they actually brainwash their followers? What's with the sleeping? And what 'special circumstances' unite all the members? All will be revealed!

So, what do I make of all this? I believe the article did a reasonable job of generally describing the oddities surrounding the Rebirth Congregation cult.

However, I was frustrated by the roundabout writing and the vague intimations designed to encourage people to read the second part, because it meant most of the mysteries went unsolved. The sentence that particularly captured my attention was:

> Some of my cleverer readers might be able to figure out what I'd spotted after examining my clumsy sketches scattered throughout this article.

It suggested that some clues to the truth were hidden in the drawings included in the piece.

I decided to cut out the pictures and look at them together. Most were top-down views of the building. As I looked, I did begin to feel that they were hinting at something.

The author had written about the building, 'It has a strangely misshapen look, more apt for a work of contemporary art than a religious facility.'

I took the drawings with sections of the hall layout and put them all together to create a complete picture, like a jigsaw puzzle. When I was complete, it did, indeed, have a very distinctive appearance.

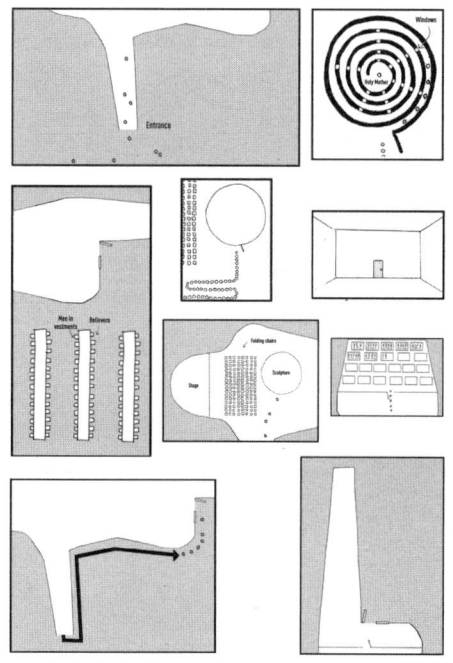

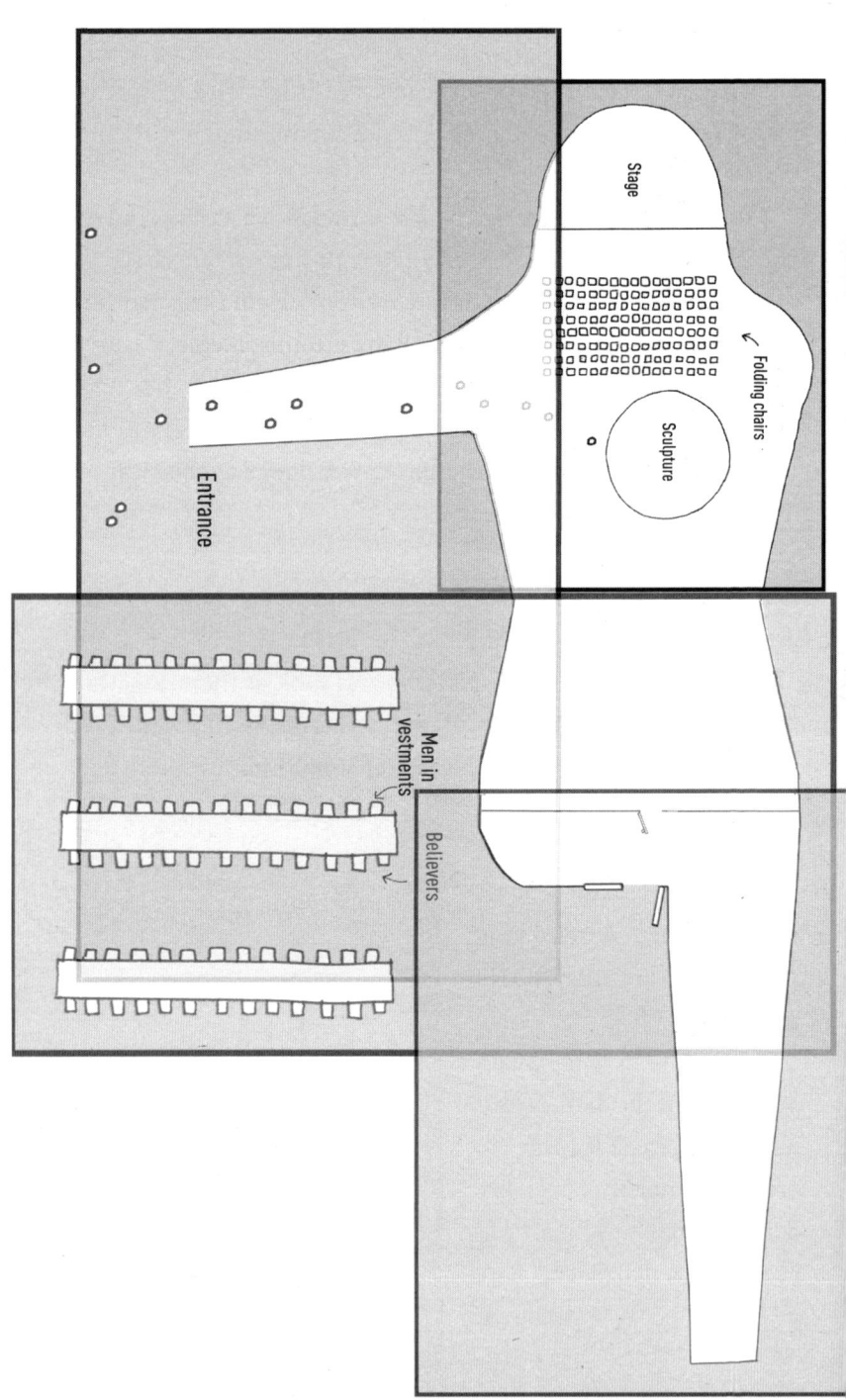

There was no mistaking it. It was a human figure. And not that of just any human.

| The Holy Mother was missing her left arm and right leg.

The image of a woman missing her left arm and right leg was right in front of me on the page. It was unmistakable. Clearly, the Hall of Rebirth itself was designed to represent the Holy Mother's body.

That understanding would eventually help me lift the veil on the other mysteries of the cult.

Finally, I suppose I should add that the Rebirth Congregation broke up in 1999, and the Hall of Rebirth was torn down the following year.

END OF FILE 6: THE HALL OF REBIRTH

FILE 7
Uncle's House

Excerpt from a young boy's journal

24TH NOVEMBER

I stayed inside all day today. Mummy didn't come home again. I miss her.

I was hungry. I was so hungry that I went to the kitchen and ate a piece of bread.

25TH NOVEMBER

Last night, Mummy got cross with me for eating bread without asking. I had to get on my knees and say I'm Sorry a hundred times. Mummy slept until late. When she woke up, she squeezed me tight. I didn't feel sad, but my eyes got all wet anyway. It felt funny.

26TH NOVEMBER

I kept saying I was hungry, so Mummy told me to Be Quiet then she pinched my nose so I couldn't breathe. I thought I should breathe with my mouth, but when I did she told me No Cheating! I was embarrassed because I cheated. I got on my knees and said I'm Sorry.

27TH NOVEMBER

A man came this evening and Mummy told me to call him Uncle. Mummy and me went to his house. It was the first time. I was a bit scared. We rode in the car and got there right away.

Uncle's house is much bigger than our flat and on the left side of the door it has a big flower bed and I thought that was really nice. We went inside and there was a hallway in the middle with lots of doors.

We went through the closest right door and there was a big TV and a table. We could see the flower bed and the house door from the window. From the big window on the other side I could see cars driving past. That was cool.

We ate dinner in that room. We had rice omlet and it was delicious. I ate until I was full and Mummy didn't even get angry at me.

After we ate dinner we went into the hallway and then to the next room. Uncle said This Is Your Room, Naruki. The room had a bed. It was the first time I ever slept in a bed. I was so happy.

And I could see the cars going by from my window, so I thought it was a fun room.

28TH NOVEMBER

When I woke up, I ate breakfast with Mummy and Uncle. We had runny eggs and fried ham and it was delicious.

After that we went out into the hallway and to the room next to the eating room. It had a big window where we could see the flower bed. There was a bicycle in the middle of the room. Uncle called it an exersize bike. I tried it and it was fun.

That room had another door. I opened it and there was an empty room. There were two windows. I could see the flowers from one and a river from the other.

In the evening, Uncle drove us home in his car. I was sad when he said Bye. Later, Mummy got angry because I didn't say Thank You to Uncle. She pinched my nose so I couldn't breathe. Using my mouth was cheating, so I tried hard to keep it closed.

[…]

24TH FEBRUARY

Mummy came home at lunchtime. She laid down in bed, so I covered her with a towel and she said Thank You and hugged me. After that I laid down with her.

In the evening, I wanted to make dinner for her and me, so I spread jam on some bread and put it in the toaster. But it got burnt and black. I didn't want her to find it so I went to throw it in the bin but she saw me and got angry. She told me No Cheating! and I was embarrassed because I was a cheater.

25TH FEBRUARY

Mummy told me that we're going to Uncle's house tomorrow, so I started to feel excited. But if I have too much fun at Uncle's house Mummy will get angry after we go home, so I will be careful not to have too much fun.

26TH FEBRUARY

Mummy and me went to Uncle's house. I was happy to see the flower bed. The three of us went to a shop to eat ramen. It was yummy, but I wish we could have had a rice omlet like before.

After I'd had my bath, he and Mummy got into a fight. Mummy started crying. Uncle told her I was too skinny and he felt sorry for me. After they made up, Uncle said he would pay Child Support and Mummy said Thank You.

27TH FEBRUARY

Breakfast was corn soup and a fried egg. It was so tasty. After that, I wanted to pedal that bicycle that doesn't go anywhere again. I went to the room next to the room for eating and pedalled it. I'd just eaten so my tummy started to hurt.

After that, I opened that other door, but that room was gone. The river was flowing right there. I thought that was weird.

That evening, Uncle drove us home. When we said goodbye, I was so sad I wanted to cry, but I made sure to say Thank You. Uncle smiled and patted my head.

[…]

3RD MARCH

There wasn't any bread in the kitchen, so I couldn't eat again today. I was so hungry my tummy hurt, so I licked my pencil and chewed some of it up. My tummy hurt less after that.

4TH MARCH

Uncle rang us. I picked up and he said Put Your Mother On, so I did. Then she and Uncle had a row over the phone. When she hung up the phone, she told me we won't be seeing him again. That made me sad.

5TH MARCH

After Mummy left, Uncle came to our flat. He told me to come with him, but I was worried that Mummy would be angry, but Uncle told me it would be all right. He said Let's Eat Rice Omlet Together! so I decided to go with him.

We ate rice omlet at his house, and it was yummy. After that, we watched TV together. Uncle told me You Can Stay Here For Ever and Go To School. I thought I would like to stay if Mummy could live with us, too.

After that, Uncle took me to a room at the end of the hall. It was a little room with a brown doll in it. It was a bit scary. Uncle said This Is the Heart of My House. Never Lock This Door. I didn't understand that.

6TH MARCH

After Uncle and me ate lunch, a car came to his house. Mummy and a man with yellow hair got out. Mummy and that man had a row with Uncle. Mummy picked me up and we got into the man's car. Uncle ran after us, but the man drove fast and pretty soon we couldn't see Uncle anymore.

We did not go to our flat. It was the man's flat. Mummy said we are going to live here together. I felt like crying because I wanted to see Uncle.

7TH MARCH

They told me the man is called Eiji. Eiji gave me food, but it smelt bad and I had to spit it out. Mummy got angry at me and I had to say sorry to Eiji.

I tried hard to eat it because Mummy doesn't want Eiji to get angry, but it was so nasty that I was sick. Then Eiji got angry at Mummy. I said I'm Sorry 100 times.

8TH MARCH

My tummy hurt and I felt like I was going to have diarea, but if I make trouble Eiji will get angry at Mummy so I held it in.

[…]

16TH MARCH

Eiji told me I have to live in the closet now. Mummy cried and said I'm Sorry, and that made me feel like crying too, but I kept it in. Mummy sneaked me a piece of bread and I tried to be quiet when I ate it.

17TH MARCH

Sitting in the closet all day hurts my back and my bum, but if I make any noise Eiji hits Mummy so today I tried hard to stay still. I kept watching funny TV shows in my head because I was bored.

18TH MARCH

I made noise so Eiji hit me. Mummy cried and told him to stop, so he hit her too.

19TH MARCH

I heard Eiji shouting and Mummy screaming. I put my fingers in my ears so I couldn't hear.

[…]

12TH APRIL

I didn't eat again today. I'm hungry. My tummy hurts. I tried to think about fun things so my tummy wouldn't bother me, but it didn't work. I want to go to Uncle's house and eat a rice omlet.

13TH APRIL

My tummy doesn't hurt anymore but it feels like all tight now. My spit tastes bad.

14TH APRIL

Mummy gave me water. It tasted sweet. But water never tastes like anything.

15TH APRIL

I can't stay sitting up, so I pushed my head into the corner of the closet and lay down. I want to sleep in a bed.

16TH APRIL

Mummy gave me a rice ball but I couldn't swallow it.

17TH APRIL

My eyes hurt and I can't hold the pen right.

18TH APRIL

It feels like everything is spinning even lying down.

19TH APRIL

My body hurts.

20TH APRIL

I can't see very well.

21ST APRIL

I want water.

THE JOURNAL ENDS HERE

AUTHOR'S NOTE

On 8th May 1994, the body of nine-year-old Naruki Mitsuhashi was found in a flat in Ichinomiya, Aichi Prefecture. Police determined that he died due to complications from malnutrition. The body showed signs of repeated and prolonged violence, attesting to Naruki suffering daily physical abuse.

Naruki's mother Saori Mitsuhashi and her partner Eiji Nakamura were convicted of Caregiver Neglect Resulting in Death. Saori was sentenced to eight years' imprisonment, while Nakamura was sentenced to fourteen years.

In 1996, the journal Naruki kept until just before his death was published as *The Lonely Death of Naruki Mitsuhashi*. This file consists of excerpts from that publication.

END OF FILE 7: UNCLE'S HOUSE

FILE 8

The String Phone

12TH NOVEMBER 2020

Interview with Chie Kasahara

The location Chie Kasahara chose for our interview was a stylish café in a residential neighbourhood near her home in Gifu Prefecture. She stared at the menu, her brow furrowed, for a good ten minutes before she finally settled on rosemary tea and a Mont Blanc.

Kasahara was working as a freelance illustrator and currently living in a flat with her mother.

She was nearing forty but had an almost girlish air when we talked. Perhaps it was her breezy bobbed hairstyle and slow, carefree manner of speaking.

When her tea and dessert arrived, she clapped her hands with a delighted 'Oh, it looks just scrumptious!' before taking a tiny bite.

We had met to talk about the house she'd lived in as a child.

. . .

Kasahara was raised in a two-storey detached house in Hashima, Gifu Prefecture.

Hers was a family of four, with her father, mother and brother. Her father was the leading salesman at an import car dealership, earning far more than most other families in the neighbourhood. However, she told me they never had the lifestyle of a 'well-off' family.

KASAHARA: My dad was a real piece of work. He spent basically all he earned on himself and didn't leave anything for the family. So, the rest of us lived like paupers. Mum had to work part time every day just to pay for dinner.

And then Dad would go out until all hours of the night, come home reeking of alcohol, and fill the house with his snoring. Selfish prat.

Of course, by that time they had separate bedrooms.

AUTHOR: And your mother just accepted it?

KASAHARA: I wouldn't say she accepted it, no, but she was too timid to say much of anything. Back in those days, you know, men were the king of the castle. But she unloaded everything she couldn't say to his face on my brother and me.

She used to say, 'I never should have married a man like that.' And I would wonder, Well, why did you? But I think maybe now I understand it a bit.

My dad was mostly awful, but every once in a while he would show a hint of kindness. He was also handsome for his age and, I guess, a bit of a ladykiller, even as a middle-aged dad. I know he had been really popular with women when he was younger. I think mum was just sucked in by the charisma.

But even with all that, Kasahara said there were some memories of him that she treasured.

KASAHARA: When I was in fourth grade of elementary school, my older brother went to boarding school, so we started living apart. I adored my brother, and he'd always doted on me. I was really broken up about it. But I had a bigger problem than that.

I was scared of everything. I was terrified to sleep on my own at night, so he used to let me sleep in his room, even when he got older. I'm sure that must have been a bit of a pain for him.

AUTHOR: And it must have been difficult for you after he left.

KASAHARA: It really was. I told Mum there was no way I could sleep alone, and she just said, 'You're a big girl now, so buck up.' I might have been a big girl, but scary is scary, you know?

AUTHOR: Parents can be a bit cold about that kind of thing.

KASAHARA: Right? And kids can't really push back. All I could do was try to put up with it. Anyway, it's what happened next that's important.

One evening, my dad came to me, a big grin on his face, and said, 'I hear you're afraid to sleep alone.' I guess Mum mentioned it to him. I was sure he was going to make fun of me, so at first I was cross, but then he held out a paper cup. 'If you get scared, use this to talk to your old man.'

I took it and realized it was a string phone. Oh, do you think people still know what those are?

A string phone is a simple toy made of two paper cups connected by a length of string. When you pull the string tight and speak into one cup, it transmits the sound to the other cup and the person at the other end can hear it.

If nothing interferes with the string, you can even communicate with someone hundreds of metres away.

But if the string goes limp, or is obstructed by something, the voice will not carry.

KASAHARA: He was all full of himself, like, 'This is my own discovery! A string-phone intercom!'
AUTHOR: What did he mean by that?
KASAHARA: It might be easier to understand if you look at this.

Kasahara took an old floor plan out of her bag.

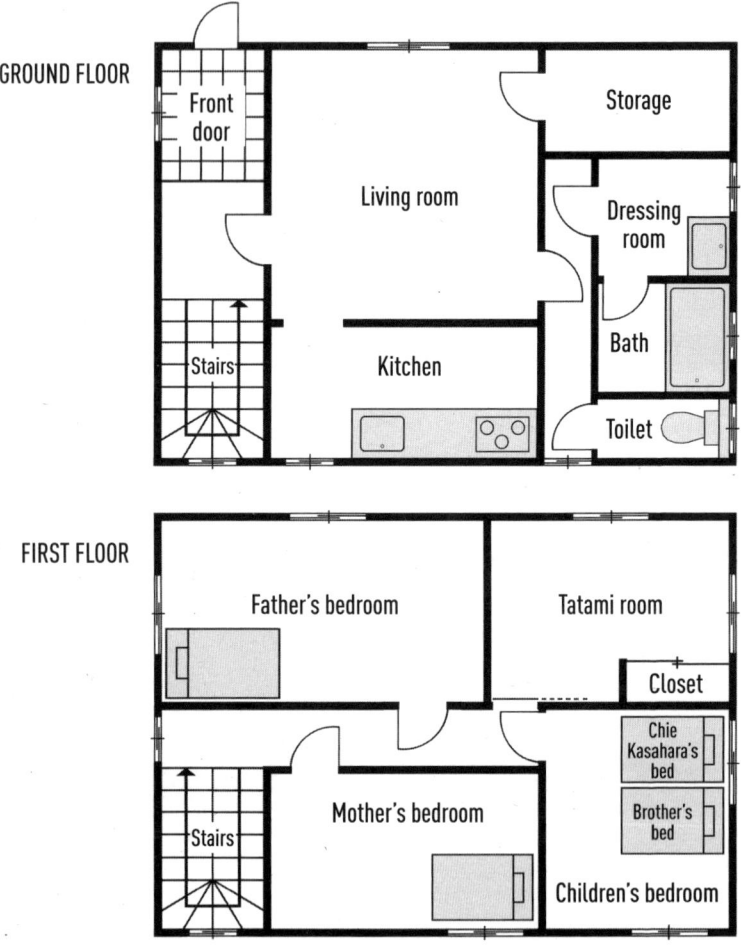

AUTHOR: Is this your childhood home?

KASAHARA: That's right. Mum dug it out for me yesterday after I asked her about it. I never dreamed she'd actually kept it, though. It takes me back, I must say. Anyway, here's my old room.

The bed by the wall was mine, and my brother had the one next to it. My dad's room was just down the landing, so the string phone could run straight between our two beds like this.

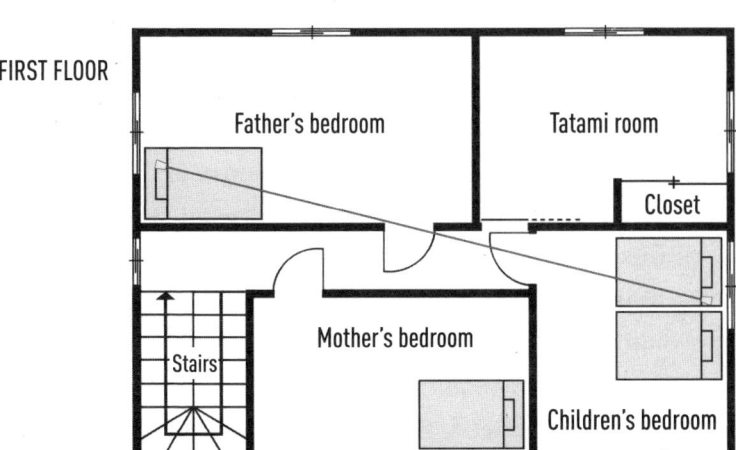

AUTHOR: So, each of you would have a cup, and you could speak to each other from your separate beds.

KASAHARA: Exactly. He said, if I was too scared to sleep, I could talk to him until I drifted off. When he first told me about it, I was a bit embarrassed, but also happy. I secretly thought it was a wonderful idea. You know, that was before the days of mobile phones or what have you, when you'd just have the one phone per house.

Lying in bed, talking on the phone! It was like something out of a Hollywood film. Of course, now, I think it would have been simpler just to let me sleep in his room.

AUTHOR: But I can see how talking over a string phone might be a bit more fun for a child than sleeping together. It feels more playful, more like a game.

KASAHARA: Exactly! The man's whole life was a game to him. That's why he couldn't be serious for a minute and why the whole family had to suffer. But much as I hate to say it, the fact that he decided to include me in this game made me really happy. I guess I was just as much a fool as Mum, in a way.

AUTHOR: And did you two talk on the string phone every night?

KASAHARA: Not at all. Like I said, Dad would stay out to all hours of the night and pass out almost as soon as he got home, so we really only used it four or five times in all. But it was a lot of fun when we did.

In the evening, I would be lying there awake, and my door would open just a crack, and a paper cup would pop through it. I'd pick it up and put it to my ear.

On the other end, Dad would say, 'Good evening, Miss Night Owl,' and I'd answer, 'Good evening, Mr Drunkard.' It was a thing we did.

AUTHOR: What kinds of things did you talk about?

KASAHARA: At first, we'd just chitchat, but after while I'd start to talk about all my worries, and more sensitive stuff, too. For some reason, I could say things over the string phone that I couldn't in person.

And it seemed like my dad's voice over the string phone was warmer and more loving than any other time. I even told him all kinds of secrets. I think Dad ended up knowing more about me than Mum ever did. It really was a clever idea. I think he must have made his way in life using clever little tricks like that to get to people.

However, one night, the father–daughter string phone chat took an odd turn.

KASAHARA: So, this one night, I was talking to Dad on the string phone. It was just before ten at night. I remember that he was different from usual. It was like his voice was trembling, and the things he said were incoherent.

AUTHOR: What do you mean, 'incoherent'?

KASAHARA: I'd ask him something, and he'd answer, but none of it made much sense. And there was this noise or something. Some kind of rustling on the phone.

After a few minutes of meaningless back and forth, he finally snapped at me, 'Go to bed. Good night!' and dropped the phone.

AUTHOR: That does sound strange.

KASAHARA: Doesn't it? And usually, once we'd finished, he would come and get the cup from my room. But that night he didn't. He just left it lying there.

I thought if I left it like that, Mum would get angry and say it was in the way, so I pulled at the string until Dad's cup came through the door. I put the phone in my drawer and went to bed.

Pretty soon, though, Mum came bursting into my room.

'We have to get out! The house next door is on fire!' she shouted. She dragged me from my room. My dad was already on the landing. The three of us ran out of the house, and people from the neighbourhood were already gathering in the street outside, staring anxiously at the house next door.

The house next door to Kasahara belonged to the Matsue family.

It was a family of three, a couple in their thirties and their elementary-school-aged son. They had apparently been on friendly terms with the Kasaharas.

KASAHARA: Flames rose above the rooftop, and through the windows all I could see was billowing red fire. Hiroki, the Matsue boy, was a year younger than me. A kindly neighbourhood woman was holding him, and he was weeping miserably in her arms. I'll never forget that night.

AUTHOR: And what of Hiroki's parents?

KASAHARA: They didn't make it out. They died in the fire…

They found the bodies a few days later. It really was a shock. Our families were fairly close, and Hiroki's father used to take me to music performances at his church.

His wife was a young, beautiful woman. It's just unbelievable that she'd ever commit suicide…

AUTHOR: Suicide?!

KASAHARA: So, it's not really something anyone likes to talk about, but… The fire was apparently caused by Hiroki's mother setting herself on fire. It was on the local news. She doused herself in kerosene in the first-floor tatami room and lit it.

Kasahara pointed at a room on the floor plan between us. I was suddenly confused.

AUTHOR: Hold on, I thought this floor plan was for your home?

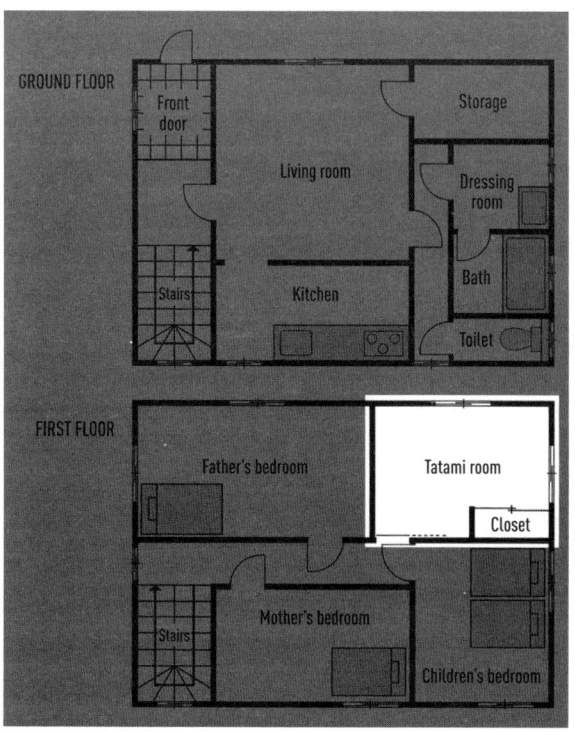

KASAHARA: Oh, right, sorry. I should have mentioned.

We lived in a housing development area filled with mass-produced ready-built houses. So, all the houses in our neighbourhood had the same layout. Everyone used to joke about them being 'clone houses'.

AUTHOR: Ah, I see. So, the Matsue house would have had the same layout as yours.

KASAHARA: Right. So, when the news said she was in the tatami room, I knew exactly where she'd been. Here, on the first floor.

Kasahara said that the remains of the Matsue house were torn down and the land put up for sale, but, naturally, no one was interested. Orphaned, Hiroki went away to live with his grandparents in another prefecture.

It was a terrible incident, but the one silver lining was that the fire didn't spread, so the Kasahara house suffered almost no damage.

However, it ended up having an unexpected impact on their lives.

KASAHARA: After that, for some reason, my dad started acting bizarrely. He went from shallow and carefree to dark and withdrawn. He was like another man entirely.
AUTHOR: Do you think it was the shock over your neighbours' deaths?
KASAHARA: I wonder. I never would have thought him the type to mourn anyone.

Not long after that, Kasahara said, he simply disappeared.

KASAHARA: All he left behind were divorce papers and a letter on the living-room table.

The letter itself was this cold, businesslike thing: 'I will pay a divorce settlement of twenty million yen' and 'I will sign the house over to you' and so on. It was quite a surprise. Mum wasn't sure if she should believe it, but then he sent a contract transferring the title deeds to her name.
AUTHOR: So, your father did what he promised in the letter?
KASAHARA: He did. Mum said it was the first promise he'd kept since they married. She'd long fallen out of love with him by then, so the divorce itself didn't seem like much of a blow. The bonds of matrimony are fragile things, I suppose.

She said that the money her father left them changed their lives. They were much more comfortable than before. Freed from the stress her husband had caused, Kasahara's mother became more cheerful, and the house was a brighter place to live in.

But then, one day, Kasahara discovered something odd.

. . .

KASAHARA: It was the same year my dad left, during our big year-end house cleaning. I decided to go through my room and get rid of anything I didn't need. I opened up that wardrobe drawer, and there it was. The string phone.

> Usually, once we'd finished, he would come and get the cup from my room. But that night he didn't. He just left it lying there.
>
> I thought if I left it like that, Mum would get angry and say it was in the way, so I pulled at the string until Dad's cup came through the door. I put the phone in my drawer and went to bed.

KASAHARA: It was there, just the way I'd left it that night, with both cups stacked together. Seeing it like that reminded me of him, and I just couldn't help it. Tears filled my eyes, though I didn't really feel sad or anything. It struck me as so strange. I remember thinking, Why am I crying? I was happy living alone with Mum, and I never liked him that much anyway. But the tears just kept coming. And I wanted to hear his voice. I suppose I missed him, selfish, irresponsible, preening jerk that he was.

That's why I did what I did next, I think.

Kasahara took the string phone to her father's room.

His bed was just as he'd left it.

Kasahara put one cup on her father's bed, then took the other to her room. One last time, she was connecting her room to her father's with the string-phone intercom.

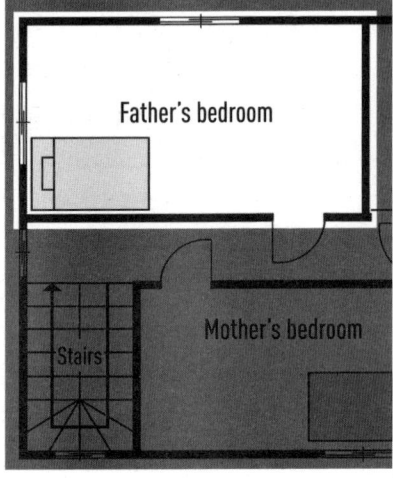

KASAHARA: I crawled into bed and put the cup to my ear. Of course, I couldn't hear anything. But after a while like that, I really did feel better. Oddly comforted.

My tears dried at some point and my mood recovered. I decided to go back to cleaning up. I knew it was silly to keep dwelling on my memories. I got out of bed and started to gather up the string phone again, and I noticed something odd.

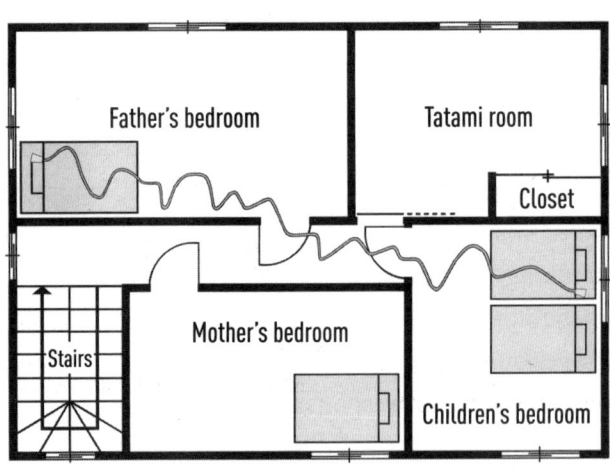

KASAHARA: I don't know why I didn't realize it earlier, but the string lay on the floor, all squiggly.

AUTHOR: It wasn't pulled straight?

KASAHARA: That's right! Which is weird, you know? String phones won't carry a voice unless the string is taut. The distance between my pillow and my dad's hadn't changed, so the string should have been pulled out straight, even if it wasn't stretched tight.

AUTHOR: I see…

KASAHARA: So, the string must always have been too long. I never should have been able to hear Dad's voice. And it's not like the string could have got any longer while it was in my drawer. Isn't it odd?

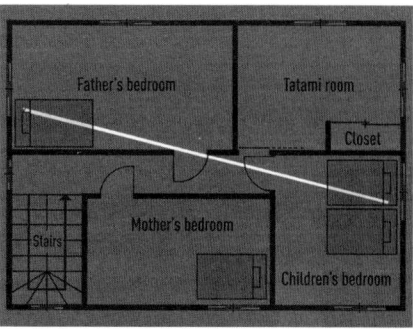

From Kasahara's bed, the farthest point a string phone could be stretched to was, in fact, her father's pillow.

AUTHOR: And you actually had talked to your father using that string phone?

KASAHARA: Yes, I had. I'd heard his voice, no mistake.

AUTHOR: So, your father must have been talking from a different room, right?

KASAHARA: But look at the floor plan. It couldn't have been any other room, could it?

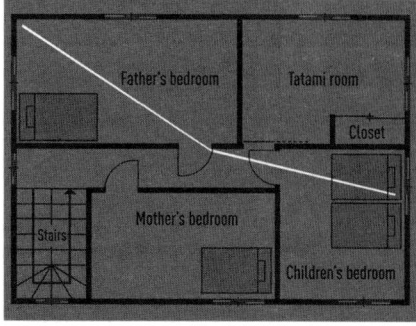

Had her father's cup been moved any farther away, the string would have made contact with the door frame, and they wouldn't have been able to talk. (Obstructions block the vibrations of the voice in the string.)

There really was nowhere in the house other than her father's bed from which a string phone could have run to Kasahara's bed. So, if the string was too long to have allowed her father to talk to her from his bed…

KASAHARA: There's only one explanation. My dad was talking to me from outside the house.

Indeed, I couldn't see any other explanation. But her room was on the first floor.

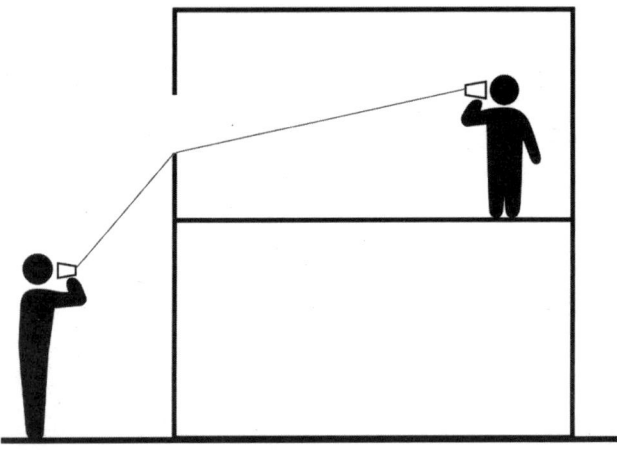

If the string phone ran outside to the garden, it would catch on the window frame and be blocked from carrying his voice.

If there were another two-storey building of the same height nearby, for example, it might have worked. But that would be too much of a coincid— Even as the thought formed, I realized what exactly Kasahara was getting at.

AUTHOR: You're talking about the Matsue house.

KASAHARA: Right. My dad was using the string phone from the first floor of the house next door.

Once I had the idea, I just couldn't let it go. I got a tape measure and checked everything. The length of the string. The length of the hallway. The distance to the next house. And it all added up to a sickening conclusion. When that string was pulled tight and I was holding one cup while lying in my bed, the other cup must have been in the tatami room of the Matsue house.

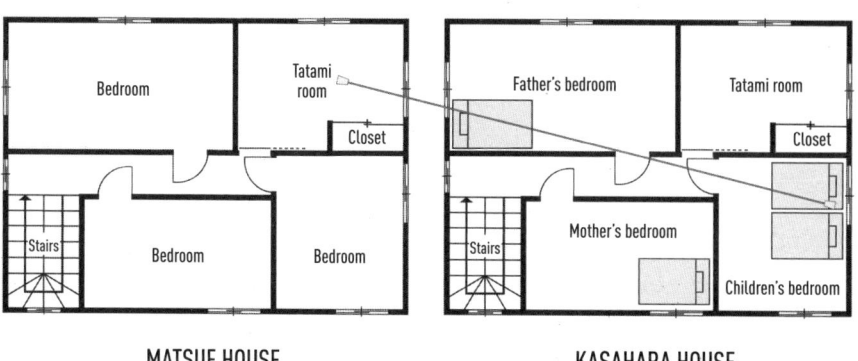

MATSUE HOUSE   KASAHARA HOUSE

> So, it's not really something anyone likes to talk about, but… The fire was apparently caused by Hiroki's mother setting herself on fire. It was on the local news. She doused herself in kerosene in the first-floor tatami room and lit it.

KASAHARA: I don't think he was there every time we spoke. Maybe he changed the length of string. But, at the very least, the last time we used it—the night of the fire—my dad must have been in that room.

Remember, that night he had been acting strangely. His voice was shaking, and his answers were incoherent. I'm sure he had something to do with the fire.

AUTHOR: But you heard on the news that it was the mother's suicide that caused the fire, right? How could your father have had anything to do with it?

KASAHARA: Was it really suicide?

AUTHOR: If it wasn't, then what...?

KASAHARA: Murder. I've spent years thinking about it, and I think my dad was committing murder while he talked to me on the string phone.

The bizarre contrast between her casual tone and the dark things she was saying sent a chill down my spine.

She went on speaking in that same voice.

KASAHARA: There was only about a metre between our houses. It was summer, so they probably had the windows open to let the breeze in.

My dad was a track-and-field runner in high school, and he liked to brag about his athleticism. So, maybe it wasn't that difficult for him to make the jump. I know I couldn't have. I would have been too frightened.

AUTHOR: You're saying that your father jumped in through the tatami-room window, killed Mrs Matsue and set her body on fire, all while talking to you on the string phone?

KASAHARA: Which would certainly explain his incoherent conversation. Then, he could have climbed back home through the windows again and pretended that he knew nothing about it all.

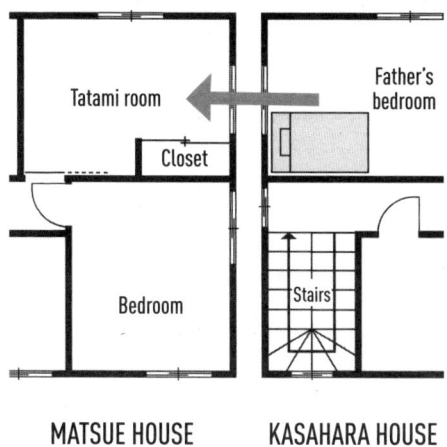

MATSUE HOUSE   **KASAHARA HOUSE**

AUTHOR: A murder made to look like suicide through self-immolation...

KASAHARA: I don't know his motive, but our families interacted a lot. There could have trouble between the parents that we kids never noticed.

    There are all kinds of things I can't explain, like whether he only held a grudge against Mrs Matsue, or if he wanted to kill the whole family, or why he made it look like she set herself on fire. But there's one thing I am sure of. Dad wanted me to be his alibi.

AUTHOR: So you could say that you and he were talking at the time of the crime.

KASAHARA: Exactly. He must have figured that if I told that to the police, it would prove his innocence in their eyes.

AUTHOR: I wonder. I actually think 'we were talking on a string phone' would have made for a pretty weak alibi. It might have been stronger if he'd come and talked to you in person right afterwards, but in general, testimony from family members, particularly by children about their parents, is not considered very useful in court.

KASAHARA: Is that so? I didn't know that. I doubt my dad did, either.

He wasn't the type to do much research before he acted. He just went full steam ahead at whatever he wanted to do.

AUTHOR: Was your father ever questioned by the police?

KASAHARA: Not even once, as far as I know. It sounds terrible in this context, but he was always lucky that way. I imagine he was convinced he had a plan for a 'perfect crime' and did it without even a second thought.

But afterwards, when he'd actually killed her, I don't think he could bear the guilt. He probably left us to run away from it. It really was a shock to me, too, the idea that he would use both the string phone and me as tools in committing murder.

. . .

After her discovery, Kasahara had kept her doubts bottled up inside, not sharing them with anyone.

Until the day came that she learnt of her father's death. It was two years after the fire, in 1994.

KASAHARA: That really was suicide, apparently. He locked himself in a little room deep in his house, sealed all the cracks and gaps with tape and took an overdose of sleeping pills. I heard there was some weird doll found beside his body. It's all just so… messed up. I think he must have been suffering from mental problems towards the end.

AUTHOR: When you say 'his house', you mean he bought a new one after he left yours?

KASAHARA: Right. After the divorce, he moved into a pre-owned house in Ichinomiya. I saw it for the first time on the day of his funeral. It was a single-storey house with a big flower bed by the front door. I talked to a neighbour, and they told me he'd had some renovation work done on the place not long before he died.

AUTHOR: Do you know what kind of renovation?

KASAHARA: Let's see… It was something odd. Like, reduction or something? That's right, they said he'd had one room completely removed.

One room completely removed? That rang a bell somehow.

KASAHARA: Oh, right, I found something else weird at my dad's house. When we were going through his things afterwards, we found a single picture of a little boy. He was at my dad's new house, eating a rice omelette. He was dreadfully thin and covered in bruises.

AUTHOR: How sad…

KASAHARA: It was heartbreaking to look at. He wasn't the son of any of our relatives or acquaintances. But still, I felt like I had seen that face somewhere before. It took me a while to recall, but his picture had been on the news.

His name was Naruki Mitsuhashi. He died from neglect. And I still have no idea how he was connected to my dad.

END OF FILE 8: THE STRING PHONE

FILE 9
Footsteps to Murder

12TH NOVEMBER 2020

Interview with Hiroki Matsue

A month after my interview with Chie Kasahara, I found myself in a rental workspace in Gifu Prefecture, waiting for my next subject. He arrived five minutes early.

He had sculpted hair and an expensive suit. He could have been a poster boy for the successful businessman in the prime of life.

Hiroki Matsue. The only child and sole survivor of the Matsue family, Kasahara's childhood neighbours. Looking at this middle-aged man, I could see no sign of the boy who had once watched his family home burn, weeping in the arms of a neighbour.

After Matsue lost both his parents in that fire, he had gone to live with his grandparents. They had been both keen on education and financially well off, he explained, so he had been able to go to a good university. He had been taken on at a brokerage firm directly after graduation and was now in his sixteenth year with that same company.

MATSUE: I have to say, I was surprised to hear from a writer investigating that fire. What got you looking into it, after all this time?

AUTHOR: I was thinking about writing an article about the dangers of fires in private homes, and my research led me to your house. When I looked into the news reports, there were some things that got me curious about it, and I just wanted to look deeper.
MATSUE: Hmm. OK.

I was, of course, lying.

The real reason was that I wanted to find out if Chie Kasahara's father was actually a murderer.

To be perfectly honest, I didn't really buy into her story about her father sneaking into the Matsue home, killing the mother and starting a house fire all while talking to her on the string phone. I wanted to learn all I could from the Matsue side, so I set up this interview with Hiroki.

. . .

I started by asking about the scale of the fire, when it started, and about any damage to neighbouring houses. What he told me was pretty much the same as what Kasahara had said.

Finally, the conversation turned towards my true interest.

AUTHOR: Do you know how the fire started, Mr Matsue?
MATSUE: The police said it was my mother's committing suicide, by setting herself on fire.
AUTHOR: And what do you think about that?
MATSUE: I think they're wrong.

He said it matter-of-factly.

AUTHOR: You believe there was another reason?
MATSUE: Yes. My mother was the victim. That fire wasn't caused by suicide. It was arson.

My heart skipped a beat. It seemed Matsue thought the same as Kasahara!

AUTHOR: Do you have any idea who might have set the fire, then?
MATSUE: I've spent years going over everything that happened, and now I think it must have been my father.

It was not the answer I had expected.

AUTHOR: What led you to that conclusion?
MATSUE: I can tell you what I think, but what does this have to do with your research? If you're just snooping into it for some gossip rag, I'm leaving.
AUTHOR: No, no, it's nothing like that. I'm serious about this article. I promise you I won't turn it into any kind of gossip column or anything like that.
MATSUE: Hmm. I see. Are you prepared to swear on your life? I am unforgiving with people who act in bad faith.
AUTHOR: I swear.

Matsue took a memo pad from his bag and sketched something in biro. I recognized the floor plan he showed me.

It only took him about five minutes to complete his floor plan. It was, of course, essentially the same as Kasahara's. It differed only in the placement of furniture. The room layout was identical.

I was surprised at Matsue's powers of recall.

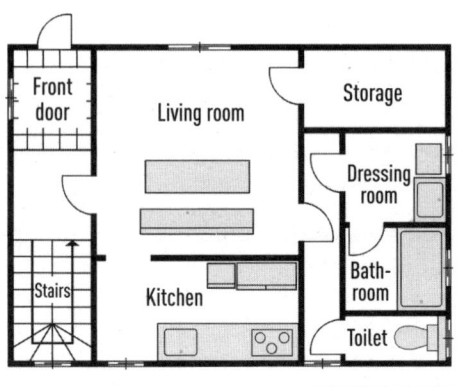

GROUND FLOOR

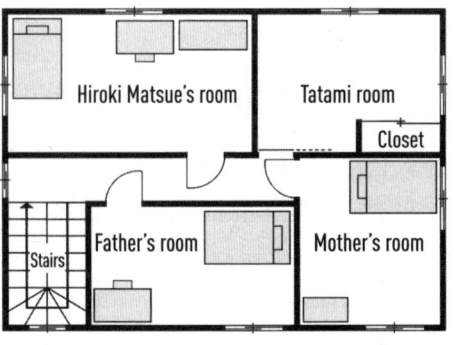

FIRST FLOOR

Note: This is the author's reproduction of Matsue's drawing.

AUTHOR: You're good at that.

MATSUE: There was a time in my school days when I wanted to become an architect. I gave it up when I heard you couldn't earn a living.

So, let me tell you what happened that day.

The evening of the fire, I was alone in the living room on the ground floor, watching television. Mother and Father were in their rooms upstairs. That was their habit after clearing away the dinner dishes.

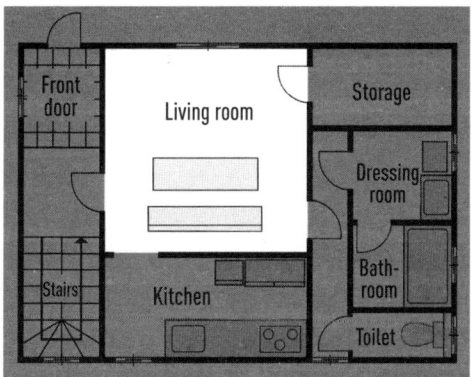
GROUND FLOOR

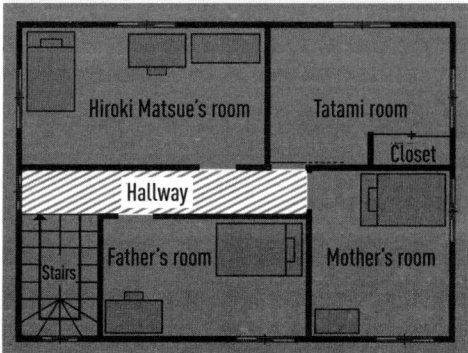
FIRST FLOOR

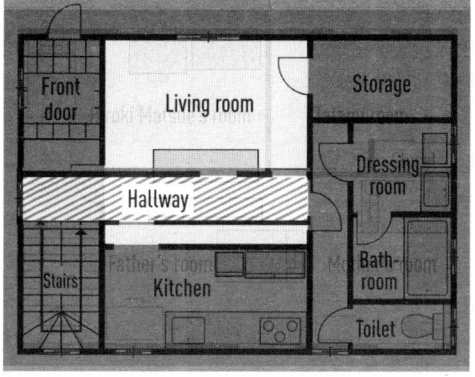

MATSUE: As you can see from the floor plan, the first-floor hallway runs right over the living room. My mother and father had very different treads, so I could tell who was walking upstairs and where they were going just by the sound.

That evening, I heard footsteps. The Sunday Sports programme had just started, so it was right around ten at night.

My father left his room upstairs and walked towards the right side of the plan. He went past the door to my room, meaning he was heading for one of the rooms farther down the landing.

I remember thinking that was strange. The only rooms that way were the tatami room and Mother's room. The tatami room was unused and basically empty, so he wouldn't be going there. Which only left Mother's room, and I couldn't imagine what would take him there either.

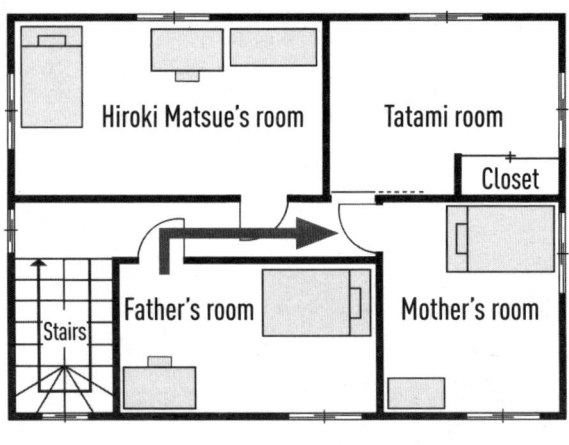

FIRST FLOOR

AUTHOR: Was it really that odd for him to visit her room?
MATSUE: I suppose it wouldn't be for most couples, but my mother and father didn't get along at all. They hardly spoke, and I got

the feeling they couldn't really bear the sight of each other. Looking back, I'm sure that sex was totally out of the question. I think the only reason they didn't divorce was that my mother had no financial independence and my father was incapable of any housework. They were just going through the motions. So, yes, it was incredibly rare for either to go to the other's room. It made me a little nervous, actually. Like, I imagined something must have happened.

AUTHOR: I see…

MATSUE: And then, about thirty minutes later, I suddenly heard footsteps racing away from Mother's room and down the stairs, then my father burst into the living room.

He was in a panic and started yelling, 'Fire! Get out!' He grabbed my hand, and we ran out the door.

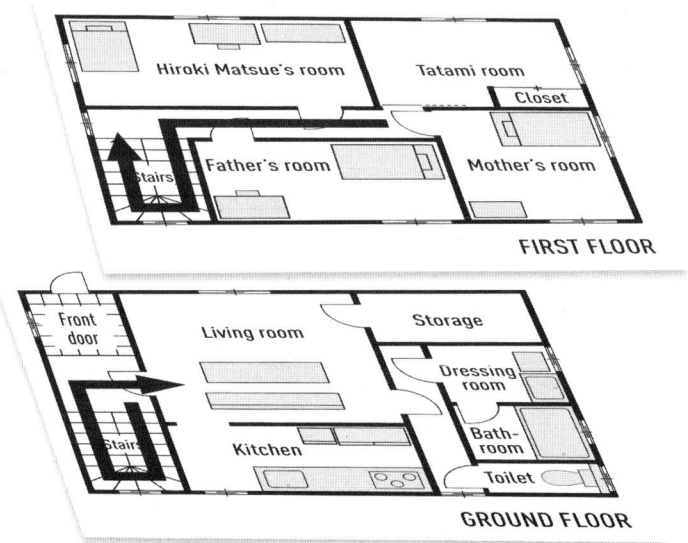

AUTHOR: That must have been a shock.

MATSUE: It certainly was. Outside, my father gave me a hundred-yen coin and his crucifix pendant and told me, 'Run to the phone box on the corner and call for a fire engine. The number is 119. Understand? Put in the coin, dial 119, and tell the person you need a fire engine. After that, just do what they say and answer their questions. I'm going to go look for your mother. For some reason, she wasn't in her room.'

Then he ran back into the house. I couldn't see the flames from outside, so I assumed one of the rooms in the back must have been on fire. So, I ran as fast as I could to the phone box.

I was just a kid, and it was my first time calling the fire brigade, so it must have taken about ten minutes. After I hung up and went back, I saw people from the neighbourhood gathering outside, watching my house. Smoke was pouring out of the windows.

I remember how an old woman from across the street found me and comforted me. In the end, neither of my parents made it out of the house.

Matsue took a silver pendant out of his breast pocket. It had the figure of Jesus Christ on the cross.

MATSUE: My father was a devout Christian. His faith was everything. He was a pacifist, too, and used to march against war and the death penalty and things like that. He told me he wanted to have me baptized as well, but my mother was opposed to it, so it never happened.

I ended up your typical non-religious Japanese person, celebrating Christmas with champagne and going to first prayers at the local shrine on New Year's Day. But I keep this with me, always. It's the only keepsake I have of life before the fire.

He stared silently at the pendant for a moment before going on.

MATSUE: They found my parents' bodies two days after the fire. My father had collapsed on the stairs. The police said he must have passed out while desperately searching the house for my mother.

They told me, 'He never had a hope of finding your mother, with her hidden like that.' It was like they were making excuses for him.

AUTHOR: 'Hidden like that'? What does that mean?

MATSUE: She was in the tatami-room closet.

AUTHOR: The closet?!

MATSUE: They never put it on the news, but she was found lying face up in the closet. A kerosene can was nearby. I suppose that's why they determined it was suicide.

AUTHOR: So, the theory is that she hid in the closet, doused herself in kerosene and set herself on fire?

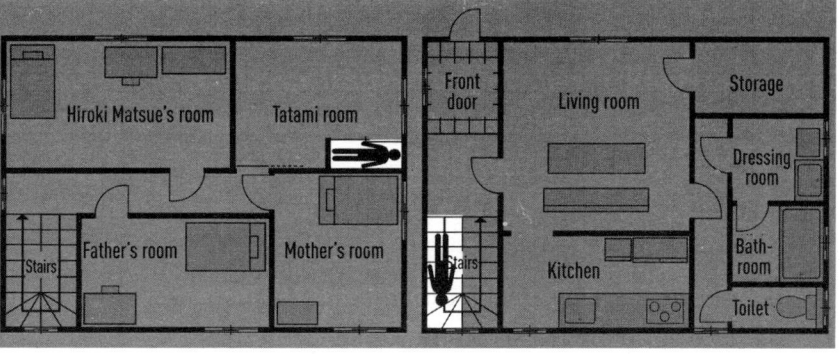

MATSUE: Yes. That's the one they came up with, anyway. But I know the truth is different. Because I heard my father's footsteps.

I know that just after ten that night my father walked from his room towards that side of the house. Thirty minutes later, he rushed downstairs and took me outside.

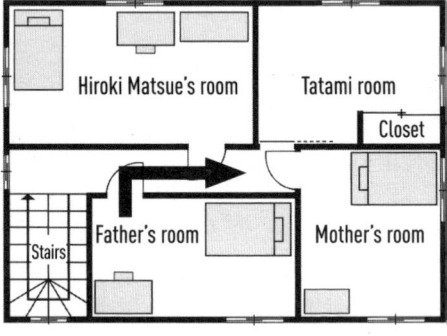

JUST PAST 10:00

What did he do for those thirty minutes? He must have been somewhere close to my mother. Why didn't he stop her committing suicide?

There is only one answer to both of those questions. He killed her.

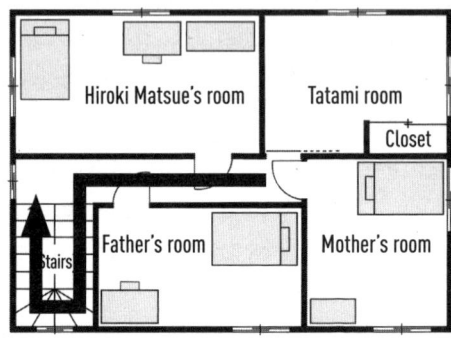

AROUND 10:30

He went to her room just after ten. He gave her sleeping medicine or something. I don't know how. Maybe he mixed it into a drink and took it to her as a nightcap. He might have asked her to talk one-on-one, like a couple, for a change.

When she was asleep, he took her to the tatami room, put her in the closet, doused her in kerosene and set her on fire. It was murder by arson. Their relationship was already miserable. Maybe he just couldn't bear it anymore.

That would certainly explain those thirty minutes.

But then…

AUTHOR: Why would your father go to the trouble of carrying her to the tatami-room closet to set her on fire?

MATSUE: I think that was for my sake.

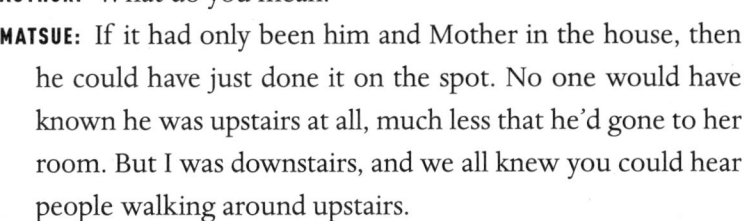

AUTHOR: What do you mean?

MATSUE: If it had only been him and Mother in the house, then he could have just done it on the spot. No one would have known he was upstairs at all, much less that he'd gone to her room. But I was downstairs, and we all knew you could hear people walking around upstairs.

And I'm sure he wanted to protect me. He doted on me. I know he would never have put me in danger. I'm sure of that much. That's why he took me outside before he even set the fire.

FATHER'S ACTIONS THAT NIGHT

Put mother to sleep

Took Hiroki outside

Returned to house, set fire

AUTHOR: Your theory, then, is that your father made sure you were safe before he ever set the fire. He only set it after he went back inside. But what does that have to do with putting her in the closet?

MATSUE: It was an excuse. His plan was to escape after setting the fire, leaving my mother to die while he made it to safety.

After that, it would have been just me and him. And when I got older, I might have asked him why he couldn't save her.

AUTHOR: Ah…

MATSUE: If I had asked him, he would have wanted some excuse, some way to convince me. He would have been the one saying, 'I never had a hope of finding your mother, with her hidden like that.'

> 'I'm going to go look for your mother. For some reason, she wasn't in her room.'

MATSUE: He had made sure to say 'she wasn't in her room' to prepare the way.

AUTHOR: It makes sense. But he didn't make it out…

MATSUE: The fire must have spread faster than he'd anticipated, and the smoke must have overcome him on the stairs. The only thing to say is, 'As you sow, so shall you reap.'

Matsue described the deaths of his father and mother as if he were discussing events he'd seen on the news, like it had nothing to do with him. But his casual tone was belied by the fact that his fists were clenched tight and hard as stone.

They spoke volumes about his true feelings.

·   ·   ·

MATSUE: If I'd told the police any of this back then, maybe they would have investigated further, or treated my father as a suspect. But I didn't say anything.

I didn't stay quiet for my father's sake, but because I didn't want to be known as a murderer's son. The whole thing is just so pathetic. A man murdered his wife by burning her alive but couldn't even get out before dying himself, like some kind of fool... I could never live with the shame of that getting out.

The truth is, I never intended to tell anyone about it. But...

He suddenly gave me a sharp glare.

MATSUE: Do you know why I decided to tell you about it today?
AUTHOR: Uh...?
MATSUE: Because this is where you end. How could I ever let you leave this place alive, knowing what you know?
AUTHOR: Wha—?! Wait, please, I promise!
MATSUE: People like to say that stockbrokers are liars. I'm not proud of it, but it's more or less the truth. When you've been a liar as long as I have, you learn to see through other people's lies. You're not planning on writing any article about 'fires in private homes', are you?

I couldn't hold back a gasp.
I broke out into a cold sweat.

MATSUE: I knew you were lying from the very start.

I told you, didn't I? I said I'm unforgiving with people who act in bad faith. Is lying to the survivor of a tragic fire acting in good faith?

AUTHOR: I… That is…

MATSUE: Remember how you swore on your life? Time to uphold that oath.

AUTHOR: No! Please, let's just talk this through!

Matsue's grim features finally broke into a grin.

MATSUE: Heheheh… Hahahahahah! Oh, that was great. You should have seen your face!

AUTHOR: Huh?

MATSUE: Sorry, I'm sorry. I just wanted to tease you a bit. Don't worry, you're out of danger. For now, anyway!

I couldn't wrap my mind around what was going on. My heart was still pounding in my chest.

Matsue wore a mischievous grin as he watched me gape in confusion.

MATSUE: The truth is, I knew all about you before you even got in touch. Chie Kasahara told me.

AUTHOR: Ms Kasahara?!

MATSUE: We're still friends. We ran into each other by accident about five years ago and ended up going for drinks. The conversation eventually led to the fire, of course, and we both revealed our theories. I was so surprised by hers! The idea that her father might be the murderer was a real shock. But I had to admit, it was possible. Ever since, we meet up and hang out or have dinner sometimes.

AUTHOR: But her father might have killed your parents! Doesn't that bother you?

MATSUE: Why would it? It's not like she did anything. Honestly, there's no one else I can open up to about it all. No one else could ever understand the trauma of that night as well as she does.

AUTHOR: I suppose that makes some sense…

MATSUE: So, in the interests of full disclosure, she got in touch last month.

She told me that some shady writer-type tracked her down to ask about the fire. 'I told him about you, so he might come to you next,' is what she said. I had to laugh when you did exactly that.

AUTHOR: She saw right through me.

I was beginning to feel bit of resentment towards Ms Kasahara.

MATSUE: Boy, it was so hard to keep a straight face that whole time. What was it? 'I was thinking about writing an article about fires in private homes' or whatever?

AUTHOR: I'm sorry. Please, just forget everything I said…

MATSUE: You need to practise lying.

AUTHOR: I suppose I do.

MATSUE: But, really, it's not nice to lie to people who've lost their homes and families to a tragedy like that.

His tone was light, but there was no smile in his eyes.

AUTHOR: I truly am sorry.

MATSUE: I suppose I'll let you off this time, on one condition.

AUTHOR: What's that?

MATSUE: Find out the truth behind that fire. It doesn't matter what it is. Even if it turns out that my father was a murderer, or that Chie Kasahara's father was. Or that it was neither of them.

We just want to know the truth.

· · ·

After Matsue left, I stayed behind in the workspace and arranged my thoughts in order.

Both Chie Kasahara and Hiroki Matsue had their own theories about the fire in the Matsue house. But, to be honest, I couldn't wholly accept either one.

HIROKI MATSUE'S THEORY	CHIE KASAHARA'S THEORY
Murderer = Mr Matsue	Murderer = Mr Kasahara
Put wife to sleep, led son to safety, set wife on fire	Sneaked into Matsue house through window, killed Mrs Matsue while talking on string phone
Was too slow to escape, died	Then set fire

Mr Kasahara's behaviour on the day of the fire was suspicious, that much was true.

But it struck me as totally unrealistic to try to fake an alibi by talking to your daughter on a string phone while you commit murder. On the other hand, Hiroki Matsue's proposed scenario was more realistic. However, I had other concerns about it.

The thing that really gave me doubts was the act of arson.

There are many, many ways to kill people, so why would he have chosen fire? He burnt down his own house just to kill his wife? It was far too much of a sacrifice, in my opinion.

I felt like the truth had to be something else. There must be a third option, other than Kasahara's or Matsue's theories. And I had to find it.

My mind made up, I left the workspace behind.

END OF FILE 9: FOOTSTEPS TO MURDER

FILE 10
No Escape

25TH JANUARY 2023

Interview with Akemi Nishiharu

Hidden in the underground level of a mixed-purpose building in Nakameguro is a small izakaya, tucked away like some kind of speakeasy.

It's a tiny place, with only eight counter seats, but it has been a favourite for neighbourhood businessmen dropping by for a drink on the way home from work for over forty years.

In January 2023, I visited it for an interview with the owner. We had scheduled our talk for an hour before opening. I stepped inside and saw a man of around fifty in chef's whites standing in the kitchen, readying ingredients for cooking.

When he noticed me, he bowed low and showed me to a small break room in the back. It was only about three tatami mats in size. A woman sat there, drinking sake. This was my interview subject, Akemi Nishiharu.

She told me she would be turning eighty soon but still stayed up late, talking with her regular customers every night. She was the epitome of a classic bar hostess. She had run the place alone with her son, Mitsuru, ever since it had opened forty-six years ago.

AKEMI: I turned the kitchen over to Mitsuru twenty years ago. Now I'm just some old lady who drinks with the customers.

And they seem to like it, if you can believe that. These days, people are lonely, just looking for someone to drink with.

Mitsuru! We've got a guest! Tea and pickles! Hurry it up, now.

Before I could refuse, Mitsuru had already rushed to the kitchen to brew some tea.

AKEMI: Forgive him. He's a hell of a cook, honestly. He's turned out good enough. Up to middle school, he couldn't even take a bath alone. Ah, but they grow up so fast. If only he'd find a wife to look after him, I could die easy.

Akemi gave a belly laugh then.

A jolly mother and a hard-working son. Normally, they'd strike me as a heartwarming family. But there was darkness in their past.

Once, Akemi and Mitsuru had lived in a flat from which there was no escape.

· · ·

Akemi was born in Shizuoka Prefecture in 1944.

Her family was poor, and she says she remembers stealing produce from local fields to quell her hunger pangs.

Her father was a construction worker who seemed to relish taking out the stress of the day by beating her. When she was fifteen, her mother died, and before long she became the victim of sexual abuse, as well.

Akemi fled home as soon as she graduated middle school.

She made her way to Tokyo to find work, ending up in Kabukicho, Japan's biggest red-light district. The nation was in the middle of its great post-war economic boom, and people and money flowed through the nightlife spots like a river. Akemi lied about her age and got a job as a nightclub hostess.

AKEMI: Those days really were something. Nowadays I'm a wrinkled old rag, but when I was young, I was quite the looker, I tell you. On top of that I knew how to talk to men, and I could drink like a fish. Before long, I was the bar's number-one girl. In my heyday, there were months when I took home over a million yen. In those days, that was enough to buy a luxury car flat out. But, well, the good times never last.

When Akemi was nineteen, she got pregnant with a customer's baby. The man had claimed to be owner of a small company and sweet-talked her with dreams of settling down and raising a family with her. Akemi had taken him at his word and was ready to get married.

But the night she told him she was pregnant was the last time he ever showed up at the bar. Not long after, she heard an odd rumour: he wasn't any kind of business owner at all. He was a simple office worker with a wife and child at home.

AKEMI: I don't hold it against him. I was a fool to believe a drunken barfly's chat-up lines.

I was just nineteen, though, and didn't know how the world worked. And so, I ended up having Mitsuru on my own. I wasn't worried much. I had plenty of money.

But I got to thinking about my future and didn't think we could go on just living off of savings. So, I figured I'd open my own place. I'd be a bar owner.

I'd hire young girls and teach them how to deal with customers, then just sit back and watch the money flow in. Course, now I know I was just fooling myself.

I didn't know a thing about running a business. I opened up shop and ended up just watching the money flow out the door. I should have thrown in the towel right away, but I held on, thinking things would work out. I started piling up debt.

When I was twenty-seven, I finally accepted that it was over, and I declared bankruptcy. But that only gets the banks off your back. I'd borrowed more than a bit of money from some more dangerous characters, too.

You try telling the yakuza that you've declared bankruptcy and can't pay them back... They packed me and Mitsuru into the back of a car and took us to a room.

They called it an *okito*. A storehouse.

. . .

Once, Japan had legal brothels, where women would live and earn money by selling sexual services to men. But the government passed a law banning prostitution in 1958, so they mostly vanished from the streets.

They were replaced by businesses like 'soapland' bathhouses or 'delivery health' call-girl services, which still sell sex but exist in legal grey zones largely ignored by the authorities. And then there were these *okito*, secret brothels run by organized crime groups.

The *okito* where Akemi and Mitsuru ended up was a remodelled two-storey block of flats in the mountains of central Yamanashi Prefecture.

There were four rooms on each floor. Gangsters lived on the ground floor and kept watch, while the first floor was filled with women debtors like Akemi.

AKEMI: The reason they used an actual block of flats was cover. They could just pass it off as a bunch of women living there and having sex when their partners visited. Which isn't illegal at all. Of course, the police would have figured it out in a second if they actually checked, but back then the police tried not to mess with the yakuza. They more or less let them get on with it.

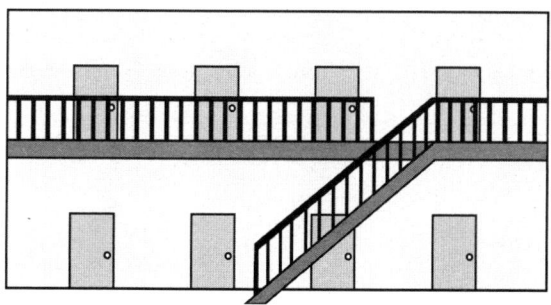

Akemi and Mitsuru were put into a corner room on the first floor.

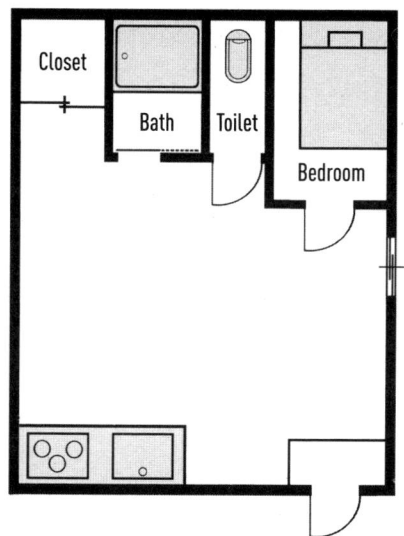

AKEMI: It was an old tatami room that reeked of mould. It had a toilet, a bath and a closet, with a simple kitchen. The gangsters brought us bento boxes every day, but they were always cold, so we used the hob to heat them a bit. Then there was a little bedroom.

I doubt I have to tell you, the bedroom wasn't really meant for sleeping. It was a dark little room with a bed and, you know, toys. It was there for customers.

It had proper walls, so the only saving grace was that I could do business without Mitsuru seeing. Of course, I'm sure he figured out what his mother was doing every night.

I glanced towards the kitchen. I was sure Mitsuru could hear Akemi's voice, but he didn't react at all. He just kept to his work. I felt bad for him and regretted this choice of interview location.

AKEMI: Customers always came late at night. And they always came in big, expensive cars. That *okito* only served rich folks.

Each night cost about a hundred thousand yen. Of course, the gang pocketed ninety per cent and the other ten per cent went towards the loan. And we were trapped in that room until the loan was all paid back. I say 'trapped', but they didn't actually lock us in. That would have openly been kidnapping and would have ruined the smokescreen they kept up for the cops. They had another way to keep us from running.

Akemi explained that although the doors weren't locked, there were always gangsters watching over the ways in and out. They lived on the ground floor and kept watch in shifts.

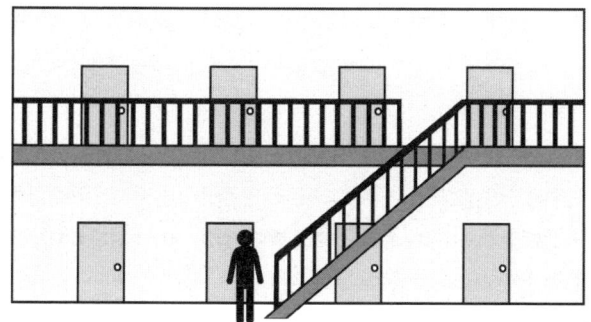

The four women and their children living on the first floor were powerless, and Akemi says that even if they had worked together to try and make a run for it, they would have been no match for armed gangsters. The yakuza knew that, of course, but they took other precautions to keep them obedient as well.

AKEMI: Each of our rooms had only one window. It opened onto the flat next door.

The windows between flats could be opened to allow conversation, but they also enabled closer observation. If a woman could prove that her neighbour was planning an escape, the yakuza would forgive half her remaining debt. So, in other words, they set them up to watch each other.

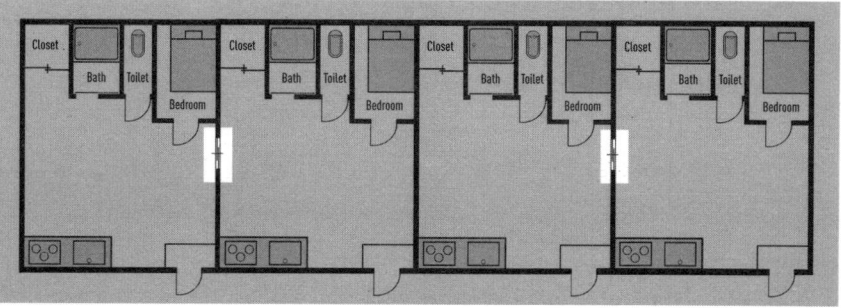

AKEMI: But it's not like you could actually prove something like that. We didn't have cameras or recording equipment. And as for the whole forgiving debt thing, no one believed for a minute the yakuza would keep their word.

If anything, the whole idea was only effective because it made people afraid of being wrongly accused. Anyway, our neighbour was a decent woman, so I didn't worry about that.

Akemi said her neighbour was six years older than she.

AKEMI: She was a beautiful woman, name of Yaeko. She had a daughter, eleven years old. We were both well aware of how hard it was to raise kids in such a terrible situation, so that whole nonsense of trying to prove the other was going to run away never crossed our minds. No, we'd just open the window and chat.

Akemi said that Yaeko had one distinguishing feature.

AKEMI: I didn't even notice it at first, you know, but Yaeko was missing her left arm. She said she'd lost it in an accident just after she was born.
AUTHOR: Could you tell me a bit more about her?
AKEMI: Well, let's see, you know we used to talk about our pasts and such when the kids weren't around. She'd had quite a life.

Yaeko had been brought up in a wealthy family. But when she was around eighteen, they told her something shocking.

AKEMI: She'd been abandoned as a baby. They found her in some hut or something, out in the woods.

So, those folks she thought were her birth parents had in fact adopted her. It's not that unusual a story, I know. But it shocked her, I suppose, and she ran away from home. She told me she still resented the both of them.

AUTHOR: But what reason did they give her to resent them? They might not have been her birth parents, but they took her in and raised her, right?

AKEMI: I couldn't say! I suppose there was something only she could understand. Anyway, I made an effort not to dig too deep. It wasn't my place to interrogate the woman.

So, after she left home, she came to Tokyo to look for work, but it was hard going with her handicap and all. She scraped by with part-time clerical work or some such, I think.

But then came the big turning point.

When Yaeko was twenty-one, she fell in love with the president of the company she was working for, and he proposed.

AKEMI: And just like that, she was the boss's wife. Isn't that something?

She had a baby right away, and everything seemed grand... Or so she thought. But life has a way of bringing pitfalls, don't it?

The 1965 securities slump drove the company out of business, and her husband killed himself. Left her just a pile of debt. So, the yakuza dragged her and her daughter off to the *okito*.

AUTHOR: What terribly bad luck...

AKEMI: Isn't it just? Through no fault of her own. Not like me.

Akemi threw back a drink with a grimace.

AKEMI: But, you know, Yaeko taught me that no matter how bad your luck gets, you have to keep your heart pure. And we owe her such a debt. She saved Mitsuru's life.
AUTHOR: She did? What happened?
AKEMI: Well, it was about six months after we got to the *okito*.

. . .

The women were not normally allowed to leave their rooms at the *okito*. If they needed to go out for short periods, they were allowed to, but under one condition: they had to swap children with one of the other mothers.

Let's say that Family A and Family B are neighbours.

If Mother A wants to go out, she has to take Child B from next door with her. While she's out, Mother B watches Child A to make sure he or she doesn't run away.

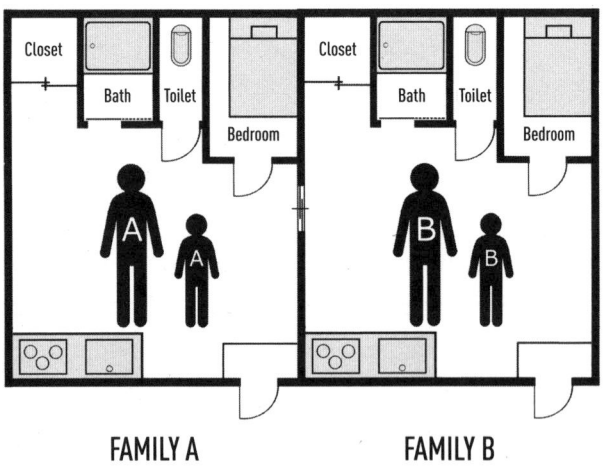

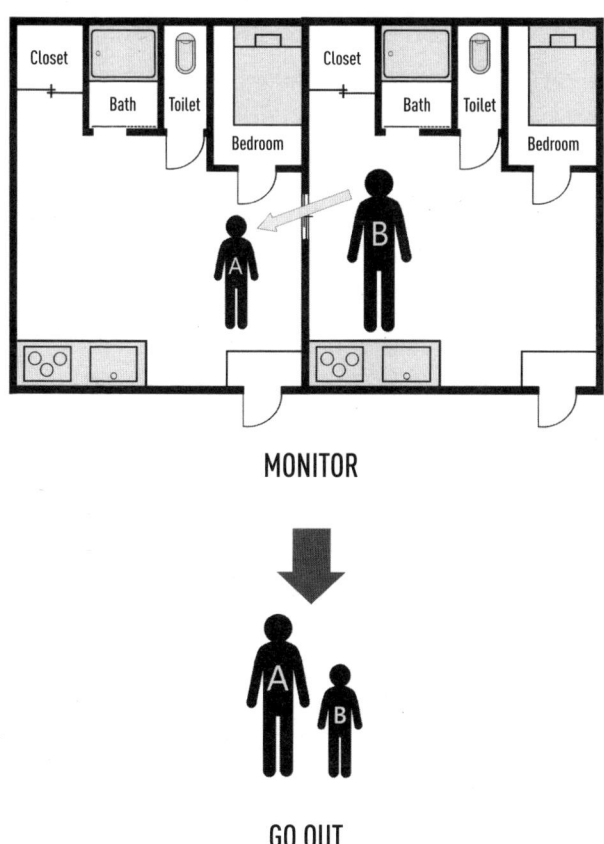

MONITOR

GO OUT

Mother A won't run away because she's left her child behind. Child B won't run away because he'd be scared to be separated from his mother.

So, in other words, one of the family members was always held hostage to ensure the other's obedience. It was as good as putting shackles on their hearts.

If, for the sake of argument, Mother A were willing to abandon her own child and run away, the rule was that Mother B would have to take on her debt, so no mothers would be willing to trade children in this way unless they really trusted each other. Akemi and Yaeko did trust each other, so they sometimes took advantage of the system.

They could go wherever they wanted, as long as they were back before dark, so they usually took each other's children to the park to play.

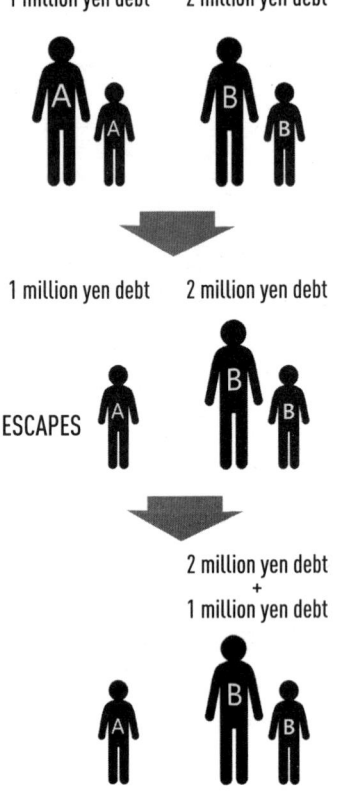

But on one such occasion, tragedy struck.

AKEMI: One day, Mitsuru asked to go to town. He wanted to see the big buildings, he said.

AUTHOR: Big buildings? Didn't you say that this *okito* was in the mountains in Yamanashi?

AKEMI: Well, yes, it was in the mountains, but not totally out in the middle of nowhere. A two-hour walk would get you to the city proper.

Yaeko said, 'If Mitsuru wants to go as bad as all that, I'll take him.' So, I gave in and let him go. The two of them got their bentos and bottles of tea from the guards, and one even lent her a map. Yaeko said they'd be back by three, but they weren't home by sundown.

Akemi could only sit and worry, until finally a guard came to her. 'They're both in hospital,' he said in a surprisingly gentle voice for such a tough guy.

It seemed that Mitsuru had mistaken a signal at a crossing and walked out into traffic. Yaeko pushed him out of the way just as he was about to be hit, but the car got her instead.

AKEMI: That was the only time in my life I ever prayed. I was beside myself with fear. Soon we found out that Mitsuru was fine. I just about fainted with relief. But then, to think of poor Yaeko ending up like that…

Mitsuru got off with a few scrapes, but Yaeko was terribly injured.

Her right leg had been trapped under the car, cutting off the circulation for too long. The limb had died and had to be amputated.

Already missing her left arm, she had also lost her right leg.

AKEMI: I had no idea how to make amends. When Yaeko came back from the hospital, Mitsuru and I knelt and apologized over and over. We could have done it till the day we died, and it never would have been enough, but Yaeko didn't say a word of blame. In fact, she said she was sorry for letting the boy stray into harm's way…

I'm not the type to go around admiring people, but Yaeko… She was different.

I still consider her a role model. Still wish I could be like her. Course, I'd need a hundred more years to learn to be half as decent as her!

Their parting came suddenly.

AKEMI: At the time, Yaeko had a regular customer. Man name of Hikura, he was. The son of some construction company big shot. He was head over heels for Yaeko. It seems he went and paid off her debt. Not out of the goodness of his heart, of course. He took them both off somewhere, mother and daughter.

I saw him through the window when he came, and he struck me as a real piece of shit. Just the kind of man who'd use Daddy's money to buy a woman. Worthless. Skinny as a rail, not an ounce of life in him, and a beak on him like a buzzard. A disgusting pervert, he was.

And even so, him being the president's son and all, he got to take over the company and now he's Mr Chairman. Ah, what a world we live in. Still, I suppose if he hadn't come along, she and her girl would have been trapped in that place even longer. So, some good came of it.

Akemi managed to pay off her own debt the year after Yaeko left. She and her son finally escaped the *okito* after three terrible years. At the time, Akemi was twenty-nine, and Mitsuru was nine.

They both went back to Tokyo, and she worked at restaurants until she'd saved up enough of a nest egg to open this bar. After years of hardship, she and Mitsuru finally managed to make it through.

They never saw Yaeko again.

. . .

Our interview ended just ten minutes before opening. I handed her an envelope containing a few thousand yen I'd prepared in thanks for her time and hurried out of the room.

As I was leaving the bar, I gave Mitsuru a greeting, my heart full of guilt for having asked his mother to share such difficult memories.

He only bowed silently, avoiding my eyes.

On the train home, I read back over my interview notes. As I did, I found myself bothered by several points.

> That *okito* only served rich folks. Each night cost about a hundred thousand yen.

Even in today's money, a hundred thousand yen per session was an incredible price to pay for sex. No matter how rich he was, I couldn't imagine any man paying that much.

> There were four rooms on each floor. Gangsters lived on the ground floor and kept watch, while the first floor was filled with women debtors like Akemi.

That meant that each brothel could only have four sex workers. That was certainly not a very efficient way to run a business, even for gangsters.

I thought that Akemi must have been misremembering some parts of the story. It had all happened fifty years ago, after all. It would only be natural if some of her memories had got confused.

I didn't think she was out and out lying to me, though. Why would she be? But perhaps she was hiding something. Something important, something that got right to the heart of her story…

I started to read back over my notes one more time.

END OF FILE 10: NO ESCAPE

FILE 11

The Vanishing Room

JULY 2022

Record of investigation and interview with Ren Iruma

'For a dream, it just felt so realistic. I can still remember how cold the floor was and what the walls felt like.'

I was talking to Ren Iruma, twenty-four, freelance designer.

We knew each other through previous work projects, and I'd sent him a copy of *Strange Houses* on its publication. He had called me a year after that with an odd story. 'I read your book. I know, I know, you sent it ages ago,' he'd said. He'd gone on to tell me about an odd experience he'd had in his childhood home.

IRUMA: I'm originally from Niigata Prefecture. I lived with my parents until I graduated from school. When I was a kid, I had a really weird experience in that house.

It was the year before I started elementary school, so I must have been five or six. You know how fuzzy and fragmentary memories from that age can be, right? It's like that.

The memory starts with a terrible feeling of dizziness.

IRUMA: I know I was inside the house, but I can't remember exactly where. For some reason, it was like the whole world started spinning. It was hard to stand up, so I had to squat down to keep myself from falling over. When the dizziness passed, I looked up and saw a door in front of me.

I remember being confused, like, 'Wait, since when is there a door there?' I walked over and pulled it open, and there was a little room. Not just, you know, small, but tiny. The floor couldn't have been more than one metre square. I doubt three adults could have fitted inside. The ceiling was pretty high, though.

I stepped in, and I remember that it was chilly against my feet. So, it probably had lino flooring or something. There weren't any windows, and the wallpaper was pure white. It was such an odd little room. While I was looking around, trying to figure it out, I noticed a small wooden box on the floor. I opened the lid and... something terrifying was inside.

AUTHOR: What was it?

IRUMA: That's the problem. I just don't remember what it was. I think... I kind of remember picking it up in both hands. It was something thin... It was really hard... I was so scared that I put it right back in the box and ran all the way back to my own room.

I started reading my favourite comedy manga to try and calm myself, and then my parents came home.

AUTHOR: So, they were out when all this happened?

IRUMA: That's right. With them home, I felt much more courageous, so that night, I thought I might try to get another peek into that room. But it was gone.

AUTHOR: The room had vanished?

IRUMA: Exactly. I went around and opened every door in the house, trying to find it again, but there was no trace of that odd little room. I even asked my parents, but they just said I must've dreamt it. I admit, it does seem a bit unreal.

But, for a dream, it just felt so realistic. I can still remember how cold the floor was, and what the walls felt like.

AUTHOR: Hmm... And you never found that room again?

IRUMA: Never. It was just that one time.

A room that appeared only once. It certainly did have a feel of the paranormal about it. The most convincing explanation, though, was that it was all just a dream, as his parents had said.

But still, I wondered why he had contacted me after reading my book.

IRUMA: At some point, I just convinced myself that I did actually dream it. But then, when I read that book you sent me, I started thinking there might have been another explanation. There was a hidden room in *Strange Houses*, right?
AUTHOR: Right. The entrance was hidden behind a Buddhist altar.
IRUMA: When I read that part, I started to wonder: what if...?
AUTHOR: What if that room was hidden, too?
IRUMA: Exactly. I know, of course, that the idea of a totally normal family home having hidden rooms is pretty out there. But if what happened that day wasn't a dream, I can't think of any other way to make sense of it.

I keep trying to think of other possibilities... For example, maybe Dad had the room put in for fun when they were building the house? I mean, having a hidden room feels like something out of a storybook.

But we didn't have an altar, so how did they hide the room, or, rather, the door, you know?
AUTHOR: If what you remember really happened, the door appeared and disappeared.
IRUMA: Right. Like, how is that kind of magic possible at all, you know? So, what I really want to ask is for a favour. Will you help me look for it?

AUTHOR: Hmm.

IRUMA: Come on, you and me. We can go to my old house and look for that room. You're writing a sequel, right? You can use this in it!

AUTHOR: Wait a minute. I appreciate the offer, of course, but we can't just barge in on your parents and go rummaging through their house…

IRUMA: It's fine! Dad's living there alone now, and he still works during the day. The house is usually empty. I go back and let myself in all the time.

AUTHOR: Yes, but you're family. I'm just some stranger.

IRUMA: Don't worry about it! I take some of my designer friends back with me sometimes. We have barbecues in the garden and stuff. I'm an only child, so the old man is soft on me. He lets me do whatever, so me bringing someone round is no problem at all.

In the end, I gave in to Iruma's insistence—and, I must admit, my own curiosity—and we decided that the two of us would travel to his childhood home the following week.

. . .

After I hung up the phone, I went back over what he'd told me.

A room that appeared only once in his childhood… If it wasn't a dream, why only once? That was the question we wanted to answer.

The room had appeared the year before Iruma entered primary school, when he was six years old. He had turned twenty-four in May 2022, so the room had appeared eighteen years before that…

So, one day in 2004, something had happened in that house. Once I'd got that far, something occurred to me.

After a simple internet search, I found what I was looking for. If I was right, then maybe we could find that hidden room.

· · ·

The following Monday, he picked me up at Tokyo Station in his car, and we set off for Niigata Prefecture. As he drove, I asked him some things I'd been wondering about.

AUTHOR: So, you said your father is living alone in your old house.
IRUMA: Yes?
AUTHOR: I hope you don't think I'm prying, but, what about your mother?
IRUMA: They're divorced. It happened the year I went to university. It wasn't a bad break-up or anything, but they were never that close, either. When they told me, it just felt like one of those things.
AUTHOR: Do you still see your mother?
IRUMA: Oh, sure. The two of us had dinner just the other day. Every time we meet, she nags me about all kinds of things. 'Are you eating enough vegetables?' or 'Make sure you get your check-up!' You know.
AUTHOR: Mothers can be like that. It's a good thing to have someone who cares.

Iruma's house was in a quiet corner of a town called Myoko, surrounded by bucolic countryside.

It had a modern design with large windows and a stylish white-and-navy exterior. The couple had bought it newly built the year they married. When their son was born eight years later, they'd had major renovations done.

AUTHOR: Nice place.

IRUMA: My dad's a bit obsessed with aesthetics. He gets so fussy about things.

AUTHOR: Hmm. Does your father work in design, too?

IRUMA: Well, I suppose he does, in a way. But not anything artistic. He's in product design for a metals company. I think he said they do something related to rare earth elements, but I didn't understand half of what he was talking about.

Right, that's enough talking on the doorstep. Let's get inside.

He took out a key and unlocked the door.

Inside, the house fairly gleamed with glossy flooring and white papered walls. It had the same modern sensibility as the outside.

It was eleven in the morning. His father wouldn't be home until around eight that evening, so we had plenty of time. To start with, he gave me a tour of the house. As we walked, I sketched a simple layout in my memo pad.

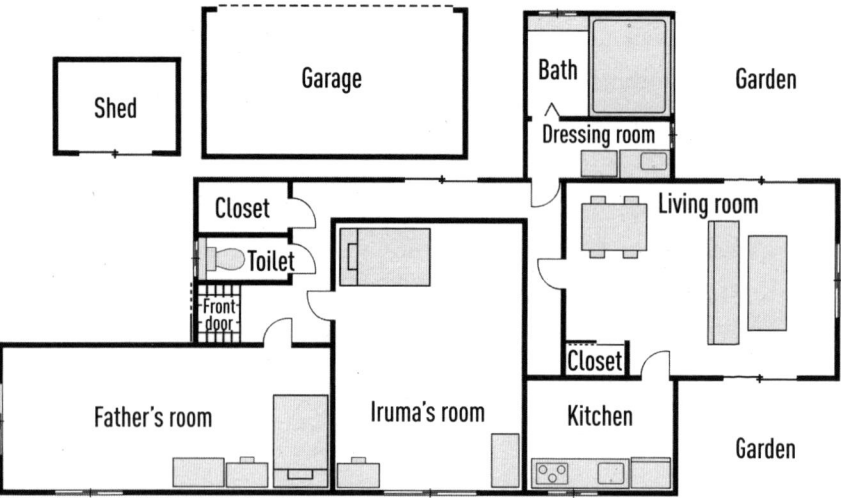

After the quick tour, he showed me to the living room and served up tea and biscuits.

It was a lovely room, with glass doors on the north and south walls offering a view of gardens on both sides.

AUTHOR: I'm getting the feeling that your family is quite well off…
IRUMA: No, no, not at all.
AUTHOR: But I've never seen a living room opening onto gardens on two sides like this.
IRUMA: Oh, that's just because we're in the country. No one could afford so much garden space in the city. So, anyway, what do you think, now that you've seen the house?
AUTHOR: OK, let's get down to it.

I laid out the sketch I'd made.

AUTHOR: I didn't spot any suspiciously positioned furniture that looked like it could have been blocking a door… So, let's compare your memories to this layout sketch and see if we can get a rough idea of where the hidden room might have been.

From what you told me, these are the key points of your memory:

(1) You suddenly felt dizzy, and, when that passed, there was a door in front of you.
(2) When you pulled the door open, there was a small room.
(3) The room was one metre square.
(4) When you opened a small box on the floor, there was something frightening inside. You then ran all the way back to your own room to escape.

Let's start at the fourth point. You said you ran 'all the way back' to your own room. That would imply a certain amount of distance between your room and this hidden one. It wasn't just a couple of steps down the hall.

IRUMA: That's a good point.

AUTHOR: Now, the third one. It was a square room, about one metre by one metre. So, the door would probably be about one metre wide as well.

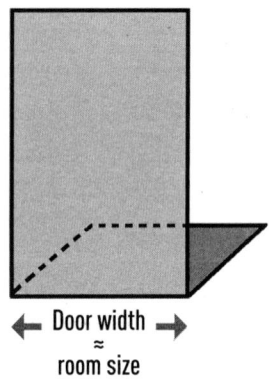

⬅ Door width ➡
≈
room size

So, then, we need to think about how that door could be hidden.

If you tried to hide a door in the middle of a large blank wall, for example, you'd almost certainly be able to see the outline.

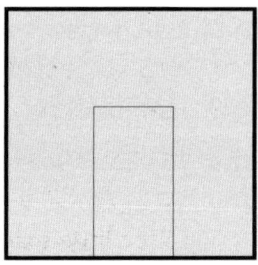

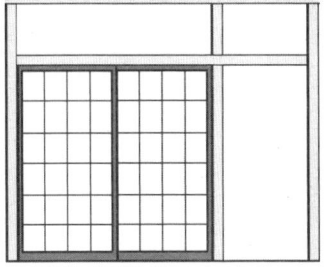
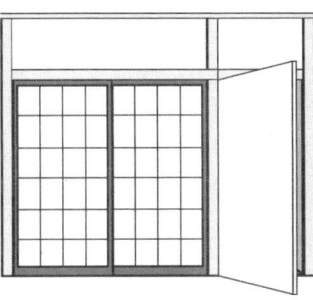
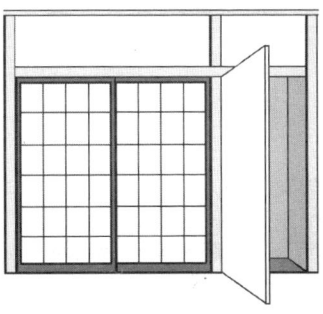
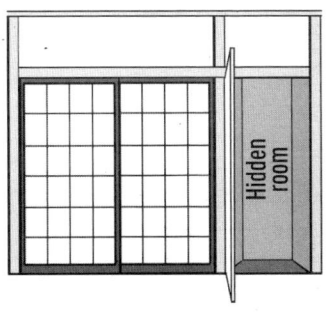

AUTHOR: So, if you wanted to conceal a door, you'd put pillars or something else on each side of it, to hide the edges. I was looking for a place like that while you were showing me round, and I spotted one possibility.

The dead end of the hallway next to the living room.

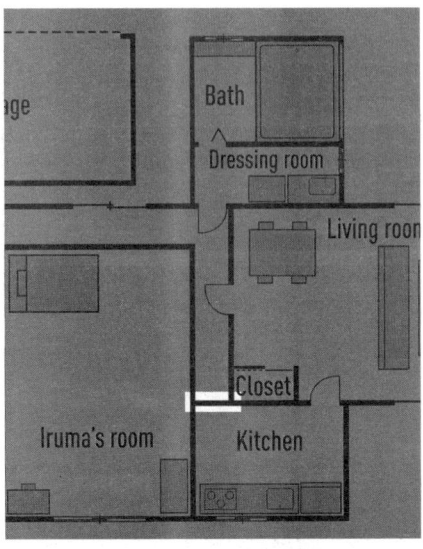

The kitchen is on the other side of that wall, so it would have been convenient to put a door into the kitchen at the end of the hallway. But there isn't one. Which leads me to believe there might be something between the hallway and the kitchen. Like a little space, for example.

237

IRUMA: Oh...

AUTHOR: Let's check and see. You go out to the hallway, and I'll go to the kitchen.

I put my ear to the wall in the kitchen.

AUTHOR: All right, Iruma! I'm ready! Give the wall a good knock!
IRUMA: Got it!

 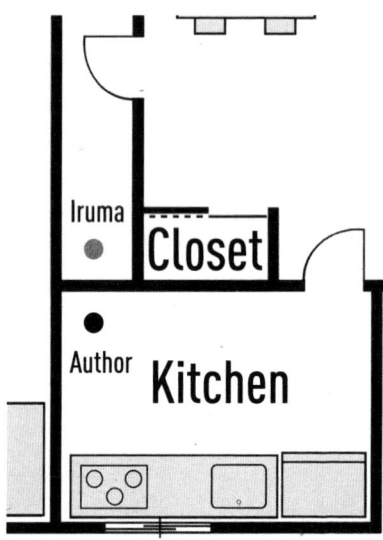

I heard a knocking sound on the other side of the wall. It sounded quiet, distant and had a slight echo. Just as I'd suspected.

There was a space between the hallway and the kitchen. A hidden room.

I rushed out to the hallway.

The wall at the end of the hallway was lined—left, right and top—with thin wooden slats. If my guess was right, that wall was actually a hidden door.

Iruma braced his feet and pushed hard on the wall, but it didn't budge.

IRUMA: So, how do we open it?
AUTHOR: For that, we need to think about the second point. You pulled the door open. You didn't push it.

The door swings out into the hallway. You'd usually need some kind of handle to pull a door open, but there's nothing like that here. So, how did you do it as a child? I was hoping you could remember in more detail. Could the door have already been open a bit?

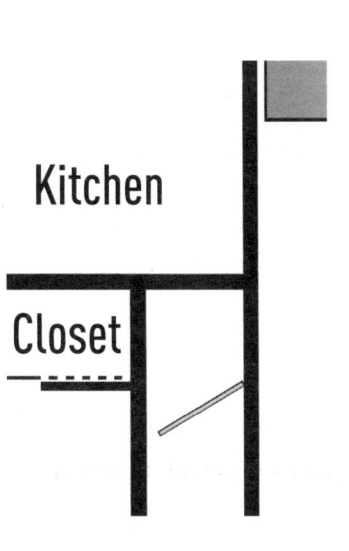

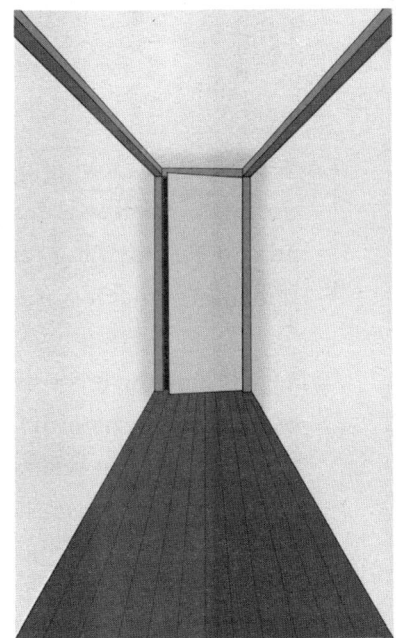

IRUMA: Oh! So, you think the door was ajar and I was able to pull it open by gripping the edge!

AUTHOR: That's what I was getting at, yes.

The reason the room seemed to appear out of nowhere was that the door had opened. It was the only way Iruma could have realized that it was a door, rather than a wall. The room never appeared again simply because the door stayed shut that whole time. That was my theory, anyway.

IRUMA: Why do you think the door opened up back then?

AUTHOR: The answer to that can be found in point number one, your dizziness. I think that has something to do with it.

IRUMA: But how?

AUTHOR: Actually, just after you called me, I had some thoughts about that. You said you remembered the state of the room very well, but you forgot what the scary thing in the box was, right?

IRUMA: Yeah, so?

> While I was looking around, trying to figure it out, I noticed a small wooden box on the floor. I opened the lid and... something terrifying was inside... I just don't remember what it was.

AUTHOR: I think the inconsistent clarity in that memory is a kind of defence mechanism.

The brain can selectively erase frightening memories as a defence mechanism, to keep you from remembering and getting frightened again later.

You said that your memory of what happened before you went into the room is also fuzzy, right?

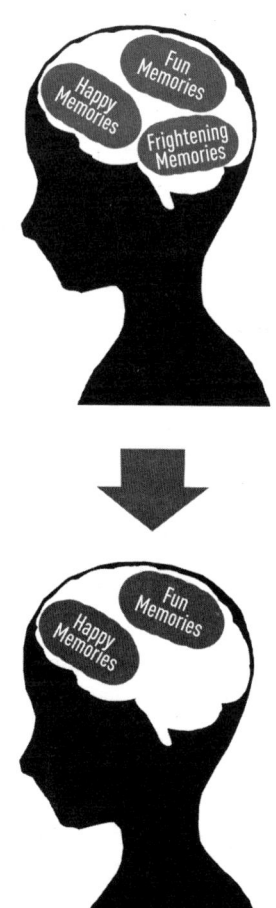

> I know I was inside the house, but I can't remember exactly where. For some reason, it was like the whole world started spinning. It was hard to stand up, so I had to squat down to keep myself from falling over. When the dizziness passed, I looked up and saw a door in front of me.

AUTHOR: You don't remember what happened before you got dizzy.

IRUMA: Not a thing.

AUTHOR: Just before that dizzy spell, I think something very frightening must have happened to you. So, your brain blocked that memory out.

IRUMA: But what could have happened to me in my own home?

AUTHOR: How about an earthquake?

IRUMA: What?

AUTHOR: I did some calculations based on your age, and worked out that the door must have opened in 2004. And, since you remembered the floor felt cold, I assumed it must have been in autumn or winter.

IRUMA: Oh! The Chuetsu Earthquake!

On 23rd October 2004, a massive earthquake of magnitude 6.6 struck the Chuetsu region of Niigata. Iruma's house was quite far from the epicentre, so the area was not as devastated as some, but still there was a lot of damage.

And that earthquake is what caused the door to open.

Iruma stood in stunned silence for a moment, a bemused look on his face.

AUTHOR: You don't buy it?

IRUMA: No, I buy it completely. What bothers me is, why didn't I ever make that connection myself? They talk about that day on television and in school textbooks all the time.

AUTHOR: You were probably too young to connect the two events in your mind. On the one hand, you had the monumental tragedy of a large-scale disaster, and on the other you had this little hidden room that mysteriously appeared, like something out of a fairy tale. The two simply didn't mix in your mind, like oil and water, so you treated them like separate incidents.

IRUMA: You might be right.

AUTHOR: If the earthquake shook the door open, I doubt it's actually locked. But since the door is wedged in between the pillars, we can't open it without a handle.

IRUMA: Ha! So, all we have to do is shake the house. Oh, but maybe we could use a suction cup to pull it open!

AUTHOR: It's a nice idea, but suction cups don't really work on cloth wallpaper.

IRUMA: Well then, I'll just go and buy a chainsaw.

AUTHOR: Please, don't scare me like that. Hmm. If they went to the trouble of building a hidden room, there has to be some way to open it.

Let's try some things. It's still only noon. We've got lots of time before your father comes home.

After that, we tried touching, knocking, climbing up into the attic... Everything we could think of. But none of it seemed to have any effect at all. Before we realized it, two hours had gone by.

AUTHOR: It doesn't seem to be doing much good…
IRUMA: Shall we take a break before we try a different tack? I wouldn't mind some tea, myself.

We headed back to the living room.

As we entered the living room, I noticed a closet in one corner. The way it opened struck me as quite unusual. It had a single sliding door that slid behind the front wall of the closet.

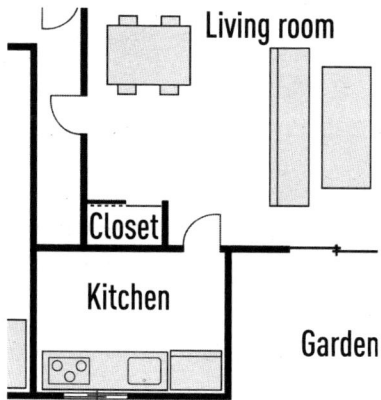

Such closets usually have what are known as 'bypass sliding doors', with two doors that slide past each other on different tracks, so that either side can be opened.

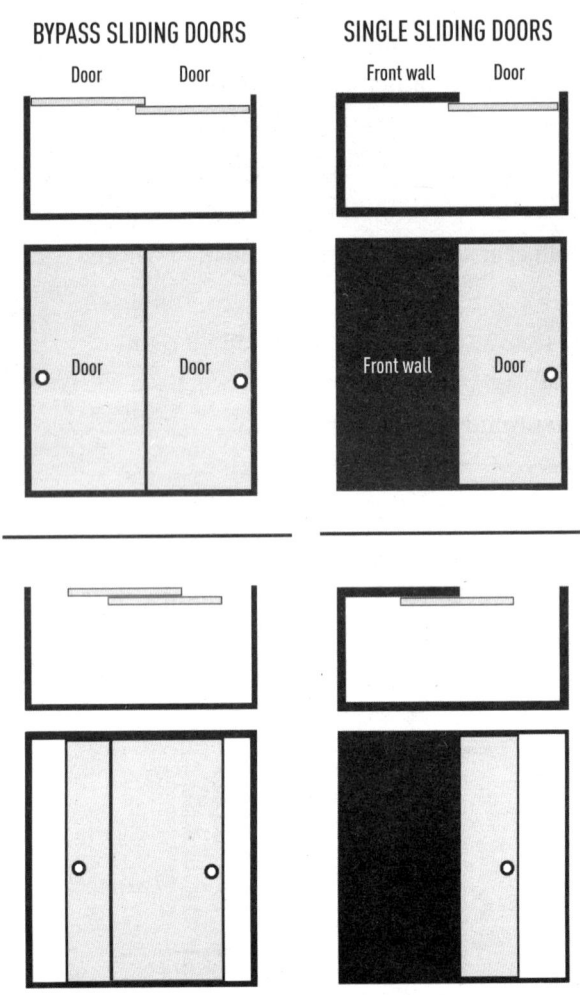

But having only one door that slid behind a closet wall would make it hard to access things stored in the space behind that front wall. Why make a closet with a door like that?

I stared at it in confusion for a moment until suddenly, it hit me.

I hurried over to the table and looked at my layout sketch.

AUTHOR: This closet and the hidden room are right next to each other.

IRUMA: Yeah, I guess they are. Could there be some kind of secret doorway or lever in the closet?

AUTHOR: I can't say for sure, but we should check it out.

We took everything out of the closet. I crawled inside the empty space and inspected every inch with the help of a pocket torch, but I didn't spot anything out of the ordinary.

IRUMA: Well? Find anything?

AUTHOR: No.

IRUMA: OK, come on out, then. No sense rolling around in the dust for nothing.

AUTHOR: Wait, there's one more thing I want to check.

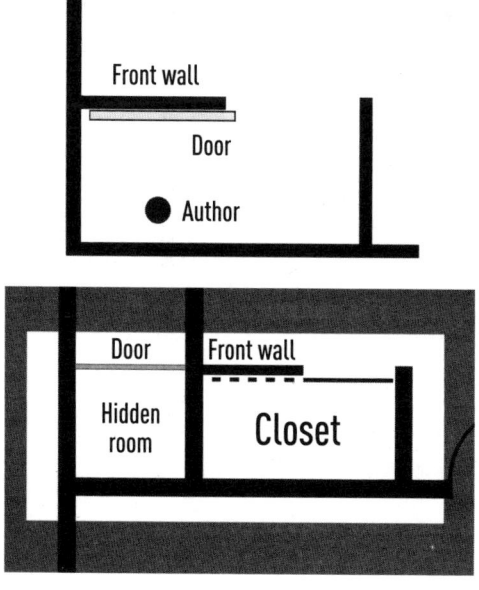

I slid the door closed from inside. Then, the light of my torch revealed a small, square depression carved into the back of the front wall.

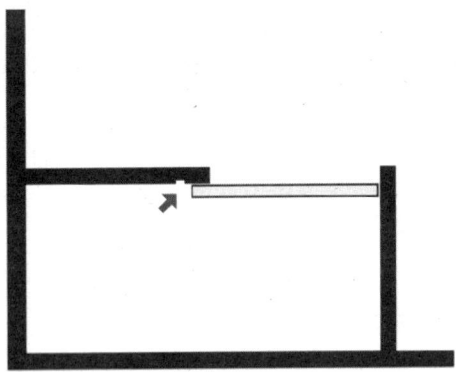

If the door was even slightly open, it would hide the depression, and, of course, no one could see inside with the door closed completely. It was a clever trick.

The depression was about one centimetre wide, and two or three millimetres deep. It looked just the right shape for a finger grip to open a sliding door.

I put my finger in the depression and pulled to the left, towards the hallway. There was a grating sound, and the wall moved slightly.

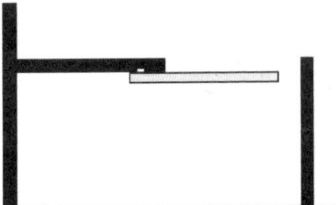

If the door is open even a little, the depression is hidden from sight.

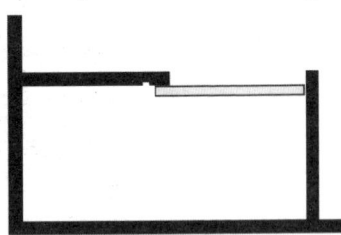

When the door is closed, the interior is hidden from the outside.

AUTHOR: Iruma! Did you see that?!

IRUMA: See what?

AUTHOR: The wall! It slid a good centimetre towards the hallway, didn't it?

IRUMA: I was looking right at it and nothing moved at all.

AUTHOR: Really?! I'll do it again. Watch closely this time.

I put my finger into the depression again and pushed. The wall slid another centimetre.

AUTHOR: Well?

IRUMA: I heard a grating sound, but nothing moved.

AUTHOR: That's odd.

The wall had slid—of that I was sure. But nothing had happened outside. Then, I thought of another possibility. Perhaps this wall had a layered construction. The outside was a fixed wall, with a moveable inner panel.

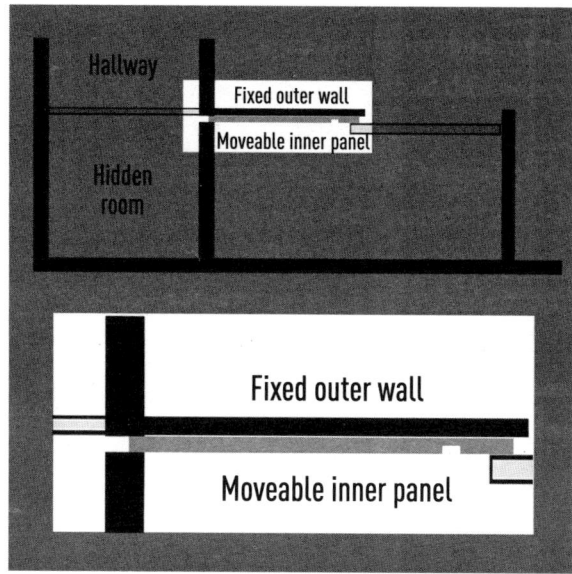

Since the interior panel slid towards the hallway, there had to be a gap in the wall between the living room and the hidden room for it to slide into.

Perhaps sliding the inner panel as far towards the hallway as possible would allow the door to the hidden room to open. I didn't know exactly how it worked, but we could figure out the details once we'd got into that hidden room.

I put my finger in the depression once more and pushed with all my strength to slide it towards the hallway. I heard the grating sound again.

For some reason, the sound suddenly struck me as wrong. How would this help open the door? I stopped and thought about it again. Something was off there. The panel was too heavy. Too hard to move. This panel was made of wood like the rest of the wall. Why would it be so heavy?

Then, a memory that had been lurking in the corner of my mind came out into the open. It was something Iruma had said when we were chatting earlier. Suddenly everything snapped into place.

It all led me to a new idea.

AUTHOR: Iruma?
IRUMA: Yes?
AUTHOR: Can I ask you go to your father's room and find me a magnet?
IRUMA: A magnet?
AUTHOR: I'm sure there's a large magnet somewhere in your father's room.

. . .

I waited for him in the living room. He came back a few minutes later, a curious look on his face. In his hand was a magnet, some ten centimetres across.

IRUMA: It was in his drawer. But how did you know he would have this?

AUTHOR: I kept thinking about how he could have opened the door himself, and it gave me the idea that he might have used a magnet as a door handle.

Now, could I ask you to go out into the hallway with the magnet, hold it against the wall at the end, and wait for a moment?

IRUMA: Why?

I explained the theory I had come up with.

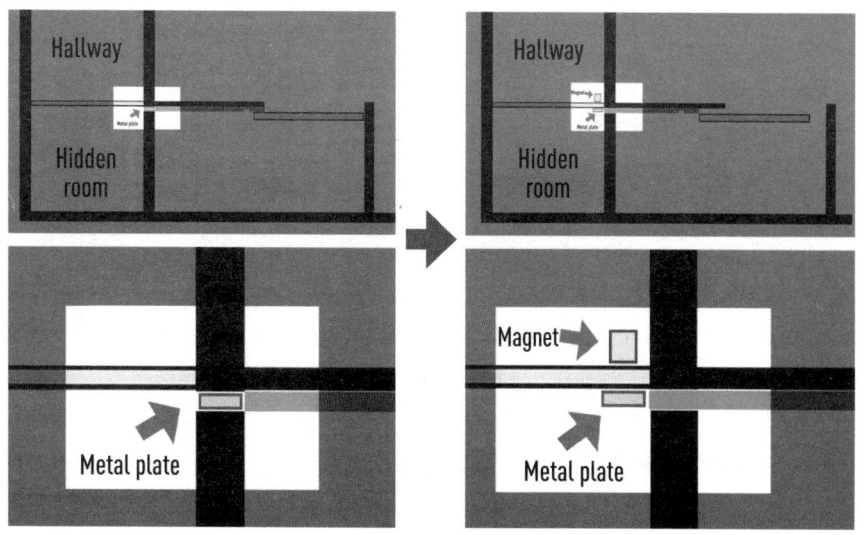

I was convinced there was a metal plate inside the wall between the living room and the hallway. Pushing the panel inside the closet must slide that plate out of the wall, so that it sat behind the hidden door. If so, a magnet held against the other side of the door could grab on to the plate and serve as a door handle.

Of course, you would need a magnet strong enough to hold on to the metal plate through a couple of centimetres of wood. Such as a neodymium magnet, the strongest type commercially available.

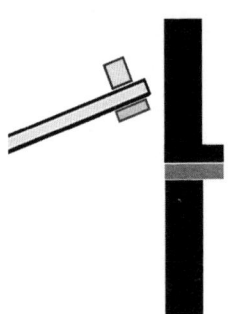

And neodymium magnets were made using rare earth elements.

> Well, I suppose he does, in a way. But not anything artistic. He's in product design for a metals company. I think he said they do something related to rare earth elements, but I didn't understand half of what he was talking about.

You could almost call this Iruma's father's field of expertise.

Before long, Iruma gave me the go-ahead from the hallway. Once more, I went into the closet and pushed with all my strength.

A moment later, Iruma shouted:

IRUMA: Whoa! It worked! It grabbed on!
AUTHOR: Right! Pull it open very carefully!

I heard a creaking sound. I scrambled out of the closet and rushed to the hallway. The door was open.

AUTHOR: Iruma! We did it!
IRUMA: Yeah...

Iruma stepped into the room.
It looked to be much as he had described it. White wallpaper. A square floor. And... the wooden box.
He knelt down and slowly reached for the lid. Even from a distance, I could see his hand shaking. Despite his obvious nervousness, he opened the box.
And inside was...

AUTHOR: Is that... a doll?

It was a finely detailed doll of a woman carved from wood. She was wrapped in cloth like the raiments of an angel, and her face, though not young, was beautiful.
But what drew the eye was not her face, but her body.
She was missing her left arm and right leg.
I stood as if bewitched.
I knew her. I knew who that woman was.
Just then, I heard Iruma mumble something to himself.

IRUMA: This doll... It looks the same.
AUTHOR: The same as what?
IRUMA: As this house. It has the same shape.

It took me a moment to understand what he was talking about.
But as I stared longer at the doll in his hands, it finally clicked. I ran back to the living room and brought the floor plan sketch back with me. I compared my sketch to the doll.

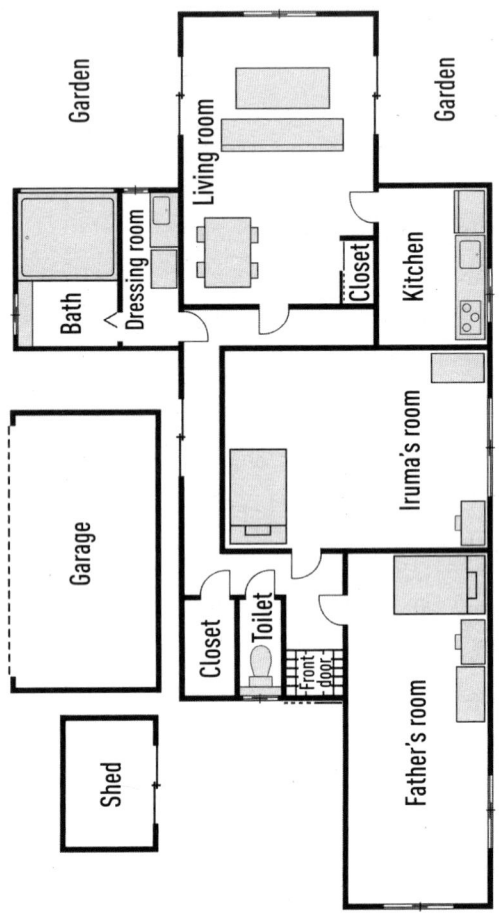

He was right. And I remembered something else.

I thought back to an old magazine article I'd read. An undercover report from inside an old cult.

That cult, the Rebirth Congregation… They'd used a building called the Hall of Rebirth for their religious practices. And their Holy Mother, the leader of their cult, had been a woman missing her left arm and right leg.

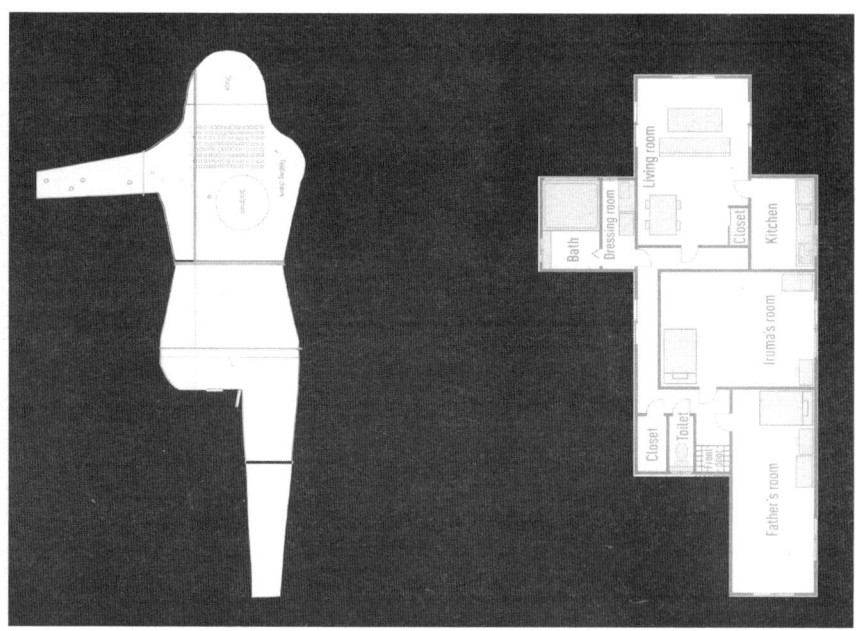

They all looked alike. The Holy Mother's body. The doll. The Hall of Rebirth. And Iruma's house.

I never even dreamt of finding a connection here, of all places, though...

Iruma returned the doll to its box and spoke in a quiet voice.

IRUMA: I guess I was right...
AUTHOR: Right about what?
IRUMA: I had this feeling when I was a kid. My parents... They got caught up in some weird religious stuff.
AUTHOR: They did?
IRUMA: This is probably part of it, right? Some kind of, what... Prayer? Ritual?

AUTHOR: Um…

IRUMA: Not that it matters. I don't have any problem with people praying to whoever or whatever they want. But… Were they really so unhappy that they had to find something like this to cling to? I guess… I wasn't enough to make them happy.

END OF FILE 11: THE VANISHING ROOM

KURIHARA'S DEDUCTIONS

After a twenty-minute walk from Umegaoka Station, I reached a small block of flats.

I carried a document wallet containing eleven files as I climbed the rusted iron stairs. They squeaked and creaked with every step. The building was forty-five years old, and it was certainly showing its age.

I went to the room at the farthest end of the first floor and rang the bell. The door opened right away.

'Come in, come in. You must be freezing.' The man who had answered the door looked the same as always. Grey pullover and baggy jeans. Close cropped hair and a patchy beard.

My friend, the architectural draughtsman Kurihara.

When I stepped inside, I was enveloped in heavy, warm air. I heard both a wall heater and a kerosene stove roaring in the background. 'Sorry,' he said, 'I can't bear the cold.' He bent over and turned up the temperature on the stove.

His flat had a small kitchen connected to a spacious living room. The living room was full of teetering piles of books, and I had to hunt for somewhere to sit.

Kurihara went to the kitchen to make tea and said, almost as if to himself, 'It's nice to see you again. We haven't sat down and talked like this since that house.'

I had first visited his flat to try and unravel the mystery around a certain strange house.

Kurihara had been able to figure out that something bizarre was happening at that house simply by looking at the floor plan. Ever since, I had rung him to make use of his deductive-reasoning skills from time to time.

AUTHOR: Thank you for all the help you've given me so far. So, not working today?

KURIHARA: Nope. I've not had much work at all lately. It seems like no one is building new houses these days. Honestly, I prefer reading and gaming to work anyway, so I can't say I'm too bothered.

He put two cups of tea on the living-room table, pushed aside a pile of books and sat across from me.

KURIHARA: So, then, these files you told me about on the phone. Shall we take a look?
AUTHOR: Right!

I pulled the eleven files from the wallet. I'd bound each into a booklet and included a summary of the information I'd turned up in relation to each.

> FILE 1: The Hallway to Nowhere
> FILE 2: Nurturing Darkness
> FILE 3: The Watermill in the Woods
> FILE 4: The Mousetrap House
> FILE 5: The House Where It Happened
> FILE 6: The Hall of Rebirth
> FILE 7: Uncle's House

FILE 8: The String Phone
FILE 9: Footsteps to Murder
FILE 10: No Escape
FILE 11: The Vanishing Room

As I mentioned at the beginning of all of this, after my book *Strange Houses* came out, people began sending me all kinds of stories about their own unusual and unexplained experiences related to houses. I ended up looking into well over a hundred of those stories.

Most of those experiences remained unexplained. In other words, I couldn't bring those stories to an end. My research was all about finding endings.

As my research progressed, it often led me away from the original experiences and resulted in some unexpected discoveries.

Then, when I went back to review my research, I noticed some coincidental connections between those discoveries, and I began to investigate those connections.

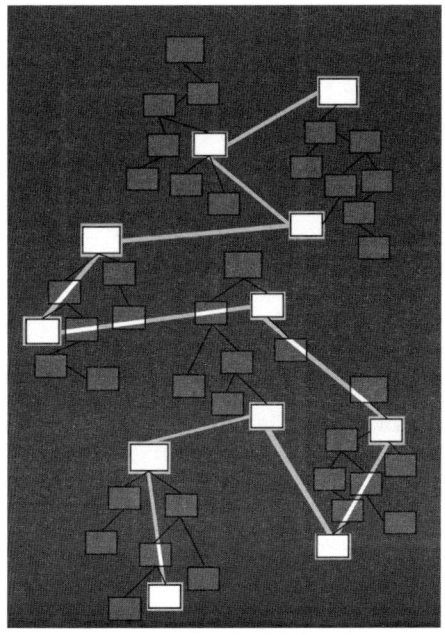

KURIHARA: And so, the end result is what we have here, these eleven files all seemingly connected by one mystery.

AUTHOR: That's right. I know that these eleven stories are all connected somehow, but I haven't been able to work out exactly how. Which is why I was hoping I could impose on you and your skills again.

KURIHARA: Hmm… Right, give me some time to read through them.

Kurihara picked up the first file.

He was the exact opposite of a speed reader. He lingered over each word as if savouring it. I sat and sipped my tea while he went through the files.

A few hours later, he closed the last booklet and put it on the table. He folded his arms, closed his eyes and sat motionless as he sank into thought. Just when I started wondering if I should say something, he opened his eyes and drained his cup of tea, now long grown cold.

KURIHARA: Now that was interesting…

AUTHOR: Well, what do you think? Did you work it out?

KURIHARA: Much of it is still just guesswork, but from what I've read, I think I can put the general story together.

AUTHOR: You can?!

THE CORE

KURIHARA: After this first read-through, there's one of these eleven files that I think stands at the core of the whole thing. Can you guess which one?

AUTHOR: The core story? Hmm. I think they're all important, but…

KURIHARA: Don't overthink it. Here, let's try mapping it out.

Kurihara tore a page from a memo pad on the table and sketched a map of Japan.

KURIHARA: File 1 happened in Takaoka, Toyama. File 2 was in Shizuoka, and three…

He muttered to himself as he plotted the points on his map. He labelled the location where each of the stories had taken place. When he finished, I saw it immediately.

AUTHOR: Oh, so that's what you meant…
KURIHARA: You see it?

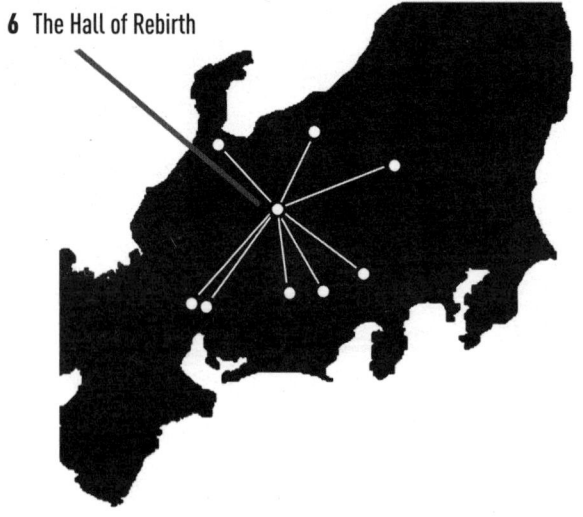

KURIHARA: Everything in these files happened in a circle centred here, on the cult's Hall of Rebirth. That suggests it's the origin. The core of the story.

He picked up the booklet for File 6.

FILE 6   THE HALL OF REBIRTH

A journalist for a magazine went undercover to report on a mysterious cult.

- The cult was called the Rebirth Congregation.
- The Rebirth Congregation had a few unusual characteristics
    - Used word of mouth and cold-calling to gather members
    - Pushed members to spend millions of yen on a mysterious 'product'
    - Held a strange rite several times a month at their Hall of Rebirth

1994—Reporter goes undercover at Hall of Rebirth to discover truth

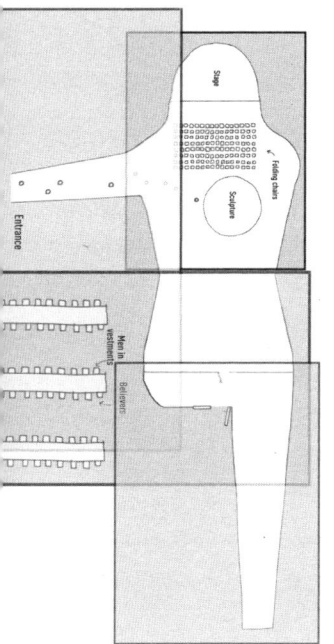

What was the Hall of Rebirth?

A religious facility in western Nagano Prefecture. A massive building designed to mimic the shape of the cult leader, the Holy Mother.

The upper section has an assembly hall with a stage, folding chairs and a shrine.

The Holy Mother waits inside the shrine.

She is missing her left arm and right leg.

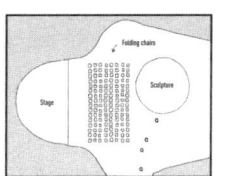

Shrine in assembly hall

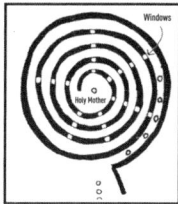

WHAT THE REPORTER SAW

- Congregation elder Masahiko Hikura speaks to members
    - Hikura was president of construction company Hikura Homes
    - Why would such an important man financially support a cult?
    - He gives an impassioned speech, saying: 'You are steeped in sin, but joining the sacrament here will purify you.'
- The journalist meets Holy Mother inside shrine.
- Suddenly, a man shows up and accosts the Holy Mother.
    - He shouts incomprehensible things, like 'You fraud! I'll seal your heart for ever!'
    - The man is immediately ejected.
- Journalist is led to room of the sacrament

What is the sacrament?

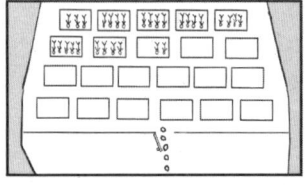

'Sleeping' is the sacrament?!

The sacrament room was a 'bedroom', where members slept overnight. Is this the sacrament?

Events of following morning

The following morning, members talk to unknown men in cult vestments in the facility garden while looking at floor plans.

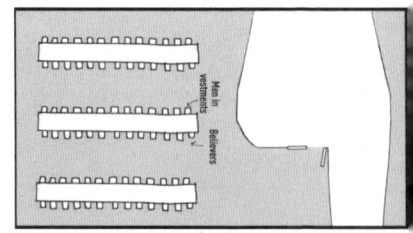

Later:

- The reporter split the article into two parts.
- Only Part One was published. Part Two was pulled for an unknown reason.
- The Rebirth Congregation broke up in 1999.
- The Hall of Rebirth was torn down in 2000.

KURIHARA: Sadly, the second part of the piece, which promised to deliver all the answers, was never published. So, all we can do is use what we know from Part One to figure things out on our own. Let's start by laying out the mysteries left unexplained in Part One.

1. Why did the ritual of the Rebirth Congregation involve nothing more than the cult members sleeping?
2. What was the several-million-yen 'product' that the cult pushed its members to buy?
3. What were those men in white vestments doing sitting across from the members at long tables?
4. What were the 'special circumstances' shared by all the members?
5. How did the members end up being brainwashed just by going through this sacrament a few times a month?

To solve those five mysteries, we need to figure out just what the Hall of Rebirth was. I think we can accept the idea that the Hall of Rebirth was built to mimic the body of the cult's Holy Mother, as hinted at in the article. In fact, similar kinds of building design aren't unheard of.

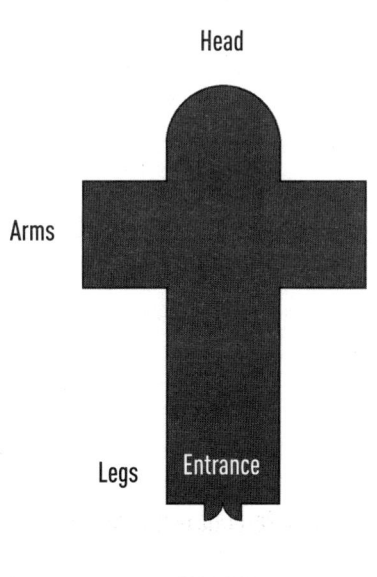

CHURCH

For example, many churches are designed to mimic the shape of the cross on which Christ was crucified. I suppose many believers like to feel protected by being inside the symbol of their faith. Anyway, there are some other interesting aspects to the Hall of Rebirth's design. First, if the whole building is a woman's body, the shrine is positioned roughly where her heart would be.

AUTHOR: Oh, you're right. So, it's like saying 'The Holy Mother lives in the heart' or something.

KURIHARA: Right. She's the symbol of the cult. So, she has to be the heart, the most vital place. Of course, the human heart is really situated much more centrally than the position of the shrine suggests, but many people think the heart is on the left of the body, and this design reflects that. That's why the shrine is farther to the left than the heart would really be.

So, not only is the exterior of the Hall designed to reflect the Holy Mother's form, but the interior is designed to represent her body too. With that established, let's consider this 'sacrament room' where the believers slept.

It's located in the belly. So those members were all sleeping in a woman's belly, just like…
AUTHOR: A baby in the womb.
KURIHARA: Exactly.

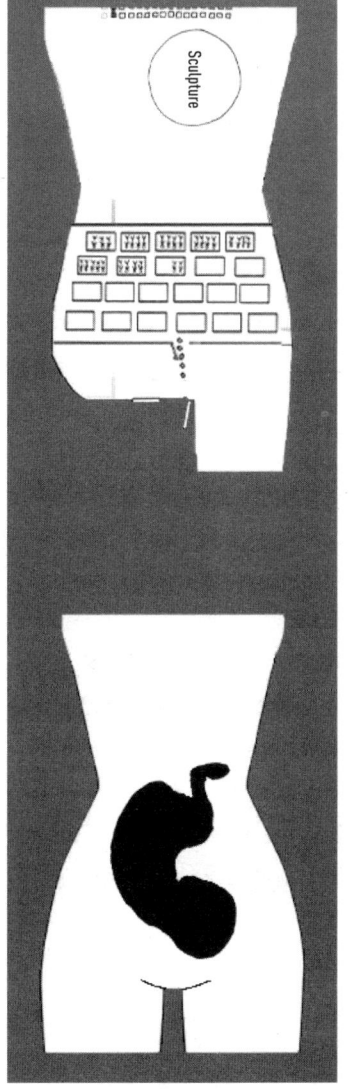

KURIHARA: The believers enter through the lower door—the vagina—then sleep in the sacrament room—the womb—and leave again through the vagina. Clearly, they're undergoing a symbolic cycle of pregnancy and birth. That solves one of our mysteries.

1 WHY DID THE RITUAL OF THE REBIRTH CONGREGATION INVOLVE NOTHING MORE THAN THE CULT MEMBERS SLEEPING?

KURIHARA: The answer is 'In order for them to truly become the Holy Mother's children.'

The sacrament of the Rebirth Congregation is sleeping in the Holy Mother's womb and being reborn as her child.

AUTHOR: So, the name of the Rebirth Congregation is really quite… on the nose.

KURIHARA: Right. Now, let's look at the appearance of Masahiko Hikura and his role in the cult.

> By your presence here, I know you are well aware. Aware of your sin, and of how your poor children have inherited that sin… Sadly, your defilement can never be erased. However, it can be lightened. Reduced. Through faith and the sacrament, you can ease your burden. Dilute your impurity here, in this hall.

KURIHARA: Those words—I'm sure you are already aware, aware of your sin—makes me believe the Rebirth Congregation members all felt the same kind of guilt.

And he goes on to say that the members are all unhappy because of the sin they bear. But, if they are reborn as children of the Holy Mother, their sin will be slightly lessened. Just a little bit. It can never be completely erased.

So, they have to keep coming to the Hall of Rebirth and keep cleansing themselves of sin. In short, the cult gathers believers who are struggling with guilt over something and teaches them how to ease it.

AUTHOR: And they do that by gathering in that room representing the Holy Mother's womb and sleeping there, over and over...

KURIHARA: It sounds weird, but the idea of 'being reborn to lessen your sin' isn't so far removed from Buddhist teaching, so it's probably easy to swallow for most Japanese people. The thing that stands out to me is bringing children into it.

> Your poor children have inherited that sin. Children born out of their parents' sin. Children of sin... And, tomorrow, you can go home, your stain faded, and introduce your children to the sacrament.

KURIHARA: When he tells them to introduce their children to the practice, I assume he means, 'Go home and have your children sleep in the Holy Mother's womb.' Which should be impossible, right? Private houses aren't built to represent the Holy Mother's body, so there's no room representing her womb. In that case, how do the believers get their own children to join in this sacrament?

The image of a certain floor plan rose unbidden to the front of my mind.

AUTHOR: They're rebuilding their houses into Halls of Rebirth.

KURIHARA: That's right! Among these eleven files are examples of people who turned their own house into a Hall of Rebirth.

AUTHOR: Iruma's parents.

KURIHARA: Right.

Kurihara picked up the booklet for File 11.

FILE 11   THE VANISHING ROOM

The search for a hidden room

- Freelance designer Iruma says that, as a child, he once found a mysterious hidden room in his house.

Visited his house to search for the hidden room.

- Iruma's childhood home was a detached house in Niigata Prefecture.
- His parents bought the house new the year they were married, then remodelled it eight years later.

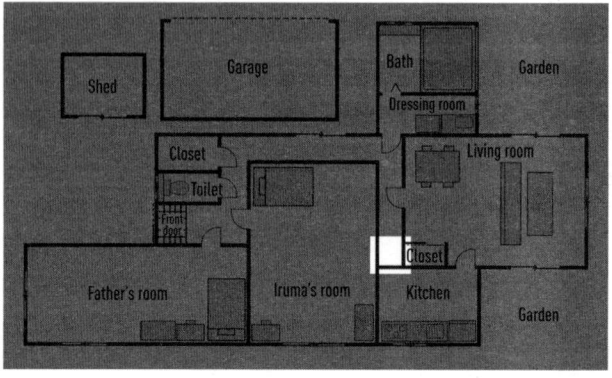

- Found the hallway dead end suspicious, investigated way to open hidden door.
- Discovered secret mechanism in closet.

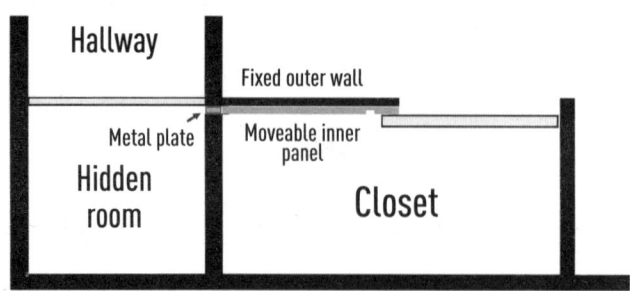

Opening the secret door

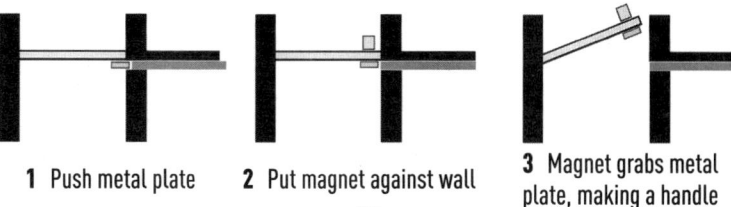

1. Push metal plate
2. Put magnet against wall
3. Magnet grabs metal plate, making a handle

What was inside the room?

- Doll of a woman, in a wooden box
- Doll was missing left leg and right arm
- Iruma said the doll looked like his house

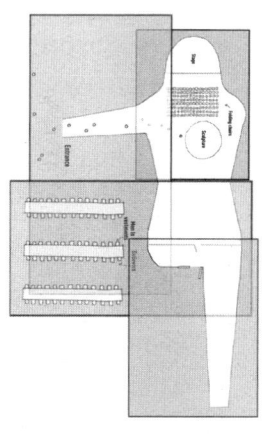

What is the connection to the Hall of Rebirth, modelled on a woman with missing leg and arm?

What did Iruma think?

'I had this feeling when I was a kid. My parents... They got caught up in some weird religious stuff.'

IMITATION

His parents had bought the house new when they were married, then had major remodelling done when their only son was born eight years later.

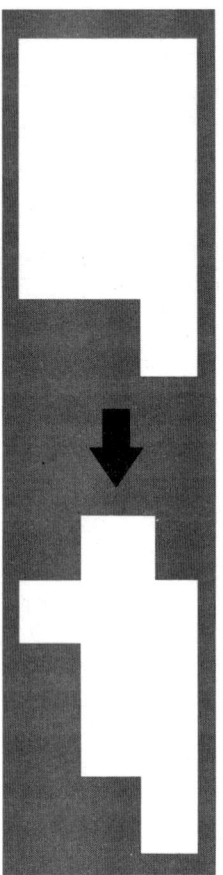

KURIHARA: The couple must have joined the Rebirth Congregation right around when your friend was born.
AUTHOR: And that's why they remodelled their house, to make it look more like the Hall of Rebirth.
KURIHARA: It was probably a completely standard-shaped house at first, but they removed some rooms so the shape of the house would reflect the Holy Mother's body. And they didn't just make changes to the exterior.

> It was a detailed doll of a woman carved from wood. She was wrapped in cloth like the raiments of an angel, and her face, though not young, was beautiful.
> But what drew the eye was not her face, but her body. She was missing her left arm and right leg.

KURIHARA: Look closely at where the doll was hidden, that secret room.
If you imagine the house as a human body, it's in the chest, just a little off-centre.

AUTHOR: The heart. Just like the shrine in the Hall of Rebirth.

KURIHARA: Which would make this hidden room the house's shrine. The Holy Mother stays in the shrine in the real Hall of Rebirth, so the Irumas kept a doll version in their own house. The doll stands in for the Holy Mother... An effigy of sorts. Like having statues of the seven lucky gods in your household Shinto *kamidana* shrine.

AUTHOR: They use a doll because they can't have the real thing.

KURIHARA: Well put! So, the next thing to look at is where Ren Iruma's bed was located.

That's vaguely near where the womb would be. So, based on the cult's teaching, when he lived in that house, he was being reborn every day as the child of the Holy Mother.

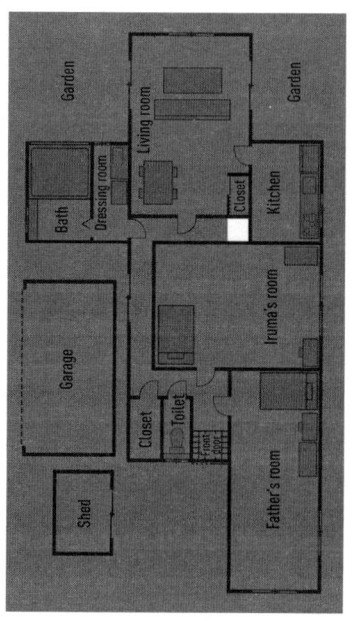

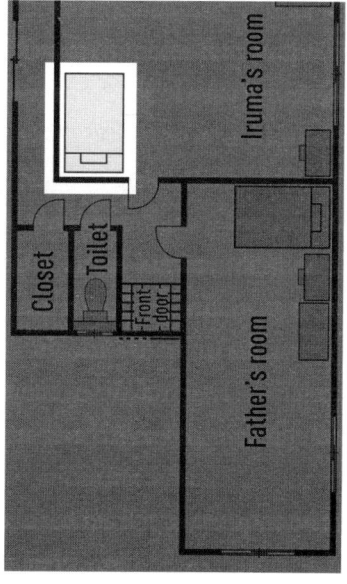

The Iruma couple joined the Rebirth Congregation soon after their first child was born. That also must mean they were dealing with guilt over some sin, some transgression.

They would have been deeply afraid when they heard Hikura pronouncing, 'Your poor children have inherited that sin.' And so, like the faithful members they were, they had their own house remodelled after the Hall of Rebirth, to lessen the sin staining their child.

AUTHOR: But how did they actually get it done? Having those rooms taken out completely, and a strange little secret room built in… What kind of company would take on such an unusual job?

KURIHARA: I imagine most builders would have refused it. And that is where the cult's profit motive comes clear.

2 WHAT WAS THE SEVERAL-MILLION-YEN 'PRODUCT' THAT THE CULT PUSHED ITS MEMBERS TO BUY?

KURIHARA: That product was houses. Or, more precisely, major house remodelling. Masahiko Hikura was CEO of Hikura Homes, a leading house builder in the region. He was in a position to make all kinds of strange construction orders possible.

So, the Rebirth Congregation was a cult that pushed its members into expensive house remodelling around its base in the Chubu region, the same region where Hikura Homes was operating.

They worked together in a mutually beneficial symbiotic relationship.

KURIHARA: Knowing that clears up the next mystery, too.

3 WHAT WERE THOSE MEN IN WHITE VESTMENTS DOING SITTING ACROSS FROM THE MEMBERS AT LONG TABLES?

KURIHARA: In a word, that was the sales pitch. Those men in white vestments were probably Hikura Homes salesmen.

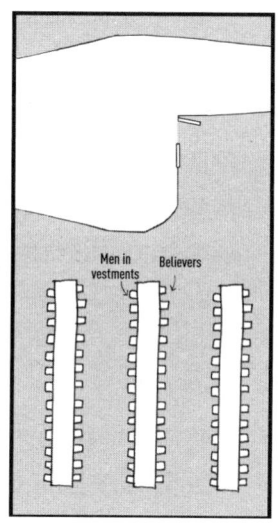

> Cult members, the people I had just spent the night with, lined one side of each, with acolytes in white vestments sitting across from them. The acolytes were speaking intently to the members across from them.
>
> When I got closer, I could see the tables between them were covered with floor plans.

KURIHARA: They must have been discussing plans and cost estimates to make the believers' houses into models of the Hall of Rebirth. The white vestments were necessary to preserve the religious atmosphere. If they'd shown up in suits, the members would have probably sensed the profit motive immediately.

So, since we've uncovered the story behind Iruma's house, I think it's obvious that there was another person in these files who was brainwashed by the cult.

Kurihara picked up File 7.

FILE 7   UNCLE'S HOUSE
Journal of an abused boy who died from neglect

- Naruki Mitsuhashi, age nine, lives in a flat with his mother.
- He rarely gets enough to eat, and his mother physically abuses him.
- At some point, a mysterious man he calls Uncle comes and invites them both to his house.
- This Uncle is kind to Naruki and gives him good food to eat.
- After that, Uncle invites Naruki to his house once every couple of months.
- At some point, Uncle notices Naruki's abuse and takes him from his mother to shelter him at his house.
- Later, Naruki's mother and a 'blond man' take Naruki away from Uncle's house.
- The blond man takes Naruki and his mother to his own house.
- The man brutally abuses Naruki, who dies a few weeks later.
- After Naruki's death, his journal is published as a book.

KURIHARA: This one was so heartbreaking, I could barely stand to read it. But Naruki left behind some very important information. Let's see if we can draw a floor plan of Uncle's house from his journal.

Kurihara began sketching out the rooms described on his notepad.

> On the left side of the door it has a big flower bed and I thought that was really nice. We went inside and there was a hallway in the middle with lots of doors.

KURIHARA: Flower bed by the door... Long hallway... Lots of doors...

> We went through the closest right door and there was a big TV and a table. We could see the flower bed and the house door from the window. From the big window on the other side, I could see cars driving past.

KURIHARA: 'The closest right door' probably means 'the first door on the right side'. It sounds like the living room from his description. The important part is, he could see the front door from the living room window.

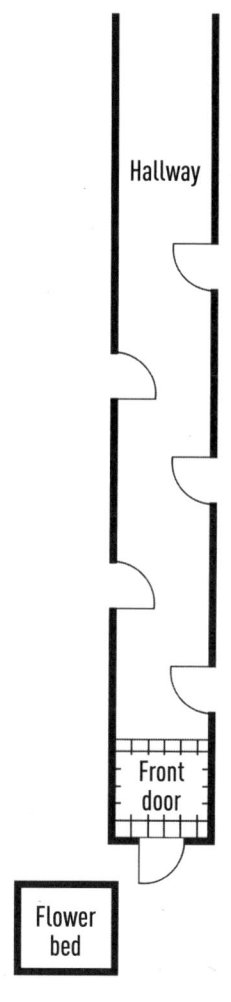

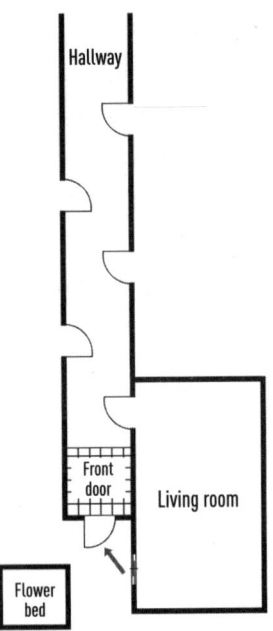

KURIHARA: So the room probably juts out into the front garden like this.

Then he talks about seeing cars going past through a window on the other side of the room, so that side must face a street. Naruki, his mother and Uncle had dinner here in this room when he visited the house, so, naturally, Naruki thought of it as a 'room for eating'.

Then, he mentions a couple of other rooms.

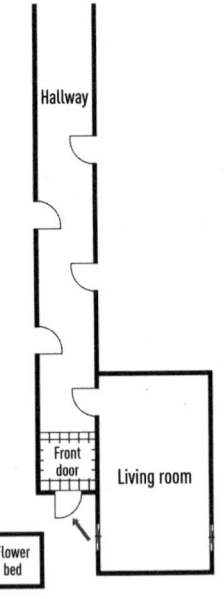

> ① After we ate dinner, we went into the hallway and then to the next room. Uncle said This Is Your Room, Naruki.
> ② After that, we went out into the hallway and to the room next to the eating room. It had a big window where we could see the flower bed. There was a bicycle in the middle of the room. Uncle called it an exersize bike. I tried it and it was fun.
>
> That room had another door. I opened it and there was an empty room. There were two windows. I could see the flowers from one and a river from the other.

KURIHARA: He describes both rooms as being 'next' to the room for eating, but they sound like different rooms. So, where were they in relation to the living room?

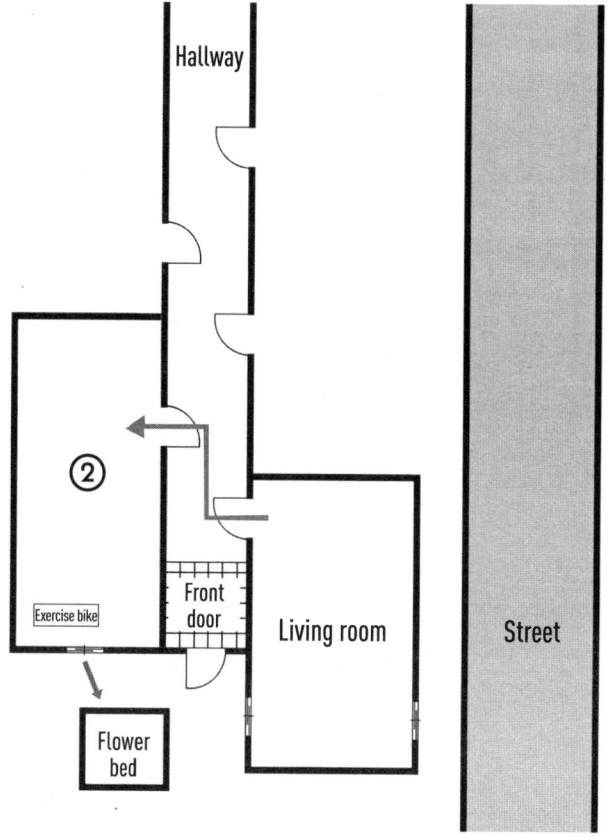

KURIHARA: To get to the room in ②, Naruki says they went out into the hallway. He also says they could see the flower bed from the window. So, that must mean that room ② is on the other side of the hallway, opposite the living room. I imagine Naruki just didn't know how to write it that way.

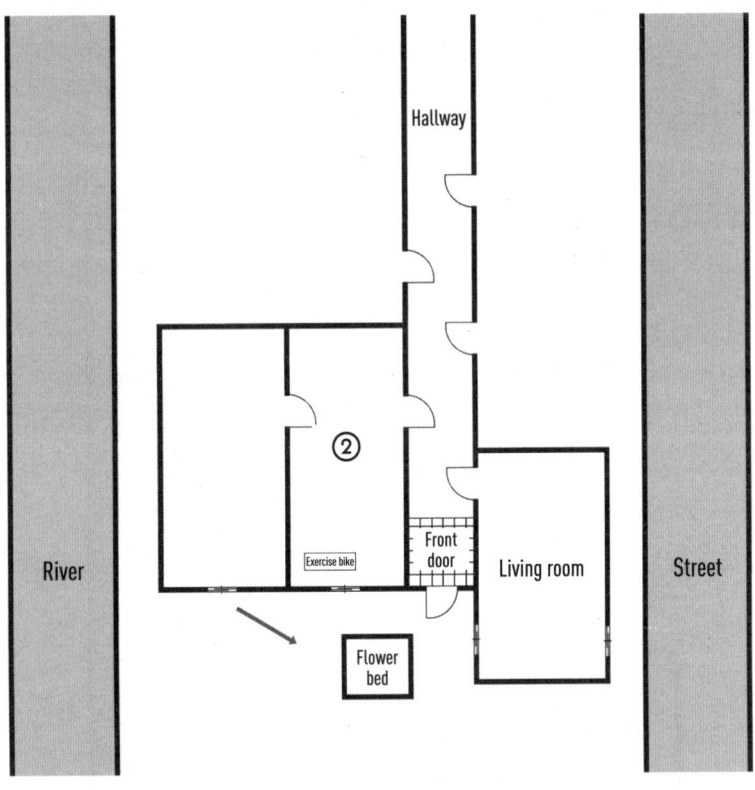

KURIHARA: Room ② had a door inside that led to another room. Naruki could also see the flower bed from that room, so I think we can put it on the left side of the floor plan. Then, there's the very important detail that he could see the river from another window. That all means we can make a pretty good guess of where ①, Naruki's room, was...

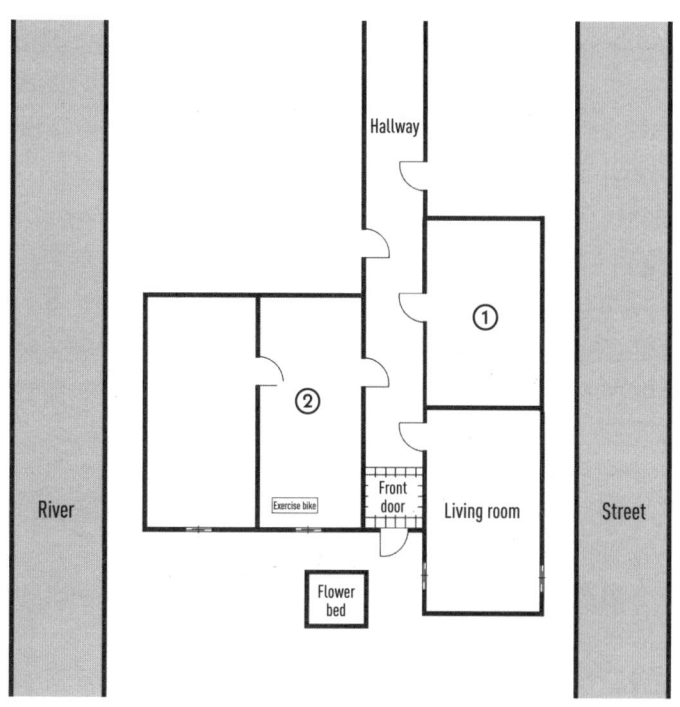

KURIHARA: I think we've got a general idea of the house's layout now.

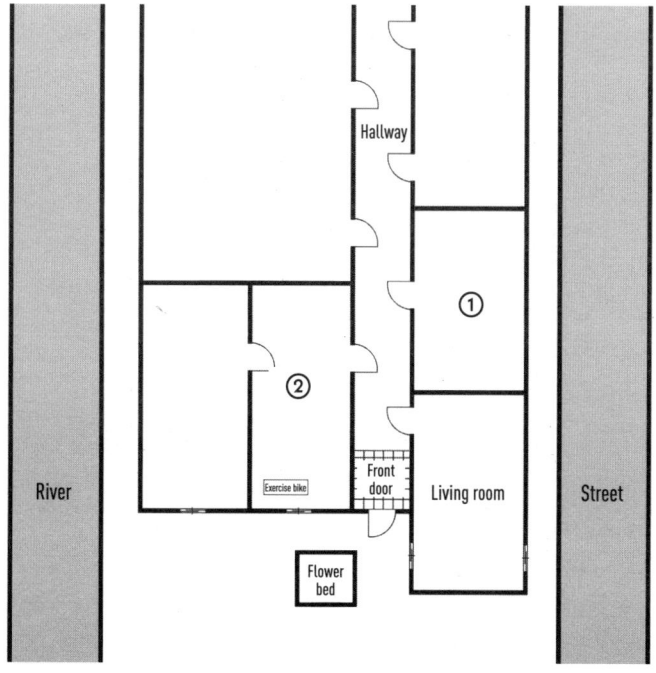

AUTHOR: I'm impressed that you were able draw the whole house from just a few mentions of the layout.

KURIHARA: That's all thanks to Naruki. I think he was a naturally clever boy. He made it all quite clear without any wasted words.

There is one point, though, where he seems to describe something rather fantastical. It's the 27th February entry, when he visits Uncle's house for the first time in three months.

> *Breakfast was corn soup and a fried egg. It was so tasty. After that, I wanted to pedal that bicycle that doesn't go anywhere again. I went to the room next to the room for eating and pedalled it. I'd just eaten so my tummy started to hurt.*

KURIHARA: From the mention of the bike, we know he's in room ②.

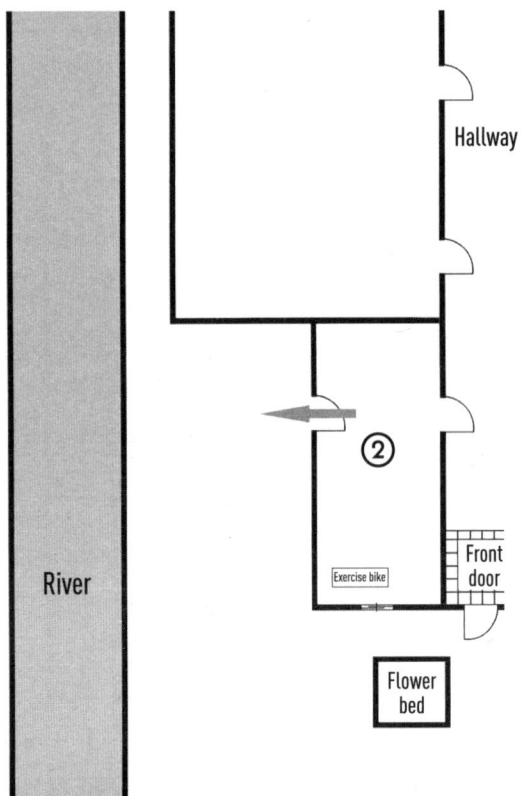

> *After that, I opened that other door, but that room was gone. The river was flowing right there. I thought that was weird.*

KURIHARA: This door must be the one that led to the room with the view of the river before. Now, though, it opens to the outside.

AUTHOR: The room had vanished?

KURIHARA: Not something you'd expect outside of a magic show. But, if we take what Naruki wrote at face value, there is one possible explanation. At some time during those three months, Uncle had some construction work done on his house. Namely, to remove one room. That would have left the house shaped like this.

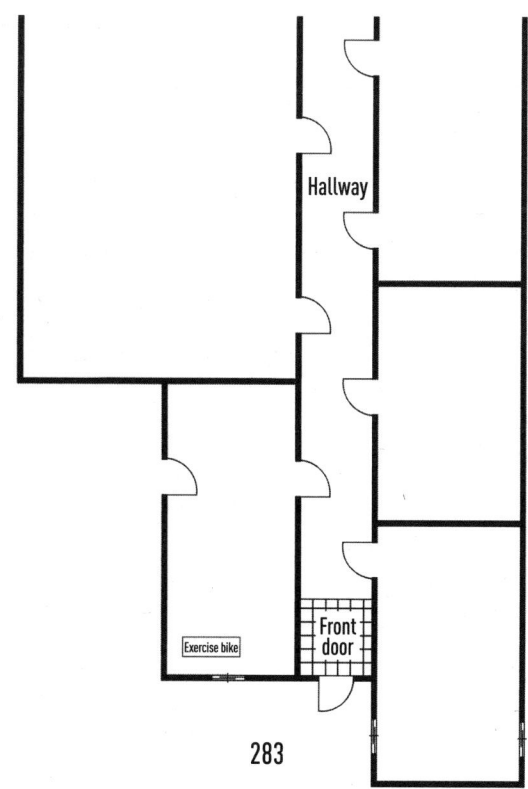

KURIHARA: Doesn't that remind you of the Iruma house?

AUTHOR: You think he had his house remodelled after the Hall of Rebirth, too?

KURIHARA: There is something else in the journal that also points to him being a member of the Rebirth Congregation.

> *After that, Uncle took me to a room at the end of the hall. It was a little room with a brown doll in it. It was a bit scary.*

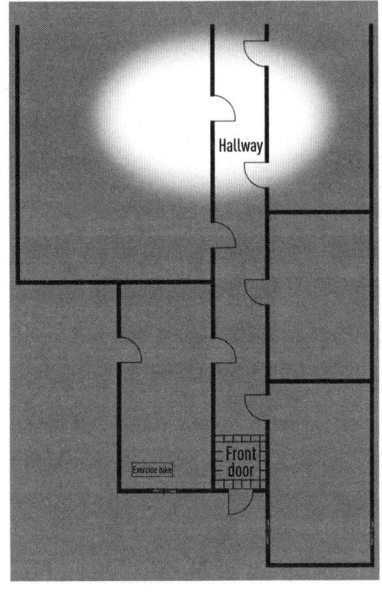

KURIHARA: Now, it's not clear exactly where that room was, but 'at the end of the hall' is enough to guess the general location. Naruki usually spent his time in the house in rooms near to the front door. So, for him, 'at the end of the hall' would mean 'the end of the hall furthest from the front door'.

That would put the room somewhere around here, in the upper section of the floor plan. In other words, near the heart of the Holy Mother.

> *Uncle said This Is The Heart of My House. Never Lock This Door. I didn't understand that.*

AUTHOR: A room where the heart would be, with a doll inside. The shrine.

KURIHARA: Uncle said it clear as day, so there's really no mistaking it.

AUTHOR: But what about that next sentence, 'Never lock this door'? What could that mean?

KURIHARA: This is the heart of my house, so never lock this door… At first glance, it does seem like nonsense. But if we consider it in relation to the cult's ideology, I think we can begin to understand.

AUTHOR: How so?

KURIHARA: The Hall of Rebirth is built to resemble the Holy Mother's body, right? They even put the shrine where her heart would be… So, if we extend that metaphor more generally, maybe they think of their houses as being alive, like the Holy Mother herself, which I think gives us a clue to understanding Uncle.

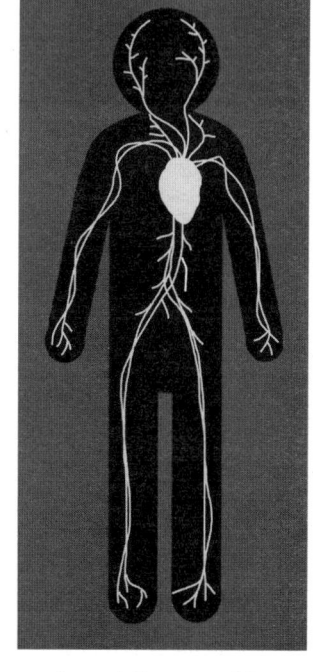

The heart keeps the body alive by pumping blood through the whole body. If it stops, or the arteries or veins around it get blocked, blood stops flowing and the body dies.

Perhaps for the Rebirth Congregation, 'locking the shrine' would be seen as 'sealing the heart'. Which would stop its energy from circulating through the house.

AUTHOR: Meaning the house would die?

KURIHARA: I think that's probably part of the ideology the cult drummed into its members. That would explain Uncle's words, and the reason there was no actual lock on the secret room in the Iruma house either.

And 'Sealing the heart...' That reminds me of something in another file. That bit in the undercover report from the Hall of Rebirth, after the reporter had visited the Holy Mother.

> A voice suddenly came ringing out from its depths. It sounded like a man shouting in anger. I listened intently and was able to make out what he was saying.
>
> 'You lied to me, Holy Mother! You promised my son would be saved!'
>
> A few acolytes immediately rushed into the shrine, and a minute or so later they dragged a struggling man from the door. It was the man who had been standing at the rear of the group after mine, whose odd expression I'd noticed. He had a striking face that would probably have been handsome were it not twisted in rage.
>
> The handsome man was still shouting. 'You fraud! If you're truly a goddess, tell me why? Why did my boy, my Naruki, have to die? I'll kill you! I'll seal your heart for ever!' The screams went on even as they dragged him outside.

AUTHOR: So, that man's outburst at the Hall of Rebirth, when he screamed, 'I'll seal your heart for ever!'...
KURIHARA: He could as easily have said, 'I'll lock your shrine closed.'
AUTHOR: I see...
KURIHARA: And if you're wondering what happened to him after that, I think this file can tell us.

Kurihara picked up the booklet for File 8.

FILE 8   THE STRING PHONE

A woman suspicious of her late father

- Chie Kasahara's father earned lots of money.
- However, this poor excuse for a father kept it all to himself to fritter away.
- Chie and her father used to play with a string phone.

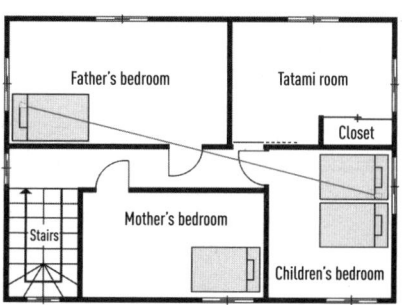

Chie's father ran a string phone between their rooms to talk when she was in bed.

Then, something happened.

- One evening, Chie was talking with her father.
- For some reason, he was behaving oddly, speaking and acting incoherently.
- Right afterwards, the house of the neighbouring Matsue family caught fire.
- Hiroki Matsue, the son, was saved but his parents perished.
- Later, Chie Kasahara heard about the fire on the local news.
  - Hiroki's mother committed suicide by fire in the upstairs tatami room.

What effect did the Matsue house fire have on the Kasahara family?

- After the fire, Mr Kasahara became quiet and introverted.
- Out of the blue, he disappeared, leaving divorce papers and settlement money behind.

- A few months later, Chie found the string phone and, missing her father, stretched it between the two rooms.

What did she notice?

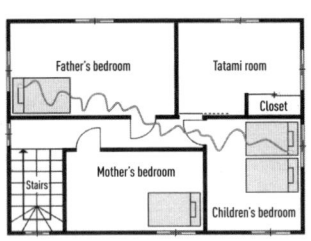

The string was oddly slack, meaning it was too long. It could not carry anyone's voice. So how did her father manage to talk to her?

Chie's answer

- The night of the fire, Kasahara sneaked into the Matsue house through a first-floor window and killed Hiroki's mother while talking on the string phone before setting the fire.
  - The string phone was an attempt to create an alibi.
  - He felt so guilty afterwards that it changed his personality (?)

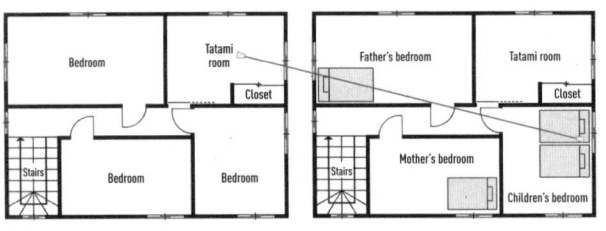

Both the Kasahara and Matsue houses were built by the same company to the same floor plan.

What happened to Mr Kasahara?

- Moved to a new house, committed suicide
- According to neighbourhood gossip, he had remodelling work done on his house not long before death.
- Chie found an unexplained picture of Naruki Mitsuhashi in father's belongings.

THREE MEN

Until the day came that she learnt of her father's death. It was two years after the fire, in 1994.

KASAHARA: That really was suicide, apparently. He locked himself in a little room deep in his house, sealed all the cracks and gaps with tape and took an overdose of sleeping pills. I heard there was some weird doll found beside his body. It's all just so… messed up. I think he must have been suffering from mental problems at the end.

AUTHOR: When you say 'his house', you mean he bought a new one after he left yours?

KASAHARA: Right. After the divorce, he moved into a pre-owned house in Ichinomiya. I saw it the first time on the day of his funeral. It was a single-storey house with a big flower bed by the front door. I talked to a neighbour, and they told me he'd had some renovation work done on the place not long before he died.

AUTHOR: Do you know what kind of renovation?

KASAHARA: Let's see… It was something odd. Like, reduction or something? That's right, they said he'd had one room completely removed… Oh, right, I found something else weird at my dad's house. When we were going through his things afterwards, we found a single picture of a little boy. He was at my dad's new house, eating a rice omelette. He was dreadfully thin and covered in bruises.

AUTHOR: How sad…

KASAHARA: It was heartbreaking to look at. He wasn't the son of any of our relatives or acquaintances. But still, I felt

> like I had seen that face somewhere before. It took me a while to recall, but his picture had been on the news.
>
> His name was Naruki Mitsuhashi. He died from neglect...

I was only just realizing it, but of course they were connected.

KURIHARA: Mr Kasahara's suicide, Naruki's death from neglect, and the undercover report on the Hall of Rebirth were all in 1994. I don't think there can be much doubt that Chie Kasahara's father, Naruki's 'Uncle' and the man who had an outburst at the Hall of Rebirth were all the same man. Putting these three files together, we can piece together the story of Mr Kasahara's life.

Mr Kasahara lived in Hashima, Gifu Prefecture. He was a top salesman at an import car dealership. He had a wife and two children, Chie and her older brother, but he spent all his wages on drunken nights out.

However, he became a much quieter, more sombre man after a fire at their next-door neighbours' house. Eventually, he abandoned his wife and family, leaving only some divorce papers and a bit of cash behind, and went to live alone.

He moved to Ichinomiya, Aichi Prefecture and bought a pre-owned house. I think we can assume he joined the Rebirth Congregation around this time. He eventually had his house rebuilt to resemble the Hall of Rebirth, in accordance with the cult's doctrine.

He invited the Mitsuhashi family to his house several times. In other words, he was having Naruki perform the sacrament.

But then, this blond-haired man showed up and took Naruki away. The man abused Naruki, and he eventually died. After that, Kasahara went to the Rebirth Congregation gathering and accosted the Holy Mother directly, telling her, 'You fraud! If you're truly a goddess, tell me why? Why did my boy, my Naruki, have to die? I'll kill you! I'll seal your heart for ever!'

But they refused to listen and threw him out...

KASAHARA: That really was suicide, apparently. He locked himself in a little room deep in his house, sealed all the cracks and gaps with tape and took an overdose of sleeping pills. I heard there was some weird doll found beside his body. It's all just so... messed up. I think he must have been suffering from mental problems at the end.

KURIHARA: He sealed up the shrine, hoping to kill his house. Why? Because the house represented the Holy Mother herself.

Mr Kasahara believed wholeheartedly in the teachings of the Holy Mother and rebuilt his house accordingly, then had Naruki perform the sacrament. But Naruki still died. The way Kasahara saw it, the Holy Mother had betrayed him.

He had tried to get his revenge on the Holy Mother by 'killing' his own house. It's so sad. Of course, it wouldn't actually pose any danger to the Holy Mother herself. It's all nonsense.

Even convinced that he'd been betrayed, he couldn't escape the cult's brainwashing. He believed to the very end that, if he killed his house, the Holy Mother would also die.

AUTHOR: But what did Naruki have to do with Mr Kasahara?

KURIHARA: I think that figuring out the truth behind the Matsue house fire will help us understand that.

Kurihara arranged File 9 next to File 8.

FILE 9   FOOTSTEPS TO MURDER

Hiroki Matsue's testimony about the fire

What does Hiroki think about the fire?

'My father started the fire to kill my mother.'

Why does he think so?

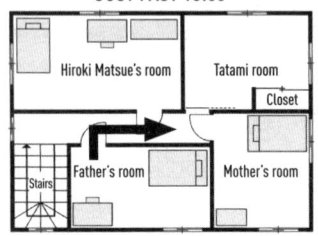

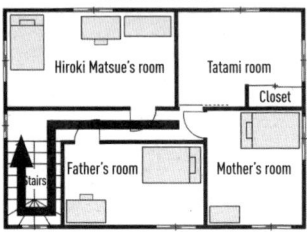

- The night of the fire, Mr Matsue goes from his own room towards his wife's.
- Thirty minutes later, Mr Matsue rushes downstairs, shouting, 'Fire!' and drags Hiroki out of the house.

  Mr Matsue hands him a hundred-yen coin and his crucifix.

  Run to the phone box on the corner and call for a fire engine, he says. 'I'm going to go look for your mother. For some reason, she wasn't in her room.'

- Mr Matsue goes back inside to save Hiroki's mother.

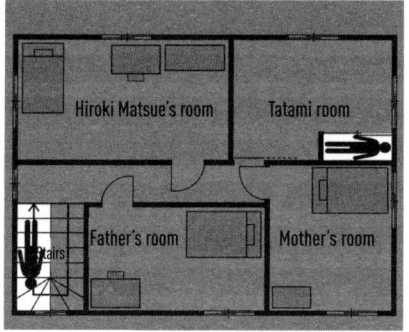

Later, both bodies were recovered. Mr Matsue had collapsed on the stairs, while Mrs Matsue was found in the closet of the tatami room on the first floor. There was an empty kerosene can next to her body, so the police declared it suicide by self-immolation.

Hiroki Matsue's Theory

- Just past ten, his father went to Hiroki's mother's room and dosed her with sleeping pills.
- Then he took Hiroki outside.
- His father went back inside, put his mother into the closet and started the fire.
- He then passed out on the stairs while trying to escape.

Why did he put her in the closet?

- To create an excuse in case Hiroki ever asked why he failed to save his mother.

What excuse?

- 'I never had a hope of finding your mother, with her hidden [in the closet] like that.'

KURIHARA: Hiroki Matsue and Chie Kasahara both suspected their own fathers of murder. I agree that both men behaved oddly on the night of the fire. To my mind, though, it's nonsensical to try to declare either one the murderer, although we should assume they both had something to do with what happened that night.

AUTHOR: You mean they worked together?

KURIHARA: No, nothing so simple. First of all, we have to clarify a few essential points.

- What was the reason for both men's odd behaviour?
- Was Hiroki Matsue's mother really murdered? If she was, who was the culprit?
- Why was the body discovered in the closet?
- If the fire was deliberately set, who did it and why?

First, let's think about the first question. Chie said:

KASAHARA: So, this one night, I was talking to Dad on the string phone. It was just before ten at night. I remember that he was different from usual. It was like his voice was trembling, and the things he said were incoherent… I'd ask him something, and he'd answer, but none of it made much sense. And there was this noise or something. Some kind of rustling on the phone. After a few minutes of meaningless back and forth, he finally snapped at me. 'Go to bed. Good night!' and dropped the phone.

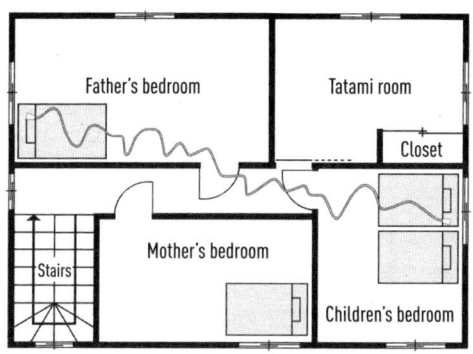

KURIHARA: From the length of the string phone, we know that Mr Kasahara was on the first floor of the Matsue house. The question is, in which room?

Chie believes he was in the tatami room. But I disagree.

AUTHOR: You do?

KURIHARA: Yes. Here, read this.

> **KASAHARA:** In the evening, I would be lying there awake, and my door would open just a crack, and a paper cup would pop through it. I'd pick it up and put it to my ear.

KURIHARA: She said the door would 'open a crack' when they talked. Doesn't that stand out to you?

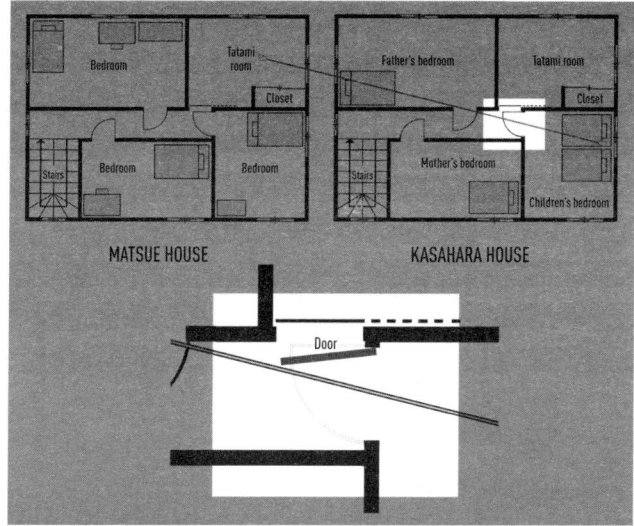

KURIHARA: To run the phone from Chie's bed to the Matsues' tatami room, you'd have to open Chie's door completely.

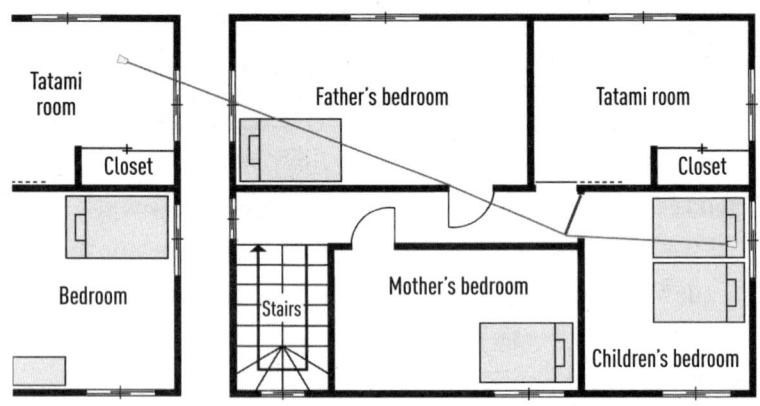

KURIHARA: If the door was only slightly open, it would obstruct the string, and she and her father wouldn't have been able to hear each other. So, on the night of the fire… Probably on other nights, too, Mr Kasahara was neither in his room nor in the Matsues' tatami room.

AUTHOR: Where was he, then?

KURIHARA: There's only one place he could have been if Chie could speak to him on the string phone with her door only open a crack, like she described. Hiroki's mother's bed.

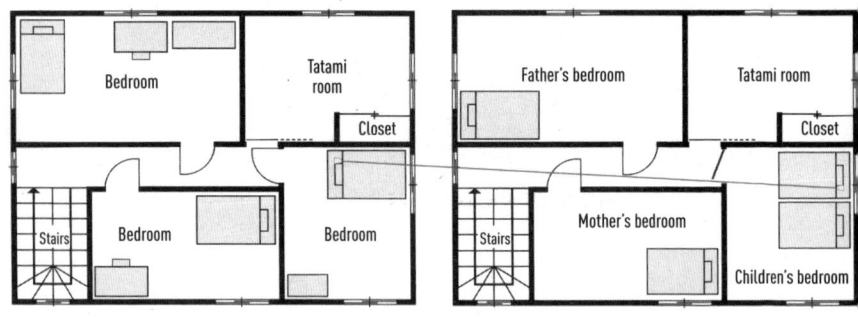

MATSUE HOUSE **KASAHARA HOUSE**

SECRETS

AUTHOR: But why…?

KURIHARA: I don't have any proof, of course, but I'd say it looks like Kasahara was having an affair with Hiroki's mother, doesn't it? Look at this:

> **KASAHARA:** My dad was mostly awful, but every once in a while he would show a hint of kindness. He was also handsome for his age and, I guess, a bit of a ladykiller.

KURHIHARA: And this:

> **KASAHARA:** And then Dad would go out until all hours of the night, come home reeking of alcohol, and fill the house with his snoring. Selfish prat.

KURIHARA: He was a selfish, shallow playboy, and one with a lot of money, too. It also sounds like he was popular with the ladies.

The files make it pretty clear that married life for both the Kasaharas and the Matsues was not at all happy.

> **KASAHARA:** But she unloaded everything she couldn't say to his face on my brother and me. She used to say, 'I never should have married a man like that.'
>
> **MATSUE:** My mother and father didn't get along at all. They hardly spoke, and I got the feeling they couldn't really bear the sight of each other. Looking back, I'm sure that sex was totally out of the question.

KURIHARA: With those two families living next door to each other, it was almost inevitable that Mr Kasahara and Mrs Matsue would end up having an affair.

And, well, I have another suspicion. A shallow man like Mr Kasahara, brazen enough to sleep with his neighbour while her husband and child were in the house, might have got tired of a simple affair. Maybe he eventually needed more of a thrill. I think that's what the string phone was for. He was talking to his daughter while he had sex with Mrs Matsue. It's sick, but people have all kinds of perverse kinks.

I'd thought that Mr Kasahara making that phone for his frightened daughter was an act of fatherly love.

Had I been wrong? Had he actually been using her as a toy for some kind of sexual gratification?

KASAHARA: And it seemed like my father's voice over the string phone was warmer and more loving than any other time. I even told him all kinds of secrets.

When I thought back on what Chie had said about those nights, I felt sick.

KURIHARA: The night of the fire, Mr Kasahara took the string phone, went through the window and into his mistress's room. But there he found a corpse.

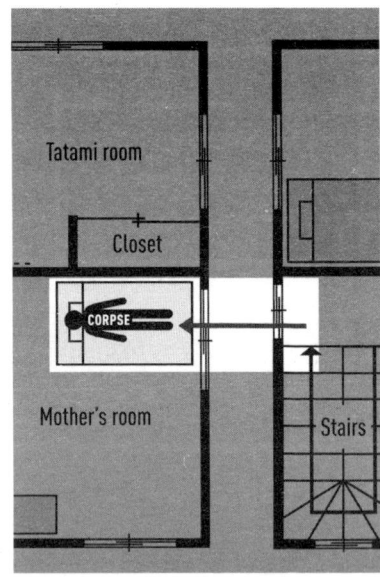

AUTHOR: A corpse?! You're saying that Mrs Matsue was already dead?

KURIHARA: I think so. I doubt Mr Kasahara had the type of personality that was capable of murder. If he did, he'd have tried to kill the Holy Mother in person, not through some indirect ritual. No, I don't think he killed Mrs Matsue, just found her body. I'm sure the shock and fear he felt explain that incoherent conversation Chie remembers.

> **KASAHARA:** I remember that he was different from usual. It was like his voice was trembling, and the things he said were incoherent.

AUTHOR: So, you think Mr Matsue killed his wife?
KURIHARA: I don't. Because he was a Catholic.

> Matsue took a silver pendant out of his breast pocket. It had the figure of Jesus Christ on the cross.
>
> **MATSUE:** My father was a devout Christian… It's the only keepsake I have of life before the fire.

KURIHARA: Hiroki Matsue's father was an especially devout Christian, which is rare enough in Japan, and on top of that he was a pacifist with an open commitment to non-violence. Of course, that doesn't mean he couldn't also be a murderer. People act against what they supposedly believe all the time. But it made me hesitant to accept his guilt.
AUTHOR: Hmm. I see what you mean.
KURIHARA: And there's another thing. Hiroki's theory is that his father went to his mother's room at just after ten o'clock,

somehow put her to sleep, and then got Hiroki out of the house to set the fire. Doesn't that sound like premeditated murder?

AUTHOR: Does it?

KURIHARA: How could it not be? Let's say he and his wife got into an argument in her bedroom and she revealed her affair, causing her husband to fly into a murderous rage. Would he really have dosed her with sleeping pills and made sure she was asleep after that? And all within thirty minutes?

AUTHOR: Right. Well, maybe it was a spur of the moment thing, but he didn't use sleeping pills like Hiroki thought. Maybe he just hit his wife over the head, or something like that, to knock her out.

KURIHARA: But in that case, don't you think Hiroki would have heard raised voices? A struggle? No, it doesn't fit.

AUTHOR: So, maybe Hiroki's father did plan the murder in advance and used sleeping pills. What difference does it make?

KURIHARA: Think about it. If he was going to plan her murder in advance, why plan it for a time when his son was in the house? He could have done it any time. And why plan to commit the murder in the house? Surely he could have come up with an idea that didn't require him to burn down his and his son's home, or to set fire to the building while he was inside it. None of those possibilities make sense.

AUTHOR: Then who did it?

KURIHARA: I think there's a hint in Chie's statement.

> **KASAHARA:** And there was this noise or something. Some kind of rustling on the phone.

KURIHARA: That rustling she heard over the string phone is key.

String phones don't really pick up background noise, which means whatever made that sound, it must have been right by the paper cup. What could that have been? Something light. Something he held near his face. Maybe a sheet of paper?

AUTHOR: But…

KURIHARA: Or a paper envelope, perhaps, placed beside the body. Mr Kasahara picked it up, opened it and took out the contents. I think you can imagine the rest, right?

AUTHOR: A suicide note…

KURIHARA: Right. Mrs Matsue, Hiroki's mother, killed herself.

DYING WORDS

KURIHARA: Mr Kasahara read the note and the content shocked him. He fled, terrified of what would happen.

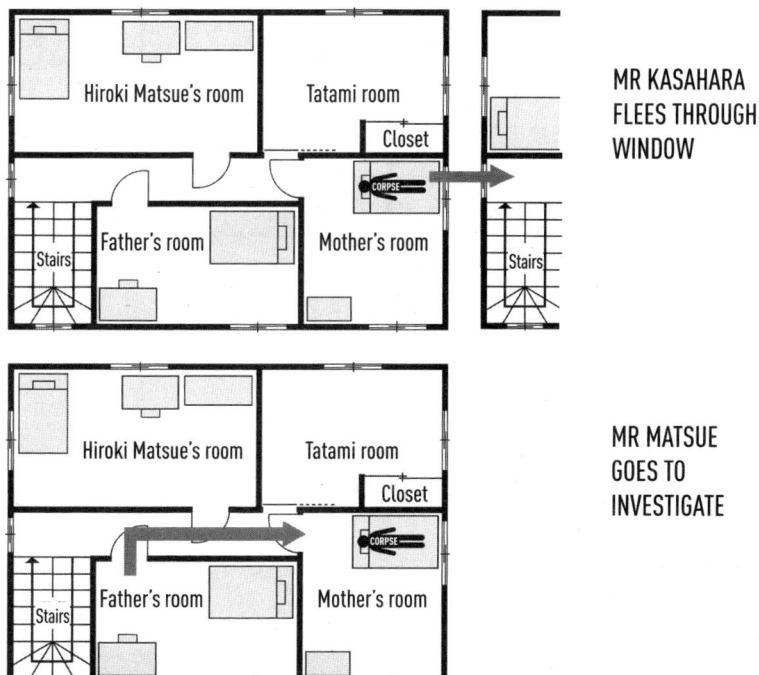

MR KASAHARA FLEES THROUGH WINDOW

MR MATSUE GOES TO INVESTIGATE

KURIHARA: I imagine Mr Kasahara must have made some kind of noise in his panic. Mr Matsue heard it and went to check what had happened, and that is when he found his wife's body and her note, just like Mr Kasahara had. Then he began acting strangely.

KURIHARA: After thirty minutes of quiet, he went downstairs to take Hiroki outside, then returned to the house. He put his wife's body in the closet, doused her in kerosene and lit the fire.

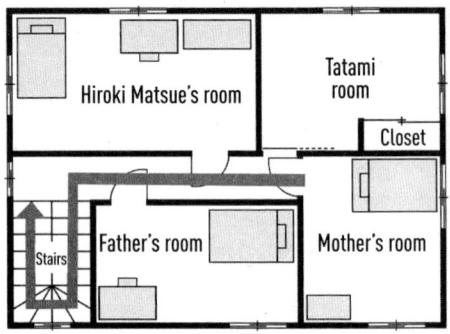

TAKES HIROKI OUTSIDE

AUTHOR: But… why? I can't even begin to explain it.

KURIHARA: When he found her body, he should have contacted the police immediately. But he didn't. Why?

I'm thinking he read something in her note that drove him to set that fire. Now, can we imagine what it might have been?

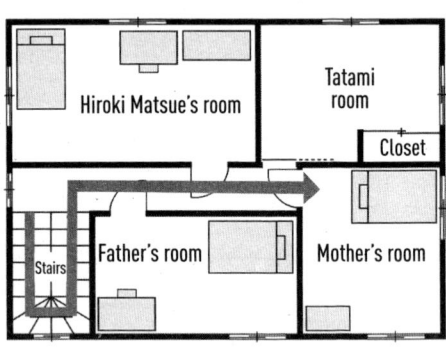

GOES BACK TO WIFE'S ROOM

Kurihara picked up his pen and drew a cross on his notepad.

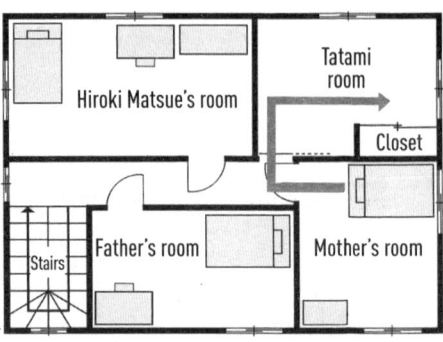

CARRIES WIFE'S BODY TO THE CLOSET

KURIHARA: I think this goes back to his religion once again. Catholicism condemns sex for purposes other than procreation. Particularly sex outside of marriage.

> **MATSUE:** I suppose it wouldn't be for most couples, but my mother and father didn't get along at all. They hardly spoke, and I got the feeling they couldn't really bear the sight of each other. Looking back, I'm sure that sex was totally out of the question. I think the only reason they didn't divorce was that my mother had no financial independence and my father was incapable of any housework. They were just going through the motions.

KURIHARA: Mrs Matsue must have been dissatisfied with her sexually repressed husband. That's probably why she ended up having an affair with Mr Kasahara.

But the key is what happened next. She almost certainly got pregnant with Mr Kasahara's child.

AUTHOR: What?

KURIHARA: She and her husband were in a sexless marriage. Her pregnancy would have instantly revealed her infidelity, and surely her strictly religious husband would never have forgiven her.

An abortion would have been possible up to twenty-two weeks, but if she spent too long unable to decide what to do and missed that limit… Well, she might have felt she had no escape.

So, mentally and emotionally trapped, she chose suicide as a way out, leaving a note explaining it all.

KURIHARA: It must have deeply hurt Mr Matsue. But I suppose there was something worse for him.

MATSUE: My father was a devout Christian. His faith was everything. He was a pacifist, too, and used to march against war and the death penalty and things like that. He told me he wanted to have me baptized as well, but my mother was opposed to it, so it never happened.

KURIHARA: He had wanted to bring his son into the faith with him, but when he read that note, it sent him into a crisis. Hiroki would go through life, knowing he was the son of an adulterer. It must have pained Mr Matsue's pious heart. And so, he decided to hide his wife's affair.

AUTHOR: So that's why…?

KURIHARA: He could have just thrown the note away, but the police would have had an autopsy conducted to confirm the cause of death, and of course that would have revealed her pregnancy. He must have decided to burn the body to make sure no one ever learnt the shameful truth.

AUTHOR: To burn the baby along with his wife…

KURIHARA: Yes. It can't have been an easy decision though. He couldn't be sure that the fire would destroy his wife's body sufficiently.

He probably spent that thirty-minute gap trying to figure out what to do, until he came up with an idea. The closet.

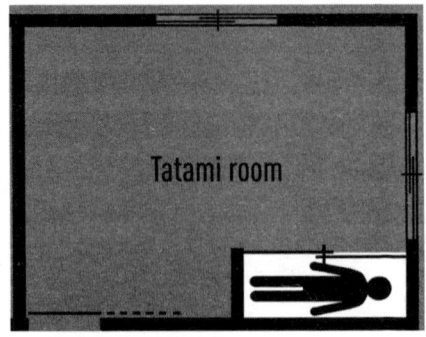

He must have imagined that burning the body in the narrow confines of the closet would concentrate the fire, making it hot enough that an autopsy would be impossible.

AUTHOR: He used the closet as a cremation chamber?

KURIHARA: That's one way to put it, but this wasn't a crematorium, just a house. You can't confine a fire to a closet. He must have known he'd burn his whole house down, but it didn't stop him.

AUTHOR: It's unbelievable. Surely, for Hiroki, losing his home and his mother at the same time would be worse than living with the knowledge that she'd been unfaithful.

KURIHARA: People are often irrational. They make stupid decisions for the sake of unquestioned beliefs, particularly where religion is concerned. And don't forget the trauma and panic Mr Matsue must have been experiencing after losing his wife…

AUTHOR: I suppose so…

KURIHARA: So, then, what became of the philandering Mr Kasahara, who set the stage for this tragedy?

> **KASAHARA:** After that, for some reason, my dad started acting bizarrely. He went from shallow and carefree to dark and withdrawn. He was like another man entirely.

KURIHARA: I think inside that selfish playboy was a cowardly little boy.

He couldn't take the guilt of knowing that his mistress had killed herself because of their affair, taking their baby with her. And that drove him to look for salvation.

AUTHOR: So that's why he joined the Rebirth Congregation.

KURIHARA: And understanding that will help us understand the heart of the cult itself.

SINS OF THE FATHER, SINS OF THE CHILD

4 WHAT WERE THE 'SPECIAL CIRCUMSTANCES' SHARED BY ALL THE MEMBERS?

KURIHARA: Let's go back and read the speech from Masahiko Hikura again.

> By your presence here, I know you are well aware. Aware of your sin, and of how your poor children have inherited that sin. Children born out of their parents' sin. Children of sin. That stain will bring profound suffering and surely drag you to hell itself.
>
> Sadly, your defilement can never be erased. However, it can be lightened. Reduced. Through faith and the sacrament, you can ease your burden. Dilute your impurity here, in this hall. And, tomorrow, you can go home, your stain faded, and introduce your children to the sacrament.

KURIHARA: Your children have inherited that sin… That assumes the listeners have children.

So, all the members of the Rebirth Congregation have children. In other words, it's a cult you cannot join without having children. And not just any children!

AUTHOR: Children born of sin… They're the children of infidelity.

KURIHARA: Exactly. There are many more such children than you'd imagine. And their parents often struggle with guilt, unable to share their burden with anyone. The Rebirth Congregation exploits that particular guilt to brainwash its members.

5 HOW DID THE MEMBERS END UP BEING BRAINWASHED JUST BY GOING THROUGH THIS SACRAMENT A FEW TIMES A MONTH?

KURIHARA: Two powerful techniques in brainwashing are instilling guilt and playing on the subject's weaknesses. People joining the Rebirth Congregation were already struggling with weakness and feelings of overwhelming guilt. It must have been a simple thing to control such people, threatening them and reassuring them in turn.

AUTHOR: I see…

KURIHARA: And by some mysterious chance, the cult's doctrine was a perfect fit for Mr Kasahara, who'd lost his mistress and their child.

> Children born out of their parents' sin. Children of sin. That stain will bring profound suffering and surely drag you to hell itself.

AUTHOR: He was convinced that Mrs Matsue's suicide was just what Hikura had warned of: suffering brought about by sin.

KURIHARA: Exactly. At the same time, Kasahara must have felt a new worry growing. Because, you see, he had a secret child with another mistress of his.

AUTHOR: Of course. Naruki.

KURIHARA: Naruki. As the Rebirth Congregation's creed seeped into him, he would have been scared that Naruki, another child of sin, would suffer similar misfortune. He was trying to lighten the burden of sin by inviting Naruki to stay over from time to time. But then, along came the blond man and took Naruki away. I'm not sure who he was, really, whether just the mother's new lover or maybe a gangster who was trying to exploit her, but it doesn't make much difference.

> The handsome man was still shouting. 'You fraud! If you're truly a goddess, tell me why? Why did my boy, my Naruki, have to die? I'll kill you! I'll seal your heart for ever!' The screams went on even as they dragged him outside.

AUTHOR: Although Kasahara had followed the cult's teachings, Naruki still died, so he turned that shock and rage on the Holy Mother.

KURIHARA: Right. And along with his senseless act of revenge, locking that room, he took his own life. It's almost enough to make me feel sorry for him for believing in such nonsense. Or perhaps he came to the decision out of regret for the things he'd done.

Kasahara had tried to recreate the Hall of Rebirth by removing a room from his house. *Removing a room… Wait…*

AUTHOR: Kurihara, wait, what about Yayoi Negishi's mother…?

KURIHARA: Oh, the Rebirth Congregation certainly had something to do with that.

FILE 1   THE HALLWAY TO NOWHERE

Mother's attitude and an odd floor plan

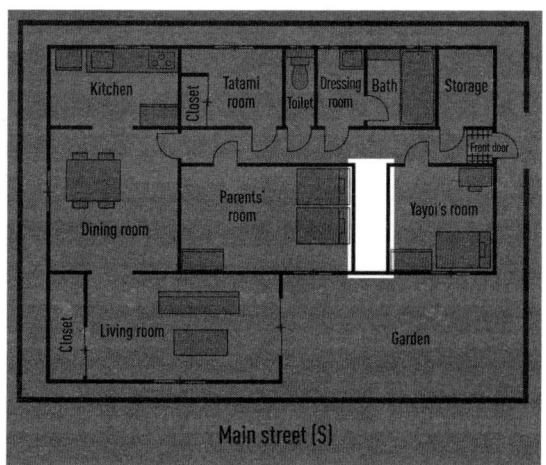

- Yayoi Negishi's childhood home had an unexplained dead-end hallway.

Was her mother's odd overprotectiveness a hint?

- Yayoi's mother strictly forbade her from walking on the main road.

What conclusion came of this?

- They had the house newly built by the construction company Housemaker Misaki the year Yayoi was born.
- The floor plan was decided by parents consulting with Misaki staff.
- Initially, the front door was located on the south side.
- However, a company truck struck and killed a neighbourhood child on the road in front of the door.

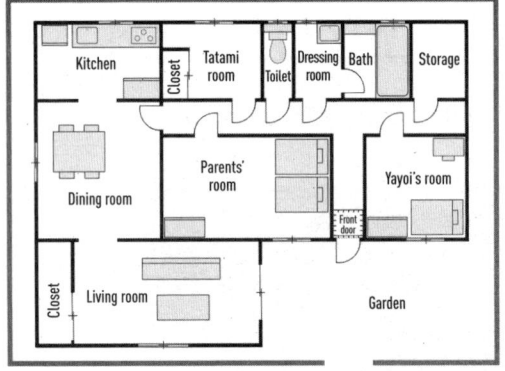

If left as is, the front door would open onto the scene of a fatal accident. Not only is that a bad omen, but they would be reminded of the death every time they went outside.

  Accident

What did Mrs Negishi propose to Misaki?

- Change the door location.
  - No view of the scene from inside the house.

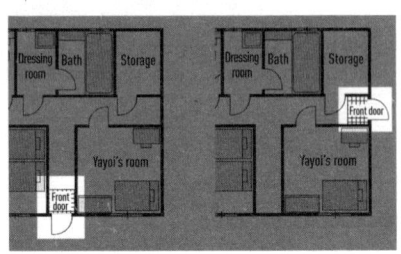

This solved two puzzles.

- The dead-end hallway was originally connected to the front door.
- Mrs Negishi's attitude towards the main road was based on fear of her own daughter getting into a similar accident.

That seemed to solve everything, until...

They learnt that a few years after the house was built, Mrs Negishi approached Misaki about having her daughter's room removed from the house.

Mrs Negishi died before it was completed, and the reason was never explained.

Mrs Negishi approached Housemaker Misaki, asking them to remove her daughter's room entirely. The first time I heard this, it made no sense, but knowing about the Rebirth Congregation, her plan was clear.

Removing Negishi's room from this house would make it look like the Holy Mother. Taking that room out would be like removing the body's right leg.

AUTHOR: I suppose that means Mrs Negishi had a child as a result of an affair.

KURIHARA: Clearly. And she ended up raising that child with her husband.

AUTHOR: What? Wait, you don't mean…?

KURIHARA: Of course. Yayoi Negishi was born out of Mrs Negishi's affair.

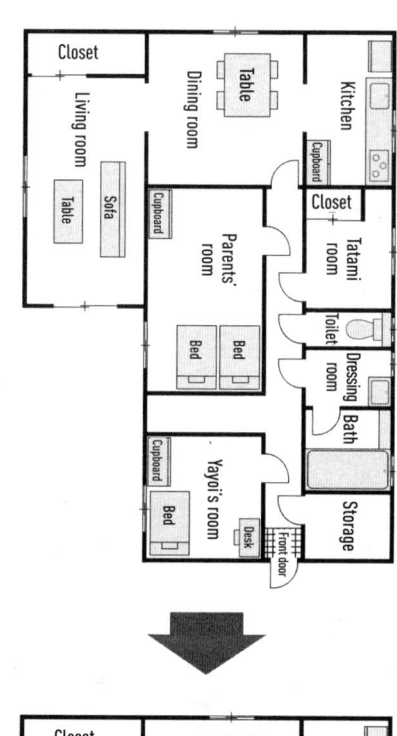

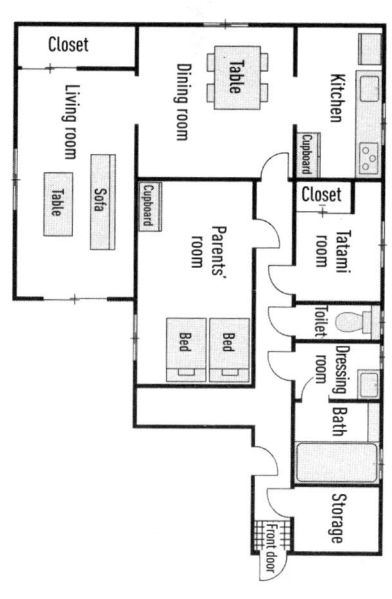

OVERPROTECTIVE

KURIHARA: The first thing that bothered me was this talk about the main road.

> Mum always said, 'No matter what, you're never to go on the big road. If you have to go anywhere in the neighbourhood, use the lanes.' The pavement along that main street was really narrow. I could see the danger, of course, but we didn't live in a big city or anything, so the traffic wasn't very heavy. I always thought she worried too much.

KURIHARA: Yayoi's mother was normally cold and strict towards her, but when it came to accidents, she became overprotective. What could explain that difference?

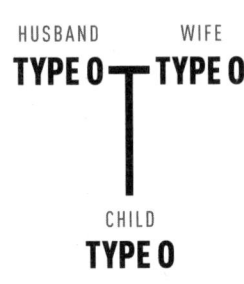

I started to think that what she was really afraid of was of her daughter being seriously injured in an accident, which might require a blood transfusion. And then they would know her blood type.

AUTHOR: Why would that matter?

KURIHARA: Many cases of infidelity have been revealed by children's blood types.

For example, a man with blood type O and a woman with blood type O could never have a child with blood type A.

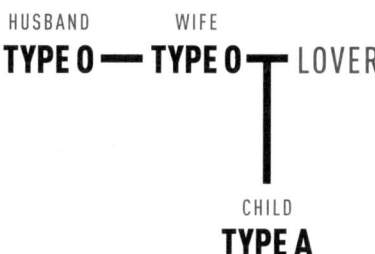

KURIHARA: That child would have had a father with type A or AB blood. In the not-too-distant past, hospitals always gave newborns blood tests, to the point that there was actually a trend of divorces immediately following childbirth when the tests revealed infidelity.

AUTHOR: So, she worried that Yayoi's blood type would reveal the affair she'd had… But, hold on, you just said they used to check all newborns' blood types. Why wasn't the affair revealed then?

KURIHARA: I imagine that the circumstances of Yayoi's birth meant they couldn't do a type test.

> **NEGISHI:** Like I said before, I was born prematurely. Two months before the due date, and by caesarean. From what they told me, it was a risky birth for both mother and child.

KURIHARA: Being born that prematurely meant her body was not developed enough for a test to be done safely.

Premature babies are quite small and so have a correspondingly low volume of blood. That means there's not much leeway to go running inessential blood tests, like to find out blood type. Of course, it was pure chance that Yayoi was born prematurely, but for Mrs Negishi it was lucky indeed.

Pregnancy from affair

Decide to have baby while hiding the truth

Joins the Rebirth Congregation

KURIHARA: Mrs Negishi got pregnant with her secret lover. She decided to have the baby and pass it off as her husband's. But I imagine that secret was a heavy burden to bear. Then, she learnt about the Rebirth Congregation and found comfort in its doctrine.

She followed the doctrine in secret, like Japan's medieval 'hidden Christians', without her husband ever knowing. But then came the unthinkable. The accident.

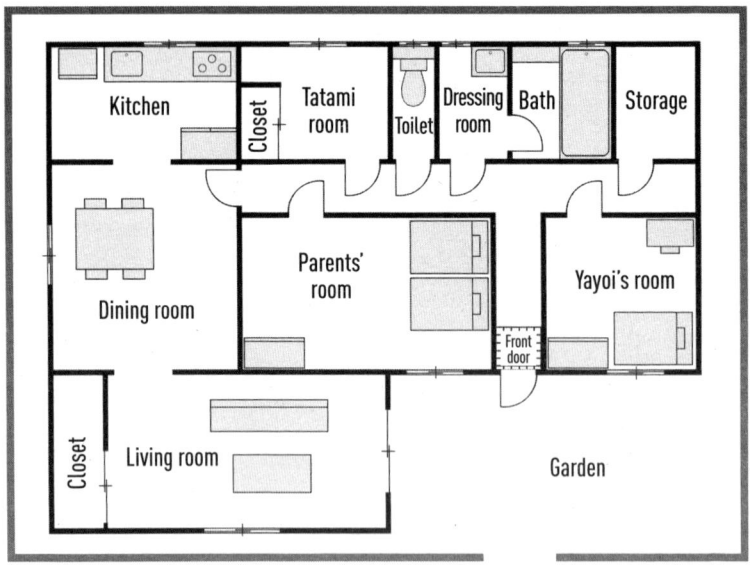

● **Fatal accident**

KURIHARA: A Housemaker Misaki employee struck and killed a child right by their house. In front of their door! I think that's when she first noticed.

Moving the front door would help make the house more like the Hall of Rebirth. A lucky coincidence. So, she took the idea to her husband.

> Ikeda said that Mr Negishi was in a rage over it. But it was Mrs Negishi who seemed to take it the worst. Then, she proposed an alternative plan. She suggested that construction of the house could continue only if the location of the front door was changed.

KURIHARA: So, Yayoi being born prematurely so that a blood test could not be

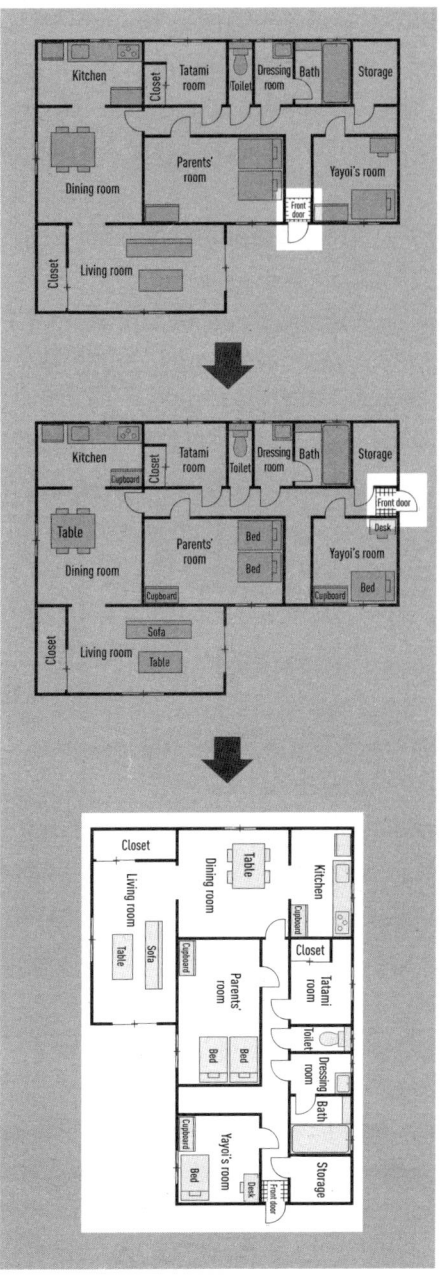

carried out was the second lucky coincidence. But then, that good luck resulted in a different set of worries.

I think Yayoi must have become something of a sword of Damocles hanging over her mother. Accident, illness, blood donation… She never knew what might reveal her daughter's blood type and possibly expose her sin.

That anxiety drove her dependence on the cult's doctrine. She fell deeper and deeper into the Rebirth Congregation, and, as she did, something began to prey on her.

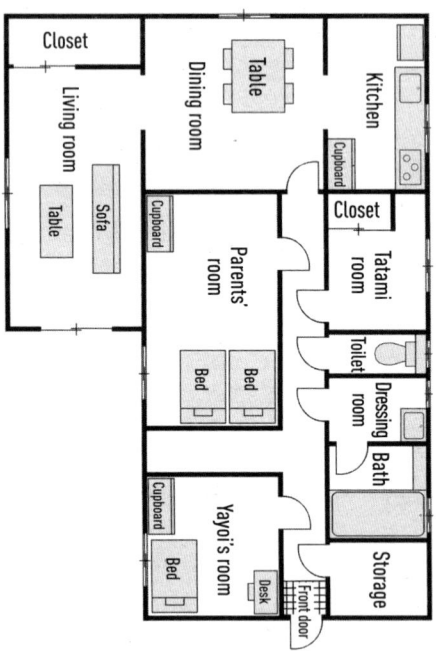

KURIHARA: Her house wasn't similar enough to the Hall of Rebirth. That's what she must have started to think. It didn't look like the Holy Mother. So, she started to squirrel away money for more construction work.

NEGISHI: First there was the money—an envelope in my mother's drawer stuffed with 10,000-yen bills. Sixty-eight of them… When Mum was still healthy, she worked part time at a bento shop.

KURIHARA: No matter how much she scrimped and saved, though, part-time work at a bento shop would barely be enough to get a few hundred thousand yen.

The Rebirth Congregation seems to be selling something that costs in the range of millions—even tens of millions—of yen.

KURIHARA: The cult was looking for millions of yen, at minimum. There was no way she could swing that much. She gave up on paying the Rebirth Congregation to do it and gave Housemaker Misaki a try.

IKEDA: The fact is, about five years after the house was built, your mother came to us one day, without your father. She had the strangest question. 'Can you tear out the room at the south-east corner?'

KURIHARA: Given Housemaker Misaki's responsibility for the accident in front of her house, she probably hoped they would take on the work at a cut rate, but the company quoted a much higher price than she could afford. She ended up struggling with her anxiety until her premature death.

AUTHOR: You might be the wrong person to ask, but still, I'm going to. Do you think Mrs Negishi truly loved Yayoi?

KURIHARA: The heart of the Rebirth Congregation's doctrine was playing on people's desires to 'save' children born from infidelity, so I do think there was love for her daughter there.

But... Well, from the positioning of the rooms, there might be another way to look at it.

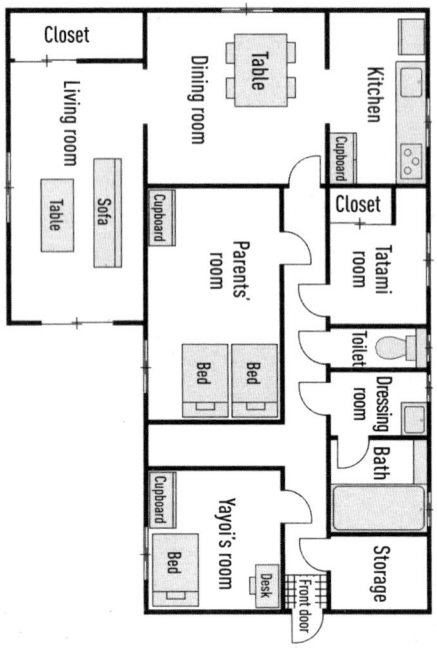

KURIHARA: The ideal layout for the cult was, as I understand it, to make the child's room a 'womb'.

But, looking at the Negishi house, Yayoi's room is nowhere near that spot. It's clearly the 'leg'. I'd say that Mrs Negishi's bed is closest to where a womb would be.

It may well have been that she was hoping to save herself, rather than her daughter. But, well, I'm just speculating here.

BREAK

KURIHARA: I think that makes it clear how the Negishi, Kasahara and Iruma houses were all linked to the Rebirth Congregation.

AUTHOR: So, we have to assume one of the Irumas also had an affair.

KURIHARA: Yes, and I imagine their circumstances were the same as the Negishi family's.

AUTHOR: You think Ren was born from his mother's infidelity?

KURIHARA: I do. However, the Iruma house is unusual in that the father was also involved in the construction. So, they both joined the cult. I guess Mr Iruma was aware of the affair.

AUTHOR: What a tolerant husband…

KURIHARA: Maybe he was one of those 'anything for the child' types. Though, if we wanted to entertain some irresponsible speculation, there is also another possibility.

> The couple had bought it newly built the year they married. When their son was born eight years later, they'd had major renovations done.

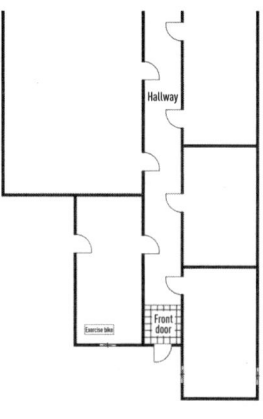

MR KASAHARA'S HOUSE

THE IRUMA HOUSE

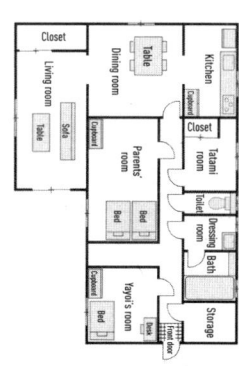

THE NEGISHI HOUSE

KURIHARA: Your friend was born eight years after his parents' marriage. That's a little late. Now, this is just a possibility, but perhaps his father is unable to have children.
AUTHOR: Like, physically? Meaning he's infertile?
KURIHARA: Exactly. And the couple was desperate for a child. So... Oh, let's leave it at that. It's all just wild speculation anyway.

Kurihara stretched his arms above his head.

KURIHARA: Well, that's the first half of the battle. Let's take a little break before we get to the second half. Shall I make some tea?

BIRTH

I looked out the window over my steaming cup. It was getting dark outside.

KURIHARA: So far, we've been working on figuring out what kind of cult the Rebirth Congregation was. From here on, I think it's time to talk about where it came from and how it broke up.
   Now, any talk about the Rebirth Congregation must include the Holy Mother. We need to figure out the history of how she became the cult's figurehead.

Kurihara opened the booklet for File 10.

FILE 10   NO ESCAPE

Mothers and children trapped in a hellish brothel

- Izakaya owner Akemi Nishiharu was a popular bar hostess in her youth.
- She got pregnant by a deceitful customer → Was left a single mother
- Opened own shop but racked up massive debt through poor management
- Declared bankruptcy at the age of twenty-seven, was taken to an *okito* with seven-year-old son Mitsuru

What are *okito*?

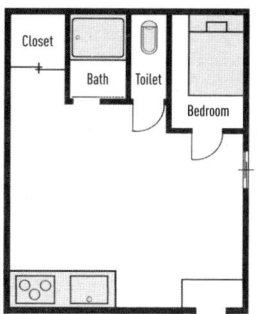

A word for a particular kind of brothel run by crime organizations. The gangs would remodel a block of flats and force indebted women to live there as sex workers, servicing customers in the flats. A portion of the income would be used to repay their debts. They would not be allowed to leave until the debts were repaid.

Rooms were built to prevent escape

Neighbouring rooms had windows so women could keep watch on each other.

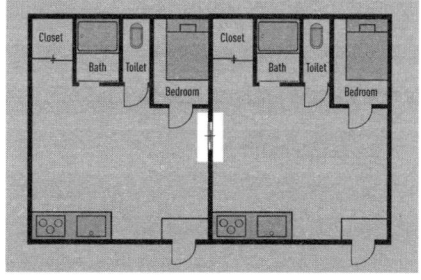

- Akemi's neighbour was a woman named Yaeko
- Yaeko was locked in with her eleven-year-old daughter to repay a debt, just like Akemi
- Yaeko was missing her left arm.

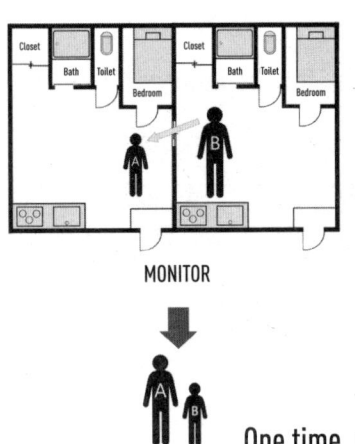

The *okito* usually forbids any outings, but under some conditions inmates are allowed out.

The main condition is that a woman must take her neighbour's child with her and leave her own in exchange.

Akemi and Yaeko occasionally took advantage of the system.

One time, disaster struck

- Akemi's son Mitsuru said he wanted to go to town, so Yaeko volunteered to take him.
- The day of their trip, Mitsuru misread a crossing signal and walked out into traffic. A car was about to hit him.
- Yaeko rushed to push him out of the way, saving him at the cost of her own right leg.

What of Yaeko after that?

- A regular customer repaid Yaeko's loan and took her and her daughter from the *okito*.

Who was that customer?

- Successor to the Hikura Homes family.
- Yaeko most likely married (was forced to marry?) him.

KURIHARA: So, this woman named Yaeko lived next to Akemi Nishiharu in the brothel she called the *okito*.

Yaeko was missing her left arm, and then she lost her right leg saving Akemi's son Mitsuru. A woman missing her left arm and right leg… From the files you have here, I think we can be safe in assuming that this Yaeko went on to become the Rebirth Congregation's Holy Mother.

AKEMI: At the time, Yaeko had a regular customer. Man name of Hikura, he was. The son of some construction company big shot. He was head over heels for Yaeko. It seems he went and paid off her debt. Not out of the goodness of his heart, of course. He took them both off somewhere, mother and daughter… And even so, him being the president's son and all, he got to take over the company and now he's Mr Chairman. Ah, what a world we live in.

KURIHARA: She said he was the chairman now. So, he must have been Masahiko Hikura. That was how he and the Holy Mother met.

Now, I want you to think back on what the Holy Mother told the members in the shrine in the Hall of Rebirth.

> You know my story. I was born a child of sin. I lost my left arm to my mother's sin. I lost my right leg to save a child of sin. With what is left of this body, I wish only to save you and your own children. Now, it is time for rebirth. Over and over again.

KURIHARA: 'I lost my right leg to save a child of sin.' That must be referring to the traffic accident. She did throw herself into traffic to save Mitsuru, which is how she lost her leg. But what makes Mitsuru a 'child of sin'? That, too, is explained in the files.

> When Akemi was nineteen, she got pregnant with a customer's baby. The man had claimed to be owner of a small company and sweet-talked her with dreams of settling down and raising a family with her. Akemi had taken him at his word and was ready to get married.
>
> But the night she told him she was pregnant was the last time he ever showed up at the bar. Not long after, she heard an odd rumour: he wasn't any kind of business owner at all. He was a simple office worker with a wife and child at home.

KURIHARA: Mitsuru's father was a married office worker. Meaning, Mitsuru was born of an affair. A child of sin.

> **AKEMI:** Well, let's see, you know we used to talk about our pasts and such when the kids weren't around. She'd had quite a life.

KURIHARA: The Holy Mother and Akemi used to chat with each other at the *okito*. That's when she heard about Mitsuru's father.

AUTHOR: So, that wasn't just spiritual-sounding gibberish the Holy Mother was spouting in the shrine. She was talking about real events.

KURIHARA: Right. From which we can extrapolate…

> I was born a child of sin. I lost my left arm to my mother's sin. And I lost my right leg to save a child of sin.

KURIHARA: When she said, 'I was born a child of sin. I lost my left arm to my mother's sin,' she was telling the truth, too. So, what exactly was she referring to this time?

> **AKEMI:** She'd been abandoned as a baby. They found her in some hut or something, out in the woods. So, those folks she thought were her birth parents had in fact adopted her. It's not that unusual a story, I know. But it shocked her, I suppose, and she ran away from home. She told me she still resented the both of them.

KURIHARA: A hut in the woods. That should remind you of something else.

Kurihara picked up File 3.

FILE 3 THE WATERMILL IN THE WOODS

A watermill with an odd contraption

- In 1938, the pampered daughter of a steel magnate, Uki Mizunashi, was staying at her uncle's house when she found a strange watermill in the woods near the house.

Unique features of the watermill

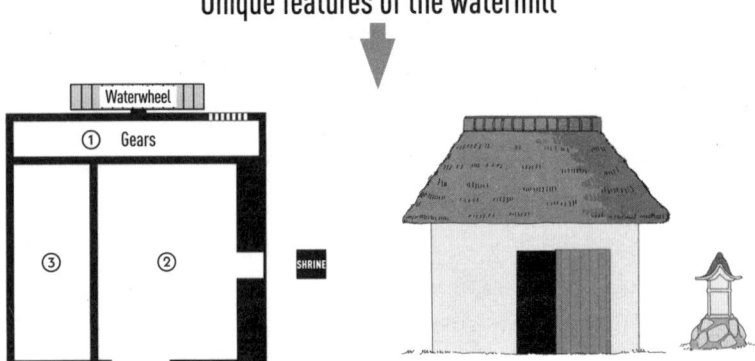

- There was a shrine nearby, inside was a stone statue of a goddess holding a round fruit in one hand.
- The building had three rooms. ① The room of gears ② The room with a door ③ The sealed room
    - Room ② had an alcove in one wall

Uki notices a trick

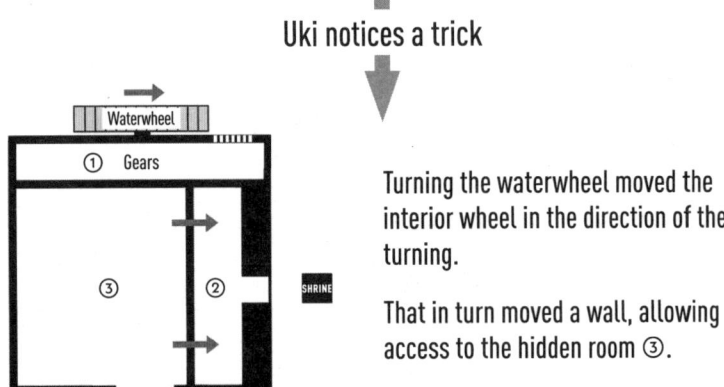

Turning the waterwheel moved the interior wheel in the direction of the turning.

That in turn moved a wall, allowing access to the hidden room ③.

What was in room ③?

Uki said she found the 'corpse of an egret'.

On seeing it, she ran away.

That evening, Uki had planned on asking her uncle's family about the watermill, but then...

The 'baby' at their house was doing poorly.

The baby 'had been struggling from the operation, and the stump of its left arm was festering'.

As a result, she missed her chance to ask.

What did Uki come to think later?

- The watermill had been built as some kind of religious penance room.
- Transgressors would be sealed into room ② and the waterwheel turned.
- The wall would approach and the repentant would be forced to curl up inside the depression in the wall.
- The shrine was outside the depression, meaning the repentant would be bowing to the goddess.

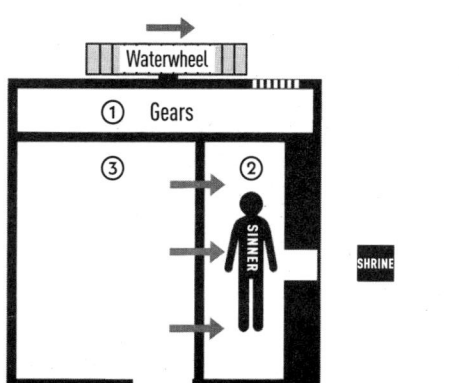
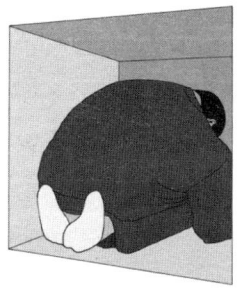

KURIHARA: This watermill in the woods that Uki Mizunashi found... What do you think that was? One thing we need to look at is this section here:

> I examined the surroundings once more, and noticed that there was a small, shrine-like structure to the left of the building, so I walked over to it.
>
> It had a lovely peaked and gabled roof and was still relatively new. The wood was clean and pale. Inside was a stone statue. It was a woman, or goddess, holding a round fruit in one hand.

KURIHARA: 'A goddess holding a round fruit in one hand.' Anyone with deeper knowledge of Buddhism in Japan would have recognized that goddess. Kishimojin.

AUTHOR: Kishimojin? I think I might have heard the name before.

KURIHARA: She was introduced to Japan from India via China, of course. She was originally called Hariti and is considered a protector of children. Statues often have her holding a pomegranate in one hand and cradling a baby in her other arm.

AUTHOR: She watches over children?

KURIHARA: That's the belief. However, Uki only mentioned a fruit. Presumably, this statue was not holding a baby.

AUTHOR: Is it rare to see Kishimojin statues not holding a baby?

KURIHARA: Well, naturally there are all kinds of regional variations, but if the statue is holding the fruit, she should also be holding the baby. They go together.

So, why was the statue outside the watermill not cradling a baby? Looking at the watermill, I think I have an idea.

The statue was located near the alcove in the watermill.

I call it a hole, but it did not go all the way through the wall. Indeed, it was more of an alcove—a perfectly square depression in the centre of the wall, large enough that I felt if I curled up, I could fit my whole body inside.

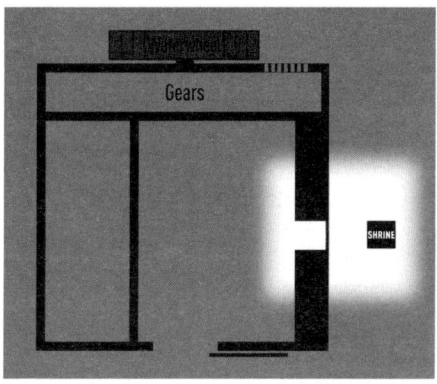

KURIHARA: I think that alcove was made to hold a baby.
AUTHOR: To hold a baby?
KURIHARA: Yes. That's what I've concluded from reading this file.

He pointed at File 5.

FILE 5   THE HOUSE WHERE IT HAPPENED

A woman's body was discovered over eighty years ago.

- Kenji Hirauchi bought a pre-owned house in Nagano Prefecture.
- Investigating the house's history revealed a terrible truth.

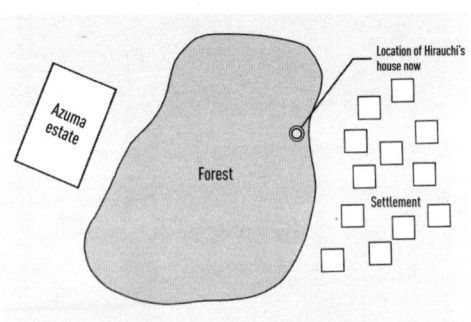

- The spot where the Hirauchi house now stands was once covered by forest.
- There was once a large house, the Azuma manor, on the west side of the woods.

What happened at the Azuma manor?

- The lord of the manor, Kiyochika, started an affair with the maid Okinu.
- When it was discovered, Kiyochika's wife went into a rage and ordered Okinu killed.
- Okinu escaped into the woods.

Where did Okinu go?

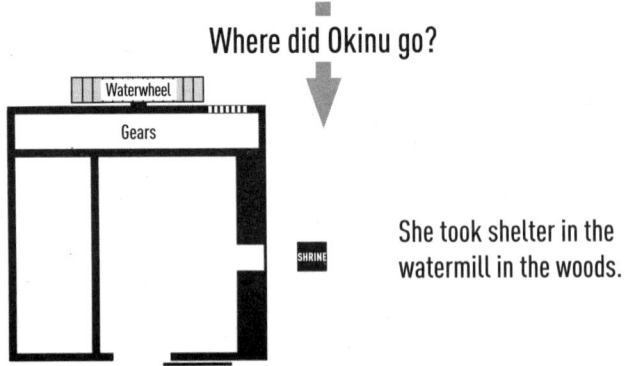

She took shelter in the watermill in the woods.

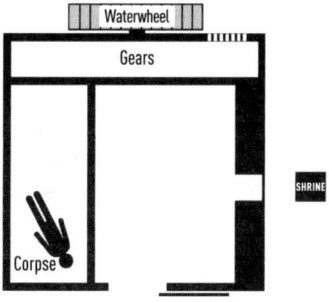

- However, with nothing to eat, Okinu starved to death in the watermill.
- Was the 'corpse of an egret' Uki Mizunashi saw actually Okinu?

Decades later

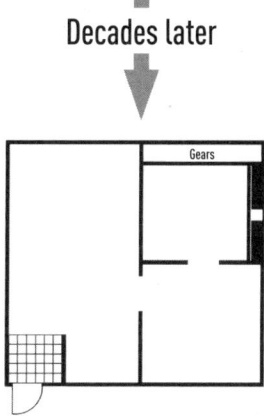

- Some person, for some reason, rebuilt the watermill into a windowless storehouse.

A few years later

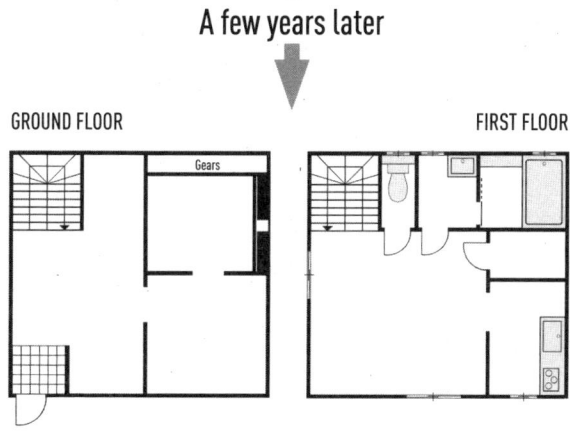

- An upper floor was added and the building was put up for sale.

KURIHARA: What if Okinu was pregnant with Kiyochika Azuma's baby…

AUTHOR: What?!

The idea had never occurred to me before. But it's certainly not out of the question. Kiyochika Azuma loved Okinu, and Okinu loved him. Their having a child together would be perfectly natural.

KURIHARA: Okinu would have had to leave the manor anyway, when the baby started to show. And with nowhere else to go, perhaps Kiyochika built some place just for her and the baby. A birthing house. I imagine he had his own private carpenters do the work.

But a simple birthing house wasn't enough. Okinu's child was also Kiyochika's, so there was a question of inheritance. If his wife found the baby, she'd have it killed. So, he would have built a hiding place into the house as well.

AUTHOR: The alcove…

KURIHARA: That's what I think. It's close to the statue of Kishimojin. He had the statue sculpted without a baby cradled in its arm so that one of Kishimojin's hands would be free to protect his own child. It shows just how much Kiyochika cared for Okinu and their baby.

And, eventually, Okinu did give birth in that house. The problem is what happened next. When Uki discovered the hut, the baby was gone and the egret, meaning Okinu, was dead. Where did the baby go?

There is another passage in Uki's memoir that stands out as important.

> That evening, after dining with Uncle and Auntie, I meant to ask them about the watermill. It was not their property, of course, but, as it was so close to their home, I thought they might know something about it.
>
> However, the moment I began to speak, the baby began to cry in the back room and Auntie rushed to check. It had been struggling from the operation, and the stump of its left arm was festering.
>
> Over the next few days, their time was taken up at the hospital, so in the end I was unable to ask about the watermill before I returned home.

KURIHARA: Uki was twenty-one at the time. I assume her uncle and aunt would have been at least middle aged. For them to have had a baby, in those days, is a little odd. Not impossible, but still…

I'm wondering if they found Okinu's baby and took her in.

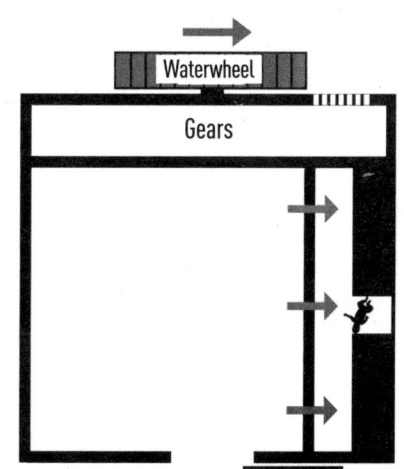

Okinu gave birth alone in that watermill. Her post-delivery recovery did not go well, and she realized she was going to die. She probably wanted to hide her baby to keep it safe before she died. She used the very last of her strength to turn the waterwheel and close the wall over the alcove.

But there was something she didn't notice.

Her baby must have reached out for her mother with her left arm, which got trapped and squeezed by the wall.

GODDESS

KURIHARA: After Okinu died, Uki Mizunashi's aunt and uncle discovered the hut and saved the baby.

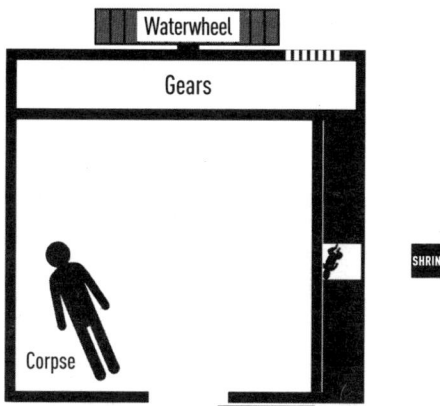

KURIHARA: The two went for a walk in the woods or something and stumbled on the watermill. Just like Uki, they discovered the trick with the waterwheel, then found Okinu's body and the baby. The baby's left arm must have been necrotic after being trapped by the wall for so long.

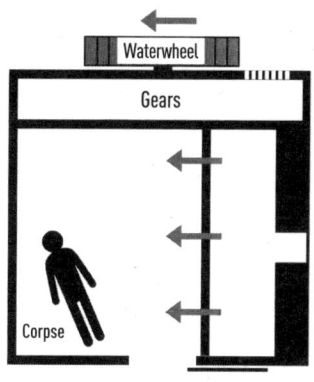

The two left the wall closing off the left room, to hide Okinu's body out of respect for the dead, then took the baby home. The baby's left arm had to be amputated due to the necrosis.

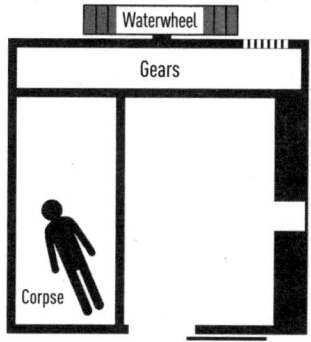

Then they adopted Okinu's baby as their own. They named the baby Yaeko.

> Yaeko had been brought up in a wealthy family. But when she was around eighteen, they told her something shocking.
>
> **AKEMI:** She'd been abandoned as a baby. They found her in some hut or something, out in the woods. So, those folks she thought were her birth parents had in fact adopted her. It's not that unusual a story, I know. But it shocked her, I suppose, and she ran away from home. She told me she still resented the both of them.

KURIHARA: That 'something shocking' was likely the secret of her birth, as I just described. Yaeko was overwhelmed and left the house.
AUTHOR: Why would she have resented the couple who raised her as their own?
KURIHARA: That, I don't know. There must have been some family issues.
AUTHOR: Hmm...

> **AKEMI:** So, after she left home, she came to Tokyo to look for work, but it was hard going with her handicap and all. She scraped by with part-time clerical work or some such, I think.
>
> But then came the big turning point.
> When Yaeko was twenty-one, she fell in love with the president of the company she was working for, and he proposed.

AKEMI: And just like that, she was the boss's wife. Isn't that something?

    She had a baby right away, and everything seemed grand… Or so she thought. But life has a way of bringing pitfalls, don't it?

    The 1965 securities slump drove the company out of business, and her husband killed himself. Left her just a pile of debt. So, the yakuza dragged her and her daughter off to the *okito*.

KURIHARA: After she left home, Yaeko got married, had a baby and was left with her husband's debt after his suicide. She was then imprisoned in the *okito*.

AKEMI: At the time, Yaeko had a regular customer. Man name of Hikura, he was. The son of some construction company big shot. He was head over heels for Yaeko. It seems he went and paid off her debt.

KURIHARA: And so she married the soon-to-be president of Hikura Homes, Masahiko Hikura. I honestly don't know if that was cause for her to be happy, or something regrettable.

    At the very least, she had found a place of stability and wealth for life… Or so she must have thought. But the story didn't end there.

Kurihara opened File 2.

FILE 2   NURTURING DARKNESS

Hikura Homes and poor design

- In 2020, a young man killed his family at their home.
- There were rumours that he did it because of the house's layout.

What was wrong with that layout?

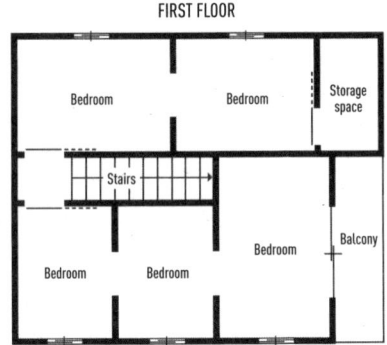

- Too many rooms
    - The elimination of typically necessary buffer spaces like hallways made the house feel cramped and uncomfortable.
- Too few doors
    - The residents had no privacy.
- The design of the house led to the family getting in each other's way all the time.
    - Led to friction and conflict between family members.

All these little issues built up...

Did they nourish the darker aspects of the boy's nature?

What did Hikura Homes do?

- Went to work on the media to keep the floor plans from circulating.

Why go so far?

- Hikura once suffered from a loss of consumer confidence and a drop in market share after baseless rumours about CEO Masahiko Hikura spread in the media.
- That helped rival Housemaker Misaki to pull ahead, and for the next ten years Hikura failed to regain ground.

What did Hikura learn from the experience?

- Develop a comprehensive media strategy.
- Use the media to hide negative reviews of their sub-par housing from the public eye.

Who is leading Hikura now?

President Akinaga Hikura — Father and Son? — Chairman Masahiko Hikura

IIMURA: Let's see… I think it was when I was still an apprentice… So, maybe the late 1980s?

There were some dark rumours going around about the Hikura president. That he'd abused some little girl when he was young. They turned out to be unfounded, in the end, but the TV and tabloids were all over it for a while, so everybody heard about it. These days I guess you'd say it 'went viral' or whatnot.

And rumour being so powerful, it even hit Hikura's market share. There, I have to admit, I feel a little bad for them.

Then along came Housemaker Misaki, their biggest local rival, to take advantage of it all and expand their share of the market. It took Hikura over ten years to regain all that lost ground.

And I guess the lesson they took from that was, the truth is powerless against the media.

KURIHARA: In the late 1980s, Hikura Homes lost consumer confidence and market share as a result of misinformation, which of course caused financial trouble. Then-president Masahiko Hikura struggled to turn the company's fortunes around, and he finally struck on the unorthodox idea of using religion.

Japan was in the middle of a huge spiritualism boom, and fringe cults were popping up everywhere.

It's hard to believe now, but there was a time when Shoko Asahara, the founder of the Aum Shinrikyo cult, was a guest on TV variety shows. Then, in 1995, Aum Shinrikyo committed their terrorist gas attack in Tokyo and everything changed. To that point, though, most people simply thought of cults as a cool, if slightly suspicious, subculture phenomenon that was popular with progressive young people.

I think Hikura founded a cult as a secret side business to develop a new customer base.

AUTHOR: Are you serious?! Hikura founded the Rebirth Congregation?

KURIHARA: Looking at it that way connects a lot of the dots.

> Before long, someone took the stage. However, it was not the leader of the cult, the Holy Mother. It was a suited man in his mid-forties.
>
> Deep frown lines in his brow, sunken eyes and a prominent aquiline nose. I had seen that face before. It was Masahiko Hikura, the president of one of the region's largest construction companies, Hikura Homes.
>
> I had heard rumours that the Hikura Homes president had some important role in the Rebirth Congregation cult and was supporting it financially.

KURIHARA: Don't let this mislead you. I can't picture such a large, well-organized cult allowing a mere financial donor to take the stage and preach to their believers in place of their spiritual leader. It's hardly in keeping with the whole religious front.

How could Hikura get away with something so presumptuous? Well, it wouldn't be presumptuous at all if he were actually the founder.

AUTHOR: That does make sense…

KURIHARA: So, when Hikura founded this cult, he installed his own wife, Yaeko, as the 'leader'. He was probably inspired by Japan's own history, because in ancient times people with physical disabilities were often revered as divine *kami*.

AUTHOR: I saw that mentioned in the article, but is that true?

KURIHARA: It is. There are records and images all over Japan of *kami* with one eye, one arm or one leg. Why? Many folklorists have come to the conclusion that it was because children born with such disabilities were often placed into this spiritual role.

AUTHOR: I never knew…

KURIHARA: There is even evidence that good-luck Fukusuke dolls, with their unusual proportions, originated in an old folk belief that children born with dwarfism would bring prosperity to their family. It does seem that people considered unusual bodies to have mystical powers.

And that is why he felt Yaeko was so suited to the role of Holy Mother, the *kami* in his cult.

> I had heard that the Holy Mother was in her fifties, but she looked to be no older than in her early forties. Her features were finely sculpted, her long hair was black and lustrous, and her skin was smooth and clear.
>
> Her right leg was missing below the hip, while the left leg she used to balance herself on her simple stool was long and slim. She was utterly motionless. She wore only a simple white cloth wrap, leaving her barely covered. I don't know if I would call the vision she presented 'sacred', but she had an unusual beauty that drew the eye like a magnet.

KURIHARA: Hikura built the whole Rebirth Congregation around her body and her life history.

A cult that seeks to save children born out of extramarital affairs by having them sleep in the leader's 'womb'... I get the sense that Hikura should have been a novelist or artist rather than a businessman.

AUTHOR: I wonder how Yaeko herself felt at being pushed into playing the figurehead.

KURIHARA: I have no idea. But since Hikura paid off her debt, I doubt she had much choice in the matter. She could only sit in that shrine and say the lines she was given.

> You know my story. I was born a child of sin. I lost my left arm to my mother's sin. I lost my right leg to save a child of sin. With what is left of this body, I wish only to save you and your own children. Now, it is time for rebirth. Over and over again.

KURIHARA: The sinful mother in her story must be Okinu. She was a maid in a noble manor, and she had an affair with the married lord of the manor. And the Holy Mother was born of that affair. And, in fact, she had lost her arm to her mother's carelessness.

> Finally, I suppose I should add that the Rebirth Congregation broke up in 1999, and the Hall of Rebirth was torn down the following year.

KURIHARA: The cult had managed to attract a significant membership, but did not last very long, for a number of reasons.

The Aum Shinrikyo terrorist attack turned public opinion against cults in general. And more believers, not just Mr Kasahara, probably started to suspect fraud.

Then, in the late 1990s, Japan went into a recession, and there were simply fewer people able to pay for such construction work.

But the biggest reason was that Hikura Homes didn't need the Rebirth Congregation anymore.

AUTHOR: Why not?

KURIHARA: Look back at File 2.

> **IIMURA:** And rumour being so powerful, it even hit Hikura's market share. There, I have to admit, I feel a little bad for them.
>
> Then along came Housemaker Misaki, their biggest local rival, to take advantage of it all and expand their share of the market. It took Hikura over ten years to regain all that lost ground.

KURIHARA: It took Hikura over ten years to regain all the ground. In other words, they did, eventually, regain that ground. How did they do it? That's in File 1.

30TH JANUARY 1990 | MORNING EDITION

A fatal accident occurred yesterday, 29th January, around 4 p.m. in Takaoka, Toyama Prefecture. The victim was local elementary-school student Yunosuke Kasuga (8). The boy was walking along the main street when he was hit by a truck backing out of a work site. The truck was loaded with construction materials. The driver reportedly said, 'It was hard to see, and I just didn't notice the boy.' The man is an employee of Housemaker Misaki and…

KURIHARA: An employee ran over and killed a child in front of a customer's property. Such a serious accident was big news. Housemaker Misaki's image must have taken a serious hit, and Misaki was Hikura Homes' primary rival in the Chubu region.

AUTHOR: When their rival lost their footing, Hikura Homes had an opportunity to restore its market share.

KURIHARA: The rumours against the president had already faded from the public consciousness, and Hikura Homes had learnt from that experience how to use the media. It was only a matter of time before they retook the lead.

With their primary business back in the ascendancy, the value of the Rebirth Congregation to the company started to decrease, and soon they broke it up.

With the cult dissolved, then, what of the Holy Mother?

Kurihara picked up File 4.

FILE 4   THE MOUSETRAP HOUSE

Why did Mitsuko's grandmother fall down the stairs?

- When Shiori Hayasaka was a child, she went to stay with her friend Mitsuko.
- Mitsuko was the Hikura Homes president's daughter.

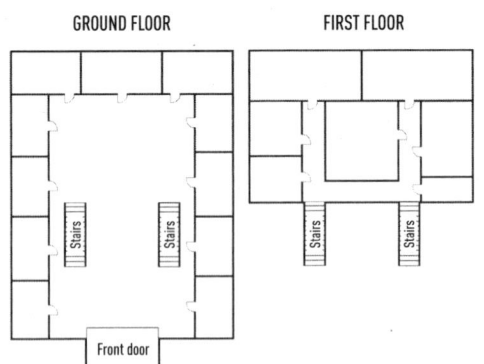

The house was a mansion that Mitsuko's father built just for her grandmother.

Mitsuko had a large bookcase in her room.

Hayasaka opened it up and peeked inside while Mitsuko was using the toilet. For some reason, the manga that they had bonded over weren't inside, which Hayasaka found odd. That evening, while Mitsuko was sleeping, she tried to look inside again, but the door was locked.

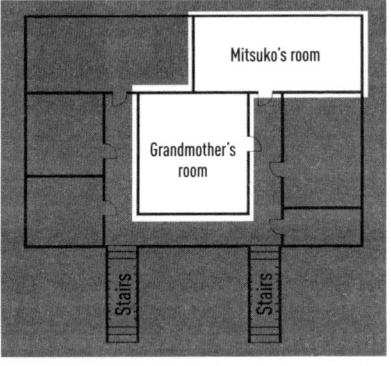

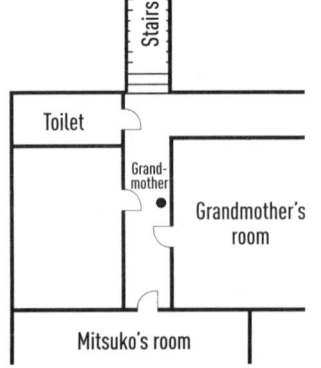

The next morning, when Hayasaka was on her way to the toilet, she found Mitsuko's grandmother in the hallway. The old lady was struggling to walk, supporting herself against the wall with one hand. Hayasaka offered to help, but she refused and sent the girl on ahead to the toilet.

When Hayasaka was washing her hands, she heard Mitsuko's grandmother fall down the stairs.

Hayasaka's Theory

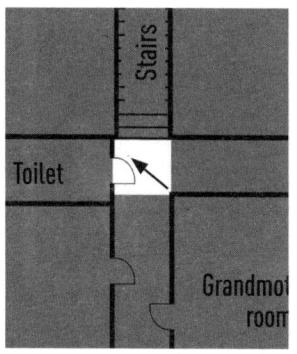

There is nothing for anyone standing at the top of the stairs to hold on to.

Mitsuko's grandmother lost her balance and tumbled down the stairs.

Why?

Mitsuko took her grandmother's 'walking stick' and hid it in her bookcase late that night.

Conclusion

- The Hikura president built the house specifically to kill the old woman, who held significant power in the company and so was an obstacle in some way.
- The area at the top of the stairs was intentionally designed to be dangerous.
- However, since Mitsuko's grandmother used a walking stick, she had managed to avoid the trap.

Mitsuko sets off the trap

- Most likely, her father, the company president, encouraged her to hide the walking stick.
  - Did the president make his own daughter accomplice to a crime?
- Hayasaka believed that she was invited to sleep over to provide Mitsuko with an alibi.

GRANDMOTHER

KURIHARA: Based on Shiori Hayasaka's age, I think this must have happened in 2001.
That's about two years after the cult disbanded.

HAYASAKA: When Mitsuko opened the door, a lovely, sweet fragrance came wafting out. I think Grandmother Hikura must have been burning incense. Inside, the room was decorated with beautiful furniture and paintings, and her grandmother sat in a chair reading. She seemed far too young and beautiful to be called 'Grandmother,' though.

She was wearing a long skirt that hung to the floor, hiding her legs completely, and was wrapped in a flower-patterned cardigan. She had long white gloves on her hands.

KURIHARA: That elegant grandmother that Hayasaka met at Mitsuko's house… She was wearing a skirt long enough to hide her legs and long white gloves, even in her own room. Clearly, to hide her hands. Why? Could it be that she had a prosthetic arm and leg?

AUTHOR: So, you think Mitsuko's grandmother was the Holy Mother?

KURIHARA: Masahiko Hikura and Yaeko had a son, Akinaga. Akinaga is now president of Hikura Homes. His daughter is Mitsuko. So, yes, it all connects. Yaeko was Mitsuko's grandmother.

The question is, what exactly was Yaeko's standing within the Hikura family?

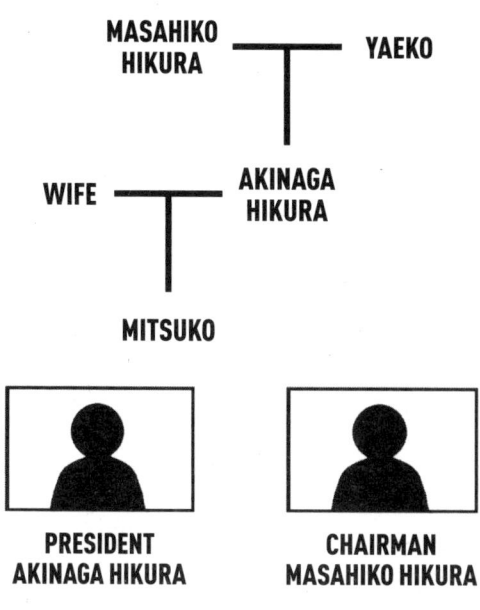

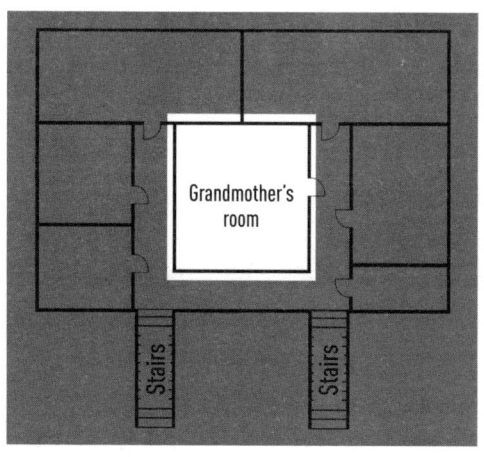

KURIHARA: From the floor plan, it's clear that Yaeko's room did not have any outside walls. Meaning, of course, it had no windows.

This was all just a few years after the Aum Shinrikyo attack, and cults were targets for public ire. At that point, it would have been very bad for the Hikura reputation if the fact they had a former cult leader in the family became public knowledge. Even so, Akinaga couldn't erase her completely.

So, they hid her from the eyes of the world within this lavishly decorated prison. This room's design reveals everything about her position.

AUTHOR: How cruel.

KURIHARA: I'm sure Yaeko must have simply wanted to live out her days in peace. But that was not enough for the family. After Yaeko fell to her death, Hayasaka came up with her theory.

> Mitsuko sneaked into her grandmother's room in the middle of the night, took the old lady's walking stick and hid it in the bookcase. The next morning, when her grandmother woke up to go to the toilet, she looked for her stick but couldn't find it.
>
> So, what did she do? The toilet was close, so perhaps she thought she could make it.

KURIHARA: It's an excellent idea, but I think there's one small error. It wasn't a 'stick' that Mitsuko hid in her bookcase: it was a prosthesis.

AUTHOR: Ah, of course.

KURIHARA: So, that morning Yaeko woke needing the toilet, and went to put on her prosthetics, but, for some reason, the leg was missing.

She had little choice but to try to get to the toilet on one leg.

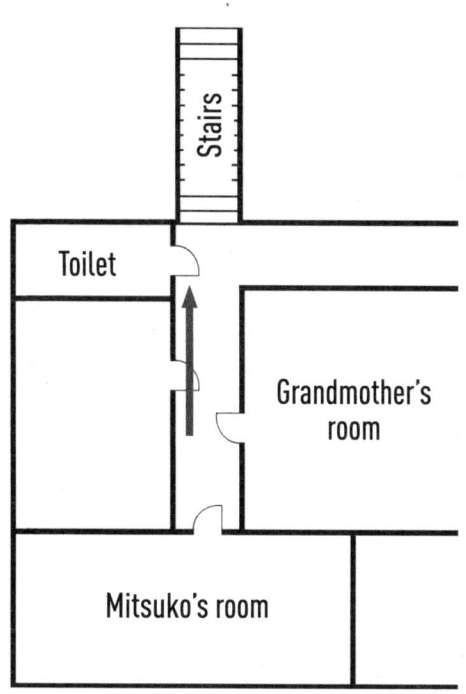

KURIHARA: If she'd walked along the left wall of the corridor, she wouldn't have needed to cross that dangerous area at the top of the stairs, but she walked along the right side. She had to.

That was because her left arm was a prosthesis. She was almost certainly not confident about keeping her balance on one leg while supporting herself against the wall with a prosthetic arm. And, well, we already know the rest.

AUTHOR: So, it's true? Akinaga used his own daughter to eliminate Yaeko, who he saw as a burden?

KURIHARA: I don't want to believe it, but yes. Maybe trying to keep a family business successful breeds this kind of darkness.

HYPOTHESIS

KURIHARA: I think that explains most of it. Any questions?
AUTHOR: Well, there is something about the Hirauchi house…

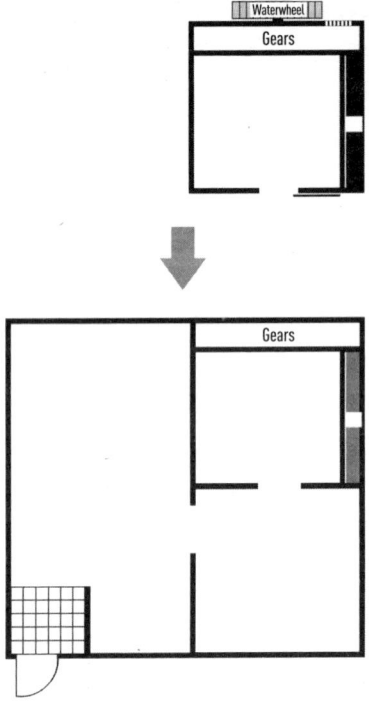

AUTHOR: I agree that it was clearly built over the old watermill. But who did that, and for what reason?
KURIHARA: I think Hikura Homes constructed the house as some kind of tourist destination for the cult members. 'Come and see where the Holy Mother was born.' The watermill itself was probably too small, so they expanded it to fit more people in.

WOMAN: Oh, it must have been twenty years ago or so. They did a lot of work. The house has two floors, right? When we moved in, it only had one. I remember thinking when they were all finished, 'Oh, they doubled it!'

KURIHARA: But then, the cult probably dissolved before they got the house up and running. With no other use for it, Hikura added toilets, a kitchen and a bath, then put it up for sale as a house. Hikura really was always focused on business, after all.

After that, Kurihara treated me to dinner, and I left his apartment. It was already dark out.

I mulled over all Kurihara's deductions on the walk to the station. I found myself more and more impressed at how he had put together such a consistent story just by reading the files.

But there were still things that bothered me.

I didn't think Kurihara was wrong. But I felt like there was something he was missing. Something important.

I got to the station, then stepped into a café outside the ticket gates and decided to read back through the files again. When I did, I found one small contradiction that I hadn't noticed before.

Why? What could explain it? I was sure my notes were accurate… After thinking about it for a moment, I came up with a new theory.

I took another look at all the files all together, reconsidering them in the light of that new idea. When I did, I was surprised at how puzzles I had thought already solved took on a different aspect, and a new story began to emerge.

SON

28th February 2023　　　　　　　　　　MEGURO, TOKYO

I sat waiting in a private room at a restaurant. I was going to speak to someone who most likely knew the most important truth of all. Someone who could explain this entire chain of events.

Finally, the door opened, and he stepped inside. He wore a thick black jumper and black trousers. Completely unlike the clothes he'd worn the last time we'd met, of course.

Mitsuru Nishiharu… The only son of Akemi Nishiharu, former prisoner in the *okito*.

AUTHOR: I'm sorry for calling you out like this.
MITSURU: Not at all. The shop is closed today. Yesterday, too.
AUTHOR: It is? I thought you were open every day.
MITSURU: That's always been our policy, yes, but Ma's been feeling unwell lately, so we've had to shut our doors for a few days. Our customers only come to see Ma, anyway.
AUTHOR: But you're an excellent cook, yourself. Surely some of them must come for the food, right?
MITSURU: Not at all. I don't know what Ma told you, but I'm not much of a cook, not really.

I've never had any training. I just learnt some recipes from cookbooks. I'm thinking of closing the shop entirely, actually. I'm worried about Ma's health.

AUTHOR: Permanently?

MITSURU: Yes. Of course, once I'm finished there, I can't imagine finding another job at my age.

Mitsuru smiled faintly.

I hadn't noticed it when I'd visited his shop, but there was grey mixed into the black of his hair, and his face was deeply lined.

MITSURU: So. What was it you wanted to talk to me about?

AUTHOR: Ah, yes, right. There's actually something I'd like you to look at first. It's a file I compiled from the interview with your mother. I imagine you heard most of it that day, but still, if you wouldn't mind reading through it?

Mitsuru flipped through File 10, reading it with no visible reaction.

AUTHOR: Well, what do you think? Is there anything in there that bothers you? Anything that's flat out wrong?

MITSURU: What about you? If you're asking me, then there must be something that strikes you as off.

AUTHOR: Yes. It's this part right here.

> **AKEMI:** Well, let's see, you know we used to talk about our pasts and such when the kids weren't around. She'd had quite a life.

AUTHOR: 'When the kids weren't around.' That's what your mother said.

But that can't be right. The *okito* only let its female prisoners leave if they swapped children with a neighbour.

If you went out, then you would have been with Yaeko. And, if Yaeko's daughter was out, then she would have been with Akemi.

So, when could your mother and Yaeko have been alone long enough for meaningful conversation?

MITSURU: Maybe it was when we were in the toilet or the bath…

AUTHOR: I can't imagine you both going to the toilet at the same time and staying there for very long all that often. The same goes for baths. Your mother even said so.

WHEN A WANTS TO GO OUT

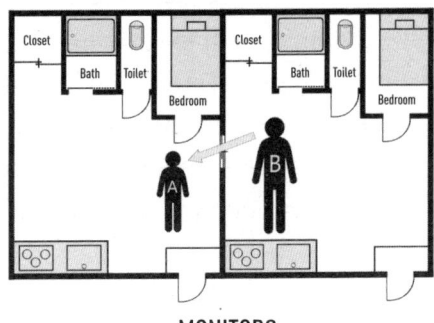

MONITORS

GOES OUT

WHEN B WANTS TO GO OUT

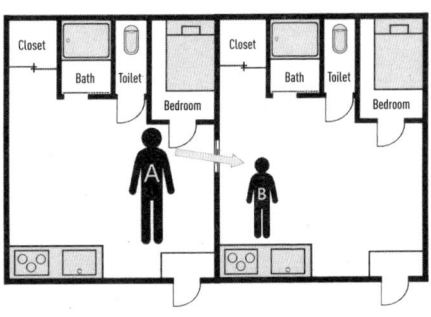

MONITORS

GOES OUT

> **AKEMI:** He's turned out good enough. Up to middle school, he couldn't even take a bath alone.

AUTHOR: You left the *okito* when you were nine years old. So, back then, you were still taking baths with your mother.

MITSURU: Ah, right.

AUTHOR: So, what were you and Yaeko's daughter doing when your mothers were talking? I considered all kinds of possibilities and found one that I think explains it. If I'm wrong, I do hope you'll forgive me. The one being prostituted at the *okito* wasn't Akemi, was it? It was you.

Mitsuru sat quietly for a moment, his expression pained. He began sniffing and clearing his throat. Finally, in a quiet voice, he began to speak.

MITSURU: Don't think badly of Ma.

THE LIE

The next day, I headed to that apartment in Umegaoka once again.

Kurihara poured tea as we spoke.

KURIHARA: I see. So, the *okito* was a brothel serving paedophiles.

> **AKEMI:** Customers always came late at night. And they always came in big, expensive cars. That *okito* only served rich folks. Each night cost about a hundred thousand yen.

AUTHOR: That price, a hundred thousand, is much more than a normal brothel would charge, even by today's standards. Back then, it would have been even more excessive. So, the customers must have had a serious reason to pay so much.

The fact that they only came late at night was not only to hide that they were paying for sex, but also because they would have been in serious trouble if anyone learnt they were buying children for the night.

> The women were not normally allowed to leave their rooms at the *okito*. If they needed to go out for short periods, they were allowed to, but under one condition: they had to swap children with one of the other mothers.

AUTHOR: On the face of it, it doesn't seem like there would be any benefit to the gangs from letting their prisoners leave the *okito*, even for short periods. So, why did they allow it? I think it must have been a bare minimum of concern for the children's physical and mental condition. Basically, they were keeping their stock healthy.

KURIHARA: But why did Akemi lie about it?

AUTHOR: Mitsuru explained that, too.

'Don't think badly of Ma. If she'd refused the yakuza, they'd have killed us both. We didn't have any choice...

'Ma acts bright and cheerful for customers, but that's not at all what she's really like. Every night when it's just the two of us, she still weeps and apologizes. Over and over. "Mitsuru, I'm so sorry about it all. Forgive me for being such a terrible mother." Even after all these years.

'I hope you'll forgive her for lying to you at that interview. I think that was for my sake. She's worried that people will look at me differently if they find out I was forced into child prostitution.'

Mitsuru also told me the truth about the traffic accident.

AUTHOR: It seems that when Mitsuru and Yaeko went to town and Mitsuru ran out into traffic, it was actually on purpose. Being forced to do what he did every night was just too much. He told me he was trying to kill himself.
KURIHARA: I see...
AUTHOR: And, given that the *okito* they were in was for child prostitution, some of Akemi's other words take on a different meaning.

> **AKEMI:** At the time, Yaeko had a regular customer. Man name of Hikura, he was. The son of some construction company big shot. He was head over heels for Yaeko. It seems he went and paid off her debt. Not out of the goodness of his heart, of course. He took them both off somewhere, mother and daughter.

KURIHARA: So, the one Masahiko Hikura wanted wasn't Yaeko, it was her daughter.
AUTHOR: Yaeko's daughter was eleven at the time. I looked it up on the net, and Hikura is now seventy. That would make him twenty back when he took Yaeko and her daughter away from the *okito*. A nine-year age difference between him and the girl. Not terribly odd in married couples. Not when both parties are adults, anyway.

I imagine that as soon as Yaeko's daughter came of age, he married her openly.

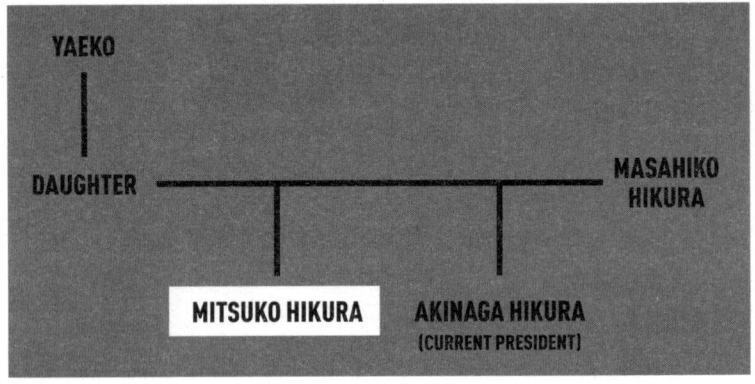

AUTHOR: This Mitsuko in File 4 is most likely the daughter of Masahiko Hikura and Yaeko's daughter. That would make the current president, Akinaga, Mitsuko's brother.

KURIHARA: So, it changes nothing about Yaeko being Mitsuko's grandmother.

AUTHOR: Right. And if we accept all this, those rumours that went around in the 1980s about the Hikura Homes president abusing a girl when he was young weren't unfounded after all.

> **IIMURA:** Let's see… I think it was when I was still an apprentice… So, maybe the late 1980s? There were some dark rumours going around about the Hikura president. That he'd abused some little girl when he was young.

AUTHOR: The facts that he had once used child prostitutes, and had gone on to take one as his wife, leaked somehow.

KURIHARA: That would certainly make setting up his wife's mother as a cult leader a risky move by Hikura.

AUTHOR: It would, yes. But… setting aside the rumour stuff, I still think there's something odd about a business founding a cult for profit.

KURIHARA: You do?

AUTHOR: Oh, I mean, it's not that I'm saying you're wrong, of course. I don't deny the fact that Hikura was running the Rebirth Congregation. It's just… I feel that even if he was one of the executives or whatever, he wasn't the one in charge.

KURIHARA: Meaning there was someone else behind it?

AUTHOR: Right. This is still just supposition, but… I think it was his wife, meaning Yaeko's daughter, who really set up the cult.

KURIHARA: Why do you think that?

AUTHOR: You should read this one again.

I handed him File 4.

> **HAYASAKA:** She was wearing a long skirt that hung to the floor, hiding her legs completely, and was wrapped in a flower-patterned cardigan. She had long white gloves on her hands.

AUTHOR: Yaeko covered her prosthetic limbs with a long skirt and gloves, even in the house. And then there was this…

> **HAYASAKA:** She had her back to me, facing the stairs, her right hand resting on the wall. She was trying to walk, but looked as if she might fall over at any moment. I think she must have had a problem with her legs.

> She was still wearing that skirt, so long it dragged on the floor. I was worried that it might trip her up, so I rushed over to help.
>
> She tried to wave me off and said, 'I'm fine. The toilet is just there.' But I couldn't just leave her like that, so I told her that's where I was going as well, so we should go together. I tried to lend her my shoulder to lean on, but she insisted. 'Never you mind me. Go on ahead. Wouldn't want you to wet your pants!'

AUTHOR: Ms Hayasaka never realized that Yaeko was missing her left arm and wore a prosthetic. Which meant she must still have been wearing her long gloves over that arm.

Even late at night, with her prosthetic leg missing and needing to go to the toilet, she still made sure to hide her missing limbs. In her own home. I can't help but think she felt ashamed of her own body.

AKEMI: I didn't even notice it at first, you know, but Yaeko was missing her left arm. She said she'd lost it in an accident just after she was born.

AUTHOR: From what Akemi said, it even took her a while to notice Yaeko's missing arm. I think that was intentional. Yaeko must have tried hard to hide the fact, such was her shame.

> Her right leg was missing below the hip, while the left leg she used to balance herself on her simple stool was long and slim. She was utterly motionless. She wore only a simple white cloth wrap, leaving her barely covered.

AUTHOR: And if that were the case, it must have been terribly difficult for her to expose herself like that to all those strangers.

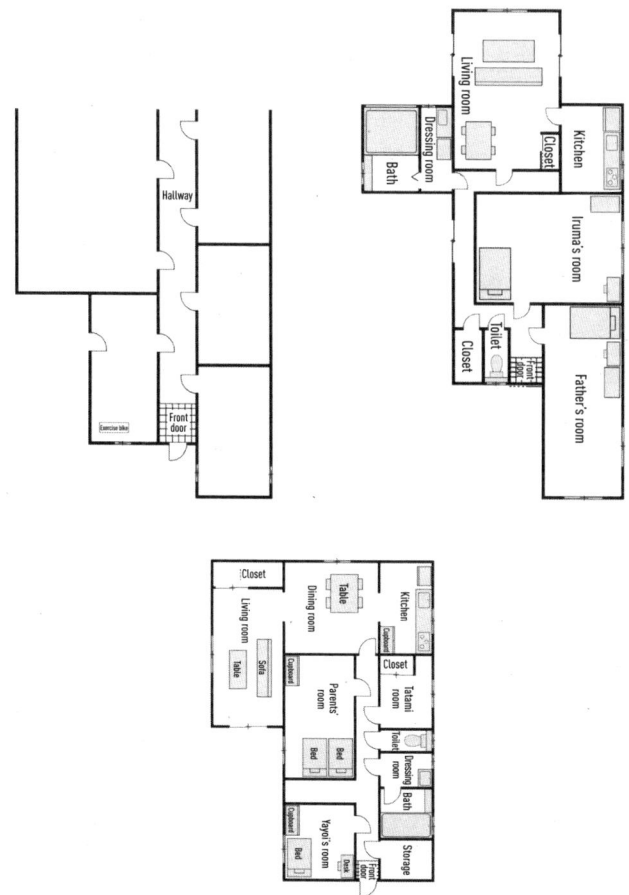

AUTHOR: And then they went on to build houses in the shape of her body all over the country… Almost like intentional public humiliation.

So, I had an idea. What if the real point of the Rebirth Congregation was to torment Yaeko, on a massive scale?

REVENGE

AUTHOR: Mitsuru says he doesn't resent his mother for what happened, but I doubt everyone could be as forgiving as he is.

Yaeko's daughter might have held a grudge against her own mother for being forced into sexual slavery. And she created the Rebirth Congregation to get revenge. Or, rather, she had her husband, Masahiko Hikura, create it.

KURIHARA: But why do you think he would have agreed to use company resources on a plan driven by something so personal and emotional as revenge?

AUTHOR: I don't think he was in any position to refuse her. She knew better than anyone that he had a history of paedophilia.

I doubt Yaeko felt able to say no, either. Her guilt for what her daughter had gone through meant she could only do what she was told.

KURIHARA: So, her daughter was in complete control of them both.

Kurihara took a slow, thoughtful sip of tea.

KURIHARA: Based on what you just brought me, I feel even more confident about another idea I had.

AUTHOR: Which is?

KURIHARA: After we last spoke, I kept thinking about why Yaeko would have felt such animosity towards her foster family.

> **AKEMI:** She'd been abandoned as a baby. They found her in some hut or something, out in the woods. So, those folks she thought were her birth parents had in fact

> adopted her. It's not that unusual a story, I know. But it shocked her, I suppose, and she ran away from home. She told me she still resented the both of them.

KURIHARA: I'm sure it would be a shock to anyone to suddenly learn they were adopted like that. But to run away from home and hold a grudge against your family for years? That seems excessive.

I think they might have told her more. Everything. Not just that she was adopted. And that thought reminded me of something in your files.

Did you bring File 3 with you?

AUTHOR: Yes, I brought them all.

> It was a snow-white bird.
> A female egret lay dead on the floor. Some terrible person must have trapped it in there as a cruel prank. Unable to get out, it had starved to death. Judging by its condition, it must have been in that room for some time. Its feathers were falling out, the tip of one of its wings was missing, its flesh was rotting, and a pool of scarlet and black fluid spread out around it.

KURIHARA: This part here: 'the tip of one of its wings was missing'. It was so brief I didn't pay it much mind. But, on reconsideration, it's odd, isn't it?

Your editor friend surmised this egret was a metaphor for a woman's corpse. I agree. If we pursue the metaphor further, the 'missing wing tip' actually refers to an amputated hand.

AUTHOR: Oh, good catch.

KURIHARA: When Uki Mizunashi discovered Okinu's body, it was missing one hand. Why? I think there's a hint in this section here.

> That evening, after dining with Uncle and Auntie, I meant to ask them about the watermill. It was not their property, of course, but, as it was so close to their home, I thought they might know something about it.
>
> However, the moment I began to speak, the baby began to cry in the back room and Auntie rushed to check. It had been struggling from the operation, and the stump of its left arm was festering.

KURIHARA: They didn't tell Uki that they had discovered the baby in the watermill. Why did they keep that a secret?
AUTHOR: Hmm...
KURIHARA: I think maybe they felt guilty about something related to the baby.
AUTHOR: Why would they feel guilty?
KURIHARA: Say, for example, when her aunt and uncle found the watermill, Okinu was still alive.
AUTHOR: What?
KURIHARA: She had just delivered her baby, and, clutching it in her arms, she begged them for help. So, what did they do?
AUTHOR: You don't mean...
KURIHARA: Uki's story doesn't mention the couple having any other children. Perhaps they wanted children but couldn't have their own. Then they found this woman on the verge of death, clutching a baby... I can imagine a certain dark temptation.

A chilling image rose in my mind.

Uki's aunt reaching out to take the baby. Okinu holding on to her daughter with the last of her strength. Desperately clutching the child's left arm…The baby screaming. The uncle taking up some bladed tool—say, a woodcutter's axe… and bringing it down on Okinu's wrist. When it was over, they turned the waterwheel, sealing Okinu in that hidden room before leaving her behind.

KURIHARA: So, the question is: why did the baby's arm have to be amputated? Perhaps it was because her mother had gripped too tightly, cutting off the blood for too long.

PLACE OF REST

KURIHARA: All of which makes me see that house in a different light.

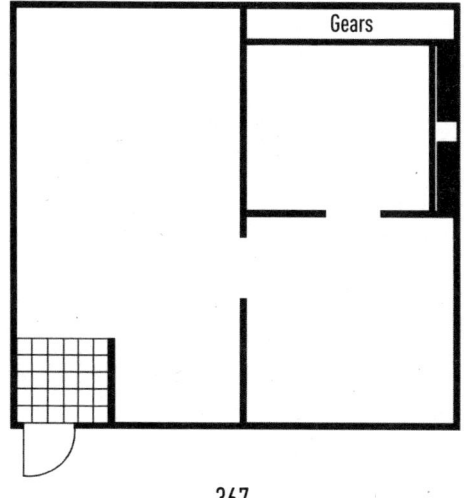

KURIHARA: Why did they build it around the watermill?

I told you that I thought Hikura had intended it to be some kind of destination for Rebirth Congregation members. But I may have been wrong about that. Perhaps it was the Holy Mother who wanted the house built. That's what I think now. Look at the floor plan again.

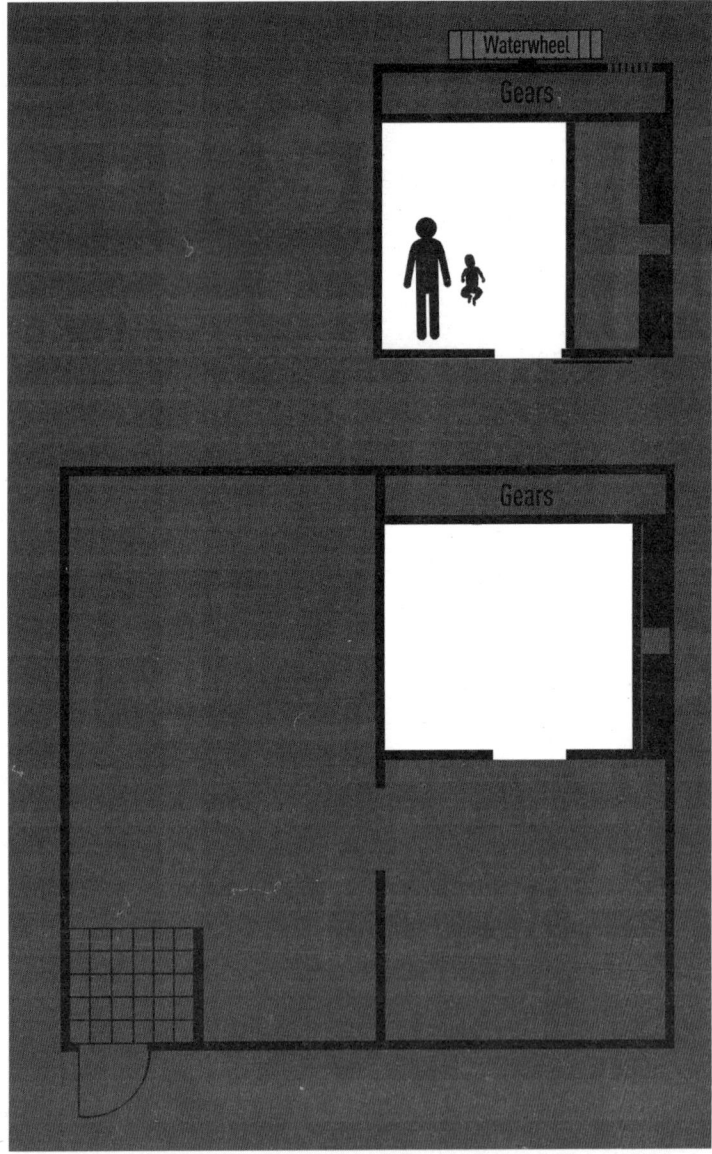

KURIHARA: The newly built part seems to wrap around and protect the room where Okinu died. Now, let's think about how Yaeko was feeling. I'm sure she was simply exhausted.

AUTHOR: By serving the cult?

KURIHARA: By her whole life. It was chaos from the start. First, her trusted parents revealed the truth of her birth and her lost arm, causing her to run away from home, despite all the difficulty she knew she would face, living with her disability.

Then came her marriage, her daughter's birth, her husband's suicide, her imprisonment in that brothel deep in the mountains, where her daughter was raped nightly, and, eventually, the loss of her leg in a car accident…

After that, her daughter was essentially bought by some company president's son. Yaeko finally had a stable position and financial security, but I doubt she ever felt anything like happiness. I'm sure Yaeko struggled with guilt over what happened to her daughter every day of her life. And then came the Rebirth Congregation, on top of it all. Her daughter's revenge.

She was installed as the cult's leader, forced to show off the body she was so ashamed of, openly abused as a fraud. But she endured it all, because of what she felt she owed her daughter.

In the end, she was taken away and shut away in a room with no windows, like some piece of unwanted furniture. How must she have felt then?

AUTHOR: I can't begin to imagine…

KURIHARA: Yaeko was simply tired of living. I think her only wish was to go back to her mother.

> **WOMAN:** Oh, it must have been twenty years ago or so. They did a lot of work. The house has two floors, right?

When we moved in, it only had one. I remember thinking when they were all finished, 'Oh, they doubled it!'

If that was the case, the building wouldn't have had any amenities like a kitchen, a toilet or a bath before then. It wouldn't have been fit to live in.

KURIHARA: This was the spot where Yaeko's mother had once held her in her arms. Yaeko had it built up like a fortress against the outside world, somewhere she could finally find some peace, in the dark, away from prying eyes, and go to sleep. I think this house was built as a place for her suicide.

· · ·

On a bright spring day, I arrived by train at the tiny station of Takasaki City in Gunma Prefecture.

It was two months after my last visit to Kurihara's apartment, where we had talked about this story. The winter had passed, and a warm breeze was blowing.

I took a bus from the station for about twenty minutes, arriving eventually at a small elderly care home on the outskirts of town.

I waited in front of the entrance for two hours before, at last, a woman came out to meet me. Her hair was pulled back in a bun, and she wore a thin cardigan over her uniform. When I greeted her, she gave me a little bow.

The name tag at her breast read Mitsuko Hikura.

CULPRIT

After talking to Kurihara, I had considered all the mysteries of the eleven linked files solved. But then, reading back through them, one nagging question started to bother me.

Who actually killed Yaeko?

Kurihara and Shiori Hayasaka both believed that Mitsuko's father had tempted her into being his accomplice. But there was one part of that theory that bothered me.

Would a thirteen-year-old girl actually agree to help kill someone just because a parent told her to? I found myself desperate to talk to the woman herself and find out what had really happened.

I learnt that on graduating from high school, Mitsuko Hikura had broken ties with her family to live on her own. From that point on, she had zero contact with either her family or the company. It took me a lot of time and effort to track her down. I cast my net wide and called in favours, and I finally found her working as a carer for the elderly. I had the feeling that her chosen career held deep significance.

I emailed to arrange an interview, but she was wary. Unsurprisingly, she refused at first, but after a few rounds of emails, I flat out told her that I wanted to know the real reason that Yaeko died. She told me that she would speak to me during her work break if I came to the home.

MITSUKO: I'm sorry I'm late. I had trouble fitting my break in today.

AUTHOR: Not at all. I'm sorry for interrupting you when you're so busy.

MITSUKO: Shall we talk over there?

She pointed towards a small playground across the street from the facility. It was the middle of a weekday, so there were no children to be seen. We crossed the street and sat on a peeling park bench. I noticed a large bruise on her arm, and she saw me looking.

MITSUKO: That happened this morning. A dementia patient grabbed my arm and squeezed the hell out of it.

AUTHOR: Is it all right? Shouldn't you put a dressing on it or something?

MITSUKO: Stuff like this is a daily occurrence in my work. If I stopped to bandage every little bump, I'd be walking around like a mummy.

Mitsuko laughed at the image.

As the daughter of a wealthy family like the Hikuras, she should want for nothing. Why would she throw all that away and choose such difficult, unglamorous work?

THE FINAL PIECE

MITSUKO: I think I first noticed how odd my home life was when I entered primary school. When my friends talked about 'family', it was like the word had a different meaning from what I knew of my own. At the time, I lived in a huge house in Nagano Prefecture. It was me, my father, mother and grandmother, along with my brother Akinaga and a whole staff of servants.

Father doted on Akinaga, took him on work trips and all kinds of places. My brother was always clever, and, he being the oldest, I suppose Father wanted him to get experience, so he'd be able to take over the business someday. I was a girl, and not particularly bright, so I was mostly just… there. Like part of the background.

My mother spent all her time locked up in her room, not talking to anyone. I always found her so beautiful, but she was somehow unapproachable. So, the only one in the family that I could be close to was my grandmother.

I called her Granny Yaeko. Whenever I went to her room, she'd say, 'What now, Mitsuko?' and then she and I would play for hours.

I'm sure you already know, but Granny Yaeko had a prosthetic arm, so she couldn't do anything very complicated. Still, we used to sit and giggle over simple games and things you could do one handed. Drawing, or batting balloons about, you know. It was the only pleasure I had in that house.

Mitsuko stared into the distance and sighed quietly.

MITSUKO: I was basically an outcast in my own family, but sometimes Father would come and talk to me, like he was coaxing a cat with a treat. Each time he would have some expensive present for me and would come in close with a big grin. And every time, he would ask me for a 'favour'.

The first time I remember, I think I was around six years old. He brought me a huge teddy bear and said to me, 'I need a favour. This Sunday, a man is going to come round with a big camera. I want you to tell him, 'The other day, we all went on a trip together. We're a very close family.' Of course, we'd never taken a family trip, and we weren't at all close. But I wanted that teddy bear, so I said I'd do it.

That Sunday, some men did bring a big camera to the house. My mother even came out of her room dressed to the nines. She, my father, brother and I all lined up for the camera, and I told the lie my father wanted, just as I'd promised I would.

That footage ran on the local station a few days later. I thought I'd done a good job at the time, but, when I watched it, I was so stiff that I thought it was obvious I was just reciting lines. I suppose the adults all thought it was nerves from being on TV for the first time.

The station added some kind of silly voiceover, like 'Little Mitsuko, the Hikura Homes princess, was pretty as a delicate hothouse flower. She was a little nervous, but with her family backing her up, she finally worked up the courage to speak to the camera!' They'd turned me into a mascot for the company, trying to improve its public image.

The favours kept coming after that. Each time, I would lie to the interviewer and smile innocently for the cameras. If I'm honest, I knew that what I was doing wasn't exactly right, but I didn't see how it could hurt anyone, so, I guess I just didn't think it mattered. And then… Well.

One day, father came as usual, but this time the smile when he asked for his favour looked different. Forced. The favour itself was different, too, and I didn't really understand, but I agreed.

I suppose I should explain that at the time we had a chef working at the house named Mr Inoue. He was a cold man and not at all intimidated by my father or mother, but his cooking was top drawer. One day, just like my father told me to, I stood in front of all the staff and my family, and said in a big, loud voice, 'The other day, Mr Inoue took my clothes off and touched me all over.'

I remember how the room seemed to simply freeze, in an instant. The next day, Mr Inoue was just... gone. Even as young as I was, I understood that I had been responsible for that.

He had been framed for a crime that never happened, and all because of what I had said. I was filled with terrible regret. And I began to hate my father for making me do it.

The next time was about six months later. Father came once more to ask me for a favour. Another lie for the cameras, just like always. But the incident with Mr Inoue had made me rebellious, and I only pretended to agree. I was planning to betray him.

That day, I told the truth to the cameras. I said we didn't get along at all, and that we'd never taken a single family trip. It was my first sign of rebellion, and my father was utterly shocked. He stood in front of the cameras in a panic, his face pale as a sheet. The sight of it filled me with triumph. *Take that!* I thought.

But, at the same time, I felt a chill. I thought I could feel someone's gaze on me, and I turned to see my mother glaring daggers.

That evening, we had beef stew for dinner. I usually loved beef stew, but for some reason, it seemed off that night. I could only eat about half. There was nothing wrong with the flavour. It was more that my tongue felt weird. Tingly.

Afterwards, when I went to brush my teeth, I suddenly started vomiting. Everything I had eaten came back up. I spent the next five days in bed with a high fever, nausea and diarrhoea. It was terrible.

The whole time I was in bed, Granny Yaeko sat and held my hand. Surprisingly, even my brother came to see me, and my father was the one who dealt with the doctors. Of all my family, it was only my mother who never once visited.

Thinking about that night, I seem to remember that when the server brought me the beef stew, his hand trembled slightly, and he wouldn't look at me. I think someone must have ordered him to put something in it.

Not my father. I'm not trying to defend him, but he was simply too weak and timid to do something as bold as to try to poison his own daughter.

And the only other person who could order the servants to do anything was my mother.

I didn't know it then, but my mother was the one who actually controlled Hikura Homes. She was using my father like a puppet. I did know, though, that whenever the servants had to talk directly to her, they were in constant terror, desperately trying to gauge her mood. And the only one of them who had ever been able to talk back to my mother was Mr Inoue, who had worked for the Hikura family for decades.

Once he was gone, there was no one at all who would resist her.

After that, Mitsuko says she lived in fear of when the next 'favour' would come.

MITSUKO: When I moved on to middle school, I was sent to a girls' school in Gunma Prefecture. My father was the one who decided that, and he built a house for me to live in. When I heard that Granny Yaeko would be coming to live with me, I thought to myself, *They're getting rid of us.* I'd grown too big to have any value as the company mascot, and Granny Yaeko, well… She'd outlived her usefulness by then, too.

Away from my parents, though, I didn't have to be afraid of the favours anymore. Life at the Nagano house was heaven compared to the suffocating atmosphere in my old home.

I made a friend at school. A girl named Shiori. I was the one who spoke to her first. I remember she just seemed approachable. She had a lonely feel, kind of sad, and that was something I could understand as the family outcast. We would talk, and we even kept an exchange notebook. That was the only time in my life I felt like a normal kid. I wanted those days to go on for ever.

But then, one day just before the summer holidays… My father came to visit.

He sat in my room, his smile more forced than I'd ever seen, and said to me,

'Mitsuko. I have a favour to ask. This coming Saturday morning, would you hide your grandmother's prosthetic leg somewhere?'

Mitsuko says that was the first time she was told the secret purpose of the house.

MITSUKO: At first, I thought it was some kind of sick joke. But my father... He looked ready to cry. He had this pleading look on his face... And as I looked at him, I grew convinced that my mother had told him exactly how he would be punished if I refused.

Inside, I was screaming, *I don't want to! I can't!* But I couldn't say it. When I tried, the misery of those five days in bed seemed to come back to me. If I refused Father... Or, rather, Mother... Then I was sure she'd actually kill me this time. I was terrified.

You can think I'm the worst person alive. I won't disagree with you. I said I would do it. I weighed my grandmother's life against my own, and I chose mine.

ATONEMENT

MITSUKO: I invited Shiori to stay over that night. I wanted someone near me. I really am the worst, dragging my friend into that nightmare. But I simply couldn't bear it alone.

When I was sure Shiori was asleep, I sneaked out of my room and went to Grandmother's room. She was already asleep.

I picked up the flesh-coloured rubber leg from beside her bed and took care not to make any noise as I left. When I did, I heard a rustling sound behind me, like skin on a blanket. I froze in place. I was too scared to turn and look, so I just stood there. But I didn't hear anything else, so I was convinced she'd just turned over in her sleep or something, and I went back to my room.

I hid the leg in my bookcase, locked the door and got back into bed. After a while, my heart finally slowed down. Then, I was able to really think about what I was doing.

I was trying to kill my own grandmother. At that thought, before fear, before guilt, it was simply grief that overcame me.

She was only one in my family who had ever been kind to me. Granny Yaeko, who used to giggle with me as we drew and played. Granny Yaeko, who had sat holding my hand the whole time I was sick. And if I didn't do anything, I would lose her. The only real family I had.

I got out of bed, opened my bookcase… And put the leg back.

AUTHOR: What?

MITSUKO: I went back to my grandmother's room, put the leg beside her bed, returned to my room and… I felt so odd.

I had gone against my mother again. I had no idea what would happen to me next. But I wasn't afraid. I think I was too happy about having chosen of my own free will to protect my grandmother.

It was the first time I had ever put myself in danger to help someone else. I felt elated. Invincible. And I fell asleep.

Mitsuko's hands were clenched into tight fists in her lap.

MITSUKO: But, as you know, the accident still happened. Granny Yaeko tumbled down the stairs and died, just the way my mother wanted. It was so strange. She wasn't wearing her leg. When I saw that, I thought, *Granny Yaeko died to save me.*

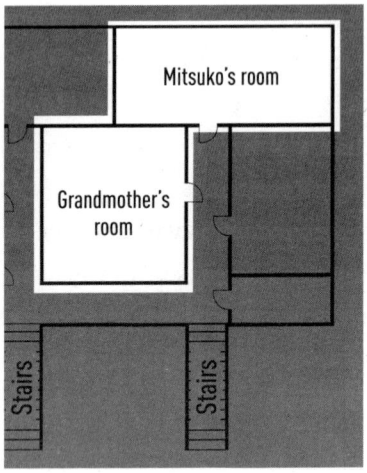

MITSUKO: My room was next to hers, with just a thin wall between us. She could have overheard Father's instructions. Or maybe he had chosen to speak to me in my room on purpose, to make sure she heard. He had really been speaking to her, rather than to me. She knew what would happen to me if I refused or messed it up. So, she… died for me.

Grandmother fell down those stairs on purpose to protect me. That's what I believe.

From then until the day of her funeral, when we collected her ashes, I apologized over and over in my heart.

It was obvious to me just how deeply she had cared for Yaeko. But… Somehow, it seemed as if she were being too frank about it all. Too matter-of-fact.

MITSUKO: After the funeral was over, and I went home for the first time in so long, I noticed something odd. Grandmother's leg was missing from her room. She hadn't been wearing it when she died, so it should still have been in her room. I searched and searched, but it wasn't there. Then, a terrifying thought occurred to me.

I rushed to my room and tried to open the bookcase. It wouldn't open, though. It was locked. I took the key out of the pencil case in my desk drawer and opened it. And there was the flesh-coloured rubber leg.

It was as if all the strength drained from my body. No one else knew where I kept that key. So, the only person who could have locked that door… was me. No one else could have put the leg in there.

AUTHOR: How could it have happened?

MITSUKO: I didn't actually take the leg back to Grandmother's room. That was a dream.

> I had gone against my mother again. I had no idea what would happen to me next. But I wasn't afraid. I think I was too happy about having chosen of my own free will to protect my grandmother. It was the first time I had ever put myself in danger to help someone else. I felt elated. Invincible. And I fell asleep.

MITSUKO: My own life was too dear, so I had agreed to kill my grandmother, but I couldn't bear to believe that I was so pitiful, so weak. My desire to be a better person, my thoughts of 'If only I had done differently. If only I had been better…' expressed themselves in a dream, and somehow I convinced myself that it had been true.

I don't know what answer you were hoping for. But the one who killed my grandmother was… me.

Mitsuko stood and turned away from me.

MITSUKO: I ran away from the Hikura family because I could not bear living in fear of the next 'favour'. I left when I graduated and paid my way through carer school, working part time. I chose this work because... Well, I'm probably hoping for forgiveness.

She touched the bruise on her arm.

MITSUKO: The reason I asked you to come during my work break was so you could see me like this, as a carer.

I wanted you to think that I truly regret letting my parents manipulate me into killing my grandmother. That I'm seeking atonement by seeking to do good in difficult circumstances.

But after telling you all that happened, I think I've come to understand something else.

I've just been running from my own guilt by playing the victim. I don't really care how you write my story, not anymore.

I couldn't find the words to respond. All I could do was stare after her as she walked back towards the care home.

**COMING SOON FROM
PUSHKIN VERTIGO**

STRANGE MAPS

UKETSU